A BED OF ROSES

Everyone, including her grown-up daughter, expects Fran to marry Michael, a kind, supportive solicitor, her friend for years. But on the morning of her wedding Fran hesitates. Should she say 'I do' and fade into the fabric of a life which is safe, sensible and familiar? Or should she say, 'Actually, no thank you' and bolt with Josh, an artist, her evening class teacher, a man she hardly knows, a man with a failed marriage and a teenage daughter. But a man who made her heart sing. A man who promised her a bed of roses. A man who said it was time for her to live for herself. But can anyone ever really live for themselves? Can they leave behind their obligations, their past? And will the future be a bed of roses? In this heart-warming novel, Margaret Graham traces the consequences of Fran's decision. Consequences that irrevocably change not only her own life, but all those closest to her.

A BED OF ROSES

Margaret Graham

CHIVERS PRESS
BATH

First published 2000
by
Hutchinson
This Large Print edition published by
Chivers Press
by arrangement with
Random House Group Limited
2001

ISBN 0 7540 1549 1

British Library Cataloguing in Publication Data available

Printed and bound in Great Britain by
REDWOOD BOOKS, Trowbridge, Wiltshire

For Colleen
An absolute star

CHAPTER ONE

'So, the man goes into the doctor's surgery with a shteering, sorry, steering wheel sticking out of his flies.' Fran paused and tried to sip her Mongolian Sunrise, but the startlingly pink cocktail umbrella was everywhere. While her daughter Jane and best friend Linda waited, she squashed it shut and gulped the cocktail in one. Across the table Linda did the same and obviously wished she hadn't. They really should have had coffee to round off the meal, but Linda had decided Fran's geriatric hen night could not end on such a whimper.

Fran rose above the burning in her throat. Around them diners tucked into desserts, served on Clarice Cliff lookalike plates. Would this gallant new art deco corner restaurant 'go' in their conventional little market town once the introductory prices had risen? Who could tell what worked and what didn't? Who could tell? She gripped her glass too tight, trying to grab hold of her spinning thoughts.

Linda said, 'Hope you approve, Fran. I always thought I'd like *mine* somewhere like this.'

Is this what weddings were all about? Bringing the dreams of others to life? Was that reason enough?

Fran watched Jane sip her cocktail carefully. It was the one she had started the evening with. Where was the young girl of yesteryear? Gone to motherhood, twice, and wifehood to Ken. Well, perhaps that said it all. Jane murmured, 'I thought you'd choose the Italian place round the corner

1

from the office, Linda. It suited me. After all, it's different in the evening.'

While Jane and Linda discussed the merits of Luigi's evening ambience Fran gripped her glass even tighter. She'd had one too many cocktails. Well, that wasn't quite true. The cocktails had joined the large gin she'd poured herself in the privacy of her sitting room as she'd waited for Linda, as though she was going to a gory death. When the taxi hooted she had somehow gathered up a smile and made herself hurry down the drive. Again Jane drank the merest sip.

She must try to emulate some of her daughter's carefulness. Yes, that's what she must do. Frantically she peeled the silver paper from an after-dinner mint. It might absorb the alcohol, but what about the panic?

Linda was tapping her arm. 'Go on, finish the joke before you're quite unable to speak.'

'Joke?'

Jane sighed. 'Something about a steering wheel, but it's fine by me if you've forgotten. You seem to be coming out with the most extraordinary things these days, Mother. I suppose we must put it down to stress, but why I can't imagine, when I've done most of the wedding preparations. Do you know, Linda . . .'

Linda cut across Jane: 'Go on, Fran, you've started so you might as well finish.'

Did one really have to finish? Was it in the rules? Fran pressed her lips together. No, she must not ask that question. She had decided. Absolutely and completely. She would not ask that question of herself or anyone else. She felt sick, felt the sweat on her forehead. She really must get a grip.

2

'Mother, are you feeling all right?' Jane's voice was concerned. 'I didn't mean to upset you, I was teasing. Finish the joke. I'm sure it's funny and I haven't minded doing the wedding preps, really.'

Fran heard her own voice as though from a distance, so quiet, so slow. 'I'm just not sure about it.' But, no, she must not speak her thoughts and she wasn't sure her daughter was teasing. She'd been uptight and difficult, even more so this evening as though she was on edge. But wouldn't anyone be, taking on the wedding arrangements as she had insisted on doing?

Had she felt Fran would mess it up, that she'd let the side down, that Ken's colleagues would be less than impressed? Did she still fear that she would? Well, would she? Shut up. Just shut up.

Linda's arm was around her, hugging her. 'It'll be a cracker, just give us the punchline.'

Fran shook free. 'No.' Her voice was loud enough to make the couple at the next table look up from their meringue. Fran rubbed her engagement ring with her thumb. 'I'm just not sure about Mike, the wedding, the rest of my life.'

Linda sat back, shocked. 'You daft trollop. What bride hasn't said that the night before her wedding?' But her voice was shaky. 'Don't be daft,' she repeated, pulling her close. Her breath was warm in her hair, her grip too tight. Fran could hardly breathe. She needed air, space. Yes, that was it, some space. To think.

Jane was tugging at her sleeve, leaning across the table. 'Mum, come on, Uncle Mike's ideal for you and you for him. For heaven's sake, you've known him all your life. It's the obvious thing, and I've never seen him so happy and content. Linda's

3

right. I remember getting the wobbles and it was only the drink. Come on, everyone's watching.' Jane snatched a look to left and right. Fran drew herself upright. She was behaving so badly, unforgivably. It must stop.

Jane was calling for the bill and Linda was insisting, 'No, this is on me. You chat to your mother, keep her on course.' She was using the voice reserved for weeping clients: half sympathetic, half 'let's keep this under control, he is still the father of your children'. Any minute she'd press the buzzer for coffee and Fran would rush in with a brimming cup, like the good little secretary she was, and at the end of the day they'd both feel like a wrung-out rag with the distress of handling the debris of so many marriages.

But this wasn't the office. This was her hen night and she wasn't weeping. She was a tipsy idiot, someone who should have known better. Who *must* know better.

Linda's tip was generous. She'd accept no contribution and the waiter hurried to phone for a taxi. Did he want them out of the place, fearful of a scene? They left the Clarice Cliff diners, the muted decor, and waited in the early spring night, just under the phoney vine-leafed porch. At last Fran could draw in great gulps of cool air, but still her head ached, lurched, spun. 'If we were energetic young things we'd find a club to round the evening off?' Linda's voice held half a question.

'Well, you're not and mother was out last night. Quite absurd. Do you know, Linda, I needed a final decision on Pimm's or sherry and where was she? At her art class. I mean, honestly. The wedding in three days time, and she's faffing about with paint

4

again. So I called Uncle Mike and he said to stick with sherry.'

Linda's arm was interlocked with Fran's and now she whispered against Fran's hair, 'I fear she'll be collecting Zimmers for us before long and incidentally, I can't tell you how much Mike is looking forward to this masterpiece you've promised for his present. He was bursting with it when he chaired the partners' meeting this afternoon. I feel he's rather hoping it's a portrait he can secrete in the attic to keep him forever young. It isn't abstract, is it?' Linda looked down the road. 'Where is this darned taxi?'

'Yes, you should let us have a look, Mother. It *isn't* like that other stuff you've done, is it?'

'It's not stuff. The act of painting is what is important, the end result doesn't have to matter.'

'Um,' said Linda, as she had done when first introduced to the paintings stacked in Fran's spare room.

'I just sort of fell into the freedom from the need to imitate reality. Think of Pollock's action paintings, all those frenetic whirls and globules of paint. Doesn't that do something to you, doesn't it unlock something, make you start to look inside yourself?'

'You said it didn't matter about the end result and who's Pollock, or is it some other joke you're about to launch into?' Jane was bored. Linda was listening, but clearly only with one ear, just as before when Fran had tried to talk about her art, which might have led to *him*, her teacher, Josh. Which might have led . . . Who knew where?

Fran shook her head. 'Well, I know I said that, Jane, and the end result doesn't have to matter but

5

if it does, if it reaches out and touches someone else, sparking a longing, a remembrance, a . . .'

'I'll pop back in and ask them to phone again, shall I?' Jane was checking her watch, but she didn't move. Across the road youngsters were jostling and laughing as they walked to the club.

Fran dug her hands deep into her pockets. Jane was right, she was a boring old fart and she wished she'd never smelt linseed oil, never picked up a palette knife, never . . . 'It was your idea,' she blurted out to Jane. 'It'll give you something other than the wedding arrangements to think about, you shaid.' She sounded childish.

'Shaid?' Linda laughed.

'I know, I know,' Fran said. 'I'm sorry, Jane. I shouldn't . . . I'm grateful you took the planning off me.'

Jane checked her watch again. 'Well, we were getting nowhere with the two of us trying to sort it; no one knew what the other was up to. You have to admit it's worked very smoothly under my control. Administration is my forte, after all.'

Fran looked at her more closely. Her forte, said in that tone? Surely they weren't back on that whirligig again? Hadn't she made herself quite clear last month? She rubbed her forehead and at that, Jane avoided her eyes. Fran was glad of Linda's arm.

Linda said, 'Are you all right, Fran?'

'I think so.' Because she wouldn't be if her daughter started pressuring her about babysitting the grandchildren again while she returned to work.

The taxi was swooping round the corner. It shuddered to a halt. All three got in the back.

'We'll drop the drunkard first, then you, Jane, then me. OK everyone?' Linda's voice was bracing. Fran looked from her to Jane, who sat in the middle. She seemed taller. It was the hump. It had created a throne.

Fran grabbed the door as the taxi rounded the corner faster than she ever would have done. Jane's weight rested on her for a moment. 'Mum, I was offered that job I went for last month.'

Fran stiffened. 'And?' The taxi was on the straight now.

'I've taken it.' Before Fran could speak she rushed on: 'We did talk about it and you did say you'd think about it. After all, I might not get another offer so everything depends on you looking after the kids and I know you won't let me down, especially when I've worked so hard on the wedding. Ken's going to make a gate through into Uncle Mike's so all you need to do is pop across in the morning. It's perfect, you can see that. It's as though it's meant to be. Everything's dovetailing. You *can* see that, can't you?'

Fran could not believe what she was hearing and, momentarily, lost her voice, but then she gasped, 'But that's *not* what was decided. Not. Not.' She was shouting now and Linda flapped her down. Fran felt quite sober as she added more quietly, 'I said I thought you should leave it for now. You are so tired, Jane. You have two very small children, one not yet six months, and it shouldn't be necessary with a husband who is a solicitor, an associate, for God's sake, in Mike's firm and earning a decent wage.'

'Salary, Mother.'

'For heaven's sake, Jane. Look, just wait for a

7

while and then we'll think again, I said. How can I look after them when I have a job myself, I said?' Her head was splitting. Was she spelling it out enough? Had firmness distilled into anger? Well, why shouldn't it?

Another corner. Again she felt Jane's weight, but this time she heard her wail as well: 'Mother, you don't need a job and I do. We have bills to pay, a huge mortgage, and there is none on Uncle Mike's house *and* you'll have the income from yours when you let it, which will give you this independence you mentioned the other week. After all, we're going to be one big family and it's what families do, and you didn't say you wouldn't, and yes, you said to wait, but it is a month later.'

At last she drew breath and Fran knew her daughter's tears weren't far away. She could hear them as she had always been able to and it should have softened her, but it didn't. 'Besides, Mother, Uncle Mike thinks it's a good idea. Ken confirmed it with him last night. He's known it was on the cards.'

Fran stared out of the window, feeling as though she was being submerged, drowned, sucked beneath waves. Linda said gently, 'Actually, Mike did run it past me when he arrived at the office this morning and it does make sense, you old warhorse. Don't you remember we talked about the conundrum of the boss's wife working as a secretary? It could prove tricky with the other girls, we said.'

Did we? Did we really? Fran couldn't remember but then she'd been too busy studying her own navel, daubing paint on to canvas, discovering another world, another part of herself, and him.

8

Him.

Again she rubbed her forehead, trying to sound light-hearted as she said, 'I don't know, I take a day off and what happens. I need hardly bother to exist, you all manage my life so well.' The anger had become rage that made her clamp her lips shut.

But no, it was she who was out of step. Why not give up work after marriage to a wonderful man? Why not look after children she adored? Why not do as everyone expected, as she would probably have expected—six months ago? But Mike informing Linda as though she were invisible, as though . . . ?

'Mum?'

Fran saw Linda silence Jane with a tap on the arm as the taxi drew to a halt in front of her semi-detached suburban villa. Jane was groping for a tissue, saying, 'Please don't be cross, Mum. After all, you can paint whenever you like if you don't work.'

'As long as I can hold a brush with a babe on one hip and a toddler on the other.' Fran's voice was ice-cold. *She* was ice-cold, so terribly cold, and she should not have said that. It was unforgivable. Everything she did, and thought, and wanted was unforgivable and she couldn't help it. 'Thanks for the evening,' she said to Linda, but nothing to Jane as she left the taxi.

She walked away from them but their voices were still with her; their plans for dragging her further into *their* future. No, *her* future.

She could barely find the keyhole, but finally she did, entering, throwing off her shoes, trying to stop everything for a moment, everything and everyone. She shut the door, leaning against it, before somehow climbing the stairs, needing to be where she could cling to that other world just once more.

In the spare room she breathed deeply of the oils, the acrylics, the turps, the linseed, calming at last, touching the canvas of the last painting he would ever help her with. He. Josh. Her teacher. She had brought it home last night. It was unfinished, just as the course would be unfinished. Gently she traced the palette strokes.

By Saturday it would be dry. Her abstract phase would be over: that startling unexpected time of awakening that had begun with her first daub of paint on oil board. 'Just be,' he'd told the class as they stood at their easels. 'Relax. Just open yourself to the canvas. Do what comes naturally.'

He was the most beautiful man she had ever seen. His voice was kind, his movements gentle, his laugh lit every fibre of his being. She felt she'd known him all her life. She had taken up her brush.

'Go on,' he had urged them. 'Dredge it up, spit it out, get rid of it, turn whatever it is that each one of you would rather forget into shapes and colours. Go for it.'

She'd balanced the brush, then instead she'd picked up the palette knife and almost as though she was in another world she'd slashed great sweeping spirals of red, dragging up out of black darkness. 'Action, emotion, raw and unconfined,' he had said, appearing behind her, then falling silent. He murmured, 'Such powerful anguish.'

Then she saw what she had painted, and was astonished and frightened. 'Go on with it,' he'd said quietly, before moving on to the next student. 'I'm here for you.'

So it began, this strange transference of energy

10

and emotion into overlapping chaotic form. So began the release of creating, not observing, the release of opening herself to the canvas as she had never done to anyone or anything before. From that first moment he had stood alongside her, never questioning, just appreciating, being there. From that first moment began the time of *him*.

She could hear his words now, his voice in her head, feel his fingers overlaid on hers as he guided her knife or brush. His words, his voice, his hands which steadied her as the layers unpeeled, savage, raw, cleansing, until her first husband had seemed just a cipher, or almost. Each week she had gone and each week she had not wanted to leave that art room when the class was finished.

Enough. These few months had to be enough. She must take one last look, then step back. For a long moment she stood there. Yes, she could paint again, but it would be nothing without Josh. Nothing. Everything would be nothing.

Eventually Fran made her way downstairs, passing the dining room on whose table gifts were accumulating. It was all so terribly unreal, but how could she say that when this was her reality?

She paused by the Womble Linda had sent in honour of dear, safe Mike's tidiness. She reached out, touching it, digging her fingers in. 'This is my world,' she said aloud.

In the small square kitchen she put on the kettle, found the cocoa, then replaced it. Instead she brewed a hot toddy from the miniature of Scotch that Linda had said was for wedding morning nerves. She added honey to disguise the taste. It was one she couldn't abide but Linda had forgotten. So if she could forget, and its reasons, one could obviously forget anything.

She walked through to the sitting room, holding the mug with both hands, sitting in *her* chair opposite the television and next to the gas fire. She was still in her coat. She should phone Mike as she had promised.

She bent her head, smelling the honey, trying to ignore the Scotch. It was no good. She discarded the mug, pushing it as far from her as the coffee table allowed, then she stared at the paint on her fingers.

Just before Christmas Mike had asked for one of her paintings as her wedding gift to him. She had painted a conventional representative study of law books. Josh had said it had all the life of a stuffed cabbage, but in spite of its destination he had taken the palette knife and shown her how to perform a miracle, one which had drawn the rest of the evening class around the easel.

The painting was wrapped and ready, propped against the dining table. But how could she survive for the rest of her life with the evidence of his existence in Mike's sitting room? There was no alternative and she must never again drink as she had done tonight, or she might split apart at the seams, and too much would be said and seen.

She phoned Mike. It rang, once, twice, three times. On the fourth, the answering machine would clock in, but the message Mike and the real one chimed in together. 'Don't hang up,' Mike shouted.

'I won't,' she promised.

'We're yin and yang,' Mike had said the afternoon he proposed.

'Yin and yang, my Aunt Fanny,' Josh had muttered when she told him, snatching her palette

12

knife from her and tackling the books.

'I just wanted to hear your voice,' Fran said into the now quiet phone.

'I'm glad. I've missed you and you missed *Horizon*, which was exploring global warming, but never fear, it's taped. You'll enjoy it.'

She said, 'Will I? Mike, we need to talk about my job.'

'No need, I've set the replacement wheels in motion.'

'Ah.'

'Linda seemed fine about it,' he soothed.

'Ah.' But she had more to say. 'So everyone's happy?'

Mike said, 'Oh, I didn't mean it to sound like that. Of course she's sad that it's the end of an era, but like all of us she wants what's best for you, so in that respect she's fine.'

Fran reached frantically for the toddy after all, gulping it down. What is best for me, Mike? she wanted to ask. In the past he had always known, always been there for her. He was such a good man, a genuinely good man, and she had been content and none of this was fair on him. So it would pass and one day it would be the same as ever between them. She clutched the mug. One day.

Mike said, 'Cocoa time?'

'Sort of. Are you fine, Mike? Are you happy?'

He laughed gently. 'Of course, and to make it perfect the curtains arrived today and the plane tickets at last. The caterers are falling into place on the vegetarian choice, but I expect Jane told you that. The plumber's coming in to service your boiler on Friday, ready for the tenants. Jane will let him in, but I expect she told you that too.'

It was reassuring to know a couple of things had slipped her daughter's mind. What a bitch of a mother she had become.

'Goodnight, my dear,' Mike said. Gently she replaced the receiver. She could drink no more of the toddy. She let it hang from her hand, staring at the shelf of art nouveau glass she'd begun collecting when it was still cheap. One item every year—a celebration of her widowhood. It was time she gave it to Jane; after all, Crown Derby already took up Mike's display case.

The phone began to ring. She buried her head in her hands. On it went. On and on until it wore itself into silence.

She dialled 1471.

It was Josh, as she had known it would be, but she didn't return his call.

*   *   *

Jane was relieved that Linda had insisted on dropping her off next. It meant she would pick up the tab. Ken had given her fifteen pounds for the evening and would expect change, and why not? They weren't made of money, that's why there was all this rush about a job, as her mother would finally see when her head was clearer. If not, Uncle Mike would talk to her and make it all right, as he always did.

She hurried up the drive, skirting the individual shrubs that lined the front lawn, which the bedroom light threw into sharp relief. She had planted daffodils in their shadow. She liked the feel of the earth beneath her hands. When she was

14

growing up her mother had shared the gardening with her, saying how she found the relentless march of nature reassuring. Jane hadn't understood as a child, but she did now.

At the front door she checked her watch again, as though that action would somehow turn back the time to 11 p.m. She tapped lightly. Perhaps Ken had fallen asleep? In which case she could fetch the spare key from behind the garage and slip unnoticed into bed. Not that she was criticising him, because he was quite right to think that she could not be trusted with her own key. After all, she had twice mislaid it. He blamed her mother for leading by example. 'Why on earth you both can't put them on a hook or something,' he'd complained. 'And wear gloves while you're gardening. You'll ruin your hands.'

Ken loomed at the glass, reaching for the catch. She waited as the door opened. He stood there and for a moment his beauty took her breath away. She said, 'I'm so sorry, it took longer than we expected to find a taxi. We were out by eleven. Ask Mother.'

He smiled, hushing her as he pulled her into the hall, kissing her cheek. Surprised, she leaned against him for a moment. Weddings. At theirs he had looked so wonderful and said she was the most beautiful girl in the world. She *must* get into shape. She still had another half-stone to go. His bare shoulder was smooth and he smelt of baby soap, and her heart shouldn't sink that he wasn't wearing his pyjama top. 'Did you have a good time? That's the main thing.' He shut the door.

She said, slipping off her shoes, feeling the deep pile of the new carpet. 'It was fine and Linda paid, even for the taxi. Oh, my poor feet.'

Ken was fixing the safety chain as she hurried through into the kitchen. He followed. 'Your camomile's in the mug. So you had fun?'

There was water in the kettle. She clicked it on. 'Not as much as if you had been there.' She busied herself attacking Ken's dishwasher rejects that he had lined up for her on the drainer, hearing the swish of his slippers on the tiles as he came up behind her. She tensed, then felt his lips on the back of her neck. 'Bring your camomile to bed when you're finished, eh?'

She nodded. He kissed her again and left. Swiftly she scrubbed the insides of the mugs and the bowl, dried them. She put away the bowl and hung the mugs facing the same way. She put new tea towels on the range bar, standing back, checking, then poured water into her camomile mug.

At the end of the garden she could see her godfather's house. It was in darkness. In a little over ten days her mother would be installed. That would make everything better, it would take the pressure off. For a moment she closed her eyes, wanting her there now, within earshot. They could garden either side of the fence at the weekends. She would always remember to wear her gloves and she'd jog, or go to the gym. No, not the gym, it cost money.

Ken would get closer to Uncle Mike. It would really be as though they were one family. Sunday lunch over there, not at her mother's. There would be talk of Gilbert, Gilbert, and *Swanton*. Yes, there was no reason why Ken couldn't build up to heir presumptive, especially as Mike's real son-in-law was a civil engineer and not in the running. How relieved Ken had been when that had come up at one of Mike's firm's parties. Their lives had been so good, once, and they would be again. Soon, they would be again.

'Jane,' Ken called from the bedroom.

She scooped out the herbal tea bag, squeezed it, put it in the compost bin under the sink, then placed the mug on the tray he had left out. She climbed the stairs, taking care not to spill any tea, checking that the pictures were straight, that the towels in the bathroom were just so, forcing herself not to pause outside the children's room.

It was dark in the bedroom. She felt her way to the bed, placing the tray on the table, sitting up against the pillows she knew he would have placed against the headboard, as well as one behind to stop the creaking.

Later, while he slept, she left the room as she always did, easing open the children's door, smoothing down Harry's cot sheet, stroking his unbelievably soft cheek, and pulling up Lucy's duvet, kissing her. Mother was right. In a perfect world they'd be too young to be left while she worked, but Ken was also right in that he couldn't cope with the mortgage alone any more. It was all getting out of hand. She felt the tremble begin but not as badly, because there was an end in sight.

*   *   *

Linda asked the cabby for a receipt at her brightly lit house. Mike had said she could put the fare in as expenses; his contribution to the evening. But that was Mike all over. She shut the front door behind her, aware of the carefully orchestrated sounds of her house. Her mother's only valuable possession,

17

the grandfather clock, ticked as laboriously as it had done when she was alive. The radio in the sitting room chattered away, the boiler drummed. And the lights were reassuringly bright. All little tricks she had learned to fill the emptiness of spinsterhood. Was that the term used today?

She doubted it. Probably she was acknowledged as Ms, a career woman who had chosen independence above the kitchen sink. Well, balls to that. It was simply that long ago she had chosen Mike and he had eyes for no one but Fran.

She slung her jacket over the banister, then stood quite still for a moment until the inside of her head caught up with her, knowing she must drink water, reflecting that *she* wouldn't be nervous if this had been her pre-Mike hen night. Instead, she would have been disgustingly eager, panting almost. But drink did strange things to people and dear old Fran so seldom over-indulged.

Or was there more to it? Fran had been so preoccupied recently, but why not, when you were sorting out one life to begin another? No wonder she'd got stuck into her painting; it must have been a bit of light relief from finding tenants and dear old Jane yammering on about sherry or Pimm's. That girl needed a good holiday, not a job, Fran was quite right, but it would all get sorted once everyone was playing happy families.

Linda sighed. It was what she seemed to do a lot lately and this one went from the top of her head to her toes.

She made her way unsteadily to the sitting room, turning off the radio, hesitating by the flashing answer machine, finally pressing *play*; so glad, then, that she had, because it was Mike. 'Linda, I know you're not there, of course, but while the thought has not yet dropped out of the bottomless pit I laughingly call my brain I thought I'd better just tell you that Mrs Veroni's finally going for a divorce and she'd rather a woman handle it. I'll send a memo tomorrow, of course. Sorry to be so senile, I just seem to be concentrating on one thing at the moment—no prizes for guessing what.'

Linda saved the message, stupid woman that she was.

CHAPTER TWO

'Why can't you, Josh?' Catherine snapped on Friday evening, holding the receiver between shoulder and chin while she applied a last coat of dark, deep nail varnish.

'Just too much on this weekend.'

Catherine, Josh Benton's ex-wife, stared across at her lover, who was sitting in the white leather armchair opposite and hadn't even heard the phone, hadn't missed a beat, hadn't looked up from the laptop even for a moment. Perhaps he was joined to it by some sort of umbilical cord. She shut her eyes against the image.

'Cath?' Josh's voice nagged at her. Her nails finished, she replaced the top and waved her hands in the air. Quick-drying my aunt Fanny. 'What you really mean, Josh Benton, is that there'll be too much coming off in that bachelor pad. For goodness sake, you only have Emily every two weeks...'

'That's because it's all you'll allow. It's

ridiculous, when you're only an hour away.'

'Don't try and change the subject. I bet I'm right, I bet you'd rather "do" some tart than see your own daughter.'

At last Roger showed an interest, looking up startled, worried.

Josh sighed down the receiver. God, that really got to her. That sigh he had made an art form. Roger shook his head slightly and returned to the laptop. He could change his face for a start, because if Em wasn't being 'teenage sat' at Josh's they couldn't go to that charity concert. At that glorious realisation Catherine relaxed, smiling at the mute television, sinking back into the armchair, loving the smell of leather.

She blew on her nails, touched one to her lips. OK, so perhaps it was quick-drying after all. She ran her hand through her ash-blond hair, then remembered her overdue roots.

Josh said, 'Quite frankly, Cath, if we're talking of tarts, I think you've the monopoly on that sort of thing, so get off my back. I can't take it at the moment.' His voice sounded weird, small, hurt, rather as it had done when she'd left him.

Catherine sat straighter. 'What's wrong?'

'Absolutely nothing.'

'It's a very big nothing from the sound of it. Someone dumped you, have they?' Her voice was harsh enough for Roger to look up again, worried, and in his eyes she saw the concern. She must be careful. He mustn't think she still cared for Josh. Anyway, she probably didn't. Besides, no one else could hurt Josh. He'd said she'd torn him apart, said he could never . . . She'd wondered over these last few months, but surely . . .

20

She stared at the huge fern Roger had inherited from his aunt, suddenly feeling as though the world had shuddered to a halt. She'd wondered, but never really . . . Her stomach twisted; she felt clammy. She stared across at Roger, the ghastly, rich Roger who was watching her with that little-boy-lost look. That 'love me, not him' look.

She smiled, raised her eyebrows, pointing to the phone, mouthing: 'Such a pain, he's dripping his problems all over me.' Roger nodded, smiling tentatively. He was handsome in a very regular sort of way: good eyes, cheekbones. She'd hooked him away from some sensible little girl in the same accountancy firm. It had been as easy as running a hot knife through butter, or slapping on paint with a palette knife. Her stomach lurched and now she shouted, 'I suppose you want me to snivel your rejection to Em.'

Again Roger looked up. She ignored him as Josh shouted back, 'No need, I've just rung your annexe and spoken to her. She told me you'd slipped next door with the rent book. Still keeping up the façade? God, you're such a bitch, Cath. Such a bloody bitch.'

Bastard. Catherine pressed the TV volume control. Loud, louder, loudest. Roger was frowning. She mouthed: 'Anything to drown him out.' Then aloud to Josh: 'Oh, sod off. Don't blame me if you can't get your life sorted.' She hung up, sank her martini and reached forward to pour another. Roger's anxiety seemed to spread all over his body. Well, lucky him, because hers did too, but she couldn't show it.

'Surely there's no need for that?' Roger said at last. 'Once a relationship is dead one should be able to talk, not row.' There was a slight shake in his voice and he was fiddling with the laptop lid.

She swirled her drink around the glass. Knowing that hers would shake if she spoke too soon. Round and round, and at last she felt her heart slow. Only then did she say quietly, 'He's too busy with his own stuff to take Em, so now we'll have to cancel the concert. He's never cared a toss about anyone but himself. I mean, night after night I'd be on my own. Neglect is a dangerous thing, Roger, a very dangerous thing.' She paused, in control again, smiling, opening her lips slightly, knowing he liked it.

Roger snapped shut the laptop and came to her, sitting on the arm of her chair. She rose, walking to the fireplace, placing the glass carefully on the mantelpiece. She'd chosen the marble, just as she'd chosen the white decor. After all, she was an interior designer; it was what she did. What she still did, not that Josh could know. Not that he could realise that she and Em lived here, and Em was only in the annexe feeding the cat. But that wasn't just for the sake of his maintenance, it was because it had been a mistake to leave. One day she now knew she wanted to go back, but wanted to be able to say, 'See, I've been a tenant, that's all, darling Josh. I'm back, we've both had time to think, to miss one another. Now we can move on.' And what's more, she'd have Roger's money tucked away.

She flicked the Florentine lighter. If he wouldn't have Emily he must be terribly upset. She felt sick. That voice. He'd called her a bitch. He'd never done that before. But she had been his wife and he still loved her. He'd said so; he was always saying so. She replaced the lighter. But no, not recently.

Roger was behind her now, cupping his hands round her breasts. How could he possibly believe he set her on fire? She leant back against him. 'I'm sorry, darling Roger. But I'm lonely. You're so busy all the time and I thought we'd have such fun.'

She felt his breath on her ear. She squirmed out of tongue's reach, turning, hugging him to her. He said, his breath clammy and hot against her neck, 'We will, I was going to wait until after the concert to tell you, but I've been offered a transfer to San Diego. It'll be wonderful, it will be a proper beginning for us. We can stop the pretence, be a real family.'

She could smell those ghastly cheroots he smoked at the office, which she insisted were not brought over the threshold, just as she'd tried to forbid Josh and his friends. San Diego?

Roger gripped her tightly. 'Josh will give his consent to us taking Em, won't he?'

She could feel the tremble spreading to the whole of her body. What the hell was going on? Everything was changing, galloping. She couldn't think. Family? With Roger? She shut her eyes. San Diego?

CHAPTER THREE

On Saturday Fran woke up in her daughter's spare room at dawn. It was the morning of her wedding. For far too long she lay just staring at the ceiling while the house came to life around her. Far too soon Jane brought tea and a glittering smile. Then there was the shower and a pretence of picking at toast.

Far too soon also, the mobile hairdresser arrived, a girl who had lived next door to Jane when they had had their first house and who still offered her favourable rates. She offered to make up Fran. Jane accepted. At last they were gone, on to the next victim: Joyce, Ken's mother.

She was alone at last. It was noon and the day had become fine and clear. It was noon and therefore an hour before the wedding. Jane called through the bedroom door, 'Would you like some coffee, Mum?' All Jane's rancour had subsided in the face of Fran's acquiescence. All Fran's despair was muted in the face of inevitability.

'No, darling, I'm sorting out the layers.' Fran held the dress to her then, taking a breath as though diving into a pool, she dressed.

It was suitably off-white, which seemed to be called ivory these days, but either way she felt like a meringue, although her sleek reflection in the mirror belied that. She had said the same in the shop. Fearing that her commission was about to whizz down the drain, the bridal gown manageress had said it was because she wasn't used to the floating nature of the silk layers. Were most of her customers used to it, then? Fran had asked. Did they come here often?

The woman had been amused. Even Jane had laughed.

Out in the garden Ken was shouting to Lucy. Well, not shouting exactly, but his voice held that edgy tone which had arrived hot on the heels of his firstborn. It was down to financial strain, Jane had repeated last night, which was why she needed to

24

work.

So Fran had repeated, 'Why not downsize, return to a more modest semi? It's done for me, for you and me, all these years.' Jane's look had spoken volumes. Fran adjusted her neckline. After the proposal last year she had just wanted to slide off to a Register Office but Mike had hankered for church; he liked the ritual.

She found cleanser on the dressing table, pulled a tissue from the box and savagely rubbed at the make-up the hairdresser had trowelled on. Hot on the heels of church had come Lucy's dream of being a bridesmaid. Naturally, then, Ken had decided to kill several hospitality birds on the back of Mike's bankroll, so the reception had been like Topsy: it had growed and growed.

Outside, the swing was still and empty. Inside, Lucy, her granddaughter, would be changing. At the bottom of the garden the fence panel to the far right had a large cross chalked in white. It was where the gate would go. *The* gate. The *gate*. The gate through which she, Mrs Michael Wells, would tippy-toe to babysit her grandchildren. Now don't start.

She turned her back, folding her arms, creasing her dress. 'Put your arms at your side,' her mother had chastised her first time round. That had been a big wedding, all glisten and fluster, all as it should be, but her mother would have been better served saying that to David, the bridegroom. Not then, of course, but in the years that followed. But her mother hadn't known. You didn't go around telling. You thought it was your fault, that one day you'd do everything right and it would stop, and David would become the person he had once appeared to

25

be.

In spite of herself Fran was shaking. She sat on the nearest twin bed, pushing aside the tissue paper. The funeral had been all glisten too, but that had been due to the rain and the roads which had gleamed. Her parents had been distraught and so, too, had their friends—except for Linda and Mike, for they had come to know—and Fran, who could have Sylvia Plathed a stake through David's coal-black heart.

The shaking stopped and now Fran reached for the small jeweller's box Mike had delivered last night. Though Jane would not allow him to see Fran. It was bad luck. She undid the white satin ribbon, flipped up the lid and admired the gold locket. Inside, Mike, dear thoughtful Mike, had placed a photo of himself and one of her. She remembered the day they were taken. They had been in the Lake District, eating scones in a tearoom and watching the water lapping the bank. He had asked the waitress to take the photos and then proposed, as she had known he would. It seemed comfortable, sensible, predestined.

She snapped the locket shut, holding it in her hand, feeling its cool weight. The chain drooped, swung.

Mike had helped her with maths homework at school. She had thrown confetti for him and Muriel. He had tied cans on David's car. Later Linda, under his auspices, had handled the conveyancing on *her* suburban villa over on the east of town, the one she had bought with David's insurance money, the sort her daughter now thought below the salt.

Mike was her closest friend, more so, even, than

26

Linda. He was safe, unchanging, with no secrets. They had slept together on a regular basis for, oh, two, three, four years. Regular being the operative word. Every Saturday night. It took a quarter of an hour, give or take a couple of minutes. On Sunday they might have lunch at her house, or in a pub. Then there would be a walk, or gardening. Once she hadn't minded: the sex or the walk, or the lunch, or the gardening.

She placed the necklace round her neck and secured it. Rising, she moved to the mirror.

The phone rang. She stopped breathing. But then it had been ringing all morning and it had not been Josh.

It would be picked up by Joyce, who had taken up a phone monitor's position at the hall table. There was the sound of running feet on the stairs, then Ken's hurried tap on the door. 'For you, Fran. Some friend from college. But keep an eye on the time; we can't be late.'

She snatched up the bedroom extension, calling, 'It's the bride's prerogative.'

Ken's laugh was good to hear. It made her feel comforted, because this wedding was already cheering everyone up, easing everyone's lives. Everyone's? Ken said, 'You know what I mean and Jane says remember to stand up, or you'll crease.'

She held the receiver to her ear, with both hands because she was shaking so badly. 'Yes, who is it?' Although she knew perfectly well.

'Do you have to ask?' His voice was desperate.

'I can't do this, Josh.'

'Then don't.' But they both knew what she meant.

'I'm putting the phone down.' But she didn't.

27

'I'm in love with you.'

She shook her head and whispered, 'Josh, you can't know that.'

'But I do and you are in love with me.' She could see him, his eyes so dark and deep, his hands so finely formed, his fingers so long, the height of him, the essence of him, and she couldn't bear any of this. 'This isn't a game, Josh, this is . . .'

Frantically he cut across her: 'I know it's not a game. A game is something you play.'

Jane called in the distance, 'Lucy, come back at once and let Marcie finish your hair.' Lucy was having it up, like Fran. It suited neither of them, only the occasion.

'Fran, this is driving me mad, I'm losing my mind. I'm behaving atrociously, yelling down the phone at my ex-wife, snapping at my mates. I'm in love with you.'

He mustn't say it. He really mustn't. She whispered fiercely, 'Well, how would you describe my behaviour if I walked away from all this? Wouldn't that be atrocious, in fact, utterly unforgivable?'

'At least it would be honest, because right now you're walking away from the person you could be. You're at the start of discovering yourself. This is your time, our time. You've been Jane's mother for twenty-five years, Mike's friend for eternity, Linda's secretary since the dinosaurs ruled. I bet by now you've arranged to look after those children. Fran, listen, you must let them sort out their own problems. You did. I did. You're not doing them any favours. You can't go on being there for them for ever. At some stage you are allowed to be Fran. Besides, your daughter shouldn't be in that house if it's such an effort. Mike won't want to live a lie. Don't be scared all your life, Fran. You can trust me. Skid out of the rut. Be brave. Be happy. You have that right.'

'You've said all this before and I've told you I've made my choice.' She sat down. Her dress could damn well crease. 'To change things would make no sense and be too selfish.' She was barely audible.

'It doesn't have to make sense and since when did making a choice equal selfishness, especially when you've been true to your obligations for so long? Look, Fran, beloved Fran, just think a moment. Just give me that. Have you ever passed someone in the street and wham, a moment of recognition? You both know something's happened, something that could change your life. If you pass on it's too late and you'll always remember you let it go.'

'It? What is it? It could be even more of a mistake than this.' She mustn't listen to him or she would weaken.

'Ah, so what you are about to do is a mistake, is it? Listen to yourself, Fran. Yes, we could be a mistake too, or it could be a bed of roses. I would die for you, Fran. I would do all in my power to create that bed. Don't pass on by, Fran. Please.'

'Goodbye, Josh.' She replaced the receiver. She could hardly raise her hand to her locket.

Outside the swing was still empty, the white cross gleamed. The daffodils were in flower beneath the leafless sumac. Everything was as it had been; everything, and she had no right to be crying.

At least it wasn't a bridal car, there wasn't even a white bow tied to the aerial, just Ken behind the wheel, sucking mints. Everything was squeaky clean, neat, but then everything about Ken was. They were following Linda and she could just see the top of Lucy's head. She would be sitting on the back seat, strapped on to her booster seat as though it were a throne. For a second she thought of the hen night and Jane in the taxi, the arrangements everyone had made on her behalf.

Fran looked down at her bouquet. Dusky pink silk roses and just one living, breathing red rose, which she had discovered on the doorstep when they left the house. Jane had decided it was a gesture from a neighbour and worried that she had committed a faux pas by not inviting them. Ken had said, 'They should have put in a card, then we could at least thank them.' He was always so anxious to do the right thing.

Quietly Fran had taken it from Jane, inserting it into her bouquet.

'It doesn't go,' Jane had objected.

'It's staying,' Fran insisted, aware of Linda's curious gaze, but pretending not to be. Did she suspect? Was Josh watching as they left?

Ken drew up smoothly at red lights. Mrs Mawes from number 11 waved. She would be on her way back from posting her weekly letter to her grandchildren in Australia. She was a good woman, content with her place in this microcosm of society; well-liked and respected. This could be her in twenty years' time. The notion helped and almost overrode . . .

The lights changed; they turned left. She could have found her way through these familiar streets blindfolded. 'I suppose it's already almost my home,' she murmured.

Beside her Ken nodded, 'A real step up for you. We're all going to be together. It will be splendid.'

She touched the rose. It had a powerful scent, too powerful. She groped for the electronic window control. The window eased down. Ken used his control to override her. The window closed. He said, 'We don't want to mess up your hair, do we?'

'We might not, but I don't give a shit.' She stopped as he flashed her a shocked glance. His cravat was too bunched. She shook her head. 'I mean, no. I'm just hot, a bit flustered.' Ken returned to the business of driving, armed with a confused silence which suited Fran.

After five minutes they drew up in front of the church. Linda had parked in the bay and was puffing up the path carrying Lucy. Her smart grey silk suit blended rather well with Lucy's pink. Would Mike carry her over the threshold? But no, he'd have more sense with his bad back.

She sat while Ken hurried round and opened her door. The flourish was embarrassingly out of character. Linda had set Lucy down in St Margaret's porch, and was rearranging her dress. Fran searched the churchyard. He wasn't there. She should be pleased, but for a moment she felt that she was going to sink to the ground. Ken offered his arm, 'Right, here we go, then.'

Together they walked up the path, her son-in-law taking the place of her long deceased father. Were her parents looking down? If so, they'd be delighted at the safe harbour she was heading towards. She looked across to Muriel's grave. Would she? Probably not. She'd been a rather difficult woman, but who was she to point the finger? She had not been exactly sweetness and light these last six months. She felt ashamed.

Lucy called from the church doorway, 'Come on, Grandma, hurry up.'

Ken's grip on her arm tightened. He waved his daughter silent. Lucy sought Linda's hand. Ken quickened his pace. The organ was playing some interim music. She had asked to enter to anything other than 'Here comes the bride', as that had been played at her last wedding. Would her wish be granted? Was the good fairy at least that much on her side?

Arriving at the open doorway Linda fiddled about with the wedding dress, then kissed her cheek. She was almost in tears, but grinned. 'If your mother were here she'd be welling up, so I'm just surrogating.'

'Idiot,' Fran murmured, kissing her again. She sounded quite normal.

Ken was counting. '. . . Nine, ten. Come on, then. Linda, you go on in and signal the organist. Lucy, get behind your grandmother. Fran, remember left right, left right along the back of the pews to the font, then a pause before setting off down the aisle to the altar, just like the rehearsal.'

Around them the birds were singing. The organ began 'Here comes the Bride.'

Fran looked over her shoulder at Lucy, but she was really searching. Beyond them was the churchyard, still bathed in the thin March sun, and nothing more. 'Ready, darling Lucy?' Her voice shook.

Ken squeezed her hand encouragingly. 'You look wonderful, Fran. You'll be fine.' Could he feel her trembling as she took his proffered arm?

He had straightened his cravat without her noticing, and now they entered and the light was stained red and blue, and there was the sense of many prayers said, some of them by her, for this was the church used by semi-detached and detached alike. This was where Jane had been christened, and Lucy and Harry too. Here was assembled her past and present. It steadied her.

She lifted her head as they approached the font. Their many guests rustled in welcome. There were hats in profusion, the smell of flowers and burning candles. Yes, it was as it should be.

Just then Lucy trod on her hem. Ken stopped. Fran turned, reaching for Lucy's hand. 'Come on, darling, we'll all go side by side, shall we?'

Beside her Ken sighed, then smiled as the guests laughed gently. They took up position in front of the font. Way down, as though seen through a dark tunnel, stood Mike, turning to look at her. The vicar was beaming. Jane was smiling in the left-hand pew and lifted her camera. Flash. Committed, transferred on to celluloid.

Behind Fran the door opened, then closed again. Her heart did the same. It was him. She knew without turning it was Josh. She shouldn't look. She should walk away from the font towards Mike. She must take that step, now.

Ken wasn't moving. Lucy stood still. Why? The signal. The damned signal from the vicar. Come on. Come on. She heard Josh's footsteps. She looked only at Mike. Closer, closer. Then they stopped. Began again. She heard Linda's whisper:

'Of course there's plenty of room.'

Now she looked. He stood in the last pew, next to Linda. His face was drawn and in pain. His hair was longer than was suitable for her world, his duffel coat out of place, the rose in his lapel heartbreaking. Linda was staring at that rose but now Josh's eyes held hers and how could such love exist between two virtual strangers?

Ken squeezed her arm. She saw the vicar's signal. Ken whispered coyly, 'You can catch up with Linda later, you have a more important date.'

He hadn't even seen Josh. How could he not see someone who was everything?

He was urging her forward, Lucy was pulling at her hand and so she walked away from Josh towards her world and she thought she would die.

Down the aisle bathed in that red and blue light, past Mike's daughter Cheryl, the spit of her mother. The children were the spit of Mike's son-in-late Mark. Cheryl and Mark didn't like Fran, didn't like the wedding, wouldn't sit in the front in case it was seen as support. They had used the kids as an excuse, saying they might disrupt the service. Linda said she reckoned they'd hoped their father would sell up, downsize, shed some capital their way. Fat chance of that happening now 'mother of Jane' was moving in.

How could one's head fill with such things? How could the mechanics of walking occur when there was no will?

Fran was a third of the way down now, level with some of Jane's old school friends, one or two of Fran's and Mike's. In front of them were their concert-going friends. She thought she knew them inside out. Did they think that of her? Her mouth was dry. She thought she might faint but it didn't happen and she longed for it, too, for then it would stop.

Here were Mike's neighbours, her neighbours, part of the fabric that had propped her up all these years, but did they like abstract art which freed you from the constraints of conventional subject matter, and furthermore touched the deep, dark past and began to ease it up by the roots? Had they opinions on jazz? Had they ever tried cannabis? What did they think of today's world, tomorrow's? They were good people. They thought Fran Major was set in stone, that this was a nice and proper tying of ends; a progression; a widow and widower heading for mutually tended rose beds with 'his' and 'her' secateurs.

She was making a great many people happy.

Was Josh still there?

Each step was taking her further towards Mike, to the life she'd always known. Away from him. Shut up. Just shut up.

She was two-thirds of the way now. Ken's parents nodded at her. Ken's colleagues from the Crewkerne branch were alongside, while Mike's and Linda's Yeovil partners and associates were lined up on the other side. Three of them played bridge with Mike, while the wives played whist. They were glad there would be a fourth. She hated cards. Soon she would be a wife, a whist wife. Dear God.

Mike was smiling at her. Her shoes rubbed: satin shoes that Jane had thought suitable. Jane, who had snapped in the bridal shop, 'If you hadn't taken to wearing these absurd boots with those long skirts all the time they wouldn't feel tight. It's ridiculously arty at your age.' Jane, who had wanted the evening class to be whist but whist was full. Art had a cancellation.

She faltered. Whist?

Harry was crying in Jane's arms, as he so often did. She loved them but she'd brought up her own child and she didn't want to bring up Jane's children. She stopped. Ken squeezed her hand. 'Don't worry, Harry's fine, Jane can cope,' he whispered. I just need to think, she wanted to shout. She walked on.

Each week it would be whist on Wednesdays. Each week *he*, Josh, would take his class. Each week he would stand with his students, taking time to draw them out, to make sure they gave of their best. Each week he would sit with them in the break, squeezing his polystyrene cup of coffee, perhaps telling them of his time in Paris.

Would he still be so alive? Would his eyes meet another's? Would he forget her? Perhaps not, although he would take another's palette knife, showing rather than taking over. But would he make that other prepared to die for him? Would *it* ever die in that other?

But how did you describe *it*? How could you weigh *it* against all else?

She was almost at the altar. Mike was holding out his hand. His cuff was white. Josh didn't own a white shirt. His were dark-blue, or reds with the sleeves rolled up. His arms were tanned, his hands painted miracles on the canvas and she wanted them to do the same to her, wanted them to touch her, stroke her. She didn't want to end her days not knowing what . . . She was disgusting.

She took Mike's hand. It was warm, safe, known.

36

She and Josh had met outside class just once. They had walked in the park one February lunchtime, his long, multi-coloured scarf trailing in the wind. He had talked of Simon, his most talented full-time student, of cubism, of abstraction in Russia in the 1920s, which had become constructivism and spread to Europe culminating in art deco. Did that restaurant know that? She did and it excited her. He had talked of the power of art, how it could free you from the past and the present. But it couldn't, not quite. Dear God, it couldn't.

He had spoken of his teenage daughter, Emily, who lived with her mother but whom he loved to distraction. His hands had weaved scenarios in the air. His arm had brushed hers. There. *It*. She could feel it now as she stood next to Mike; as the vicar smiled at them both; as Lucy slid into the pew alongside her parents; as the vicar began his address.

There. They had both stood quite still in the park, with the cold wind cutting through them. So close but not touching. Just there. She had known from the start he was the beginning, and ending, of something. Something that she had waited for all her life. Something to do with the mingling of hearts, or lives, of the extension and discovery of self. And she knew he had recognised her too, from the first moment.

And, that day in the park, she had walked away. Of course she had walked away. He had called, 'Don't discard this. Don't pass on by.' But it was nonsense.

He had stood at her easel each week after that, as usual. He had performed miracles for Mike's

37

wedding present but he had said, 'We can't ignore this. It's too important.' But it was at the wrong time; all at the wrong time. The train was set in motion.

How could you hurt these people, and their dreams for you and themselves, when it was you who had changed, and how could you take the risk for yourself, and how could you leave the food uneaten, the speeches unsaid, the cake uncut?

'Who gives this woman . . .?' the vicar droned. Harry wailed. Ken was loud and eager.

The vicar asked Mike, 'Do you, Michael Trevor . . .'

Mike was looking at her, his grey eyes so familiar. Eyes that had met hers over the maths books, the A levels. In the silence after he'd proposed he'd said, 'Say no, if you must. We'll always be friends. But it seems right and I do love you. We're like yin and yang.' It had been like slipping into a pair of slippers, long shaped to her feet.

This week, as she left the class for the last time, Josh had said, 'There are so many minutes, hours, years that we will not now live together.'

She had replied, 'We might not have worked.'

He had shaken his head. 'You know that's not true.'

Mike was staring at her. For a moment she didn't understand, then she heard Jane's fierce whisper, 'Mum.' The vicar cleared his throat. He was smiling encouragement, mouthing, 'Do you Frances Adele . . .?' He had obviously said it once already.

She turned back to Mike and couldn't bear the kindness, the dawning knowingness. She just couldn't bear any of it and took a great deep breath, that sounded thunderous to her, that seemed to ignite every nerve in her, that had a force nothing could stop.

She said, her voice hoarse, her hand gripping Mike's, her voice for him alone, 'Actually, no. Actually, I can't. I've changed. My life has changed, Mike. I'm so sorry. So terribly, terribly sorry. I love you, but not . . . I thought I could.'

Mike was bending close, his lips had clamped shut as they had when he'd broken his leg in his O level year. He was gripping her hands tight: very, very tight. The vicar was closing his order of service, clearing his throat, trying to catch the eye of the organist. All around were mutters, rustles, the anticipation of scandal. Mike nodded, suddenly letting her go.

'What's happening?' Ken's father, Sydney, brayed to his wife.

'Mother,' Jane called.

Harry's wails became full-blooded cries.

Mike said, 'Would it help to talk?'

'Don't be kind,' she whispered, then walked away from him, gasping for air, looking to neither side, her shoes pinching. Clip, clip. Get on the carpet, woman. Deaden your exit. The organ wheezed, started, then died. What did you play for a bolter? Shut up. Just shut up. Why didn't the top of her brain shut up? The guests were turning to one another, then back to her.

She heard Jane call again and again, 'Mother, wait.' She heard her running, felt her hand on her arm. She shook free and now it was she who ran, holding up the layers of silk and running. It was like some bloody farce. Stop swearing.

Past Cheryl she ran. Cheryl who was shaking her head, then Linda, who was standing in the aisle, her hand up, waving Jane back. What did she think it was, a road junction? Linda caught her arm, held her fast, her face pale and anxious. 'What the hell's going on, Fran?'

Fran wasn't sure. She looked around. All these faces, all these friends but without Josh they were invisible. Where was Josh? He was by the open door. The light was streaming in. 'I can't do it,' she shouted to Linda. 'I've got to go with him.' She nodded at the man she was *sure* she loved more than life itself, more than all of this. Sure or thought? But what if . . . ?

Linda looked from Josh to Mike. She released her grip, shaking her head. 'Well, go on, then, make a run for it, but your timing's crap, you silly old fool, and we're going to be stuck with the canapes for ever. Who the hell is he?' Her voice was strange, shaking, as Fran's had not; quiet as Fran's had not been.

Fran thrust her bouquet into Linda's hands, snatching at the rose. 'Look after Mike.' She wouldn't look back towards the altar. She reached the door, reached Josh, who took her hand, gripping it very tightly. They ran towards the car park, her breath jolting in her chest, so that she felt as though she was half weeping, sounding as though she was, knowing that she was. Jane screamed after her, 'Mother, how could you do this to me? Are you insane?'

Oh, God. Oh, God. The gravel was moving beneath her feet. Josh said, 'I love you. I'll always be with you. Always. Trust me.'

40

CHAPTER FOUR

They drove out of the car park in his ancient Fiesta, her heart beating as though it would explode. She was panting, laughing, crying. His hands were shaking on the steering wheel. Her dress was bunched up. They turned into the main road, hurtling along, breaking the 30mph speed limit. Outside the Spar a pedestrian made as if to flag them down. He was pointing frantically to her door.

Josh steered into the kerb.

'Don't stop. Please don't stop.' Her voice was hoarse and high.

Josh leaned across and his voice was as distorted. 'It's all right, it must be your dress, caught in the door. I'll open, you gather up.' He sounded as though he'd been running.

The pedestrian rushed over. It was Mr Price, who delivered the parish magazine to Mike. Josh flicked the handle, pushing open the door, Fran scooped, Mr Price stared. 'A change of plan,' Josh explained, shutting the door sharply, sitting back in his seat, putting on his seat belt. 'Be safe,' he suggested to Fran as he indicated and started to draw out, but it was into the path of another car. A horn blared, Josh braked. 'Idiotic. I didn't see it.' He dragged a trembling hand through his hair, checked his mirror, drew away. Mr Price stared after them open-mouthed.

Fran plugged in her belt. Be safe? Now she was trembling. What the hell had she done?

They drove out of town on to the A303. She

stared ahead. Neither of them spoke above the rattle and roar of the car. She couldn't find enough complete words, although there were the start of many. There were images, or fragments of images. There were sounds, or bursts of sound. There was the pressure of Mike's hands on her, Jane catching at her arm, Linda's grip. Her voice and the canapes, the hats. Lucy. They drove and drove.

She was hot, so hot. She wound down the window. It was still a fine day. She expected it to have moved on to the darkness of night. She was too cold. She grappled with the handle. Her hands were weak, too weak to grip. Her mouth was dry, her mind was falling apart. What had she done?

'Let me.' He reached across and closed the window, his eyes on the road. His hands were still shaking and his voice sounded as though it was caught in his throat. He half turned, trying to look ahead and at her at the same time. She waved him away. He caught her hand, turned to the front and suddenly they were hanging on to one another as though they had nothing else; and now they hadn't. She had cut herself adrift. She was terrified, exalted. 'This is the best day of my life,' he said fiercely. 'But it must be the best and worst of yours.' He kissed her hand. It was the first time she had felt his lips. He said, against her skin, 'I'll make it the best for you too, I promise.'

She moved her hand within his, laying her palm against his cheek. 'Josh,' she said, as though she had never said the name before. 'Josh.' They had only touched for a reason before: 'Try the brush this way. Use the palette knife here.'

He half turned again, kissing her palm, flicking a glance into the mirror, then ahead, indicating at the first lay-by sign, turning, braking carefully beneath overhanging trees which were just beginning to bud, switching off the engine, undoing his seat belt. In the silence he turned, undid hers, easing it over her arm. She hardly dared move. He pulled the pins from her pleated hair. His face was so close. His fingers brushed her neck, traced the shape of her eyes, her mouth. He was closer still and his eyes never left her, and now he was kissing her eyes, her cheeks and finally her mouth; gently, slowly and all their shaking stopped.

They kissed again and again, and now, slowly, gently, they held one another, she with a sense of wonder.

He said, 'I can't believe how I feel. It's as though for the first time everything is hugely vibrant. It's as though I've been practising, that's all, practising until you came along.'

Then they were crying, both of them, with a sort of relief, a huge inescapable joy, until a lorry pulled in behind them and the driver made his way to the hedge, squeezing through just to the left of them. Josh pulled away, dragging out his handkerchief, wiping her face and his own. Then he half laughed, raising his eyebrows, nodding his head towards the hedge. 'Being severely practical, that guy's got a point.'

She hit him, because she'd just been thinking the same thing and how could she push through any hedge, go to any loo in a wedding dress? Well, she could do anything if she could bolt from a church and sit here, in a small rattletrap, with a man she barely knew. So, after the lorry left, she did just that, returning to the car while Josh did the same, and as she settled herself she let the joy take over, let the sheer elation carry her, push away the risk, the guilt, the thought of Mike and his clamped mouth, his long-ago broken leg, but back it came.

Mother, how could you do this to me?

Would it help to talk?

Josh returned, removing his duffel coat before he clambered back into the car. He was wearing his maroon velvet jacket over his navy shirt, and deep-green moleskin trousers. Again he gripped her hand. This time he kissed each finger, while she leant forward and kissed his temple. His skin was cold from the fresh wind that was blowing but still he smelt of that mixture of paint, turps, linseed, tobacco and just him.

Mother how could you do this to me?

Would it help to talk?

She'd done it. *She*'d done it. She must find a way to live with it. *She* must find a way to live with it. *It*. What was it? Love? It had to be. After this.

He put his arm round her. A Renault pulled in behind them. The driver was on his mobile phone.

She laid her head on his shoulder. It felt good. She closed her eyes, took a great breath, holding it, forcing herself to see and hear Jane, to see and hear Mike clearly, slowly, replaying once, twice more. Finally she let out her breath, feeling the muscles in her neck loosen because she had leapt off a precipice and had to learn to fly, or she would crash.

She stared up, now, at the clear blue sky, the budding oak above, and for her, too, the colours were vibrant in a way they'd never been and there was texture she'd never noticed, and now the relief was uncontainable and joyous. She said softly, 'There are crèches or Ken must sell the house.

There's Mike's bridge evening, the pattern of his life will be undisturbed and Cheryl will be relieved. It doesn't excuse me, but it makes it bearable.'

His arm tightened around her. 'I feel drunk, I think, strange, excited, nervous.'

She could see the pulse beating in his neck. For so many months she had wanted to kiss this spot. Now she did. A shaft of something reached deep, deep down. She closed her eyes. He kissed her. The shaft sliced deeper. She was like water: limp, on fire. How could she be both? She opened her eyes, swimming for the surface, clenching her hands, her nails digging into her palms. Yes, this was real. She formed her words slowly, so slowly, as slowly as her mind. 'But where on earth can we go?' she asked.

'Nowhere until we've eaten sandwiches, smoked salmon. Not as grand as . . .' He was reaching over to the back seat, his voice still not quite steady. 'Coffee from a flask. It can't be beaten.'

The Renault pulled out, passed them, roared back on to the main road.

*   *   *

They drove to St Ives, where Josh told her he had booked a small flat in one of the narrow twisting streets above which seagulls called. 'You were so sure?' she murmured as he shut the door behind them, looking at her, just looking.

He shook his head. 'I was never less sure of anything in my life, but if you went ahead and married Mike I knew I had to be away from anywhere you were, until I could bear to pass on and never know what we could have been.'

45

She checked her watch. It was just after five. The speeches would have been over, she and Mike would be changing in the room set aside for them in the hotel. At five thirty Ken would have marched them left right left right to the taxi. The flight would leave from Bristol at eight.

She shivered, looking from Josh to the room. The sloping eaves, microwave in the corner, the sink, the huge window, the lights around the bay, the sullen sea, the fading light. She stroked her creased and muddied wedding dress. She was alone in a studio flat overlooking St Ives bay with a man she had kissed for the first time this afternoon, who had supplied a flask and sandwiches which they had eaten as though food had been denied them for months, who was leaning against the door, smiling at her. Who was coming towards her now. Who was taking her in his arms.

She sagged against this man she could not believe she had never held, because it was as though she had always known how it would feel, how every other man should have felt but never had. It was as though, at long last, a void had been filled and expectation realised.

Josh whispered, as though astonished, 'I know now I've missed every moment I haven't been with you.'

Somewhere below a radio was playing. Outside a child rang his cycle bell, but nothing touched them, here, in this world, as he stripped her of the wedding dress, as she stepped beyond it, as he carried her to the bed, covered with an ethnic throw. Slowly he lowered her, joined her. Slowly he ran his hand the length of her and it was as she had imagined and longed for.

It was as though she was floating, merging, flying. Each second was full, each minute endless. His voice rose and fell. His hands were gentle, hard, urgent, adoring. His skin was soft, his muscles moved beneath her fingers. She felt she had ceased to breathe and was suspended, but not alone; that she would never be alone again. Each touch was a miracle, each kiss endless. They moved together, wordlessly now, but understanding everything the other meant. Together. Together. Faster. Faster. There were no barriers between them. They were totally one, and they sank and rose together, flying, floating, soaring and then gently, tenderly sinking down to the earth together.

His arm was heavy on her, warm and heavy, and it belonged. They spoke soft words. They touched lips, bodies, fingertips to fingertips. And so evening turned to night, and she wondered at this immensity of love, which only this morning had lain dormant, untouched, unreleased, and saw the same wonder in him.

*   *   *

When she woke in the morning, the sheet tangled about her legs, he was gone, although the bed was still warm. Uncertainly she called his name, then saw the piece of paper propped on the table set for two in front of the huge window beyond which the sea gleamed. The throw around her dragged on the varnished floorboards, cool beneath her bare feet. She reached for the note: 'Gone for supplies!'

Stupid woman. How could she doubt him when they held the key to one another, when neither could live without the other? She half laughed her

47

relief, tracing his handwriting with her forefinger. He was in every loop and stroke. She stared across the bay, feeling as though she was living in a different universe, wondering if contentment like this had a name, knowing, even as she thought it, that of course it had. It was love. *It* was love. It *was* love.

She was dazzled at its simplicity and its power. It had brought her to this.

They ate lunch at a pub. She wore the top and long one-size Indian skirt he had borne back in triumph, having tracked down a small boutique-type shop a few streets in from the seafront. He had bought soft leather moccasins which he'd sized by comparing them with her wedding shoes he'd taken with him. He'd also bought champagne, and croissants which they'd eaten in bed, drinking the champagne from tumblers. The spring sun had blazed. They had made love again in its heat and then he'd pulled her to him. 'Let's go pubbing, woman.'

Now here they were, drinking lager and eating pasties, and she was still hungry. There were other people in the bar, but it was as though they were alone as she felt his thigh against hers and the weight of his arm around her. They seemed to be in their own world as she pictured the Newlyn artists that he described; their joy in everyday scenes, their use of light; as he told her that Cornwall was a marvellous bastion of abstract painting, her great new love.

'Alongside you,' she said.

At three they returned to the flat, picking up his artist's materials from the Fiesta, and instead of telling her, he erected his easel and showed her what he had meant, standing at the window, sketching, in a light linseed wash, the bay, the children on the foreshore, the upturned boat, and she gloried in it all.

The window was open, the wind lifted her hair.

'Here, try it,' Josh said. He handed her his brush. 'Sort out the breakwater for me, interpret it as you wish. I know you will anyway, but how about trying for an essence of light?' His fingers touched hers and the painting was forgotten as they sank on to the bed. His mouth was on hers, passionate and demanding. He removed her clothes and her hands were demanding in turn, in a way which was new to her. Finally they rested and she held him still, kissing his lips gently, making him wait, smiling into his smile, sinking down on him at last, as though she were another person.

But she wasn't. She was the Fran who had danced on a table when she was eighteen and unattached, only to forget and become someone who had been what others needed for far too long. Now she was free. Free to be naked with this man. Free to ignore roses that needed dead-heading, whist, grandchildren, legal files, echoes of her past. Free, gloriously free, to explore everything and anything. Free. Or half of her was. The other half thought of them all the time and something inside her was breaking.

*   *   *

That evening she left him by the window. She waited a moment by the door, watching him as he drank in the fading day. He turned, concern making his voice quiet, his hands restless. 'Please

49

let me phone for you.'

No, this was for her to do. She smiled. He gave her strength, all this gave her strength.

The phone box smelt as all phone boxes seem to. She dialled the number. It rang, once only. 'Yes?' Mike said.

She was watching the tumbling clouds above the clustered roofs, watching their shapes change as though some great artist were joyously creating from the depths of his being, or so she told herself, but really she was trying to balance her sadness at her leaving with her joy at her arrival.

'It's me,' she said and her voice trembled.

'Hello, me,' he said, as he often used to. 'I knew you'd call.'

She smiled, but wanted to weep. If only she could have cut herself in two and lived two lives but she had known he would make it easy. He was her friend. Even now, she hoped he was her friend.

'Forgive me, Mike.'

'Always.' He hesitated. 'But why?' Now his voice broke. 'Who? Why?'

Anger had crept in. But of course it would and it was what she deserved.

'Why?' she asked. How could she put into words the reason? Words would trivialise. Words were not enough. Words would hurt him, but they were all she had. 'I couldn't pass on by,' she explained. 'It was the art class. Something happened to me. It opened a door to somewhere I didn't know I had, showed me someone I had forgotten, and it gave me Josh. Something was there between us from the start. I had to take the chance. Forgive me.'

A pause, an empty pause. Was it filled with anger, regret, pain, hate? She wouldn't talk into it.

50

She would wait. At last he said, 'Dear Fran, you always did take an interminable time to make a decision, but just this once I wish you could have sorted your act out a little earlier. I'm not used to standing alone in the spotlight.' The anger had gone, a ruefulness remained.

'Oh, Mike.'

'It's the thought of you being with someone while you were with me. It's the thought of the lies.' Anger had returned.

'I wasn't with him. I had never touched him, never kissed him. There was just something . . .' She trailed off. Words were so limited, so useless.

Mike's voice sharpened with alarm now, not anger. 'Oh, Fran, my dear. But then, how do you know how it will work out? How do you know what he is really like? My dear girl, what have you done? Remember David? Look, let's just keep calm. Why don't I postpone the letting of your house, put it off for a couple of weeks? Perhaps I should cancel it altogether? What are your plans? Oh, my God, Fran, remember last time.'

Thankfully the machine was telling her she had fewer and fewer seconds. She said, 'Mike, I've got to go, I'll be in touch.' She replaced the receiver. Words were black and white. Words were sharp and asked questions that had no place in the world she had created. Not yet. Not when they levered at the deeper layers, prising up David, drawing him into her new world, when she thought she had almost painted him out, left him behind. Almost, but not really, and now that old dreadful panic was racing and she pressed her hands hard against her eyes, bringing in all the old ploys, the breathing, the counting, the hard pressure of her fingers in her

51

hair until it passed. Until at last it passed.

She took a deep breath and dialled Jane, tired now, but needing to make this last call. 'I'm so sorry, darling,' she began, but then the ball was snatched from her court and for a full five minutes Jane gave her a hammer blow by hammer blow account of the superfluous photographer, the politics of a reception without a bride, a bridesmaid without her grandmother, the bill, and it was almost a relief. 'Which Mike paid, not a murmur. That man is a saint, and who was that with you and what am I supposed to do now? I've accepted the job. Are you coming back? Are you intending to fulfil any of your obligations, your promises? How could you deprive me of a father?'

Fran rubbed her forehead. The moon had found a gap in the clouds. A paper bag was scudding along the pavement. Two boys on mountain bikes tore past with no lights. She felt chilled, alone, and pulled Josh's jacket tighter. She rubbed her cheek against the velvet of her shoulder, imagining him. She said quietly and sadly, 'Mike will always be your godfather.'

'No thanks to you.'

Fran stared up at the clouds again, and now they were racing and so was a terrible anger, an anger that took her by surprise. 'I used a childminder for you, Jane. They do still exist, you know.' It wasn't what she'd intended to say. She was going to apologise, to grovel.

'And don't you think I would have been better off with my grandmother?'

'Since your grandmother was six feet under, I hardly think so.' She had worked, struggled, protected Jane, which is what a mother did and

52

which she had never resented, but her daughter had a husband, a life. Surely she could see that her mother had a right to one too, that she didn't have to be there to pick up the pieces all the time? Or was she wrong? Probably. She didn't know and the anger was over as soon as it had begun.

'That's right, be glib. That's your answer to everything, isn't it. But at least we knew where Grandmother was, which wasn't running around behaving like some tart. The neighbours are having a field day. You've made a complete fool of yourself and us.' Jane was talking, almost screaming, in bursts, as though snatching at breaths in between.

Fran could picture her and she wanted to hold her because Jane was quite right, of course. 'Darling, I'm sorry, I know I should have sorted it out sooner. It was unforgivable and after all your help, too. I just sort of snapped. I couldn't go through with it.'

'Well, state the obvious, why don't you, and damn the rest of us.'

Stung again, Fran lashed out: 'Actually, Mike's being very kind and I know he'll find someone better.'

'Well, that won't be hard.'

For a moment neither spoke, there was just a great silence. Fran said, 'I expect it won't, he . . .'

'So who *have* you found?' Jane interrupted. 'I still can't believe it. It was like a bad film. Are you insane, or just utterly selfish? For God's sake, I suppose I'm to have a stranger for a stepfather. It's bad enough when I don't remember my real father, but to have . . .'

Desperate to stop Jane, Fran told her about

53

Josh.

Jane's voice was almost a screech. 'An art teacher, someone you hardly know? Well, that's it. Mike would have been so right, can't you see that? It would have solved everything.'

The moon was back behind the clouds. The street lights did their best. The sea was pounding as the tide came in. Fran heard herself shouting, 'For God's sake, Jane, change the record. We should be talking about how badly I behaved, not how inconvenient everything is for you. Surely you and Ken are able to sort out your lives. You're bloody adults, aren't you? I love my grandchildren, I love you, but I have a right to my choice, even if I have done it horribly clumsily, and it's for that I apologise, nothing else. Do you hear me? Nothing else.'

She slammed down the phone, pushing herself out of the phone box, taking great deep breaths, striding blindly, setting off along the front. She was not alone. There were others strolling, but these she overtook. Faster, faster.

Suddenly she stopped dead, sank on to one of the benches, staring out at the moon-rich sky, pulling Josh's jacket tighter still. What was she doing here? She felt more alone than she had ever felt in her life before, and frightened and guilty, and the confusion made her shake, because she didn't know if Josh would be Jane's stepfather. She didn't know where they would go from here. She didn't know anything about anything.

But then Josh said, as he sat down beside her, sliding his arm around her, 'I'll take you back, if that's what you want.'

How had he found her here? Was he a mind

54

reader? Would he always be near? She leant into him, clinging to him, starting to cry, heedless of the glances from the few late walkers, eventually letting him wipe her face with his oil-stained handkerchief, letting him help her to her feet and hold her tightly, so tightly.

CHAPTER FIVE

Fran slept in Josh's arms and woke to the sound of the sea and a turbulent day. He kissed her. Her eyes ached from last night and the memory embarrassed her. He saw and repeated, 'I'll take you back this minute, if it's what *you* want, but you'll have to walk if it's what Jane wants, or the neighbours, or Uncle Tom Cobbley and all.'

She wanted nothing more at this moment other than to lie here, watching the sea, hearing it, feeling his arms around her. Just that, nothing more. Again it seemed he sensed everything she felt and for a further hour that is what they did, before he slipped from the bed, dressed, borrowing his own jacket with a grin. 'Coffee? Croissants? Newspaper?'

She smiled. 'Yes to the first two, no to the last.'

He left. She dressed in the skirt, and one of his paint-stained sweatshirts which was sufficiently large to make her feel delicate and beloved. They were here, for a week, or maybe two, or perhaps three. Here, far away from real life. There was no need yet to think of the future, of the letting of her house, of her job. Well, what job? No need, because they were suspended in this moment of time. No need to think of anything and that was something she had never experienced before.

After their takeaway cappuccino and croissant, eaten in front of the window, Josh reached past her, taking the Fiesta keys from the ashtray on the windowsill, throwing them into the air, catching them with one hand and stroking her cheek with the other. 'How about a drive? I'd like to show you Lamorna, on the south coast. It's where Lamorna Birch lived and painted. Not an abstract artist, I grant you, but pretty wonderful. You might like to try playing with impressionism, you know. We'll go via Tom Ellis's neck of the woods: an abstract painter, I knew. He became a stockbroker but your work makes me think of his.' His eyes were alight with eagerness. He wore a rollneck under his shirt, because he had returned his jacket to her.

She clasped his hand. 'Lead on.'

They drove via Tom's old shack near Zennor. 'Tom liked Hilton, who saw all Cornish landscape in abstract terms, especially his evocative work. Hilton is a bit obscure for me, he was one of the "unfinished" school, but I'm sure you'd like him. Nicholson's more refined and his abstracts have more references to the outside world. Maybe he'd be easier for Jane to understand. It might be an idea to find some of his to show her, might help you reach out to her.'

She kissed him. Yes, perhaps. In due course. They left the car. She let the wind pluck at her clothes and hair, staring out across the moor to the sea, and she longed to paint the clumped rocks, the turbulent sky, the flattening heather.

'Would you like to come tomorrow, Fran, or the next day, whatever? We'll both have a go, you

56

doing it your way, me doing it mine.' He stood beside her, the wind tearing at his hair. 'Isn't there a song like that?'

'If there isn't, there should be.'

'Try not to worry about them all,' Josh said. 'Time is a great healer. Let's get on to Lamorna.'

Time. How much time?

'What about your daughter?' she asked as they drove to Lamorna, parking illegally in the car park at the Wink, where the beer was good and the pasties better, Josh told her as they walked down the valley road towards the sea. He slipped his arm around her. 'She's cool about it even though she's difficult now she's thirteen. She's known you were there, that I had hopes, and she'll be pleased, because I'm pleased, thrilled, over the moon . . .'

She laughed and put her hand over his mouth, but it was forced, and he knew and kissed her hand, then clasped it, as he walked her briskly towards the sea. So, Emily had known. It was only Fran who hadn't found the courage to tell. Stay in the present, she insisted to herself, no past, no future. Look at these hidden houses and high banks overloaded with primroses and, somewhere, the sound of the stream, and everywhere the celebration of birds who were finding great things with which to build their nests. It worked, the moment passed.

His old hessian art bag jogged on his shoulder. 'It never gets cold here, you know. Never has, never will. Paradise, it is.'

'Never? You're the oracle?'

'I'm the main man, the man who knows.'

'A sort of second sight?' They were heading down the slope and the bay lay before them, bright

57

with the sun that had broken through. There were a car park, a café, some terraced houses. Inside the bag would be his sketch pad, charcoal, pencils, enough for them both.

'Actually, not quite. Mum and Dad live a few minutes away, towards Penzance. They're potters. We could visit, if you like.' He was tentative.

She wasn't sure if she liked because she wanted no more judgements passed.

He had been watching her face and now kissed her hand. 'Meeting the son is more than enough? That's fine.' He was laughing, running her down the road, across the car park on to the slipway and the small beach. He squatted, scooping sand with his hands, making her a castle. She joined him in gouging a moat in damp, cold sand, feeling the heat of the sun on her head and shoulders. As she scooped, water seeped up, half filling it.

He kissed her mouth, then, digging his hands deep into the sand he crab-walked backwards towards the sea, making a channel for the rapidly incoming tide. 'We'll wait, watch it fill, shall we?' he called from the surf line.

It was a question, not a statement. He waited, smiling, the wind tugging at his hair. Josh did that, he asked questions and listened to the answer. It was an eternity since anyone else had done so.

She rose, dusted her hands and made for the sea wall, levering herself up on to it. 'Yes, and then we'll "do" your parents.'

Had he told them too? She didn't want to know.

He ran up the beach on to the sea-rounded stones, not altering his pace at all until he reached her, then he leant against her knees, taking her face between his hands. 'You are so beautiful,' he said

58

against her mouth. 'I love you so much, but where has it come from?'

Again it was a question. He stepped back, staring at her. 'All this love,' he repeated, 'it's bursting from me, as though it's been dammed up and I'm not frightened of it because I just know it will never empty and, what's more, it's matched by you. Do you know what I mean?' He was painting great images with his hands. 'There aren't words for it. Do you understand? Its like that moat, it's always filling. No matter what happens the water will seep in, wonderful in its relentlessness. How do I know that our love will? I just do. *Do* you understand?' His voice was urgent, his face intense as though he could hardly believe his feelings.

She caught at his hands, kissing each one, dismissing all else, for this moment, because of course she understood. He tore free, reaching for his sketch pad from his bag, his eyes never leaving her. Beyond embarrassment, she stared back and wondered if he would capture her love. But how could emotion be translated? She asked him this question.

He drew frantically, then brushed his hair from his eyes. 'I don't know,' he said at last. 'Sometimes it can, sometimes it can't. That's the anguish, but it doesn't matter. Because I will see it here.' He tapped his head fiercely with his pencil. 'I will always see it here and feel it here.' He touched his chest. 'Always, do you understand?' He had stopped drawing and took a pace forward, leaning against her knees again. 'Always.' He didn't kiss her, just looked so deeply into her eyes that for a moment she had no separate existence. At last they kissed and it was different again from yesterday, less frantic, less desperate, more certain, more deep, more . . . oh, she didn't know. He drew away at last, and they were both surprised at the daylight, the wind, the sound of the sea charging up the beach and dragging back.

Silently he levered himself up beside her and held her hand. They watched as the tide gained momentum, as the waves sniffed at the mouth of the channel, took up the scent, and rushed tumbling and tearing along the gully, closer and closer with each surge of the tide, reaching the moat, dividing, encircling, clawing at the foundations of the castle, sucking the grains back into the beach, again and again until the castle was gone, until it was as though it had never been and the tide roared on, covering the sand, heading forward across the rounded stones.

'It won't reach us,' Josh said quietly. 'It won't touch us. Nothing will do that.'

Fran stared at the foaming water, listened to the rumbling stones, the shifting pebbles, and all the while Josh's hand was warm, his arm was light but sure around her shoulders, his coat was tight about her body. At last the tide calmed, a good six feet from the wall, and settled, rattling and tumbling the pebbles beneath it. It did not reach them. It did not touch them. But things could. They could make you hide, make you nurture invisibility, acquiescence. Why was she thinking this? Josh was not David. How dare Mike? Josh was *not* David. How dare the shadows come when she had almost painted them out, when love, such a love, had reached her.

He whispered as he jumped down, 'Trust me.'

She held out her hands. He took them. She

jumped. The stones shifted, crunched. They walked back to the slipway. 'Always,' she said and allowed herself to believe in him, for the moment, and leant into him and let the happiness roar away the memories.

*   *   *

They drove to his parents' home, which was a detached cottage set alongside the road with a POTTY POTTERS sign hung above the sort of lay-by created for callers. Josh led her along a crazy-paving path narrowly avoiding the tall gnarled roses. He ignored the front porch with its huge old ship's bell and the order 'Whack me and someone will come'. Instead, he led the way round the side of the house, holding her tightly as though he feared she would bolt. But she'd already done that, she told him drily. They hugged, then he rat-a-tat-tatted on the bright-red door around which pots of leggy geraniums clustered.

'It's open,' a full-throated female voice called.

'It's your son, with the only woman he loves apart from you, you old darling,' Josh said, opening the door, ducking beneath the low lintel, dragging Fran in behind. Fran should have felt foolish, but she didn't. Instead, she felt proud.

A plump, elderly woman, wearing a long red-and-purple skirt, and flowing top, turned from the Aga, looking astonished. A sauce, clearly rich in garlic, dripped from the wooden spoon she held. An equally plump Norfolk terrier, lying on the rug at her feet, opened one eye and caught the drips on a long tongue. Josh dragged Fran past the large cluttered pine table, reaching his mother, kissing her cheek, an arm round them both. 'This is Fran, Mum. I love her and she loves me. You always said I'd meet someone and I have, and it's even better than gravy, you appalling mutt.' He stroked the dog with his boot.

His mother was looking from Fran to Josh, but then she dropped the spoon on to the Aga, calling, 'Fred, get out of that studio, you old bugger. Your son's got his act together at last.' She swept Josh and Fran into a great hug, hustling them to the table, shouting towards the open door, 'Fred, I won't tell you again. Oh, for goodness sake, Josh, go and get the old fool. He'll have his ear plugs in just in case I need him for anything.'

Josh shook his head at Fran. 'She only appears a lunatic.'

His mother pushed Fran down on to the carver. Fran said, 'Off you go.' Josh headed for the door, ducking again as he stepped out into the sunlight.

His mother patted Fran's shoulder. 'You just sit, I'll sort out a mug of something.'

'Let me help.'

'Can't help in someone else's kitchen, causes all sorts of upsets.' Josh's mother bustled to the Aga where she transferred the simmering kettle to the boiler plate, saying over her shoulder, 'Call me Jessie and tell me everything. The last time I heard from him was on Friday and, golly gee, talk about down in the mouth because you were about to trip up the aisle with someone else. Did a runner, did you? How deliciously scandalous, but I bet you've had your knuckles rapped. Coffee, tea, or herbal pee? Can't stand the stuff myself but we've camomile for Fred's nerves and cranberry for his tinkles, and nettle . . . Can't remember what that's for but he could give you chapter and verse. He truly loves his supposed bad health. Its his constant companion.' Jessie was reaching for two mugs which lived on the chimney shelf.

'Coffee, please.' Fran could feel the laughter building.

'Ground or instant?' Jessie nudged the terrier. 'On you go, Hercules. On to your bed. They're like men, a bit smelly, all tongue and under your feet, given half the chance.' She was poking her head into the larder. 'The ground is freshly bought, Fran. I'd like you to have that. Anyone who makes my darling boy look and sound so happy deserves the best.' She emerged with a packet of Colombian. Hercules had not moved an inch.

Fran said, 'That would be wonderful, I love it almost as much as I love Josh.' The two women smiled at one another. It should have sounded absurd, mawkish, but it didn't. It just sounded right.

Jessie found a pair of scissors in the end drawer of the table, and passed them to Fran, before reaching for the cafetière which sat on the overloaded dresser behind her. 'Put enough in for all four of us, while I sort things out. Now, come on, what happened?'

Fran snipped the corner of the packet, then poured the coffee into the cafetière, wondering where to start, but before she could, Jessie spoke again: 'D'you really love him?' Jessie was patting the kettle, egging it up to the boil. 'Come on, I won't bite but I'd like to know.' Her voice was very gentle and quiet. Her eyes were Josh's.

For a moment Fran thought about what she should say, but then just let it come. 'Yes, I really love him. It's not like anything I've known, otherwise I would have cut the cake, drunk the sherry, as perhaps I should have done. Or handled it all differently anyway.' The relief of talking without wounding others was incredible, that of sharing heady.

'Should? Who says what you should do or not do? Shouldn't it be what is right for you?' Jessie was stirring the pot, her voice stronger now and as casual as though they were discussing the weather.

Fran had a sudden image of that long rush away from Mike, from her life; a replay of his voice, Jane's voice, and said quietly, 'Timing is all. I left it far too late, for him and for my daughter, maybe her children, too. It was atrocious.' It was good to say it out loud.

Jessie was bearing the kettle towards the table, the handle wrapped in a spotless tea towel. 'People survive and prosper, believe it or not. Who knows what's around the corner for them, for us all? It's arrogance to feel that we are the only solution to their problems, to their lives.' Her voice was quiet, her eyes as intense as her son's. 'Allow yourself to live your own life, my dear. Yes, you could have told them, but did you really know what you were going to do? It's to your credit that you *thought* you were going to go through with it. Think of it that way. Anyway, once the bairns are up and running we can surely allow ourselves the indulgence of our own wishes.' It wasn't a question.

For a long moment they just stood quietly, assessing one another, two adults with a common link. Then Jessie reached out, touching Fran's cheek as her son so often did. 'Don't beat yourself up, my dear. It's done. You'll waver, panic, but your

64

course is set and I for one am grateful, so there.' Now Jessie poured water on the coffee grounds. 'You are chief plunger,' she said, returning the kettle to the Aga, before going to the back door and calling, 'Will the party of two come and join the rest of the world, especially now we've had a bit of a gossip.'

Just like that, Fran thought. I feel better, just like that, and missed her own mother for the first time in many years. But that made her think of Jane, so she plunged and poured, and found sugar in case anyone needed it.

* * *

Over a lunch which neatly polished off the 'one for the table, one for the freezer' casserole that Jessie had prepared, the talk was first of Fran and then of pots, pots and pots, with Fred pointing out Josh's on the top shelf of the kitchen dresser, Jessie's on the middle, and his own on the windowsill overlooking the back garden, from which he could see his beloved studio.

Fran hadn't known Josh threw pots. Jessie wiped her plate clean with a crust of her own bread, saying, 'I doubt that you know how he threw his money away, as well.'

Fred and Josh exchanged a look, with Fred shaking a finger at Jessie. Jessie leant forward. 'Don't you do that to me, Fred Benton. Fran *should* know, because while her chick has flown the nest, young Emily certainly hasn't.' She bent towards Fran. 'Having said that, you're going to have to get that Jane to grasp the fact that her wings are fully developed. There is the "no" word, you know.

We've all got to learn it. Don't let her bully you.'

'Mum,' Josh almost shouted, just as Fred tutted, 'Jessie.'

Jessie laid her hand on Fran's knee. 'This is woman's talk, isn't it, Fran. We understand that no harm is meant, that this is . . .'

'Meddling,' Josh said with finality. 'Leave her family out of it. and yes, Fran knows that I have Emily, and let me point out that she is no longer in my nest. But she is in here.' He banged his chest.

Jessie raised her eyebrows. 'Don't be histrionic, dear. Now, Fred, go and find the choc ices in the freezer. Bring at least three, but four if you feel your cholesterol can cope. Perhaps you can have nettle tea instead of coffee afterwards. Is it detoxifying? I was trying to remember earlier. We have to hope that Josh has more of my genes, Fran, or you could find yourself embroiled in just such a balancing act. How Fred ever gets any work done, heaven alone knows. But perhaps that's to do with genius. Because he is one, and a gem and I love him to bits.'

Fred had totally ignored Jessie and was deep in conversation with Josh about friends on the other side of Penzance. Jessie tutted and offered more bread to Fran, who had no room. Jessie waggled the plate towards the men, who smiled their refusal without a break in conversation. 'Then I'll just have one more tiny piece while we wait for the great one to find time to hunt down the pud.' Jessie took the largest remaining slice and tore off the crust, eating it steadily and saying, 'Fran, dear, you must come and see us as often as you can. We don't see enough young people.'

Fran smiled at the description. Linda would

appreciate that. But would she? She had to phone her. Perhaps tonight. She shrank from the thought. 'Josh sometimes brings Emily, so next time you can bring your grandbabies and Jane too, if that appeals. Perhaps Ken would find it a little . . .' Jessie looked helplessly around the room. 'Well, a little too shambolic, shall we say. That was Catherine's problem, in some respects. She liked things nice, but wouldn't get off her arse to help. She was infinitely more interested in sticking that particular part of her anatomy into the air for some little toerag to . . .'

'Jessie,' Fred warned her sternly.

'I've told you, this is girl talk.' But now the men were alert and listening. 'Basically, Catherine's a whore.'

Fran touched Josh's knee. His hand covered hers, he mouthed, 'Sorry, this happens from time to time.'

Jessie was unstoppable. 'Strange, really, I can remember when Josh first brought her down; I didn't like her then and don't like her now. I used to think it was because she was doing Interior Design but she's a nasty bag of tricks. Never could see what he saw in her, but he gave it his best shot when she told him darling Em was on the way.' For a moment the river seemed to run dry, as Jessie stared across at Fred, and now Fran could see the pain in the woman. Jessie shook herself, as though discarding dark thoughts. 'I worry, though, because they're tucked up in Roger the Dodger's den and it can't be doing Em good. He's the current lover, one in a long line, I might add.'

Josh was squeezing Fran's hand too hard and now she saw his mother's anguish reflected in him.

Jessie said quietly, 'My boy still tries too hard for the bitch. He gave her most of the proceeds from the house and moved to darling Hamdon Terrace, and'—Jessie banged the table—'and took up teaching so there was a steady maintenance for Em. What does Catherine do? Says she lost the capital trying to set up her business, so he gives up and gives her maintenance too. Will she work? Says she can't. No childcare.'

Fran thought of Jane and hoped she wouldn't work either, but wasn't that only because it would ease her conscience? Jessie was shaking a finger at Fran, demanding her attention, such was her indignation. 'She says she has rent to pay and a rent book to prove it, but she's cohabiting. Will Josh get proof? No.' She threw up her hands. 'There, I rest my case.' But she didn't, because on she swept. 'That boy of mine insists on believing her story of business losses, but I know that little madam. I know she's stashing it away like some gloating miser.'

'Mum.' Josh's voice was gentle, his grip had relaxed. 'Mum, don't get upset. Just think of it as something that has to happen to make Emily's life easier. If I don't play ball some of the time she'll badmouth me. Some of the time, remember, Mum. I have said no.' Josh's face was grim.

Jessie snorted. 'You were finding your place, your reputation was flying and then you sacrifice it to teach.' Jessie was frantic. Josh and his father exchanged a tired smile. Obviously it was not a new conversation.

Josh said, 'I enjoy it and I found Fran.'

Suddenly Jessie smiled. 'That's a perfect silver lining.'

Fred was clearing the plates, his voice firm as he said, 'Here endeth the lesson. Now, choc ices for four, I think. You will, won't you, Fran—?'

'I'd love one.' Jessie took the plates from Fred. Fran started to collect the napkins. Jessie waved her back. 'Leave them. I never manage a choc ice without half of it going down my chest. You just take hold of one of my son's hands. Far nicer than disgusting dishes and you'd only trip over Hercules who's the puppies privates when it comes to getting in the way. But I think we've discussed that before.'

Fran laughed and the room was light, warm and light, but it was strange to learn that there was so much she did not know about the man she had just run away with. As Fred nipped out of the door Josh explained, 'Freezer's in the hen house.'

'Of course it is,' she replied. 'Where else.' But of course it wasn't *strange* to discover someone had a life. What had she expected?

Over the choc ices Jessie listed the pots and the three paintings of Josh's which had sold and which she had omitted to mention when he phoned on Friday.

'Oh?' Fran was intrigued.

Josh squeezed her hand. 'I still sell down here, but that little bit of business I keep between myself and the taxman, with no murmur to Catherine, so I'm not the saint my mother makes out. You just remember that, Ma.'

Fred said gloomily, 'Don't start your mother off again.'

'I've done my breast-beating for today,' Jessie said, licking her paper, then screwing it into a ball.

Fran laughed quietly, relieved, because saints must be difficult to live with. She stopped, quiet suddenly. But were they? Going to live together? She didn't even know that. She said, 'So, you get a lot of callers to the cottage?'

Fred folded his choc ice wrapping. 'A few here, but most of our business is done at the gallery.'

Were they? Going to live together? Fran asked, 'What gallery?' Fred explained that a friend of theirs ran a gallery locally, taking in artists' work and arranging workshops. 'He's also extended the premises and has franchised out a coffee shop. It works well, brings in customers who then buy from the gallery. In fact, that's where that tyrant sitting next to you learned to throw. No, not Josh, Jessie.' He smiled benignly at his wife. 'We were both late starters, keeping on the day job; she at the bookshop, me as an accountant, until our sales picked up, not to mention our age.'

Jessie was on her way to the kettle, but shouted back, 'There you are, it's never too late to decide what you want, Fran.'

Fran nodded, the internal litany still asking that question. She leaned back in her chair, easing her shoulders. 'So how does it work? Does he buy the stuff from you?'

Fred chuckled. 'Nothing so certain. He takes a cut when it's sold and a cut of the workshops that we teach, and a cut of the coffee shop. Basically he relies on the tourist trade, or the area wouldn't be big enough.'

'Does he get good newspaper coverage?'

'He's getting better at that and extending himself into schools on a workshop basis, that sort of thing.'

Jessie plonked nettle tea in front of him, but coffee in front of everyone else, before sinking on to her chair with a sigh, fanning herself.

Josh was looking at Fran, shaking her hand slightly. 'If you're interested, you try it.' Behind him the red curtains were moving in the down draft from the leaded windows.

'What, pottery?' Jessie puffed.

Josh shook his head, stirring his coffee. 'I think it's the gallery that appeals, isn't it, Fran?'

Fran wished he hadn't asked, because what did it matter what appealed? It was what was possible and if she couldn't work for Linda it would have to be with another solicitor, something with a proper income. Real life, it was called. Plans, they were called and they'd made none, and this morning it had not mattered, but now . . . But it had only been three days, for heaven's sake. But . . Josh suddenly looked like a stranger. Jessie and Fred too. This house? She didn't even know where the coffee was kept, what village it was in.

'Fran?' Josh was insistent, shaking her hand harder. She withdrew, lifted her coffee, drank, then said, 'I don't know enough about it.'

'If you want it enough, it'll work.'

She snapped, frightened and worried, 'But things just don't *work*.' Oh, God, she sounded like Jane. Beside her Jessie suddenly stared into her coffee as though searching for the meaning of life. At the end of the table Fred was pulling Hercules's ears. Josh grinned at her. 'Look, Grouchy, you can do what you want with the rest of your life. Do what *you* want. After all, what you were saying when you left the church was "this is my time". Set up a gallery, go back to the same work, whatever. Go on, give yourself permission.'

Fran sipped her coffee again. Yes, if she wanted

71

it that badly she could sell the house and realise capital that way. But it was Jane's birthright and would, quite rightly, cause an earthquake of immense proportions on top of everything else. She could let it, though, and use the rent. But where could she live She listened instead to Josh, Jessie and Fred, who were throwing ideas around, talking over one another, assessing the merits of such a venture for Fran, as though it concerned just her. What *she* wanted, he'd said. Give *yourself* permission? Was she going to be alone?

She pushed away her mug, exhausted suddenly. But then Josh swung round. 'Look, I've some capital salted away from the sale of my stuff down here. Not a lot, but some, enough for a deposit. I'm sure we would find somewhere suitable and I've contacts in the art world. You have friends in the legal profession. Would Linda do us a decent conveyancing or leasing deal? If you don't want to sell your house, could we go on with the let? The rent would give us enough to get it up and running, and who knows, you might grow to love my little house, even though it's minus the space you have in yours.'

'Us?' she queried, then realised that Josh had sounded tentative. Had he thought she wouldn't want to live with him. Had he been tossing and turning things in his mind too?

Josh's voice was quiet, different, guarded: 'Well, not if you want to do it alone. I didn't . . .' He stopped. 'But surely we are going to do things together, surely . . . I mean . . .' Relief made her speechless for a moment and now she waved him silent, trying to find her voice, reaching for him, laughing, soaring. Jessie was patting the table, Josh was kissing her hands, Fred was saying again and again, 'Well, that was a close one.'

The third time Jessie shouted, 'Pipe down, you old fool.'

All the way back to St Ives in the car they plotted and planned, and decided that the only possible way was to live in his house and let hers. With her rent and the remains of his salary they could just about live, *and* keep the business ticking over. His parents would continue to sell his stuff down here and that could go into the pot. His excitement mirrored hers, his sense of total wonder equalled hers, his words of love interrupted hers and they had to park and kiss, and hold one another too tight for breath.

They drove on and now they both noticed the same shadows beneath the rocks, on the rocks. They pointed out the same crouching trees and he said she must keep on painting. He said she was special, that she had a real burning 'something' that reached out beyond the canvas.

He inspired her and she wished she had her easel that very moment. He made her believe she really was special. They talked of creating and the end result. She remembered how a similar discussion had bored Linda and Jane, and how she hadn't been able to defend the premise properly.

He did so for her, and it was perfect to pass between rocks and moor and trees under a looming sky, and listen as he talked of paintings which produced something that tapped into the common energies of everyone, releasing something in them, putting them in touch with something in themselves. Listening as he told her that one day their gallery, *their* gallery, must exhibit her paintings, for she was special, gifted, wonderful.

It was perfect to drive steadily towards St Ives and explore techniques, surfaces, materials and know, and accept, and savour this man who appreciated her, extended her, and in whose company she would be able to grow to appreciate and find her total self. It was more than perfection that she seemed able to do all these things for him as well and she couldn't believe that she was capable of anything so wonderful. As they crested the hill and saw St Ives spread before them, it made the fact that they were strangers insignificant, for every second they became more as one.

They parked the car in St Ives in the fading light and the gulls whirled restlessly above them. They looked at the sea and the sky, their hands clasped for minute after minute, then he stirred and said, 'Real life calls. Tonight I must phone Emily. I must tell her about progress on the love front, though not the business, not yet.'

The gulls were wheeling low, then high. Real life, perfection, swooping and soaring. Tonight they would soar and always there would be those times for just them. She said this now and he kissed her, saying against her lips, 'Always.' He reached for the door handle. 'I can tell her I will now finish the painting?'

She was still watching the gulls as she climbed from the car. 'A painting?'

They walked slowly along the front, arm in arm, 'I began work on it soon after you started the class. I thought it might work you out of my life. It just made you more real.'

She had painted something out of her life, or thought she had, but Mike had brought it back, so dreadfully easily. She said, 'The painting didn't make me real, it was because you love me and love is good. Bad things, appalling things should not become more real either.'

He looked at her and waited, but she had nothing more to say. Nothing.

'I usually phone her every other day,' he said. 'It makes me feel as though she's with me, almost. It must have been hard for Jane, growing up without a father.'

'She was very young, only four.' Fran watched the gulls swoop and soar.

'She wouldn't remember much of him then, which must make Mike important to her?'

This she could answer. 'Yes, he's been a very stable source of support.'

'So perhaps she's worried he'll withdraw. Maybe that's why she's turning this around to herself. He won't, will he?'

She dug her hands into the pockets of the blue wool jacket his mother had insisted she take so Josh could reclaim ownership of the velvet. 'No, he's a good man; protective, honourable. He loves Jane. I'm sure he won't.' But she wasn't here, not really. He touched her cheek. Instinctively she flinched away, but no. This was now. There was no need.

Josh said quickly, 'I'm sorry, I won't talk about it, it was tactless. But I'm sure Mike . . .'

They were passing the phone box. She stopped, pointing. 'Josh, you ring Emily first and then I'll try Linda.'

While he phoned she counted the gulls, then the lights as darkness came, and prayed that Jane could remember nothing of her father. Absolutely nothing.

He waited outside and she phoned Linda, who dismissed her apology, although insisting that the huge quantities of nibbles she had had to consume to prevent Ken going on and on about the waste would not be forgotten. She also promised to keep an eye on Mike, when he returned from the few days' leave he had taken. Not, of course, in Paris. A colleague had taken the tickets. He had rushed off to the Lake District.

On her return to the studio flat Fran painted, slashing, daubing, gouging. Josh sat quietly until it was over. Then he held her.

CHAPTER SIX

Emily joined her mother and Roger in the white sitting room, curling up on the sofa, wishing that Catherine had chosen something cosier than leather when she designed Roger's house. Mercifully their annexe was still very much as it must have been when the previous owners had kept it for their guests: all rustic and old-world.

'Feet off,' Catherine said as she flicked through the travel brochure.

'Oh, Mum, I've taken my boots off.'

'How many times have you been told not to wear those things in the house?' Catherine gestured towards the Doc Martens.

Roger said from behind his laptop. 'I don't mind as long as they're clean.'

Emily picked at the seam of her jeans. 'Dad doesn't care whether they're clean or not, actually.'

Offended, Roger resumed typing, but that was all he ever seemed to do. He'd taken her mother away from them and all he did was damn well type or snog. Oh, yes, she'd seen him creep up, his hands everywhere.

She flashed a look at Catherine, could see her irritation visibly building and sat straight, knowing she'd gone too far. Catherine's voice was almost a drawl when she said, 'I suppose its too much to ask of your father that he provide a good example, something that encourages a decent standard of behaviour in you.' Her laugh was hard and brittle, and it was the one that made Emily know there was more to come. 'But good behaviour is foreign to that man who cancels his access weekend at the drop of a hat, presumably for some dolly bird he has the chance of laying. Did he say who? I gather that was who was on the phone, no doubt trying to suck up.'

Emily rubbed one bare foot against the other, staring at the chrome fire guard.

Roger was shaking his head at Catherine. 'I say, that's not quite on, darling. He is her father, let's guard our tongue.'

Emily curled her toes tightly into the deep white pile, harder, harder.

Catherine aimed her drawl at him this time. 'You do what you like with your tongue, so allow me to do as I wish with mine.' Roger was already ducking down behind the parapet, groping busily for his calculator. Emily watched as her mother pushed up the sleeves of her cream cashmere sweater. Her gold bracelets clinked against one another as she reached for a cigarette, tapping it on the back of the gold-plated cigarette case she *said* she had bought last week. Had she really, or was there someone else? Again?

Emily grabbed the onyx cigarette lighter from the glass coffee table to her left and was with her mother in time to light the Rothman's. 'Sorry, Mum,' she whispered.

Her mother was looking down again at the travel brochure. 'Go and sit quietly. I've had more than enough for one day.'

Emily set down the lighter, sinking on to the sofa. Brochures? So another Mum and Roger holiday was in the offing. Would it mean she could stay with her dad or would she have to go? She hated it when her mother went topless, when she said, 'Take yours off too, Emily. Be proud of yourself.' Three weeks of boring embarrassment.

Emily looked down at her boobs. They seemed to grow a bit every day. She hunched her shoulders.

'Sit up straight,' her mother ordered. 'Why you have to wear men's sweatshirts I cannot imagine. Bottle-green is not your colour. Go on, sit up at once.'

Reluctantly Emily did so, checking that Roger was too busy to notice.

'So what *did* your father have to say for himself?' Catherine leant over and stubbed out her half-finished cigarette, suddenly looking pale. The brochure slid from her lap to the ground.

Concerned, Emily half rose, 'Mum?'

Roger stopped tapping. Catherine touched her forehead. 'Sit down and don't fuss, it's only a headache and can you wonder, when your father behaves as he does? He shouldn't do this to you. He shouldn't bring all these odds and sods, these tarts, into a home he expects his daughter to spend

78

time in. I just feel sorry for you, darling, that's all, and by cancelling your weekend, Uncle Roger and I missed the chance of a concert with Lady Longman.' She looked across at Roger. 'Sorry to be nasty earlier. Roger, darling. I'm just tired of taking responsibility for this child's well-being. Josh is such a pain.'

Emily wanted her mother to talk to her. She wanted her mother's eyes on her. She wanted Roger out. She wanted to throw the gold cigarette case into the non-existent fire. Why couldn't they have a fire? They had a fireplace and guard. Why no damn fire? This room was always too cold, or was it the colours—or lack of them? She'd never quite decided. If it were hers she'd use colour wash, tinted with oranges and browns to summon up the sun. She said, 'You could have left me alone. I am thirteen.' Uncle Roger hadn't thought it wise. In anyone else it would have been caring, but he had no right in their lives, no right at all. 'He's been in St Ives, with Fran, and don't worry, Mum, Fran's not a tart. I've seen a painting he did of her and she's old, like him, not youngish like you, and he's just told me he wanted the weekend to try and sort things out with her, and he has. They're staying for longer, and Grandma and Grandpa like her, Hercules too, and Grandma wants me to go soon, so'—she pointed to the brochure—'I could go there if you're thinking of a holiday. That would take the worry off you, wouldn't it. If you'd rather I didn't go to Dad's, though . . .'

'Be quiet.' Catherine was staring at her, her nails digging into the white leather. In a minute they'd go through and she'd shout.

Emily stumbled on: 'She's really not beautiful,

79

not like you, and if I do go to Dad it'll help with my standards, because she won't want boots on in the house.'

Catherine was on her feet, dragging another cigarette out of the case. She scooped the lighter off the table, lit up, drew in deeply. Emily wished she wouldn't. She'd get lung cancer. 'She'll be there, then, in his house?' Catherine said quietly.

'Well, yes, like you and Roger.' Emily remembered too late that this was never to be spoken of.

'We do not live together, is that quite clear?' Catherine was looming over her. 'Now go to bed. No, go to bed in *our* annexe tonight.'

'But Mum, its only eight o'clock.'

'Get to bed when I tell you.' Catherine was standing over her, her arms crossed, but she wasn't looking at her. She was sort of looking inside herself. Just staring like she had when they had seen Dad laughing, walking hand in hand with a woman in Clark's Village last year.

Emily edged from the sofa, picking up her boots. 'I thought it would help, make you feel better.'

Roger had set aside the laptop and was coming across to her mother, and she hated him. Emily reached out, pulling at Catherine's arm. 'I thought you'd be pleased that he had someone too. Honestly, she's not nearly as pretty as you. Honestly.'

Her mother shouted, 'Will you go to bed.'

Roger was smiling at Emily, that sort of 'like me' smile he always tried on with her. Well, if he had liked her so much, why had he caused all this trouble? He should never, ever have taken her mother from Dad. Never. The others never had.

80

Emily stormed from the room, slamming the door, running along the corridor, through to the annexe. She slammed the connecting door behind her, throwing her boots against the umbrella stand. She only stopped crying when the cat rubbed against her legs. Roger said it was a hunger signal, but she didn't believe that. She really didn't.

Catherine let Roger hold her, let him talk about the transfer to America he'd been whittering on about. He'd even come home bearing a pile of travel brochures to whet her appetite. Now he said, 'Darling, it's such wonderful news. I thought Josh would never take the plunge and settle with anyone. It'll make it all so much easier, and apart from anything else he'll be bound to give his permission for us to take Emily to San Diego. He'll be wrapped up with this woman—they'll be in a sort of honeymoon state, won't they—and we'll be able to live our own life, create our own family unit, with Emily. A fresh start, my angel. The western seaboard is wonderful: the light, the heat. It's just a short drive up into the mountains and down to the desert, and if I'm there I won't have to travel any more, or hardly ever. We can be together every night.'

Catherine shut her mind against that thought as he rambled on: 'It'll be so much cleaner to be open about us at last. I'm not criticising, I know you felt it would protect me financially, but they've put together a good package for this trip. Though bloody hell, I had enough before. The lie made me feel a bit bad, you know, old thing.'

Catherine let him talk, because now she was thinking of the painting. How dare Josh paint another woman? How dare he replace her and with someone older? How could he, when she'd always thought . . .? How could he do this to her, when he'd always loved her, always? When he'd led her on, wooing her back with all the maintenance? Damn it, she was almost ready to ditch Roger, now that she had enough money stashed away. How could he, when deep inside she still loved him? She'd just got sick of a life waiting for the next commission cheque to come in but she'd been younger then, impatient. He should be able to understand that.

Roger's tongue was in her ear. She did wish he wouldn't. She made the noises he expected. Now he was running his hands up and down her back. She could hardly bear it. A family with him? The thought made her want to vomit.

No one had compared with Josh. Her heart failed her. And why ring now when he could have spoken to Emily earlier, while she was out. Why rub her nose in it?

Roger was murmuring rubbish in her ear. She focused on Josh. Perhaps that was it, though. Perhaps he wanted to torment her, to make her jealous. The relief almost made her laugh out loud. Of course, she could see it all now: the cancelled weekend designed to make her ask questions, an evening phone call. He'd really got her going.

Yes, that's what it was all about. Well, at least he was getting better at game playing, the silly bastard, so maybe she'd share a bit of the pot she had built up. Share when she went back, but not to Hamdon Terrace, they'd have to do better than that. Give it a few more days, see what his next move was.

Roger was pressing himself against her. He was just so deeply unattractive, now that he was hers.

CHAPTER SEVEN

Jane polished the stainless-steel draining board with the J-cloth, standing back to check for smears. She straightened the tea towels, checked the mugs on their hooks, the position of the plants on the windowsill. In the garden Ken was extending the vegetable patch into the area he had previously decided to pave to allow easy access to the gate. He had been satisfied with her scrubbing of the fence. You would not now know where the cross had been.

Mike would be back today. There would be lights on again in the evening as though watching over them. She eased her shoulders. Almost lunchtime. A week ago at this time, she and Ken and Mike had stood in the reception line apologising for her mother and directing people to the sherry, which to her had tasted like vinegar.

She'd drunk too much of it to try to blur the shock. It hadn't. Nothing had. It felt as though nothing ever would. Then there had been the food. The table had groaned under its weight. The cake had been an embarrassment until Linda had taken it upon herself to instruct the hotel staff to deliver it to the local old dears' home. Personally she doubted that their teeth could cope with the icing.

Mike had been wonderful, circulating, holding himself with dignity. Ken had been smiling, hiding a rage which only she could see. It was the waste, the expense, the public humiliation. Not that his colleagues seemed put out, or if they were it hadn't been reflected in their appetites.

The clock in the hall chimed the quarter. Suddenly she remembered the time and flew to the fridge. She had bought his favourite, Parma ham and salad. She set the table, polishing the knives and forks, putting the dressing into a jug, the jug on a saucer, arranging his napkin and hers.

She checked that Lucy was still content in the sitting room watching *Care Bears*. 'But let me rewind it, so you can see it all again.'

Lucy put her thumb in her mouth, shaking her head. Jane shouted, 'Don't disobey me, you *will* watch it from the beginning again while Daddy has his lunch. You know he likes to be quiet when he eats.' Jane rewound the tape frantically. Come on, come on. There. She smiled, hugging Lucy, settling cushions behind her on the armchair, kissing the top of her head. 'Be a good girl for Mummy.'

Lucy snuggled up to her, smelling of baby shampoo. Her hair was so soft, her curls so bouncy, just like her own had been according to her mother. 'Was I like Dad?' she had asked. 'A bit,' her mother had replied, too busy to say more. Always too busy to talk about him.

She heard the back door open and sprang to her feet, her finger to her lips. 'Be good, darling.'

Ken was in the kitchen washing his hands. His stocking feet had made sweat prints on the quarry tiles. She handed him a towel from the radiator. 'Hard going?' she asked.

He was drying his arms, then his hands, and just grunted. She replaced the towel and took the two cling-filmed plates from the fridge. While he settled himself at the table and examined his cutlery she placed his plate before him.

He shook out his napkin, looking from the ham

to her. 'Just how do you think we can afford this?'

'I had a little left from the housekeeping. I thought you'd need a treat after all the work you've had to do today. Though I suppose you would have had to dig there, if you were laying hardcore for crazy paving?'

When he stared at her as he was doing it made her mind go woolly. He answered a question with a question. 'Have you found a childminder yet? Don't forget you start work in another week. Or is there just an outside chance your esteemed mother might be slipping back into the area, enabling you to go back to Plan A?'

She took her place opposite him. The Parma ham seemed very dry. She swallowed twice, patting her lips with her napkin. Damn you, Mum. Damn you. 'I really think Plan A is dead.' There, it was said, again.

He sighed, cutting his cucumber into precise halves. 'So, we pay out for a childminder who will take a great bite out of the money that was your sorry attempt to improve the situation.'

He'd said that last night and the night before, and it was driving her mad that she couldn't pluck a miracle from the air. 'Maisie Kent is the most reasonable and by far the most convenient. She's in Albert Street. It's just a question of whether she can squeeze in both.'

At that moment the baby alarm on the work surface nearest to the fridge crackled into life and Harry's cries filled the kitchen. She jumped to her feet and snapped it off, hurrying back to the table. 'I'm sorry,' she said as he stared at his plate.

He resumed eating, cutting, cutting, cutting until he was finished. Hers tasted like sawdust. She

85

could hear Harry in the distance. He was hungry. He would be reaching up with those plump arms . . . She made herself finish, laying her knife and fork neatly together, clearing the plates. Bringing fruit and side plates, willing him to hurry.

He peeled his apple, cut it into quarters, removed the core. She did the same with hers, keeping to his pace. Would Lucy come in? Would she say 'Mummy, Harry's crying'? She knew better. Mealtimes were sacrosanct or Ken's ulcer would return. She felt her own stomach knot. He had finished. He was wiping his hands. She wiped hers. 'Coffee?' she asked.

'I rather think so.'

Everyone had these rituals. Some people even finished one another's sentences. Everyone had their own way of living. Things just became more extreme under stress. It was a normal progression. All quite normal and if Mum and Mike . . . Oh, it could so easily have started to get better. She filled the kettle, noticing how the clouds had built one upon the other. It was going to rain. There would be no more gardening. Harry's cries were even louder.

CHAPTER EIGHT

Linda phoned Mike after six o'clock on Sunday; it had taken her this long to decide what to say.

He answered, 'Mike Wells speaking.'

She said, 'It's me.' Which is not what she'd decided to say. Cursing, she added, 'Linda. It's me, Linda, Mike. Just to see how you are?'

Oh, God, she hadn't been going to say that, absolutely not that. She hurried on: 'I mean, how were the lakes? Did you get into your stride, avoid the scree? Did it rain? It does up there, doesn't it? I absolutely love it there, myself, especially when the daffodils are out. Wordsworth did too, but then of course you know that. We all know that.' She realised Mike was laughing. What a glorious sound. People with broken hearts didn't laugh.

He said, 'The walking was good. It cleared my head.' His laughter stopped.

What about your heart? she wanted to ask. It's a week after Fran bolted and are you healed? Did you really love her? Instead she said, 'Have you any food? I find I've cooked enough for two; lamb stew. In the slow cooker.' Why not tell him the weight, the herbs, every last detail. Idiot.

'You are a dear but I'm inundated with offers. Ken and Jane, the bridge group, and I've refused them all. I just fancy a bit of time on my own. You know?'

'Yes, of course. But that doesn't answer the question. Have you food? We can't have you wasting away. I could leave the lamb on your doorstep.' Why didn't she just let it go?

'Again, what a dear you are, but I have the freezer. I stocked up for our return from Paris.' He fell silent. She couldn't think how to fill the seconds. Then he continued, 'I thought I'd come back to work on Monday. No point in staying at home and we're one man short now that Peter's taken the Paris tickets. No point at all. You know?'

What could she say because of course she knew. Unrequited love? She was the bloody oracle. She could write chapter and verse, and be damned to

87

daffodils. 'I'll see you on Monday, then. Another day, another dollar.' How crass. Was she insane?

As she began to replace the receiver Mike called, 'Linda, Linda.'

She snatched it up to her ear. 'Yes.' She had sounded too eager, she knew it.

Mike said, 'About the replacement secretary.'

'Yes?'

'Can you continue with the temp for now? I just have a feeling Fran might be back. Apparently she hardly knows this Josh. It could all go pear-shaped and I'm worried because those who've been involved with one beater can, subconsciously, be drawn to the situation again.'

It was her turn to fall silent, her stomach flipping. Slowly she said, thinking aloud, 'Yes, of course I know that, but she's had you since then, so the pattern is broken, surely.'

'Well, don't worry, I'm probably jumping at shadows, but I'll do some discreet checks. Either way, Linda, it has a good chance of failing because they don't know one another at all. Just wait, once reality strikes the cracks will show.'

'Not necessarily, love can come out of nowhere. Two souls can become one.' Linda cursed her crassness, but her mind was still half with Fran.

Mike's laugh was strained. 'Well, there is always that but put a hold on the secretary anyway, eh?'

'Of course. See you Monday.'

This time she replaced the receiver firmly, walking to the drinks cupboard and pouring a large gin, bugger the tonic. She took a sip, a big sip, well, almost a gulp, and who the hell could blame her. Surely Fran wouldn't . . . Surely Josh wasn't . . . Well, why not, these bastards didn't go about with a

88

sign round their necks. They were masters of the cover-up and those they beat became so too.

Her heart sank for her dearest friend, feeling even more as though she had failed her, for in the days that had passed since the wedding she had realised how little she had been there for Fran. She had not listened to her delight at discovering art. She had ignored the release she hinted it had given her. Yes, in those half-remembered fevered spirals and slashes Linda could now recognise the legacy of David. Fear, anger, a laying of the ghost?

So if she had even halfway left that darkness behind, surely she would not be drawn like a moth . . .

She drained her glass. 'Oh, Fran, make it be a good choice.'

She put the glass in the dishwasher and her plea was altruistically for Fran, though by tomorrow, for she knew herself too well, it would be for herself as well.

CHAPTER NINE

Fran told Stan, Josh's neighbour, where her key could be found. 'David's death certificate is in the top shelf of the bureau.'

He promised to send it recorded delivery, along with Josh's decree absolute. It was the final nail in the marriage licence application procedure, she said.

'Unfortunate choice of words,' Josh murmured, crammed up against her in the phone box. She leant further into his hug. He shouted into the phone, 'By the way, Stan, we have to stay here until we qualify, another week on top of the three.'

Stan half laughed. 'My, my, you must be heartbroken. The college are OK about it, are they?'

'As long as I'm still on board for all the painting trips I usually drag the kids along on. Oh, and the Dean wants an Easter egg.'

'Just bring back a broad smile. That would please Cindy and me more than anything.'

Josh squeezed her. 'I haven't stopped smiling since we arrived. I'm pig happy, Stan.'

Fran leant back against him. The day was sunny, the phone box stuffy. Did dogs really have a built-in instinct to use it as a latrine? That's what Mike had said when they were kids. She hesitated, then stayed with the memory because slowly she was allowing herself to accept with a lessening of guilt the actuality of those whom she also loved. They were indeed a part of her life, a life which was moving forward at a pace that was frightening. No, that was the wrong word: exhilarating, crazy, wonderful.

They strode to the pub.

'I don't ride,' she'd protested as Josh asked the barman for directions to the nearest riding school.

'Neither do I,' he'd replied, pocketing his change and pushing her lager along the shiny bar. 'Take a sip, sweetheart, then we can find a pew.' He looked at her over his glass. 'Riding is something I've always wanted to do. You've made me bold.'

The horses were placid, the saddles honest and old, the reins soft. The woman who led them along the bridlepath was red-cheeked and hearty. A golden labrador scouted ahead, running off whenever and wherever the spirit took him. He was old enough to know better. 'Like us,' Fran murmured.

'You have a lovely seat,' Josh said.

She flushed, hushing him. 'Where are you going back to?' the woman called over her shoulder.

Josh looked at Fran. 'Now there's a question.'

Fran replied, 'We're going forward, together.'

The woman looked puzzled.

Fran clarified the situation. 'We're to be married.'

'The woman guffawed. 'Oh, well, there's to be no sense out of you two for a while then. Fancy a bit of a trot? That'll sort you out for a couple of days.'

It did indeed and the next morning they bought small lilos to sit on, and instead of romps on the bed they took a gentle walk along the front before returning to sit gingerly and gaze at the view. 'Or do you think we should try pastures new?' Josh wondered, as though they'd been in the middle of a conversation. 'We could rent out both our houses, start again somewhere else.'

Jane was there in Fran's mind. 'Jane's tired. Two small children. A job. Anything could happen. One could be ill. It'll be awkward with Mike but . . .'

Emily was in Josh's mind. 'She knows my house, my neighbours. It's just far enough from Dorchester, but not too near.'

'So we stay put,' Fran suggested.

Josh kissed each of her fingers tenderly. 'I'm rather glad we're not going to ride off into the sunset.'

Fran shuddered. 'I'd rather die than ride anywhere ever again.' They were still laughing five minutes later.

The next day they walked along the cliff path. The tenderness had gone, but the stiffness was worse. It didn't matter, because it was something shared. They talked more about the future, about their children, with an increasing freedom, lying on their backs on a grassy knoll overlooking the bay.

He turned to her, blocking out the sun. 'I'm a very happy man, Fran Major. Very, very happy.'

Below them were two women walking a dog. They were like ants, out of hearing, distant, but there. 'Pretty much sums up our lives,' Fran murmured. Josh didn't need an explanation.

The next day David's death certificate arrived and Josh's decree absolute. Was it really happening? Was she to wed this man who seemed to light the sky for her?

After presenting the documents to the Registrar they drove to Land's End and stood above the thrashing waves, then joined the tourists as they wound their way round the touristy things, and all the time they talked of the gallery, and of this and that, and held one another's hands and rejoiced that the stiffness was receding, but really in the fact that they were alive and had one another, and this was how their lives would be: lived out together, going forward, creatively, innovatively, perfectly.

Each day was precious, marking a growing knowledge, a growing pleasure. Each day it was more difficult to leave their nest even to walk along the front, because they had sufficient in one another and real life seemed ever more distant.

'But this is *our* real life,' Josh said the night before their wedding, the night before they would leave this flat.

'Four weeks? It's been a lifetime,' Fran agreed.

Josh's lips were gentle as he touched her cheek, his words soft as they turned to watch the moon rise over the sea. 'It will be a lifetime. It will be life as *we* want it to be.'

They were too content to sleep that night. Every second was too precious, the thought of the days and weeks and years to come too wonderful, and they were at the window to watch the dawn and knew it was symbolic.

CHAPTER TEN

Fran and Josh had decided to marry quietly at Penzance Register Office, opting to drag in two witnesses off the street and invite no one, not even his parents. The very thought of a guest list and its inherent politics made their heads reel as they had made their plans, walking along the sand at St Ives.

'If we invite Jessie and Fred, and Jane and Ken, there would be a Swanton diatribe,' Fran murmured.

Josh smiled and continued for her: 'While to invite Jessie and Fred, and *not* Jane and Ken would be asking for a retrospective diatribe.'

So, in the company of two benign strangers, which Fran felt apt, they made their vows and never had Fran meant anything so much, never had she felt so complete. The following morning they left St Ives. In the late afternoon, from Josh's home, they informed those who needed to know. 'Blood on the floor?' queried Josh as she replaced the receiver on Jane's assumed indifference.

'No, the cold treatment, but it's understandable.'

'So, that's everyone?'

She just looked at him, because he knew it wasn't. 'Skedaddle while I talk to Mike.' He touched her cheek, kissed her mouth, put another cushion behind her, dragged up a footstool. She waved him away. 'I'm not an invalid, just a trollop.'

His kiss was harder now. 'Don't you ever say that. Never, do you understand. I won't have it. I just wish you'd let me do this for you.' He walked from the sitting room on to the patio, closing the French windows behind him, and she watched, knowing she couldn't, mustn't, wouldn't. Fran took a deep breath and another, dialling. It was the answer machine. She slammed down the receiver. 'Damn.' Her palms were damp.

On the patio she could see Josh sitting at the wooden table, talking to Stan. It was Stan who was responsible for the banner which had greeted them when they had entered the sitting room an hour ago. *Wow, way to go* hung over the mantelpiece, partially covering Josh's unfinished portrait of her.

Stan must have been keeping watch, for he had darted out of his front door, with his partner Cindy and their son Mark in hot pursuit, and played 'Bless the Bride' on his saxophone as Josh carried Fran over the threshold, understanding completely when Josh had slammed the door in their faces, calling, 'Celebrations later, you idiots.'

Now, Stan held up a can of Fosters and bowed to her through the window. She laughed, feeling she had known him all her life, just as she had known this house with its eclectic collection of paintings, books, sculptures, pots jammed on every dusty surface, and the plants which Cindy had kept

94

watered in Josh's absence. She felt at home in spite of the dark-red paint on the walls that should have closed down the room but didn't. Instead it made it vibrant and alive, like Josh, like the rest of the house with its bold colours.

Did the gene pool extend to artistic taste? Seemingly so, because even the beams were stencilled, as Jessie's were, and those same beams were also hung with hops. Where did heredity end? If she'd had a son would he have . . . ?

Josh was peering through the window now, his hand shielding his eyes. 'Everything all right, darling?'

She dragged herself back, pointing to the phone. 'He's out, so I'm trying Linda.' How did Josh sense when she was drifting near any source of darkness, any situation of need? She had told him about David as they sat drinking in the view one early evening. It had seemed the honest thing to do.

It had appeared to hurt him almost as much as David had hurt her, although he had always known there was something. Of course he had. Would speaking of it help? Probably. Would her painting alter? Probably, but the talent would still be there, he insisted. Would their life together cancel out David? God, she loved this man so much.

Her call to Linda was different, the tension wasn't suffocating, the eagerness could show. 'Hey,' she said when Linda answered. 'We did it. We married in Penzance. I'm ecstatic.'

For a moment there was silence, then Linda shrieked, 'You little monkey. God, I'm *so* glad, so terribly pleased. Thrilled. Delighted. For you, of course. Absolutely for you.'

'Well, who else would you be pleased for, you

daft great thing.' Fran shifted the cushion behind her back, propping her feet up on the footstool, settling down for the inquisition, which came and continued until Josh tapped on the window again. Cindy and Stan were alongside too, pressing their faces grotesquely against the glass. Mark joined them, and Edward with his partner Tom, both artists from number 11.

Fran laughed as much at them as at Linda who had just asked if she had actually seen anything but the ceiling of the St Ives flat. 'Look, Linda, get your thrills somewhere else, I've got to go, but come to the wedding party next Saturday. Now, back to the gallery. You're sure about doing the conveyancing. I don't want to make it awkward for you with Mike.'

'Let me worry about that and, come to think of it, wasn't the old doctor's surgery up for grabs? You know, alongside Cheap Street, next to the car park. I've heard the council want to revitalise that end, so planning could be sorted and probably a supremely reasonable lease negotiated, although they won't sell it. You won't get capital growth, of course, but you would get a return on the goodwill if you ever decided to sell; providing you make a go of it. You'll have to pay for the renovations yourself, but the rooms are a good size in those double-fronted houses. Get back to me. Don't worry about the tenant's contract on your house. I'll just reactivate it. Now, Mike was out, you say, so would you like me to phone? It might be better for him, you know, to hear from someone other than the horse.'

The relief was enormous, but Fran knew that life shouldn't be that easy. 'It had better be me, don't you think?'

Linda said nothing for a moment. Fran chewed her lip, until she heard her voice insisting, 'Actually, I think it might be rather cruel. Why don't you leave it to me and write to Mike instead?'

'Isn't that wimpish?'

'Under the circumstances I think we could use the word kind.' Linda's voice was waspish and Fran was taken aback. But of course she was right. How could she be so stupid? She imagined his gentleness, his broken heart. Now the floor show the other side of the French windows included hands against the glass. She wanted a moment to think. She turned, saw the banner.

'Fran, darling, let me do this for you and for him. You concentrate on yourselves.' Linda was back to her usual self.

For him. Yes, she'd write. She relaxed. Bless Linda. 'One day I'll do the same for you,' she said more lightly than she felt. 'Now I must go, or I'll get maudlin. I owe you, darling girl.'

'Not really,' Linda said. 'Fran, I . . .' She stopped. Fran asked, 'Yes?'

Linda said quietly, 'I hope you're deliriously happy. You really do deserve to be. It's been a long haul, and you've worked so hard at life and been a wonderful mother. Go for it, darling, and keep in touch. We must talk more, just as we used to, and if you ever need to, we can hoof out the tenants. I'll always be here, whenever and wherever. You must never forget that. Mike won't let the years count for nothing either, I just know it.'

There was a click as Linda hung up. Outside, Josh had pulled away from the glass, concerned, watching her closely. She smiled, replaced the receiver and hurried out to them, spoiling their game, slipping into the hug Josh offered. 'I'm fine,' she answered the unspoken question, returning his kiss, taking the can of lager offered by Cindy.

They sat on into the failing light, a loose little group around the old wooden table, talking, all of them, overlooked by the neat little row of two-up two-downs. When it grew too cold they moved into the sitting room, finding chairs, or squatting on the floor, or tipping books from stools while Stan played jazz on his saxophone, joined by Edward and Josh on the guitar. Tom played his double bass, which required a room to itself. 'Which is the only reason Edward and I have to share a bed.' He flounced, grinning.

It was now that she heard Josh's glorious singing voice and if that evening could have lasted for eternity she would have been content.

In the early hours she and Josh lay beneath the patchwork quilt his mother had made. 'There's so much I don't know about you,' she murmured into his neck. 'But so much I do. At last I feel as though I belong, as though I've come home.'

*   *   *

On Monday Josh returned to college and Fran wrote her letter to Mike but did not post it, because the words were stilted, too formal, too careful. It needed more thought and less caffeine. She tipped away her half-drunk coffee. It also needed fresh air. She grabbed a jacket and drove to the old surgery, peering through chinks in the boarded windows. She packed up the art nouveau in her house and the linen, her kettle and her painting materials. She put her paintings in the loft, along with all sorts of other odds and sods, because they did not express how she felt any more. She packed Jane's childhood relics and put those in the loft too, where they would be safe from careless tenants.

She hoovered, cleaned, moved the cardboard boxes out to the car. She locked up the house, feeling no regret, just eagerness to be back in her life at Hamdon Terrace. She did not even have to face her neighbour, Anne Thomas, who would have crossed her arms over her ample breast and shown her disapproval in no uncertain terms. It was her bowls day.

At the Terrace she stacked the linen in Josh's airing cupboard, the egg box containing the art nouveau found a place near the French windows, the spare kettle and various sundries, as the inventory described such things, went into the cupboard under the stairs. Her painting materials joined Josh's, near the easel in the spare room, the one that Emily occupied one weekend in two.

Dirty and itching from the fibre glass she showered, rang Linda and confirmed her interest in the surgery. Linda said she'd sort out a view and they'd take it from there. Fran spoke the words that she'd been pushing away all morning: 'Have you talked to Mike?'

Linda's voice became quieter. 'He'll be fine.'

'Is this Dr Linda's prognosis, or his?'

'M.Y.O.B. It is sufficient that the words are said, my dear old duck.'

'Less of the old. But how is he really?'

'Look, Fran, let it rest and get on with your life. He needs time to heal, that's all. Just write to the guy.' Her laugh was strained. 'Enjoy being Mrs

Benton. I'll keep you posted on the lost-love stakes.'

At last Fran was able to rewrite her letter, saying that she would give him space, inviting him to next Saturday's party to celebrate their marriage, knowing it was impossible for him to attend. She confirmed her love for him, her truly, deeply felt love, which was both separate and different from her life with Josh. Apologising. Apologising. She sealed the envelope and posted it, feeling greedy that she still wanted the best parts of her old life along with the new.

*   *   *

The following Saturday dawned clear and bright, and though Josh pulled her back when she tried to slip from the bed she wriggled free, her finger to her lips. 'Emily,' she warned.

He rolled his eyes, slapping his forehead. 'I forgot,' he mouthed. 'Hugs can be quiet.' She lay with him, but they were both alert, listening. 'Damn,' he breathed into her hair.

She grinned. 'Patience. It's not every night and besides, she's your daughter.'

He said plaintively, 'But why is thirteen such a bloody difficult age?'

She laughed, but very quietly. 'Wait for fourteen, then fifteen. You will truly see the dark side of the moon then.'

He squeezed her almost too tight. 'Thank you for welcoming her. Thank you for giving her your bracelet, thank you for letting her insist on spaghetti for the wedding feast.' He groaned again, louder this time.

She hushed him. He laughed as she slipped away, reaching for her dressing gown on the back of the door. 'Things to do,' she said.

He lay there, looking at her in the light of the morning. With Emily in the house she felt embarrassed at being naked, at being watched. From the spare room came the thunder of Bon Jovi. Josh raised his voice. 'Remember the neighbours please, Em.' It went down a fraction. Fran escaped to the bathroom, locking the door, running the shower, drowning the sound of the teenage years which she thought she had left well and truly behind.

But then she smiled as the water ran through her hair and down her body. Emily was part of Josh, she was interesting and in no way was she her responsibility. It was a bit like being an aunt or a grandmother, and anyway, it was just two days every two weeks. Only two days and then he was hers again and she was his.

By midday the bolognese was under way, Linda had arrived and was dealing with the garlic bread. The spaghetti was on stand-by for *al dente* cooking and Emily was dressed in designer gear. Linda murmured to Fran, 'Interior design is obviously doing well.'

'Not if you take heed of the ex Mrs Benton.' Fran's stomach knotted but it was for the shadow it brought to Josh.

Stan and Edward were doing their strolling minstrel turn in the garden. 'Warming up the tubes,' they said. Tom was based at the patio table, twanging his bass in between sips of lager. Fran hooked up a bin bag by the shed for the empty cans, catching the one that Stan tossed her and grabbing Josh as he tried to slip down the garden to join them. 'Not so fast, my lad. We need the plates carrying through from the kitchen. Thank the lord it's a fine day and would you weight down the napkins.'

Josh kissed her. She could taste lager and suddenly St Ives was back, but this was better. This was the present and the future, and she tossed Stan's can into the bag, hugging Josh, knowing he would hug her back, only tighter, and he did, kissing her hair, her eyes, her mouth. 'I love you, Mrs Benton, to utter distraction.'

Stan and Edward played 'The Stripper'. Linda called from the French windows, 'A bucket of water?'

Edward yelled, 'It usually works.'

Their other neighbours, Sharon and Isaac from number 5, the Wilsons and twins from number 8, were slipping through the hedge and Matt, who lived alone but had constant 'callers', as Josh called the girls who buzzed around that particular honey pot. Today he brought a new college lecturer. They had matching tints in their hair. Stan pretended to vomit. Matt said he'd see him about it later. 'You and whose army,' Stan replied.

'Army? You're bringing an army. All for me?' Edward said. Tom left his double bass in young Mark's grasp and slapped Edward with his bow. Fran felt she'd known them all her life.

Other guests were arriving and Fran took the lagers and wine they brought, putting some in cool boxes and others on the table. Some brought gifts, although Josh and Fran had said not. Emily called from the hall, 'Dad, some of the students have arrived and hey, half the staff room. I'm sending

102

them through.'

Fran greeted members of her evening class who were agog and thrilled, and shocked and delighted, and they too had brought bottles and gifts. Some of them made their way through to the garden, others admired the painting of Fran. The younger students took up position on the stairs, or milled about the kitchen with Emily.

Fran, Linda and Josh handed round olives, pineapple and cheese, and anything that hadn't been on offer at the real wedding, because many of those same guests would arrive and it was this that was making Fran's shoulders tense. Josh looked worried on her behalf and Linda issued soothing noises, while pursing her lips as she did when she had a difficult case.

Fran checked her watch: 12.15. Jane would be here any minute. It was Ken's cardinal rule that they arrive fifteen minutes after the designated time. He deemed it socially correct. But, God bless them, they were coming. She flashed a look around the room, then out into the garden. Josh was at her elbow. 'It's all right, I've warned Stan and Edward.'

'No joints,' she checked. 'You know how I feel about that.'

'No joints,' he reassured her.

'The students?'

'They'll be fine. Now relax. You're not alone. It's the two of us now, always. We'll make it all right for Jane, I promise. Look how Emily's taken it on board.' He kissed her hand. The sun caught his hair, the slope of his cheekbone.

She said, 'I love you so much.'

He held her hand tighter, slipping his arm around her, standing close as they listened to the jazz now being played. It was all so wonderful, exotic. It was everything she had dreamed her life with Josh could be. And yes, Jane and Ken were coming, and it was generous of them, and her love for her daughter momentarily overwhelmed her.

Linda was beckoning from the sitting room. Ken's car had pulled up outside. 'I'll come,' Josh said.

Fran hesitated. 'No, let me see them first, if you don't mind.'

He smiled. 'You know best. I'll listen for my cue.'

Fran pressed through the guests, appreciating their congratulations, saying that she would be back. Her voice was unsteady. Jane and Ken stood at the open front door with the children. Fran went to them with open arms. 'Come in.'

For a moment Jane's face was as cold as Ken's, but as Fran hugged her she felt her respond. 'Oh, Mum.'

Fran murmured, her eyes filling, 'Oh, darling, I'm so touched you came.' Jane tightened her grip. Ken coughed. Jane pulled back and in her place Ken offered a cheek as though bestowing a great gift, holding the baby as if it had pooped. Fran wanted her daughter back but Jane was examining the tiny but exuberant hallway and her face said it all. Fran sighed, took Harry from Ken and crouched to cover Lucy in kisses, loving the soft warm arms around her neck, the baby shampoo smell, saying, 'I've missed you all so much.'

Jane smiled down at her for a moment, but only a moment. Then the smile became something else: more a grimace, an unspoken condemnation, and Fran stood, a great sadness settling on her. At that moment Emily pushed past Fran, shaking hands

104

firmly with Jane. 'I'm Emily, Josh's daughter. I suppose that makes us relatives. I'll show you round Dad's house in a minute but right now there are a million people trying to get past you, so how about budging over.'

Jane looked at her mother. 'Relatives?' She was surprised. 'Relatives.' Her tone was cool.

Fran ignored this and led the way into the sitting room, saying, 'Hey, everyone, this is my Jane, and her lovely family.' Josh stood near the door and as everyone called a greeting Fran said to Jane, 'This is Josh. I want the two people I love most in the world to be friends.'

Josh put out his hand. Jane shook it, her face frozen. Ken coughed, shook hands, then took Harry back from Fran. Scooping Lucy up, Jane said, looking her up and down. 'Can I do something while you change, Mother?'

'I am changed,' Fran said softly. 'Josh brought me this ethnic skirt in St Ives. I like long skirts and I'm coming round to colour.'

Linda was trying to squeeze past to replenish the olive bowl. She threw a kiss at Jane. 'Lovely suit, darling. Lovely tie, Ken.'

Now Fran noticed that Jane was wearing *the* wedding outfit and she remembered too vividly the cravat. Josh gestured towards the bar on the patio. 'Please, let me find you a drink.'

Ken said, 'Orange for Jane, she's offered to drive, but a Pimm's would be good.'

Josh smiled gently. 'Wine or beer, that's all, I'm afraid. Em, fetch Jane an orange juice, please. Something for Lucy?' He was squatting, talking directly to Lucy who clung to her mother's navy pencil skirt.

Linda was calling Fran to the door, where more neighbours from her old life waited. These she brought in, taking the presents they offered, although they too had been asked not.

Mrs Thomas said crossly, 'Well, what was I supposed to do with it after that charade of yours. I don't need a Teasmaid.'

Josh heard, smiled for Fran alone, then continued to introduce Jane and Ken around, before leaving them to gravitate towards the 'previous life' clique.

Emily took Lucy to the table set up under the front window of the sitting room. 'Shall we open the presents, Dad?' she called over the hubbub of talk and music.

Josh raised an eyebrow towards Fran, who was trying to decide with Linda when to put the spaghetti on to cook. Fran hated the idea. It was embarrassing, for some had quite rightly not brought anything, but Emily and Lucy were already ripping off paper. 'Keep the cards with the gifts,' she called, the decision made for her.

She snatched a look at Jane. She was tired and drawn, even more than before the wedding. She nodded to Josh. His smile was supportive.

'I'm a selfish old bag,' she said to Linda.

'Absolutely. Quite why this time?'

'Oh, never mind.' Because little Lucy was laughing as Emily tickled her with silver parcel ribbon, and she saw Jane watching and laughing too.

'Spaghetti or not?' Linda asked, eyeing the kitchen.

'Not. Let's wait for Josh's parents. They shouldn't be long. They phoned from the service

106

station earlier, warning that the traffic was slow but they'd be bound to be here by one.'

They arrived at 12.45, bursting into the sitting room, larger than life. Jessie shrieked, 'Now where's that trollop of a grandchild?'

Those around laughed, and made a path for Emily who was scrambling out from under the table where she and Lucy had been folding the wedding paper, smooth, smoother, smoothest. 'Grandma,' she yelled, forgetting to be 'cool' for a moment, tearing across the room, her arms wide for the hug she and Jessie shared. Fred ruffled her hair. 'Grandpa,' she protested, smoothing it down, tutting as she had to reclip the side bits, remembering, now, who she was.

Fred grimaced at Fran. 'How they grow up.'

Jessie was looking around, puffing a bit. 'Where's that son of mine, Fran? He must bring the woman a drink at once.'

Josh called over the heads of the guests, 'On my way. I knew the wheels would need oiling, you dreadful old soak.'

By the mantelpiece Fran's old neighbours tutted, Jane and Ken pretended to look at the wedding presents, Harry grizzled. Fran inched Jessie towards them. It was slow going as Jessie had to field greetings, kisses and hugs every inch of the way. She extracted herself each time with the legend, 'I'll catch up in a minute and never fear, I've all the gossip on these two bolters.'

Finally they reached Jane and Fran slipped her arm round her waist. Jane had lost weight. 'Darling, meet Jessie, Josh's mum. She knows all about you and the kids, and Ken of course.'

Jessie beamed, her face almost as pink as her

lipstick, which clashed gloriously with the brick-red of her flowing silk. She spread her arms. 'So you're the other one, are you?' she bellowed.

'Other one?' Ken had proffered his hand. Fred shook it.

'Grandchild. Reckon she's that now. Not a trollop. Wouldn't dream of suggesting such a thing.'

Jane stepped back, hard up against the table. A lamp teetered, then recovered. Oblivious, Jessie flung her arms around Jane and Harry, kissing them both. Ken's body language made his position very clear and he reinforced it by taking hold of Jane by the elbow. 'Mrs Thomas needs us. We'd better move on.' His voice was enormously middle-class, as it always was when he wanted to make a point.

On impulse Fran snatched Harry from Jane, who smiled weakly. They walked away without a backward glance. Fran stared after them. Harry pulled at her hair. She held his hand, releasing the strands, then leant her head against her grandson's. 'I love you all,' she whispered.

Jessie roared off to the patio with Fred in her wake. Here she stomped to the music, her beads flying this way and that. In as little as thirty seconds Emily and Josh had joined her, while Fred produced a mouth organ from his breast pocket and took up position between Stan and Edward. Ken and Jane looked at Fran, then back at the patio, appalled and embarrassed. Fran took a step towards them, but what was she going to do, apologise?

Linda was alongside Fran. 'Well, it is a little different from the wedding *they* anticipated. Give them time, dear one.' Her arm was round Fran's waist, her foot tapping to the music. On the table behind them the lamp finally fell. 'Oops,' Linda breathed. 'Well, utterly merciful, actually. It was 'orrible.' The two women laughed.

By 1.30 the bolognese was as ready as it was going to be and Emily was pushing the spaghetti down into the pan, keeping an eye on the time. 'It needs to be hard in the middle,' she shouted at Fran over the noise of those guests who had gravitated as far as the kitchen table.

'Quite right,' Fran said as Jane whispered, 'Spaghetti at a wedding? That's absurd. Tagliatelli if you must have pasta.'

Emily brushed back her hair, stepping out of the steam for a moment. 'My mother suggested spaghetti,' she challenged.

Linda slid past Fran with the garlic bread. 'Oops again.' Her look spoke volumes.

Fran picked up a platter of biscuits and cheese. 'Take these, Jane.' It was an order, not a request. Jane tutted out. Fran checked the pasta. 'Five minutes, Emily.' That too was an order.

She walked into the garden. The day had clouded over but there was no rain. Was the music too loud? Were people trying to eat lunch, doze, entertain, garden? Would there be complaints? They were overlooked by a similar terrace to theirs. Invitations had been issued and some had been accepted.

There would be no complaints, Josh had reassured her. It wasn't that sort of neighbourhood.

'Mother.' Jane was heading towards her, her voice strident. In spite of herself Fran shrank inside. 'I've been looking at your presents. Linda's is an accounts book. "For the new business" the card says. What new business?'

Fran took her daughter's arm, needing that contact, wanting Jane to know that nothing touched their love. 'Darling, I love you. I've missed you. Try and understand about Josh and me.' Jane said nothing. Fran led her into the garden, and along to the hawthorn which Josh said had a yellow flower and glorious scent any minute now. 'The accounts book should keep me on the straight and narrow for my new venture.' She told Jane of the gallery. It all sounded flat and absurd. As absurd as her skirt.

Emily was shouting from the kitchen: 'Spaghetti's ready, Fran.'

Fran smiled tentatively at Jane. 'Coming to help serve the unservable?'

Jane was stabbing at a molehill which had appeared overnight. 'I thought it might be some sort of part-time secretarial service you were running from home. I thought we could still somehow sort out the children, because the job you haven't asked about yet is so demanding. I'm so tired, Mum, rushing to and from the childminder, and it's all so expensive.'

Emily called frantically, 'Fran, it'll be spoilt.'

Fran walked towards the house. 'Mum,' Jane called.

'Not now, Jane. Absolutely not now.' Josh heard her, heard the disappointment, frustration and guilt, because he detached himself from the stomping and headed across the narrow but long garden. Fran shook her head, pointing to the kitchen. 'Help your daughter with that damned spaghetti your ex-wife wanted us to have.'

He stopped dead, stared, then turned on his heel and headed for the kitchen without a word, while Fran helped herself to a glass of wine, smiling stiffly at Stan and grateful for Jessie's bellowed, 'Come and stomp a little.'

Fran did for a moment, ignoring Jane as she walked back into the house without a sideways glance, but her daughter looked so terribly tired and she'd lost weight. But then she'd said she had half a stone to go, though Fran had thought it ridiculous then and ridiculous now. It was the weight loss that could have made her drawn.

Jessie's beads were clicking and flying free. Fran thought of that day in the kitchen: so warm, so light, so much a family and perhaps she should have the children. But how, when so much else was within her grasp?

Josh and Emily dished up. Linda and Fran ferried platefuls through to the sitting room, distributing napkins and forks. Ken's parents had arrived and Fran worried about the bolognese; Sydney fired from his exhaust at the merest hint of an onion. She led the couple firmly outside to the patio table. Only when everyone was served did she take up position at the sink, hoping Josh would find her. He did, slipping his arms around her, murmuring, 'It was never going to be a doddle, my love.'

'I hate it when people state the obvious.'

He kissed her neck. 'An oak won't bend, so it breaks in a storm. Be a willow.'

'Sod off.'

'Really, Mrs Benton.'

Linda came in, carrying a tier of dirty plates. 'Stop that and get busy,' she ordered, dumping the plates on the draining board. 'Now, if you'd done the other gig instead, Mrs Benton, you'd have had staff to do this and we'd be cutting the cake.'

Fran stared at her but Josh roared with laughter. He kissed Linda. 'You are rather a star.'

Stan tapped on the kitchen window. 'You ready, Josh? We need your dulcet tones.' Josh was still laughing as he left the room. Linda and Fran looked at the dishes, then turned tail and followed him outside. The band played for another half-hour, then Mark, Stan's son, took control of the ghetto blaster.

In the encroaching darkness Jessie lit B-B-Q candles she had brought with her and finally, at last, Josh and Fran danced together, to Tina Turner's 'You are the wind beneath my wings', interrupted only by Ken's mobile, which he took down to the bottom of the garden, his finger ostentatiously in one ear. Josh murmured, 'Rise above it all and enjoy me, I'm a wonderful dancer.'

'My feet remain unconvinced,' she told him. He hugged her, and instantly she didn't care that her old neighbours were distant and embarrassed, that Jane was still brooding, that Ken was busy on the phone.

As the track ended Josh scooped up Lucy and danced with her, joined by Emily. Fred asked Fran for the pleasure. Jane looked worried as Stan attempted to sweep her into the fray, but Jessie snatched Harry from her arms and shooed her off. Now Jessie and Barry were jigging around the molehill and he was finding that her beads actually were suckable.

It was as Jane was at last really smiling and Rod Stewart launched into 'Waltzing Mathilda', that

Emily came out on to the patio with a huge painting wrapped in wedding paper. She called, 'Dad, can we open Mum's present now?'

Josh had been allowing Lucy to pull his black curls but at the sight of the painting he placed the child down gently. Jessie laid a hand on Emily's arm. 'Not now, darling. Later, when everyone's gone.' Her eyes were on Josh, then Fred.

Mark and Fran were changing CDs and in the lull Emily's voice was loud, 'But that's not fair, we've opened the others. Lucy, come and help.' Josh reached for Lucy but she was half running to Emily. The guests had turned and were watching.

Josh insisted, 'Later, Emily.' His voice was harsh.

Startled, Fran took a step towards him, but it was he who came to her side. 'I know what's in it.' He was pale. 'Trust me, we don't want to open it here, now.'

Emily propped the painting on the patio table, heedless of Jessie or her father.

Fred was closest and put a restraining hand on her arm. 'Later.'

'No, Mum wanted everyone to know she approved.' Emily shrugged him off and Fran remembered the terrible thirteens. There would be no stopping the child now.

Josh said urgently, 'Play some music, Mark.'

Mark was sorting through his collection. 'Any minute now, boss.'

'Now, for God's sake.' Josh's voice was again harsh as he moved towards Emily, shouting, 'Do not do this, Emily.'

Fran stared, while Linda touched her arm. 'What the hell's going on?'

They watched Josh shrug, then stop, shake his

113

head as though in despair as Emily and Lucy tore at the wrapping paper. The guests were closer, quieter. They crowded round, Fran and Linda were drawn inexorably along with them, and still Josh shook his head. Fran just stared at him and then at the painting, revealed in all its glory as the guests gasped and Jane said, 'Well, really.'

Fran was close enough to touch it. She recognised Josh's palette strokes, his naked body. Stan said, 'That woman is all sorts of a . . .' He stopped, because Emily had spun round defensively.

Linda tucked her arm through Fran's. 'So, that's what Catherine Benton looks like in the buff. I wonder if we'd recognise her with her clothes on.' It hurt. It damn well hurt to see Josh naked, painting a beautiful woman. It hurt more when it was at her wedding. At her damned wedding, in front of Jane, in front of her grandchildren.

Mrs Thomas's voice was loud and clear. 'What else can we expect, it's all very bohemian here, isn't it. All a bit seedy and quite disgraceful with youngsters present.'

At that Emily turned to Jessie, bewildered. 'Mum said it should come back to them. She said if they're starting a gallery they could lead with this. It's one of Dad's best. It is, isn't it, Dad? She said the technique should transcend anyone's fragile middle-class sensitivities. Or I think that's what she said.'

Josh said nothing, then came to Fran, taking her by the shoulders. 'I could kill her,' he whispered savagely, so quietly that Fran wondered if she had misheard.

But she hadn't and now she was as cold as his

voice had been, a deep-down cold. She shook free and went to Emily, saying, 'It is indeed one of Josh's best, Emily, and it will certainly lead the exhibition.'

She watched Jane leave the group and search for her handbag on the sofa. She heard Ken calling as he came up from the garden, 'Have I missed the toast? Sorry, a business call.'

Jessie took the painting from the table, propping it face inwards against her skirt. Jane called, 'Harry's tired, Ken. I think it's time we went.' It was 6.30.

Mrs Thomas and many of the 'old guard' took the lifeline Jane had offered. 'Yes, lovely afternoon. So kind.'

Stan grabbed a CD from his son's hand. 'Not that one, Dad.'

'Yes, this one,' Stan snapped, 'and a bit bloody late at that.' Dire Straits burst into life.

Jessie slipped her arm around Fran as they followed the departing guests to the door, murmuring, 'That Catherine is a complete cow, but Emily would have viewed it simply as art, just like the students. It's how she's been brought up. Try to do the same and don't let her get to you.'

The students were indeed looking at the painting, noting the texture, the tone, but all Fran could see was Catherine full frontal. 'Not a bit of cellulite, that's what hurts,' she murmured, smiling her farewell to Mrs Thomas and her husband, who flagged a wave as they rushed down the path. She tried to see Josh in the mêlée, but couldn't.

'Poor mother,' Jane said, standing in the porch. 'I suppose we'll see you hanging up on some wall like that soon. You must wonder what on earth you've got yourself into.' Her voice was angry beyond measure.

Ken looked puzzled as he appeared with their jackets. 'What on earth have I missed? The room is buzzing.'

'A painting by a wonderful man. A nude of his first wife and himself,' Fran snapped. 'Now, why don't you get home and put these children into their beds as Harry probably needs that sleep.'

She didn't wait to see them leave. Instead, she returned to the sitting room, grabbed up a bowl of crisps and ate too many, before offering them to those not dancing, knowing she should not have snapped at Ken and Jane. But if not at them, then at whom? At no one. It was art, that was all.

Linda handed her a drink, her eyes too concerned. Stan approached, saying, 'He's up in the bedroom. Go and have a word, there's a good girl.'

She passed the drink back to Linda. 'I'll be here for a while,' her friend said.

Fran made for the stairs, which were clogged with her fellow evening class students. One, Herbert Strawn, who was seventy and a pointillist, grabbed her hand. 'Wonderful party.'

She smiled at him, seeing that he meant it, but said nothing. She stepped between the earnest students, and their enthusiastic comments, finally reached the bedroom, opening the door, but always hearing his voice: 'I could kill her.'

Josh was at the bedroom window. He didn't turn as he said, 'That woman will never let me be. She's totally out of control.'

It was what David had always said to her. But it had been he who was out of control, he who had

116

held up his creased shirt and said, 'One day I will kill you.'

Josh swung round, raising his hand. She stepped back, her legs almost failing her, flinching. He came towards her, 'Fran, darling, I'm so sorry that this happened, so sorry you had to see the painting. I loved her then. I'm sorry but I did and she left me, and for weeks I didn't know where she and Emily had gone, and then she bobbed up, "renting" Roger's annexe in Dorchester. What bobbed up as well were the men people didn't want to tell me about. So many men, over all the years we'd been together. Men even Emily had guessed about.' He stopped. 'Come here.'

It was what David had said and each time she had gone, each time, because not to might have been worse. He could have gone past her to Jane. Mike had known better than to say it. This man didn't. This man was saying things that were disturbing the mud. This man had made her love him. This man said the same things David had. No, she would not go. This time she would just stand.

So he was coming to her, across the darkened room. It was so dark and deep down inside her she was so cold. It was a cold that was spreading and soon she would fall because her legs were so weak.

He was here, in front of her. She could not see his face. He was lifting his arms. She could not move. Then he held her gently and said into her hair, 'She broke my heart and now she does this, and she uses Emily and I don't understand why, when she left *me*, and I won't have you hurt and I won't let her make me into someone I'm not. I won't let her make me hard and cruel and full of hate. I won and I will never hurt you. Don't be frightened of me. Ever. Don't flinch from me. I'm not David. I never will be.'

Fran felt his hands gentle on her hair now. David had never, ever, been gentle. She had assumed it was passion to begin with. No, he had never been gentle and Josh wasn't a bit like him. Not yet. Perhaps not ever.

'It's a superb picture and I hate her thighs.' How strong her voice sounded.

'Yours are better, so much better, and I love you as I never loved her. We're going to have such a life together you and I. Just you and I, and we'll set up that gallery and it will be a success.' His lips found hers and were so gentle. 'Trust me,' he whispered.

*　　　*　　　*

Outside the door Emily stopped, her hand on the door knob. Just you and I.

You and I, as it was in Roger's house. She let her hand fall. She'd wanted to say sorry to her father who had never ever shouted at her before. She'd wanted to say sorry because her grandmother had explained that sometimes personal memories backfired at an occasion such as this. Emily half understood and was half angry with her mother, who had said Josh's friends would be delighted, but on the other hand she was half protective, because her mother couldn't have known so many stuffies would be here.

She turned away and went to her room. Just you and I. She sat on the bed, hugging herself, rocking and wishing the cat were here, because at least *he* was hers.

CHAPTER ELEVEN

At lunchtime a month later Linda kissed Fran goodbye outside the posh restaurant and watched her float down the street to the old double-fronted doctor's surgery which had been acquired in record time. It was amazing what could be achieved with a few contacts and a great deal of focus. She watched Fran turn and wave the keys triumphantly, before disappearing into the building. Linda breathed a sigh of relief. It was done. She barely noticed the walk back to Gilbert and Gilbert, or the brisk May wind which the weatherman had failed to mention.

Back in her office, she answered her new secretary's buzz. 'Yes, Sally?'

'Mrs P's postponed to three. You have a free, which is as well as you're fifteen minutes late.'

Linda flicked her off with a snap. Sally had missed her vocation, she should have been in the prison service. Half of her longed for the days of Fran, who juggled everything behind the scenes without feeling the need to slap her wrists. She flicked Sally back on. 'Thanks, Sally. It *was* a business lunch.'

Why was she explaining? She cut the connection, swinging her chair round, pushing the window open a little further. The breeze caught at the files and papers on her desk. She closed it slightly. Why was everything such a fine bloody line?

The sun was warm through the window. What would June be like; would it be a long, hot summer? Would Mike come to the concert with her this evening? It was the Bournemouth

Symphony and it had been a sell-out, and he had desperately wanted to go, or so she had overheard his secretary tell Sally as they crunched their Ryvita in the staff room last week. Ryvita? It made her feel guilty and that annoyed her, because she thought she'd learned to live with the extra six pounds that seemed immovable now that she had reached fifty.

She groaned, reaching for her briefcase, taking out the two cancellations that had arrived in the post this morning, handling them as though they were gold dust. God, Mahler was so dark, kind of boring. Give her Lloyd Webber any day. Never mind.

She pressed the intercom. 'Sally, see if Mr Wells is in conference. I've a few things to discuss.' Why explain again?

Mike wasn't. He could see her.

She checked her make-up in the lav, dabbing around with the blusher brush, but was that rather too much? She straightened her navy jacket. She undid the jacket and the top two buttons of her blouse. No. That was absurd. She made do with crisp and efficient, longing for Fran's glow of mutual love, great sex and a joint project. She felt as though there was a great hole in her chest, awash with envy and longing.

Thank God she had sorted the lease, secured the gallery, got the tenants in, got them on the road. For Fran's sake, too, of course for that.

Someone tried the handle of the lav. No peace anywhere. 'Coming,' she called.

'No hurry.' It was Sally. Well, it had to be. Fran, I miss you. But I'm so glad you're gone, so glad you're happy. So glad you have a chance at last, now that Mike's investigations have revealed Josh

120

as the injured party, one who acted painfully decently throughout his marriage and divorce.

The evening Mike phoned her with the news Linda had almost cried with relief, for herself and Fran, and embarked on her own project. At last.

She dabbed her lipstick with a tissue. For God's sake, he wasn't going to snog her. She straightened her shoulders as though she was going into battle and opened the door. Sally was 'queuing' against the white-glossed brick wall. The woman would have to go. Linda smiled. 'Sorry. Bit of a tidy-up.'

Sally nodded seriously. 'Makes us all feel better, doesn't it?'

Get out of my face. Linda headed for Mike's office. It was the biggest and best, but so it should be. He *was* Gilbert and Gilbert.

She shouldn't have had a second and then a third glass of wine. Fran had thought she was throwing caution to the winds in celebration of the gallery. Why hadn't she told her it was because she had two unobtainable concert tickets for a man jilted at the altar? Awkward, that's what it was, awkward and, perhaps, hopeless for as Mike had also cautioned on the phone, Josh and Fran were still in the starry-eyed period. So much could go wrong; she could still return to the fold. It was something he obviously half expected and fully hoped. Damn it to hell.

She passed the coffee machine, stopped, retraced her footsteps, poured two, using the cups Mike liked rather than the polystyrene jobs. She bore them carefully. Anne, his secretary, looked up from her word processor. 'He's expecting you and he's just had a cup of coffee.'

Damn. Mike's door was ajar. She tapped lightly

121

with her foot, feeling an idiot. 'It's me, Linda.' Well, he knew her voice, didn't he?

'Come in and I'd *love* another cup of coffee.' He was making his way to the door as she pushed it with her shoulder. He would say that, though. That was the sort of man he was. How could Fran . . . ?

He shut the door behind her. Thank God, or the Anne hotline would circulate all that was said. She placed the cups carefully on his desk, one on his side, one on hers, and perched on the edge of the clients' chair. She dug in her bag and produced the after-lunch mint chocolate from the restaurant, knowing he was partial. 'Apple for teacher,' she offered as Mike sat.

He smiled, taking it. 'I love being spoilt.'

Let me. Let me.

'Business lunch?' he said, unwrapping it, popping it in his delicious mouth. She had to stop this. Never again would she drink midday.

'Yes, at Chez André.' She didn't want to get into that. 'But it's personal.' Mike looked confused as he dropped the green foil into his waste bin.

'I mean the reason I'm here is personal.' Oh, God. She sipped her coffee. His cuffs were so white against his tanned wrists. Were his shirts laundered, or did he beaver away with the washing machine and an iron? Or perhaps his 'lady who does' did them. Let me. Let me. I'd thrash them against boulders for you, rub them against a washboard . . .

'Take your time.' Mike's voice reflected his concern. He stirred his coffee slowly. Why? There was neither milk nor sugar in it. 'Oh, no, nothing *really* personal,' She spoke too quickly. Had she slurred? Surely not. 'Oh, no, nothing serious. It's just that I have been given two tickets for the

Mahler concert by friends who are unable to make it. It's wonderful as I've been desperate to go but it's either famine or feast. First none, now two.' Shut up. She drew a breath. 'Well, I can use one, but am drawing a blank with the other. Perhaps you would like to come?'

Mike's smile was warm. 'Linda, yesterday I would have been delighted but I managed to pick up a cancellation myself. Just one. How kind of you to think of me.' He had stopped stirring and now he carefully placed his spoon in the saucer, looking at it as he continued, 'You have been so kind since . . .' He straightened his blotting pad. 'I do appreciate it, really.' His eyes were looking directly into hers now, heart-stoppingly directly. They were the deepest sensual grey. Her stomach flipped.

His intercom buzzed. He flicked the switch and his voice was the same as he spoke to Anne. 'That's kind, Anne. I do appreciate it.'

Her stomach skidded as it landed. He lifted his coffee cup, glancing at the grandfather clock in the corner of the wood-panelled room. It wheezed just as her father had done. 'Is there anything else? I've a few things to catch up on. Court makes such a hole in the day.'

She gulped the remains of her coffee. 'We're still chasing Mrs P's policies. The bar-steward solicitor is saying he hasn't received them.' She stopped, appalled. Mike was staring. 'Bar-steward?' He said the word several times as though he was trying out a new flavour. Then he laughed, a loud surprised laugh. 'Ah, bastard.' Suddenly he looked younger. She picked up her cup. 'You were going to consider taking it over once we reached the conveyance stage, but with all . . . Anyway . . .'

His eyes were on her again, those grey, grey eyes. She busied herself getting to her feet, smoothing her skirt, anything. 'You do it. Run the bar-steward, or bastard, or whatever he is, into the ground.'

His voice was savage for a moment. He looked different: hurt, enraged, damaged. Then it was gone. 'You do it,' he repeated. 'Look, if you're going tonight, why don't we share a car? It's absurd both of us driving when we're a road apart. Let me collect you and your guest, if you can find someone, and then you could have yet another drink.' He was smiling, but it was a warning too. A 'you have clients to see' warning.

Elated, humiliated, her mouth felt dry as she forced a smile. 'Thank you, Mike.'

The grandfather clock chimed the quarter-hour.

Sally ushered in Mrs Pendergast at 3 p.m. precisely and slipped a yellow post-it note on to Linda's desk, along with the glass of water she'd asked for and the paracetamol.

Linda:
I mentioned the concert to Ken, who is here for a conference on the Mainwaring case. I thought Jane might like to keep you company as you said you'd drawn a blank. Ken says she has a cold, but he is keen. If, however, you've managed to pass it on, please ignore this. Get back to me?

Ken was a shitty little gooseberry. She smiled at Mrs Pendergast, tasting the bitterness of the paracetamol, swallowing great mouthfuls of water, wishing the pounding headache would go.

CHAPTER TWELVE

Jane finished audio-typing the last of Stanley Oldfield's estimates, quotations and letters, sitting at the scarred old desk in the tatty office which must have had the same dreary green paint for more years than she had lived. The man rambled. He called it the personal touch for those desiring high-class printing but when she had to rush to catch the post it was just a nuisance. She signed for him. So much for the personal touch when golf was involved. The phone rang for the millionth time.

'Oldfield and Mason, how may I help you?' She hated that, it made her sound like a fifteen-year-old Tracy.

'Jane.' Ken's voice was hurried. She sat up straighter. 'I'll be in and out quickly this evening. I'll need the pale-blue shirt and green tie. A salad—no spring onions. Mike's off to a concert and there's a spare ticket going. It's next to Linda, actually, but it'll be better if we bump her into the single, and Mike and I have the two together. Seems ages since we exchanged more than a word or two and it'll be a chance to get back to where we were before . . . Well, never mind that.' He sounded pleased, so she was too, and not about to clarify the confusing seating logistics.

She dashed into Safeways on the way to the crèche and picked up ready-washed baby leaf salad and a piece of cooked salmon. The woman before her in the Express queue had eleven items. How dare she? Jane used her points to pay because Maisie needed cash daily after the last cheque had bounced. Jane hadn't known Ken's Visa bill had been so large, or that he had joined the gym. Was his blue shirt clean? She rushed to the car, spinning the wheels, taking a deep breath, easing her foot on the accelerator. That was better.

Lucy was already in her coat as she sat sucking her thumb in the vibrantly decorated playroom. Several other children were building a castle over by the sandpit. Maisie had yellow ribbons in her bunches today—how absurd for a woman of thirty. Or so Ken thought and he was right. Maisie looked at her watch. 'I'm sorry I'm late,' Jane said.

She gave Maisie a pound extra to make up for the thirty minutes. Maisie gave it back, smiling. 'It's not that, Jane. It's just that when you say a time children like you to keep to it. It's a long day for them both.' Harry was asleep in his buggy, but woke when she clicked him into his car seat. He cried all the way home. Lucy told her of the paintings she had done, Mrs Maisie's funny hat that she'd worn to tell the story, Sonia who'd wet her pants. Jamie who'd built a lovely castle until Jane wanted to scream.

She gave Lucy tinned macaroni cheese and Harry Farex, spooning it into his mouth too fast. He spat some out, all over the floor. She shot a look at the clock. Oh, God.

She wiped up the mess. 'Watch him,' she ordered Lucy and tore upstairs. Yes, the shirt was in the wardrobe. She checked it carefully, hanging it on the front of the wardrobe door. She found the tie.

Downstairs Lucy was calling, 'Mum, he's been sick.'

She took the stairs two at a time. In the kitchen Harry had regurgitated just a little into his pelican

126

bib. He was crying as Lucy rubbed at his face with the J-cloth which had last been used to clean the sink. Jane snatched it from her. 'For God's sake.'

Lucy blinked, froze. Jane shook her head, 'Sorry, darling, but it's a bit of a rush tonight. You sit down in the sitting room while I sort all this out, and then let's have bathtime a bit early, eh?'

She prepared Ken's salad and searched for hollandaise sauce while Harry cried and cried. There was none. But it might not matter as he was in a rush.

Quickly she tidied the kitchen, checking the mugs, the tea towels, lifting Harry from his chair. His arms came around her neck, his little body was shuddering, his face damp with tears and sweat. She checked the clock.

'Lucy.' Her voice was urgent. 'Lucy, come on. Bath.'

She hurried to the sitting room. Lucy was on her own little yellow plastic seat, turning the pages of her rag book. 'Lucy,' Jane repeated, more gently this time, loving her daughter, the soft curls, the round limbs, the concentration.

Lucy came. Jane took her hand, her dear little hand. They climbed the stairs together and she breathed Harry's baby smell.

*   *   *

Ken returned from the concert just before midnight. Jane watched the headlights slash the curtains, listened as the car idled, then died. There was the soft closing of the car door, the turn of the key in the front door. The sound of his footsteps on the stairs. The opening of the door. 'Are you

127

awake?' he asked, whispering in case he woke the children.

She eased herself up on her pillows, reaching for the bedside light. 'Good time?' she asked.

He was pulling at his tie, whistling between his teeth. 'Can't stand all that grinding classical stuff, but Mike was on good form. Very pally.'

She smiled with relief. He was unbuttoning his shirt, removing it, tossing it on to the chair, then his trousers. There wasn't a spare bit of flesh on him, he was as lithe as the day she had first seen him. It was important for a man, she could see that, to stay fit. He said they had been offering special rates for those joining the gym before the end of May.

He was in and out of the bathroom in a flash, then slipping into the bed. 'Turn off the light, darling. I'm worn out.'

She was relieved and slid down into the bed. His hand found hers and gently he squeezed it. She relaxed. 'I think Linda's got her eye on Mike,' Ken said, his voice muffled by the duvet which he liked to pull high up over his chin.

Jane couldn't catch his tone. She said hesitantly, 'That'll be good for Mike.'

He shook her hand. 'You really can be incredibly stupid. Any idiot can see that your mother and Josh can't last, so if Mike gets himself tangled up with Linda it would be a damned disaster. How could he then start up with Fran? For God's sake, do we, or do we not, want the boss of my firm, who holds my career in the palm of his hand, in our family?'

He was hurting her, twisting her hand. She could hardly think but she must. 'If Linda keeps Mike "warm". I mean, he'd never choose her over Mum, if Mum were back on the market. I mean, it's better than someone we don't know. At least with Linda we can keep an eye on things.'

His grip had become tighter with every word. She was struggling to lie still, because he didn't like her moving, didn't . . . She must be still. But now his grip was lessening. Now she could breathe. She wanted to gasp, force the air in.

'You know, darling'—his voice was soft—'you've got a point. Let's ask them for a meal, keep it simmering. It would be pay-back for the tickets and Mike's friendship is important to me, you know. I *need* that contact. Damn it, if only . . .' His grip was tightening.

She cut in quickly on his rising voice: 'I'll phone him from work. Will Saturday do? You choose the menu. I saw him over the fence yesterday; he was saying he'd been so busy recently, but was missing us.'

'He said that?'

She said quietly, 'He is the closest thing I have to a father, you know.'

For a moment there was a silence. 'Actually, in law, that position is taken by Josh now.' The grip was tightening again.

Don't say that. Just don't say that because I have no place in Josh's life. None at all. She stared into the darkness, hanging on to the fact that Mike was her godfather. Surely that meant something and he was the one whose lights she could see from the children's room. As long as she could see those there was someone close enough to . . . She slammed her mind shut. His grip was still tight on her hand, then slowly it relaxed.

He said, 'I'm bushed.' His kiss was light on her cheek. The duvet was pulled up again and almost

129

immediately he was asleep. How did men do that? How did they empty their minds? She stared at the ceiling, because she couldn't pay Maisie next week, not for all of next week now that the gym money had to be found, and she didn't know where their money was going. If only her mother had married Mike.

If only she had said something about Josh earlier they could have stopped it. But she never said anything about anything. Never. Not about anyone. If her father were alive, would Ken get so angry? Perhaps he would relax more, talk to her dad in a way that he couldn't to his own father. Round and round it went, and as always when she thought of her father it didn't help because her stomach knotted and she wanted to cry, and she didn't know why.

CHAPTER THIRTEEN

Catherine sat in her white satin dressing gown, sucking her pen and checking her figures. Well, if that CSA woman was right and husbands often paid more, if they were cohabiting, she didn't want to waste a moment.

Emily rushed into the dining-cum-sitting room, *their* room, in *their* annexe, her feet clattering noisily on the tiled floor. 'You'll be late for school,' Catherine said as her daughter rummaged through the school work piled at the other end of the dining-room table.

Emily sighed loudly. 'Have you seen my English?' Catherine returned to her figures. 'Mum, have you seen my English?'

Catherine shook her head, wishing she had more detailed information about the number of items Josh had sold through his bloody mother, but Emily had only heard the gist and even then she hadn't known what she was reporting back. Her solicitor had said best not to question her, best not to alert Josh until the letter claiming a slice arrived.

'Got it.' Emily was brandishing the green file in the air. Catherine stared at her. She was becoming so loud, so messy and clumsy. Just like her father. 'Emily, it would be altogether better if you didn't have to hunt for it in the first place. Now go to school and tomorrow try putting your hair in a plait.'

Emily practically ran round the table at her like a stampeding rhino. The kiss messed her hair, then she was gone. Catherine waited. The front door slammed. Why couldn't she just close the door? She sat quite still for a moment. She'd always said that to Josh. The pain that came and lodged in her chest was almost physical. She rubbed. It remained.

On the Ercol settee there was a discarded video tape. A trainer lurked beneath the television table. Why couldn't the girl do as she was told? It was all too much. Just too much. She treated the place as a doss-house, but thank God she confined it to these quarters, because Catherine couldn't have stood to have her concept, Roger's minimalist white, spoiled.

She brushed her hair back from her face, and for a moment the room spun and sweat broke out on her top lip. She dabbed at it, trying to focus on the figures again, but the ache was still there and she threw down the pen, not able to believe, even now, that he had found someone with her own house, with whom he was sharing a gallery, someone liked by his parents, who had made him forget her, someone to replace her.

She ran her hands over her breasts. They were still taut. Well, they should be. Forty wasn't old. Taut, but tender, familiarly tender. The sweat broke out again. She laid her hands flat on the table, cold. Very cold. She should pick up the tape and trainer. She should put the breakfast dishes in the dishwasher. She could do nothing.

There was a knock on the interconnecting door at the end of the small lobby leading off the room, the sound of footsteps on the woodblock floor. 'Sweetheart.' Roger's voice was tentative behind her. 'I'm off. Kiss?' He stood between her and the sideboard.

Fuck off. 'You better had or I'll want to know the reason why.'

She slid her figures beneath her design folder, turning, her smile ready. He was wearing the suit she had chosen yesterday and carrying the rather fine extending briefcase she had bought by mail order with his credit card. For a moment she allowed herself to appreciate the Roger who had seemed so appealing at their first meeting: the long legs, the neat hair, the air of order and wealth.

Roger kissed her mouth, but it was the same old kiss, the same old tongue. He straightened, touching her shoulder, staring into her eyes in that meaningful way he had. 'Do you think he'll let Emily come?'

God, change the record. 'I still haven't mentioned it, darling. Why, when we don't know the exact date? It's best to have the one

132

conversation.' The other trainer was beneath the Ercol armchair, she now saw.

'But if he agreed in principle we could just relax.'

She wanted to slap his hand from her shoulder but instead held it. 'Trust me. Josh likes all the "i"s dotted and "t"s crossed so there's less for him to think about.'

Roger looked worried. 'So you think there'll be a problem?'

She straightened his jacket, wanting so much to be free of him. 'Stop worrying. I know the States is more than a hour away but San Diego's not the moon. He can always come and visit, or she can fly back for a holiday, so how can he object?' Roger grinned suddenly, switching his briefcase to the other hand, searching for his car keys in his trouser pocket. 'You're right.' He kissed her hair, messing it up. What was it with people?

She waited for the door to shut, still feeling his lips on hers, hating him, hating Josh, missing him, hating Fran. Hating her. Really hating the woman because there might be nowhere to go now. Nowhere except America, for Josh had not contacted her, but perhaps he was waiting for her to take the game into his camp.

An hour later she took the pregnancy kit into the annexe bathroom and waited, sitting on the edge of the bath. She knew, of course, barely needing the confirmation before throwing the bloody thing in the waste bin. She washed her hands, splashed her face. Damn. Damn. She sat back on the edge of the bath, rubbing her belly, trying to think. She showered, towelled herself and still her mind raced, her head spun, sweat broke out and with it came the nausea.

She wrapped the towel around her and searched frantically through her writing desk, then again. It was where she kept those things Roger mustn't find: address books, letters, useful numbers. She couldn't find it, couldn't think. It wasn't fair. It just wasn't fair.

One last look. Then she rushed to the phone, stabbing out Sue's number. Sue would know. The trainer was still there, under the armchair. Of course it was. Sue's answer machine clocked in: 'This is Sue Marshall of Casu Interiors. Leave a message and I'll get back to you.'

'Sue, pick up the phone.' Catherine heard the panic in her own voice. She waited for a response from her business partner and ex-lover. It had only taken her a couple of sessions to decide that particular niche wasn't for her, but it had been fun.

Sue said, 'Hi, Cathy. Found your Heathcliffe yet?'

Catherine was sick of the joke, but laughed anyway. What the hell did it matter if it didn't sound real. 'Sue, shut up. Look, I'm up the duff again.' Damn, she'd meant to sound casual.

There was no sympathy from Sue, just irritation. 'Oh, for goodness sake.' In the background Catherine could hear the soft click of the word processor and the tone that meant that Sue was only listening with half her brain. 'I can't find the number of the clinic. Have you still got it?'

The clicking of the word processor stopped and Sue was all attention now. 'What do you mean? Oh, Cathy, get your bloody act together. If you didn't want it you should have practised safe sex, or come back to me.'

Catherine slammed the phone down. She didn't

need this. None of this. Her hands were trembling. She reached for a cigarette but the phone rang before she could light it.

It was Sue again. 'Oh, here's the number.' She reeled it off. Catherine wrote it down, holding the receiver between her shoulder and her chin. Sue said, 'There can't be any doubt, can there? Have you tested yourself?'

'Of course.'

Sue went on quietly, 'Look, Cath, why don't you keep it? There are tests to make sure the baby's all right, especially at your age.'

Catherine was feeling sick again. She pressed her hand to her mouth, wiping away the sweat. When the worst had passed she said weakly, 'Look, if I get back with Josh I can't have the kid, can I?'

Sue's voice was incredulous. 'What do you mean, get back with Josh? Where the hell has this come from?'

Catherine felt the tears starting, great long streams of them. 'I want to go home. I really want to go home and I can now. I've money. I can make it work. He won't let Emily go to America so I'll say take us both back or have none of us. I think he really wants it. He rang while I was here, to rub my nose in his new love.'

'Neither.'

'What?' Catherine shook her head, wiping her face with the back of her hand, not understanding.

'Not none of us, neither of us.'

'Oh, for Christ's sake, I didn't phone for a lesson in . . .'

'Cathy, just think. He's with this Fran, he married her, for God's sake. He doesn't want you back, not now. You have to accept that.'

She didn't want to hear this. Sue was supposed to be her friend and now the pain was coming, the awful pain. She shrieked, 'That's because he doesn't know I want to come back. That's because . . .'

Sue's voice was cool and hard. 'I repeat, that's because he's found someone else, someone to replace you, someone to make a life with. Get a grip, Cathy, leave them in peace. Give them a chance. Josh deserves it and you'll never keep your knickers on, never give him a fair deal; you didn't the first time, you didn't for me, I bet you haven't for Roger. You probably never will for anyone, ever. You cheat people, you don't know how to love, so keep the kid, if it passes all its tests. Be discreet, try and make you and Roger work. Focus on the kids. Now, I've a meeting to get to. I'll phone later about the Simmonds job. I've some ideas for the curtains.'

The line went dead.

Catherine stayed motionless for minutes. There was only the tick of the clock, the cat who was wailing to be let out, the creaks of the house. Leave them in peace? Leave *them* in peace? Give *them* a chance? She moved at last, snatching up the trainers, first one, then the other and throwing them into the hall, the video tape after them. Then she lit the cigarette. There. But her hands were shaking, bloody well shaking and who the hell cared? No one.

She inhaled deeply but instantly the sickness was back and she sank back on to the chair, dropping the cigarette into the ashtray. The tears were coming again, great racking sobs.

An hour later she rang her solicitor. Bob Walker sounded pleased, but that's how they were paid to sound. 'Bob, let's get the claim in.'

'I told you I wasn't sure if we really had a case.'

She said, 'You said don't alert him until we're good and ready.' She sipped the iced water she had poured for herself.

His voice was patient. *'You* said "good and ready". I said do not alert him as I didn't know if we should or could really do this . . .'

'Do as I instruct. Come on, Bob, remember whose side you are paid to be on.'

'Well, talking of that, it's going to cost you. You're no longer on Legal Aid. And after all, he did settle a capital sum and he has paid maintenance, *and* you were cohabiting long before him. We don't know what this other woman's income is.'

She pressed the glass to her cheek, then hurled it across the room. It smashed against the bookcase, drenching the books. What was it with everyone? 'I don't give a fuck about that. She's got a house, it's providing an income. There are just the two of them. I want a letter sent. I want their cage rattled, d'you hear. How bloody dare he?'

'Catherine, what's up?' His voice was concerned. She took a moment, remembering suddenly that trick Bob had of licking the base of her throat, remembering how he had cared, how he still gave her lunch, how he often said, 'If only . . .' She stretched, feeling better. The water dripped from the shelves to the floor. It would wipe.

She picked up the cigarette lighter. There had

been just the one time he hadn't been able to make it to the wine bar but she hadn't been sitting alone for long. Paul Davies she had named the man who had bought her a drink. 'Never use a real name,' she had told him as he bought her a second martini. 'It makes it more exciting.' She could give Paul a ring on his mobile. Yes, there was always that, it would calm her down, help her to think. Calmer, she said, 'Just send the letter.'

She hung up, changed into one of her 'shop till I drop' outfits. She'd look for something soft and a new bra, one that showed off her nipples, her enhanced cleavage, then she'd call Paul. But not today, she'd leave that until tomorrow; the day Josh and Fran received the letter.

Give them a chance? No bloody way. She'd harass that bitch into the ground, or at least until she was off and over the horizon.

CHAPTER FOURTEEN

The next day, in the entrance hall of the chaotic and soon to be finished gallery, Fran steered Harry's buggy round a ladder as Lucy caught nervously at her skirt. James, one of Josh's youngest Foundation Course students, teetered on the top, paintbrush in hand. He peered down and called, 'You again, little 'un. Great to have some sensible company. The geriatrics get boring.'

'James, you should have someone steadying that.' Fran guided Lucy along the corridor into the main gallery where Simon, Josh's star student, was hard at work. 'I've sandwiches for our lunch,

138

darling.'

James called, 'You shouldn't have, sweetness, I've brought my own.' His Somerset burr made everything seem gentle and calm. Josh could not have chosen a better part-time team and their rates were reasonable too.

Fran grinned. 'On second thoughts, James, don't have anyone steadying that, just take the tumble that's long overdue.' She pulled a face at Lucy, putting on the carrycot brake, quietly asking Simon to hang on to the ladder for the idiot.

Simon wiped the excess paint from the roller, propped it on one end in the tray, turned up his Walkman and made his way into the hall, jerking about as though plugged into a live current. Lucy put her thumb in her mouth, clinging even tighter to Fran.

'Yes, you're right, it is a madhouse, darling,' Fran said softly, picking her up, 'but it's just such a treat for me to be looking after you; we're going to have such fun.' She kissed the child's cheek. In a way it was. But four afternoons a week?

Josh had said, when she put down the phone a few nights ago, 'Surely you didn't have to agree? Look, when are you going to learn to say no? This is ridiculous. You're stretched as it is and this was supposed to be your time, our time.'

She'd defended herself: 'Well, what else can I do? Jane's right, if I hadn't changed the ball game . . . Anyway, the crèche is too expensive and *she's* getting beside herself, so I *should*.'

'Darling,' he'd hushed her. 'OK, OK, I just wish I had the money to help them out because it's such a lot for you and you are wrong. You don't *have* to.' He put up his hand in defeat as she started to

139

explain again. 'Anyway, Fran, I'll be at the gallery after college, so you'll have an extra pair of eyes. Though I'm no good with nappies and don't intend to be. You have been warned.' His tone had been light, but she could still see the frustration in his eyes.

She had gone to him. He had held her and they kissed, and when he pulled back he said, 'We can cope. This is not a problem. It must not be a problem.' It had sounded like a mantra.

She felt uneasy, even though they had made love as always.

Lucy was wriggling. 'I'm hungry, Grandma.'

Fran laughed and kissed Lucy. 'I'm not surprised, you've been so busy all morning. We've all been busy.'

'I'm hungry,' Lucy repeated. 'You said darlings were having sandwiches.' Fran laughed harder, putting her on the reception desk, which was littered with invoices, memos, faxes and sugar-free chewing gum wrappers. It seemed students and gum went together.

'Just be thankful it's nothing more exciting,' Josh had murmured. 'Don't worry, they know the "no wacky baccy" rule.'

Cardboard boxes were scattered all over the half-painted gallery floor, electrical equipment and planks were heaped at one end and in the coffee shop area. She dug into the baby bag of provisions Jane had left with Maisie, finding peanut butter sandwiches for Lucy, tutting as Simon snatched one on his return.

While Lucy sat on the desk and ate, and Harry slept, Fran checked the message pad. There were lots, mostly from the local press. She managed to return two calls in the comparative peace of Simon's humming as he painted and James's grunts as he secured the picture rail in the entrance hall, but then Harry woke, crying.

She changed him on his mat on the floor. Simon was appalled, decided he needed more cigarette papers and was gone, leaving the roller propped in the tray as before. 'You bring to mind rats and sinking ships,' she called after him.

Then James came in, wiping his hands on a rag. 'Wow, now this is when my stepmother says she needs three hands.' He took the nappy bag gingerly by a corner and dropped it in the black bin bag which was set up in the corner.

'You're a good boy,' Fran said, handing him the baby wipes to put in the baby bag, scrambling to her feet with Harry, who played with her hair.

'I like kids,' he said. 'My dad has two more by the new Mrs Walton. She's a belter too.'

Fran sat on the desk next to Lucy with Harry on her lap. Lucy rubbed at the peanut butter on her cheek. James used another baby wipe to clean her up while Fran fed Harry puréed carrots. The phone rang. James answered, writing down the message from the plumber, returning to the ladder, throwing over his shoulder the fact that he'd prime the rail today and gloss it tomorrow. 'Fine,' Fran called, trying Harry with just a little more purée. 'Just as long as you're keeping up with your college work.'

'Never fear, Mrs B.'

Simon reappeared with a pasty for each of them. 'Peace offering,' he shouted above the Walkman, leaving hers on top of the message pad, staining it with grease. She grinned, used to it by now.

Gail, an English student hoping to go into publishing, turned up in workmen's overalls and began glossing the coffee shop woodwork, turning James into a lust machine, he confided as he came through to answer the phone yet again. It was a reporter. 'Shall we swap?' he asked, his hand over the mouthpiece. Harry cried as he was handed to James. Fran found his bottle and James plugged him in, as she put the receiver to her ear.

But then Lucy began to weep. 'I want James.'

Fran put her hand over the receiver. 'Hush for a moment, darling.'

She tried to concentrate on the phone as James wedged the bottle beneath his chin and helped Lucy down. The bottle slipped. He caught it before it hit the floor. Harry screamed his rage, Lucy her jealousy. Fran completely lost the journalist's drift. As she pressed a hand to her free ear James plugged Harry in again, but he had lost interest, preferring the sound of his own voice.

'Sorry,' Fran said to the journalist. 'Bit of a crisis; there's never a dull moment here.'

She couldn't hear his response as James shouted to Lucy, gaining her attention at last: 'Walk with me, princess, while I try to persuade young Hal to like his lunch. Let's start at the planks but whatever happens we must not touch the cables, or we'll be turned to stone. Hush, now, and lead me.' Miraculously Lucy quietened. Miraculously Harry took his bottle again. Silence reigned as a tremulous Lucy led the way.

Every home should have a James, Fran decided as she absorbed the reporter's questions at last, but then Lucy touched a cable and the tears began. 'I'll phone you back,' she said to the reporter.

'Sorry, off out,' he replied.

Somehow they stumbled on with the interview. It had been like this yesterday and the day before, only not so bad for the children had still been curious, even Harry, it seemed. Today they were settling in. Tomorrow? Somehow it would work. She must keep saying that, but the tension was giving her a headache. At last it was over. 'I'll phone again if I need to check anything with you,' the reporter said.

'Make it in the morning,' she advised.

'I will, if I can, but I doubt it.' Damn.

She'd phone the *Western Daily Press* next. They were always helpful, had promised to be here for the launch and wanted to do a run-up piece, so too did BBC Somerset Sound. The list was getting longer as the time grew shorter. She checked the calendar. 'We'll do it,' she assured herself, rolling her shoulders, trying to ease the rigid muscles.

James and Lucy had edged beyond the cable for the second time. 'There, you see,' James said. 'It's only a game. No one was turned to anything.' He grimaced his apology to Fran. There was no need.

'You should be packaged and sold to harassed grandmothers,' she told him. 'Now, come in, number four.'

Relieved, James led the way back to the desk. Harry's bottle was finished, he was almost asleep. Gently she laid him in the buggy, saying to Lucy, 'See, you looked like this and I used to tuck you up just as I'm doing now.' Fran stroked Harry's hair. Now Lucy did too.

James was gathering up his things and he called, 'I've got to go to college now, or Uncle Josh will throw a wobbly and I'll never get to uni, so I'll leave you to Gail's tender mercies.' He winked at Fran. 'Be still, my beating heart,' he whispered.

'Have you written down your hours?' she asked. 'Call in on Friday for the money. Thanks so much.'

'See you, Simon,' he said, as he grabbed his scarf and swept out. Josh must have been like him, Fran thought, all those years ago. So many years without one another. So many years when she must have been barely alive. They would cope. They must cope. In a moment the phone was ringing, Lucy was tugging at her skirt, Harry stirred and there was a crash from the coffee room.

Simon called, 'You still with us, Gail?'

'No probs. Just a renegade chair.'

Fran snatched up the phone, checking the clock. In an hour he would be here and he was adjusting to the children. He could see it wasn't too much, surely he could see?

'Hold the line just a moment, please,' she said calmly into the phone, finding Lucy's colouring book in the supply box and a new set of wax crayons, lifting her on to the desk, opening it at a picture of an apple. Lucy chose a red crayon. Fran turned her attention to the caller, trying to write the details of the coffee room furniture delivery date on the greasy pad, and failing. She wrote them instead at the top of Lucy's page.

Lucy tugged at the book, jogging her. She wrote it again and ended the call. 'Come on, Lucy, we'll choose another colour and do it together.'

Simon had opened the windows either end and was glossing the lighting rail. Lucy chose a bird with very delicate legs. Should they go into the coffee shop away from the paint fumes? But there the chaos was worse and no phone was connected.

Lucy was stabbing at the bird with a deep-green crayon, then the stabs turned to swirls. Suddenly Fran was homesick for her paints. But she could return to those when things were quieter. Lucy leaned back. Fran caught her in time, kissing the top of her head, holding her tight. Yes, she could wait and she must not let the frustration show.

Lucy said, 'Forest, Grandma?'

So Fran walked her over the cables, skirting the planks, waving to Simon, pointing out where they would hang the paintings, where the lights would go on the rail and where the artwork greetings card rack would hang.

Gail called, 'Shall I put the kettle on?'

'Please,' Fran shouted as she lowered Lucy to the floor instead of the desk and, groaning, joined her with a yellow crayon. Gail brought mugs of tea through, one for Fran, one for Simon, and left both on the desk. The phone rang. This time it was the *Western Daily Press*, wanting to put the run-up feature into their Saturday magazine and needing comprehensive details which Fran was only too pleased to give them.

They spoke for ten minutes and Fran was pencilling in the photographer for Friday afternoon when Simon bellowed, 'Lucy, what on earth have you done?'

Fran turned to see Simon darting towards Lucy, his combat trousers splashed with paint. Lucy stood frozen, the crayons rolling away across the floor, her strong red slashes and spring-green circles vivid . . . on the newly painted wall next to the door.

Oh, God. As Simon reached Lucy she ran crying to Fran, who said into the receiver, 'Got to go. I'll phone back.' Lucy clung to her legs, sobbing.

145

Automatically Fran lifted her, but her eyes were on the wall, her heart sinking, her headache soaring, her muscles rigid. She said, 'Hey, it's all right, it can be painted over.'

Simon turned. 'I'm sorry, I didn't mean to shout at her.'

Fran repeated, 'It's all right.' It was to herself as well as Simon. 'Everything will be fine.'

She was patting Lucy. Harry had begun to cry. Her head was throbbing. How could it turn from an ache to a throb so quickly? The wind was channelling itself in through one window and out of the other. It was cold, but how could she shut them, with the children . . . Though they must be cold too. She hunted for their jackets.

'It'll be all right,' she repeated, but they only had ten days until the launch, for God's sake. Ten days.

Gail had arrived from the coffee room, a duster in one hand, a tape measure in the other. She had tied her long hair in a red ribbon. Gail said, 'Bloody hell, Fran.' She looked from the wall to the children. 'I bet you're glad you only had one, or you could be coping with a football team of ankle biters. Just imagine that.'

For a second Fran froze, her eyes drawn back to Lucy's swirls. Momentarily the world stood still, she didn't hear Lucy's cries, only saw the crayon marks. She could barely feel her throbbing head. She stared at the swirls. She should go home and paint; great gouging spirals, great slashing palette strokes because *he* was back, David was back, summoned by words which meant nothing to Gail, but everything to her. Words. It was always those black words which found the cracks.

She shook her head. No, No, she savagely told

146

herself. But they were said. That awful single child bit. But it was all in the past. She was tired, that was all, that was why these words dug, twisted, hurt. She concentrated on the small crying child who had run into her arms.

She patted and soothed, listening to Simon as he said, 'How about some juice, Lucy?' His voice was measured. He was trying to slow things down.

He was hunting in the box with kind hands which were paint-smudged. Now Harry was crying. She watched him; his bunched fists.

When her son had been six months in the womb . . .

Simon had found the juice. He brought it to Lucy. 'I didn't mean to . . .'

Lucy took it, her face wet, hot and red. Fran could feel the heat of her, the gulps. She kissed her damp hair.

Gail picked up the two crayons from the floor. She brought them to the desk and placed them upon it. Fran watched as they rolled. She concentrated on that but felt instead the blow to her belly and later the white, white . . .

Fran kissed Lucy's head. The phone rang. Josh called from the hall, 'I'm here. What can I do?'

He swept in, his eyes on hers, his smile for her alone. She clung to that smile and somehow found her own, and her voice, and hid everything else, everything that had escaped too easily. She murmured to Lucy, 'Hey, it's all right. We can paint over it, or maybe not. We could frame it. Make it the star turn?' She sounded as though she'd been running, but it really was all right, because he was coming to her, straight to her, enfolding them both in a hug, telling Gail to answer the phone, turning

147

from Fran, scooping up Harry and leading them into the relative peace of the chaotic, unfinished coffee shop. 'Simon, bring through more juice, there's a good lad, and a bottle for Harry,' he called.

Fran added, 'The tea too. Make sure you bring yours.' She sounded almost normal.

He did, handing the juice to Fran and his tea to Josh. 'There you go, boss. I'll brew another.' He sauntered into the kitchen, bottle in hand. Josh and Fran looked at one another and Josh patted Harry's back. 'What did we do with our lives before we met one another and sailed off into the sunset?' he said and there was no frustration, only humour and love.

Never felt safe, she wanted to answer. Deep down, I never felt safe.

Lucy gulped the juice Fran held. Fran said automatically, 'Waited, for one another.'

Josh blew her a kiss. 'Absolutely right.' But he was examining her too closely and now he was stroking her hair, his eyes asking the question.

Simon emerged from the kitchen with his mug of tea, stirring in his three spoons of sugar. 'Bad for you,' warned Fran as always. Her voice sounded tinny but no one seemed surprised.

Simon wagged the spoon at her, before licking it clean. 'Ah, but I'll need energy to repaint the wall, and I will when I've finished the rail, so don't fret. It will be as good as new.' This last bit he added in a whisper with a worried look towards Lucy. 'I'll get Harry's bottle.' He returned with it wobbling about in a bowl of hot water. 'Don't know about the temperature.'

'Si's right, it will be as new.' Josh's voice was

mild as he tested the milk. It was just right. Harry guzzled it, quiet at last. Perhaps he needed more solids, Fran thought. Josh looked down at Harry. 'However, I rather like the energy of the swirls.'

Lucy handed back the juice mug, quite empty now. Fran said quietly, 'You know you mustn't colour on people's walls, don't you, Lucy. You won't do it again, will you?' Lucy shook her head, tired. Of course she was. She needed a camp bed here. Later, when the gallery was open she could roost in the office at the back and Lucy could stay there with her, but until then she'd have to set up a system. She ran her hand through her hair. That's all it needed, a system. It was how she had learnt to live her life. For these children it must be reinstated.

Harry was asleep again. Josh carried him through to his carrycot. Fran followed, set Lucy down by the desk and took the message Gail had written on the notebook she had brought with her. Now this girl would make a good administrator one day.

Behind her Josh was looking at the wall. He came to Lucy. 'I think what you have created here is Grandma's very first original gallery painting, and because this is a place where pictures belong I think we should find a nice frame and put your name and the title beneath. It should be our benchmark painting. *We're here to encourage, to open minds.* How about that, darling? Shall we frame the wild things, the ones that sometimes escape?'

He was looking at Fran. It was a question. He, Josh, her husband, was framing her past, containing it, trying to turn it into something else.

149

He would not ask what it was. He would listen if she wanted to tell him. She dared to relax, to let her breathing regulate itself. She nodded her agreement, watching as he picked up a piece of beading to show her how he would frame it. 'What shall we call it?' he asked Lucy.

'Apple trees.'

Josh cocked his head. 'Of course.'

Fran placed her hand against his cheek. 'You're wonderful.'

Now Josh said seriously, as Fran had, 'But no more drawing on walls, only on paper.'

'Or Mummy and Daddy will be cross,' Lucy said.

'Probably,' Josh replied. 'Let's choose a picture in your colouring book and do it together in the kitchen, while Grandma does what she needs to do. I suppose O'Reilly hasn't confirmed yet? He leaves everything to the last moment.'

Fran ran her fingers through her hair. She had meant to phone O'Reilly next. He was main exhibitor and as slippery as an eel to pin down to detail. She shook her head. 'Not yet, but there's time.' Josh nodded. What else did she need to do? For a moment her mind was blank, but then she remembered Ruth, the coffee shop manager, was due. Sure enough, the doorbell rang. Simon answered it. Were they right to employ, rather than franchise out?

Time would tell. Dear old Father Time. She drew a great, deep breath, feeling as though she'd reached a far shore, and smiled at the girl Simon brought in. This was her world. *This* was her world and this was the girl Simon had recommended, all wholesome cheeks and curly hair, who had dropped out of college two years before to work in a small craft-coffee shop near the coast. She was here to talk about the launch nibbles. Such were the glorious minutiae of her life. She smiled at Ruth, as Simon hovered. Fran suspected a love affair, but said nothing.

Ruth's ideas on the launch nibbles were sound and cheap, without appearing so. Simon produced more tea and slipped out for jam doughnuts for them all. Fran felt her suspicions were confirmed.

The phone went on ringing. Harry continued to sleep. Lucy and Josh were busy doing colouring, face painting and story book reading. At 5.30 Lucy took up yesterday's position at the window to wait for her mother.

While Josh cleared up their play area Fran called from the desk, 'Come and sit with me, Lucy.' She waggled a crayon temptingly.

Lucy only shook her head and pointed to the clock. 'Mummy said when the big hand was there and the little hand there she'd come.'

It wasn't until six that Jane flew into the gallery. 'Sorry, Mother, but I thought I could do the shopping on the way.'

As Lucy ran to her mother, Fran said quietly from behind the desk, 'Lucy's been waiting since half past five. If you're going to be late, call us.'

Jane coloured, picking up the baby bag, turning the buggy towards the gallery door as Lucy grabbed at her skirt. Jane said over her shoulder, 'Mother, shopping is just so much easier without them, you know what it's like. I'm sorry.' She looked down at Lucy. 'Mummy's sorry she's late. She has crisps in the car for you. Let's hurry now, or we'll be late for Daddy's tea.'

Bugger Daddy's tea. Fran clamped her mind

151

shut and saw Josh doing the same. She heard Lucy say, as they reached the gallery door, 'Look what I did, Mummy.' She was pointing to her 'mural'.

Jane stopped dead, staring at the wall. 'Lucy,' her shout startled them all. Josh cut across whatever was about to be said next: 'We're going to frame it. It's special and will lead the exhibition. It will be a good talking point.' He put his hand on Jane's arm, but she shook free, shouting at Lucy, 'How could you?'

'Honestly, we did explain that she mustn't,' Josh said, his hand on Lucy's head now, his voice conciliatory. Ruth was clattering in the kitchen, Gail was hoovering up the coffee shop.

Jane cut across him, speaking to her mother: 'It will just encourage her. What are you thinking of? She'll do it at home now.'

Fran looked carefully at Jane, at the dark circles under her eyes, took in the pitch of her voice and remembered how she used to feel when she rushed back from work, having to switch from one world to another without pause for breath. She said gently, coming from behind her desk, 'Josh has just told you we explained this was a one-off and must not happen again. Honestly, darling, relax. We don't mind, so you shouldn't. Just think, at least we've decided not to lead with the bare bums of Catherine and Josh. In fact, that painting won't be hung at all, so every cloud has a silver lining. I'm sure Ken . . .'

'Everything's a joke to you, isn't it?' Jane pulled Lucy from the room, scraping the buggy wheels along the skirting boards. Fran winced, Josh winked and they both followed, Josh helping her down the steps. Lucy waved as Jane rushed off.

Fran leant back against Josh as his arms came round her. 'Thanks, Mum and Josh. So kind,' she mimicked. 'Forgive her.'

Josh kissed her neck. 'Strangely, I do. I remembered, just now, what it was like to drag Em round a supermarket when I first had her for weekends. Not just the shopping, the whole single bit. It nearly killed me. You're right, Jane's whacked, but she'll grow accustomed, as the song says.'

'I could wring her neck.'

'Messy,' he murmured.

She loved him to distraction.

*   *   *

An hour later she and Josh picked up fish and chips, with extra chips for Stan and Cindy, who would otherwise be round scrounging theirs. Once home they only stopped to take a bottle of chilled white wine from the fridge and two glasses, before heading for the patio. Chips were one thing. If the others wanted booze they'd have to bring their own.

On cue Stan opened his back door. 'Ah, Bisto.'

Fran settled herself back in her chair, Josh on the bench next to her, their knees touching, and opened her portion, eating from the paper using her fingers rather than the wooden fork, pointing to the extra portion still wrapped in its paper. 'Those and no others,' she ordered sternly.

Cindy was right behind Stan and took up position alongside him on the bench, asking, 'How did it go today? Were the kids conducive to preparing a gallery?'

Stan spoke with his mouth full. 'More vinegar next time, Fran.'

'Sod off.'

Stan wagged a chip at Josh, who was pouring wine for Fran. 'So that bad, eh?'

Fran laughed. 'Pretty much.' Josh rubbed his knee against hers.

Stan groaned. 'D'you remember Em, right little snot, and she wound you up and you were like a ruddy bear with a sore head. Then Em got better and now she's, well, thirteen.'

Josh shook his head as Fran slapped Stan's hand away from her glass. 'Go and get your own, we're on a budget.'

'No need,' Edward called from the other side. 'We're on our way with lagers, the real man's drink. You lot carry on with your grape stuff.'

Josh groaned. 'Did I send invites? Did I?'

Cindy and Stan took no notice, they just made room for Edward while Josh bunked up the bench, leaving a space for Tom, who wanted to know what time to come to the gallery the next day, as he had volunteered to erect the lights for them cut price. 'Not quite the stage set I'm used to,' he said thoughtfully, 'but as long as the gloss is dry I'm happy. It is, isn't it?'

Josh grinned. 'Simon's sorted it and you won't be sullied by even a hint. I just hope you've something to light, because O'Reilly's being his usual tardy, elusive self. These artist types, they're designed to age you.' Everyone laughed. He smiled at Fran. 'We still haven't received his agreement that we're to have his Russian screen prints. They're in the catalogue and it would look like amateur day if there's a big hole where his stuff should be. Should we fax him again, Fran? The trouble is, he can get arsey if he thinks he's being pestered.'

'I'm just not sure. Go on, make the decision as you know more about him.'

Josh wiped his last chip round the polystyrene container, soaking up the salt and vinegar, and thinking. Young Mark was with them now, bringing a can of coke and drinking from it.

The June evening was perfect and Fran reached across, cupping the full-flowering fragrant Old English rose given to her by Linda, which she had risked in a pot. She rolled her shoulders and looked up at the sky, remembering how Linda and she would often sit out over the years, putting the world to rights, the stars making their problems feel insignificant. She found the plough, moved on to the bright planets and it was working for her again. She frowned, then tapped Josh's knee. 'Just going to phone Linda. It seems ages since she rang.'

Linda's answer machine clocked in. Fran left a message. She also picked up their mail, sorting through it, taking Josh's out to him, waving a buff envelope she didn't recognise. 'Hey, this might be from O'Reilly.'

Josh smiled his thanks, taking it from her as he continued to explain to Stan that he really had too many for next year's course, but there'd be bound to be drop-outs. Stan was rolling some sort of cigarette but Fran was relaxed about it, for with Mark around it would be kosher. Josh opened the letter as Cindy poured more wine. Fran shook her head, because her headache had only subsided, not gone. She stood behind Josh, her hand on his shoulder. 'I don't believe it,' Josh whispered, 'How can this happen?' His voice was stunned, appalled.

Stan looked up, Cindy and Edward stared at one another. Fran said, squeezing his shoulder, 'What's wrong?'

There was no answer as Josh read the letter again, then just stared at it. Fran sat down warily. Had O'Reilly changed his mind? Stan had stopped rolling, Cindy looked from Fran to Josh. Edward and Tom were getting up. 'We'll leave you to it. We've things to do, anyway.'

Even in the twilight Fran could see that Josh had paled. Her mind was clicking from Plan A to Plan B. They'd just have to lead with the students' work and Josh's, and spread the other exhibitors' out a little. They could even hang *that* picture if necessary. 'Problems?' she ventured, putting her hand on his knee. 'Never mind, darling, we can alter the schedule.' Idiot, she should have tried harder to reach O'Reilly. There was no excuse. 'It will be fine and I'm sorry; it's my fault,' she continued.

He wasn't listening. He was still staring, his face almost contorted with rage. Then he crumpled the letter, thrust himself to his feet and almost ran into the sitting room, snatching up the phone, dialling a number. Fran's headache sharpened. Stan and Cindy said, 'Come on, Mark, these two need some space.'

Fran entered the sitting room. It was gloomy. She switched on the lamp near the fireplace. She could see the letter balled in his hand, his white knuckles, his white face. He was holding it out to her. She took it tentatively, smoothing it out.

She read headed paper—*Regarding financial support*—and almost sagged with relief because this wasn't *her* fault, it was nothing to do with the gallery, but then he was pulling her desperately to him and she could hear his heart . . . and the dialling tone. It went on and on, and as it did she read the whole letter, and was swept with anguish for him, and on second reading even more so.

At last Catherine's languid voice answered: 'Catherine Benton.' It was like being drenched with a bucket of cold water, for Benton was Fran's name now, and it was this that made her mind race, her emotions rise; that made the letter seem real and outrageous. How dare this woman hurt Josh again.

'Catherine, how could you? How the hell could you when you have been cohabiting with a bloody money machine?' Josh was shouting.

'Darling Josh, you know I don't live with Roger, I'm merely his tenant and I'm a little tired of this old record.'

'Tired,' Josh almost screamed. *'You're* tired. How do you think Fran feels, working her butt off to get this gallery off the ground and now you want *more*. Isn't it enough to run me into the ground without involving her? You're a bloody nightmare.'

'Don't swear. Look, I admit there could have been something between Roger and me, but do you really expect me to trust myself to another man after the failure of our marriage? But that's not the point, because I assume you are cohabiting, since you popped a tacky ring on her finger. I mean, she's not that past it, is she?' The tone wasn't so languid now. It was what? Wheedling, Fran decided with the small part of her brain that was still in control.

'You bitch,' Josh yelled, still holding the receiver at an angle, so that Fran could hear.

157

Catherine's voice hardened. 'Therefore your bills are halved as your income increases. If a nice house brings a nice rent, it would bring a nice price if it were sold. Just a one-off payment, that's all I'm asking, and a share of the profits from the pots and paintings your mother sells for you. After all, I tried to build up a business just like you. I worked my butt off, as you say. All to no avail, so surely you don't expect your daughter to live down to my standards when you two have sufficient to throw a wedding party, buy a new pine bed and new linen, as well as setting up a joint business? Note the joint, darling Josh. I am the one to struggle on alone.'

Josh was breathing hard. 'Look, why don't you ask for the shirt off my back as well?'

'Certainly not. I don't care for rags, I just want what is morally mine. I want the best for Emily and you should too.'

Josh was holding Fran tightly. His face was still white. 'But her clothes, they're expensive. How can you afford those if you say you've lost everything, if you're earning nothing? For God's sake, I'm not a bottomless pit, I'm a teacher.'

'A teacher who sells his stuff through his mother. A teacher married to someone of property. A teacher who can afford to start a . . .'

'All right. All right, just be quiet.' Josh was staring at Fran, but not seeing her. 'God, how could I ever have had anything to do with you?' he almost whispered.

Catherine's voice was sharp. 'Oh, next you'll be saying you never loved me; and what effect will that have on your daughter? I mean, she's going to have to share you with that woman's grandchildren, isn't she? Four afternoons, isn't it? So when do you graciously make time for her? Every two weeks. Big deal.'

Josh said, savagely quiet, 'You would not allow me more. You said you would poison my child against me if I pushed it.' He held Fran tightly. She put her arms round him.

Catherine's voice was equally savage: 'Well, what will happen now, do you think, if you won't divvy up? After all, how does another wife and two strange kids who will practically live with you add up? A fairly firm sort of favouritism, one that is remarkably close to rejection, don't you think? I do, especially if you don't want to provide for her. Get me the capital I've asked for, Josh. If she loves you she'll sell. It's not that much to ask. If she loves you as much as I did she would.'

Fran wrenched from Josh's arm, rubbing her face with her hands, over and over again.

After a moment Josh put down the receiver. It seemed so quiet and still. Outside it was finally dark.

Josh cleared his throat. 'I need to think.'

Fran ran her hand along the mantelpiece, looking at Josh's finished painting of her. 'She's bluffing. She wouldn't poison Emily. Anyway, Emily is old enough to see things as they are.'

But all the time she was thinking of Lucy and Harry, four afternoons a week and it was uneven. 'But we decided to keep the house because it's an earner for us, from now until for ever and then it's Jane's. It's all I've got to give her. Let Catherine have some of the rent. *Some* of it but only some, because we need the rest to survive. Let her have some of the profits when they come. She must

159

compromise, she has enough.'

She was repeating herself, her voice was getting higher and she was being unreasonable, she was sure she was, but how could she sell her house? What would Jane think? How would the gallery survive? 'How does she know about the bed? The linen? The grandchildren? The stuff your mother has sold? How? What else is Emily saying?' She shouldn't say this but her head was bursting. She should comfort him, hold him, give him anything to make it easy for him. She should, but she wouldn't. Couldn't.

He walked away into the hall. She called, 'Let's talk this through, Josh. For a start, you pay generous maintenance, her school fees; anything Emily wants she gets. Why do they need more money when they've more than us? Yes, everything she wants she gets.' She was talking to herself as well as Josh.

'Except a proper family,' he said, leaning his head against the hall wall. 'She wants for a proper family.' His voice was muffled.

'Catherine left you, remember that.' She couldn't bear to see him so crumpled and went to him, trying to put her arms round him, but he didn't move from the wall. He didn't turn to face her.

His voice was still muffled as he said, 'But it was none of Emily's doing. And what if Catherine has lost everything? What if she and Roger *are* over? You see, we don't *know*.'

'What does Emily say? Do you ever ask her?'

He turned now, slipping past her into the sitting room, staring out of the front window, and said, 'Of course not. How could I?'

She watched as he tapped his fingertips together, again and again. He was right, how could he? That was the measure of the man. She went to him and this time he held her, stroking her hair, then, stepping away again he reached for the phone and dialled a number. Her number?

Yes, it was, because he said, 'We need to think about this.' Fran could hear the metallic sound of her voice. He answered, 'Because it's Fran's house, not mine.' He put the phone down very carefully, staring at it, then at her.

She shook her head not wanting to see the agony on his face, the confusion because he shouldn't have said they would think about it. He shouldn't roll over and sacrifice them, her, as though she were invisible, as though *her* family were invisible.

But it's only money, only a house, she told herself. But it wasn't. 'So now it's my decision,' she said, exhausted suddenly. Did her disappointment show? Did it tear at him as it was tearing at her?

'Who else's can it be?'

She lifted her hands, then let them drop. 'Yours,' she said slowly. 'Your decision about how unimportant our life is, how unimportant I am.'

He turned away without answering, walking out into the hall, opening the front door, leaving. Just leaving. She watched as he reached the gate and walked out of sight, hands in his pockets, head down.

She crossed her arms, her stomach twisting. Just half an hour ago they had been dipping chips in vinegar, sipping wine.

He had walked away.

She reached for the kitchen phone, then let her hand drop. What would she say to Linda? I need

161

you, it's not perfect after all. Ask Mike what we can do about it? Oh, yes. Of course. Why not?

He had walked away.

She couldn't stand still. She paced backwards and forwards, then to the front door. Her hand was on the latch. She let it drop. She paced again, up and down. She made it to the patio, feeling sick, frightened, angry. She went to the spare room, digging out her paints. She stared at the board, but nothing came.

She stared out at the sky. See how insignificant you are, we all are, she told herself. None of this matters. We don't matter. Finally she went to bed and lay waiting, tossing and turning. But what if he didn't return? What if he did and wanted her to sell? What if he wanted her to decide whether to sell? How could he do this? How the hell could he do this? She beat with her fists on the pillow. She should have said yes. Of course she should. But it was Jane's. It really was Jane's.

He returned at midnight. He came and sat on the bed in the dark, taking her hand, kissing it. 'I'm sorry, really sorry. I love you. Of course she's trying it on.' He showered, came to bed, held her but somehow it wasn't the same. Almost, but not quite because she should have handled it differently. If she had done that it would have been all right.

CHAPTER FIFTEEN

Emily tore off to school late again, ignoring Catherine when she said, 'This won't do. You mustn't cause such chaos in Roger's home.'

162

'I don't mind, it brings the place to life,' he said as Emily slammed the door. He was behind Catherine, pressing too close as she wiped the sink, longing for him to go. Just go. He said tentatively, 'Are you all right? Your dates seem a bit off. You're not . . .' He hesitated.

Pregnant, she wanted to shout, pregnant is the word. She wondered if his mother had spelt s-e-x rather than say it. She said, 'It's just stress.'

His disappointment showed, only to be overtaken by concern. 'Let me take the load for you. Let me tell him about America, there's no need to wait like this and it's obviously weighing on you. I can't think why you won't. After all, we've tenants lined up and the tickets bought. It's only two weeks, darling.'

'You'll be late. Is Emily's tardiness rubbing off on you?' She softened her tone: 'Trust me, I know how to handle Josh and we'll talk later, darling.'

Roger smiled, kissing her forehead, thank heavens. He was wearing the Paco Rabanne aftershave, which made him slightly more bearable. Shame he wasn't a kipper, then she'd probably devour him at midnight, larded with vanilla ice cream.

He patted her shoulder. 'I love you.'

She could tell from the look in his eyes that he did and for a moment she weakened. He would give her a good life and she felt tired, anxious and wanted someone to look after her. He would. But he wasn't enough. Josh would be enough . . . probably.

She leant against Roger for a second. 'Drive carefully.'

'I will.' He left, whistling. She had made him

163

happy. Again she was tempted, but then the moment passed and before his car was out of the drive she rushed through to the annexe to collect her mail, just in case. There it was on the mat, a rose among the buff thorns. She snatched it up eagerly. His handwriting. She could picture the pen she had given him. Or had he another?

She returned to the main house, placing the letter carefully on the breakfast bar by the jasmine that needed watering. Had Fran packed her bags and gone back to her old life, or was she still there, guarding her house and beginning to get up his nose with her middle-aged ways? She fed the cat, brewed coffee, tried dry toast, but could cope with neither. She fingered the envelope. It wasn't fair to have to deal with all this when she wanted to vomit every five minutes. Slowly she opened it and drew out the letter.

Dear Catherine

Thank you for phoning the other night. Look, we've thought and we've talked, and if your financial situation ever worsens then of course I'll review the situation, even if it means re-mortgaging my own house. But Fran's is not part of the equation, because her house is *essential* to the establishment of the gallery and the gallery is *essential* for the eventual funding of Emily's university. I do hope you can understand the above reasoning.

As for the small additional income from sales of my work, you will see from the figures I enclose that this is *essential* for my day-to-day expenses, including the petrol used when collecting my daughter every other weekend.

Naturally I would love Emily to visit far more often but those were the terms *you* insisted upon.

If you do feel that your standards are affecting Emily's well-being, then only you can change that and to insinuate that Fran's love for me is on a par with yours is utter nonsense. It was you who left me. It was you who indulged in playmates. I doubt that you know the meaning of the word love. However, I sincerely hope that one day you will, for life without it is bleak in the extreme.

Best wishes,
Josh

The patronising bastard. Underlining as though she were an imbecile, repeating as though she could understand nothing. Oh, but she did. She understood everything. He hadn't written this, it was that cow, standing behind him like some old witch, and he had done as he was told. That was all. He'd just done as he was told. She read it again, one word at a time, slowly, painstakingly, seeing his hand on the pen, hearing the words and it *was* his voice, not Fran's, the voice he had used so often towards the end, the voice she had almost forgotten.

Shaking, she laid the letter carefully on the breakfast bar. Sweat beaded her forehead, nausea built and built. She reached the bathroom just in time, kneeling, vomiting again and again, then dry-retching until it was over. She sank back against the bath. She was tired, so damned tired. For a moment she slumped, too weak to move. Not knowing where to move to, nor what to do any more. The phone rang, then stopped. The answer machine wasn't on. It could be him. She hauled herself to her feet. Her stomach swam. She leant on the basin. It wouldn't be him.

Slowly she cupped water from the tap, drinking just a little, staring in the mirror, seeing lines around her mouth, her eyes, feeling the tenderness of her breasts. She clung to the basin and wept until her sore throat was even worse, her eyes swollen and red, her face blotchy. Wept and wept until at last she was done. Until each breath shuddered less and the nausea died away. For another moment she waited, then splashed water on her face, checking again in the mirror. Better. Not perfect but better.

She returned to the kitchen, feeling ancient. She picked up the letter carefully. She would show it to Emily, let her see the man her father was, but then she reread it and saw that he'd even taken that away. It was too clever. It said as much about her as it did about him. But she'd only kept Emily away from him for her own good. It had helped her to settle, that was all. Surely Emily would understand that.

After a moment she tore the letter again and again until it lay like confetti, white against the slate of the breakfast bar. Had he and that cow had confetti? Had they? Had they? She swept the pieces to the floor. Confetti? She wouldn't have any. It was naff and tacky. She'd tell Roger that, because she'd have to marry him now, and she'd want an engagement ring and matching wedding band, and they'd better be worth a king's ransom.

She checked her watch, sitting down, ignoring

166

the torn paper, making herself think of the ring, but all she could see was Josh under a shower of confetti, Josh with her, Josh and that damned woman together, cosily together. The minutes ticked away. But no, she was damned if they'd be left alone when she was out in the cold. She reached for the phone, then stopped. The cleaner would be here any minute. The old bag opened the door and waltzed right in as though she owned the place.

She poured herself a glass of water, then stood in the archway, looking through to the sitting room. It was this phone she used to contact the clinic. They had said she could cancel up until the last minute, because she was such a good customer. Bloody cheek, but even that didn't matter now. She sat on the arm of the chair carefully, telling the receptionist, 'I've changed my mind.' She raised her eyebrows, nodding. 'Yes, I'll have the tests, but forty isn't old these days.'

She depressed the rest, then dialled Sue's number.

Sue said, 'I've just phoned you. I didn't think you were in.'

'Never mind that, Sue. Look, I've decided to have it and stick with Roger for now. America could be fun.' Sue said nothing for a moment and in the background Catherine heard the tapping of the keyboard. 'Are you listening to me at all?' she snapped.

Sue said, 'Um. I was just wondering about GCSEs.'

'What about them?'

'Well, what's the American equivalent?'

Catherine crossed her legs, stroking the white

leather of the armchair. She was glad Paul, her little gentleman of the night, was into leather, but talk of the whip was taking things too far. 'It doesn't matter what the American brats take. Josh will never give his permission. That is something I really do know for certain.'

Now she had Sue's full attention. 'Cath, you've lost me, what are you playing at?'

'I ask, he refuses. So he gets her, or rather, they get her. Let's see how they like trying to get a stroppy teenager off to school on time. That should tear apart the little love nest and with any luck that cow will break her neck on a trainer when she does a bunk.' She laughed, but Sue didn't. Catherine sighed, slipping round to sit on the chair properly, wondering why she should listen to the lecture she knew was coming.

'But for God's sake, Catherine, she's your daughter. You can't pass her around like a package. Josh would give in if you approached him reasonably. You know that.'

Catherine was irritated. Why did people feel the need to give advice, to poke their bloody noses in? 'She can come to the States for the holidays and this way her schooling won't be affected. D'you really think I hadn't thought of exams? I'm not a complete fool, you know. Besides, she can rebuild her relationship with her father and then he can stop bleating.' Yes, that sounded good. Reasonable. She would underline the word for Josh. She would put two lines beneath, in fact.

'But you'll miss her?' It was a question.

How dare Sue. 'Of course.'

'You'll forfeit your maintenance.'

Teach your grandmother to suck eggs, why don't

you, thought Catherine, but said, 'He'll have to stump up something for the holidays. Believe me, he'll be more than willing by the time term finishes and the cow's had enough of looking after his kid.'

'But he's bound to make you stump up for the fare, just like you do, and you won't like that.'

Catherine pursed her lips. 'Oh, just drop it, Sue. What does any of that matter? Roger's got enough. He's always on about a family, about looking after me. He'll dote and I'll suffocate.' The nausea was returning. 'I've got to go.'

'So you're really going to stay with Roger, then? And what about the business? Where does this put me?'

Catherine sighed. Sue had tunnel vision. 'I thought you could finish the contract with Ashley's and we'll split the proceeds fifty fifty.'

'No way, that's only ten per cent more than it is now and I'll be doing the remaining work. Make it seventy thirty. It'll be worth it for you, in case you and Roger don't last and you come back with your tail between your legs.'

Catherine decided that she'd never really liked Sue and anyway, her work was utter crap.

'Take seventy per cent, then. I couldn't give a shit. I just hope they're satisfied and I don't expect you to come whining to me for contacts.'

There was silence at the other end for a moment. Then, in a cold, clear voice Sue said, 'What about Paul? Are you going to dump him, or is it someone else already, or as well? Putting yourself about too much at your age could make you drop your meal ticket and then where would you be? By the way, whose baby is it anyway?'

Catherine slammed down the phone. Bloody

bitch.

The front door opened. It was Mrs Stevens who practically sniffed her distaste whenever she saw Catherine. Well, let her see how far it got her when she was out of a job in two weeks, because there was no way Catherine would recommend her to the tenants.

Mrs Stevens said, 'Oh, I assumed everyone would be at work. So sorry, Mrs Benton.'

She dragged the hoover into the room, plugged it in, and roared backwards and forwards. The moment Catherine left the room the hoovering stopped. She stormed to the study and from *his* phone, the lord and master's phone, she rang Paul's mobile. The phone was only taking messages. Damn them all. She said, 'Had enough of you, Paul. Can't make our date. I wish I could say I've enjoyed it, but I'd only give you five out of ten. More work needed. Much more . . .'

*   *   *

Ken stashed the files on his desk, all except Mainwaring's. He'd try to work on it this evening to make up some time. He checked his watch: 1 p.m. He'd barely make Bristol by 2.30 but she'd wait. Mark you, she'd dig into the room bar, which would cost him an arm and a leg again. He grabbed his mac, calling to his secretary as he flew past, 'Seeing a client. I've the Mainwaring file in case anyone asks.'

Then he was gone, out into the car park. He threw his briefcase and mac on to the back seat and roared off into the traffic, which seemed intent on obstructing anyone needing to get anywhere this side of Christmas. He shoved in a Tina Tuner tape and tried to concentrate on the words. Anything other than the thought of Kate naked on the bed. Naked except for stockings and suspenders, and with the drink he liked her to hold in her hand; any drink. And he naked, except for the sleeveless leather jerkin she'd introduced him to and which he liked very, very much. Naked, doing the things they did. His breathing was shallow.

Listen to the music. Watch the car in front. Overtake it. Steady. Not much room there, but you made it. Into Bristol: grid-locked again. He checked his watch. He'd do it. Into the car park. Into reception. 'Paul Davies.' Did the stupid woman smirk when she handed him the key? What did it matter? Up into the room. He was first. He showered, lay on the bed in the hotel robe. Perhaps she'd let him soap her with the water streaming down on them both. He'd stand behind, press himself against her, slide himself up and down while he worked her with his hands, then he'd bend her over and the water would beat on them.

2.30: his breathing was shallow again. No. He found a gin in the bar and drank it neat, looking out at Bristol. At 2.45 he took out Mainwaring's file. It was hopeless. Impatiently he slid it into a drawer. Kate Smith had never been this late or if she had she'd phoned and then talked dirty until she arrived. He pressed himself against the windowsill. Press, withdraw. Press, withdraw. 2.55. Bloody traffic, that's what it was. Where did she come from? He didn't know. She was right, it made it better. He didn't know her. She didn't know him. They just knew one another's bodies, one another's mouths. He slipped his hand inside his robe.

Then, when he was almost there, in the shower he'd push her away, turn her round, force her down until her mouth found him. Then she'd lead him to the bed. She'd drink her gin, the pillows behind her, her legs wide and he'd find her with his tongue.

3 p.m. Why the hell didn't she phone? He pressed his glass to his cheek. Steady. He concentrated on the cars crawling like ants below. Perhaps she was in one of them. Maybe she had forgotten her phone. Phone? Damn it. He snatched it from his briefcase. Yes, it was off. There was one message. He listened, staring out over Bristol. Listened and then just stood, and now his breathlessness was something else. Something bloody else.

It took Ken twenty minutes to arrive at the all day wine bar where they'd met. It was Bob Walker's watering hole and six months ago he'd hoped he'd be there for a bit of a whinge about being passed over for the Yeovil office again, but *she*'d been there, all lipstick and cleavage. She'd been waiting for someone too, someone who'd never showed. Well, he bloody well wished whoever it was had.

He shouldered his way past the greenery which was draped either side of the doorway. Of course she wasn't there. The barman was new, foreign, and if he couldn't grasp what Ken needed to know, he shouldn't be in the bloody job. He gave up. 'Cretin,' he yelled, stalking back to his car, looking around. But no. She wouldn't be here.

He slammed into the car, gunned the engine, turned up the radio louder, louder. Bloody bitch. They were all bloody bitches. All taking, none of them giving. All of them. Every bloody one of

172

them.

CHAPTER SIXTEEN

That weekend Josh picked up Emily from Roger's on the far side of Dorchester, bringing her straight to the gallery where Fran was overseeing more of Tom's lighting manoeuvres. 'Getting in the way, actually,' Tom drawled, flicking a six-gun salute at Emily, who laughed.

James and Simon were in the yard at the back and knocked on the window, beckoning to Emily. She took the broom Josh handed her and joined them, doing nothing, just sitting down on the low wall, talking.

Tom winked at Fran. 'That's all they do at that age, if you're lucky.'

Fran grimaced, remembering only too well.

Once the lights were sorted they took a picnic outside, sitting alongside Emily on the wall like sparrows on a telephone wire, trying to work out how many tables the courtyard would take. 'They'll have to be the small wrought-iron ones. Plastic take up too much room,' Josh said.

'Hang on, I'm not sure how much we have left in the budget,' Fran warned.

Emily looked at her as though about to speak, then turned away.

Josh shrugged. 'What about second-hand? Tell us how much we can go up to and we'll all ask around.' The others were nodding.

Simon said, 'Or we could just use a couple of the plastic ones in the meantime, couldn't we? The

173

DIY sell them pretty cheap.'

Fran said, 'They'll still need paying for, but you're right. I'll try and sort out a kitty for it so they're installed in time for the launch, then we can overspill out here. That's if people come, of course.'

'They'll come,' James insisted. 'How many have replied?'

While Fran told him Emily leaned back, looking up and down the overgrown bank. She said, 'They'll like the jungle effect, will they?'

Josh was juggling a slice of disintegrating quiche. 'Glad you said that, Em, because we need someone to weed.' His tone was pointed.

'I expect you do.' Emily's response was cool.

James elbowed her, saying, 'You've a pair of hands on you. If the lady's not for brushing, perhaps she's for weeding.'

Emily tossed her hair, which was several shades lighter, Fran thought, or was it highlighted? If so, it would have cost a bomb. So much for living in penury. All at once she was conscious of her hair. When had it last been cut? The wedding, the one that didn't happen. It was time she had a tidy-up.

Emily drawled, flicking a glance at her father, 'But on the other hand, perhaps not, even for weeding.'

Fran stared at the sponge cake laid on top of the cool box. Slapstick appealed suddenly.

Josh stuffed the last of his quiche in his mouth, talking through it: 'It wouldn't hurt to get stuck in, Em.'

Emily's hair-tossing increased by leaps and bounds. 'It's all right for you and her, Dad. You're both past caring what you look like, but look at these.' She held out immaculate nails. 'They've taken months to grow.'

'Who's "her"?' Josh snapped.

Fran held up a bottle of diet Coke. 'Who's for a drink?'

Tom was, but James and Simon had brought cans of lager.

Fran watched as Emily held out her glass for lager, rather than make a move towards the Coke.

It was James who waved her away. 'Coke for the little 'uns. The ones who are too precious to give us the loan of their immaculate hands.' He was grinning.

'Oh, for God's sake,' Em flounced. 'So, if I do some work I get some booze, is that the deal?'

Fran stood up, brushing the crumbs from her jeans. Let the birds have something. 'I've got to get on,' she said, ignoring Josh's silent appeal for help. *Her* was going to keep right out of this, *her* was. Her role was peripheral, or so she and Josh had decided after the letter. This must be a relationship between father and daughter. It was precious. It wasn't hers.

She studied the accounts, moved a little bit of cash here and a little there. Her mobile rang. It was Jane. She sounded full of cold. 'Mum.'

Mum? Glory be, not Mother but Mum. Just as she used to. Fran smiled. 'Hello darling. You sound a bit full.'

In the background she heard Ken call. 'Nothing,' Jane said, to him, not Fran. 'Nothing, I was just wondering if Mum could have the children this afternoon, even though it's a Saturday.'

Fran's heart sank. She'd said not. Really not, because this must be Em's time. She said apologetically, 'Darling, I can't. There really is too much to do this particular weekend and Josh does need some time with Emily.'

'Fine.' Jane was short. 'Fine.'

But it obviously wasn't. 'Look,' Fran said, dragging her hand through her hair. 'Maybe next weekend, though . . .'

'I said it was fine.' Jane's voice was harsh.

'Can't Ken have the kids for a couple of hours so you can get your head down, darling? Take a Beecham's. Can't . . .'

'Fine. I said it was fine.'

'Look, why don't I take a break from the gallery and come and see you instead.'

'No. No.' Her voice was harsh again. 'No. For goodness sake, Mother, don't make a production out of it. I'll bring them on Tuesday as usual.'

It wasn't a question. Before Fran could answer the line went dead. She stared at the figures, not seeing them. What was it with the younger generation that they were so in your face, so sure they deserved special treatment? In a way she envied them, because they were not going to allow anyone to push them around.

'Dad, I told you I will *not* weed. No, not even with gloves.' Emily's shout reached her. She snatched a look through the window. Josh was holding out marigolds and a hand fork. Emily was obdurate, standing with arms crossed. James, Simon and Tom were packing up the picnic. Silently Fran chanted St Ives, St Ives, St Ives.

The doorbell rang, and without pause the front door opened and Linda called, 'Is this a bad time?'

Fran rushed into the entrance hall and tried to drag her in. 'You little ray of sunshine, come and brighten our day.'

Linda shook her off, laughing. 'Can't stop. Just thought I'd see how things were going.'

'Well come in off the doorstep at least.'

'If I do that I'll be here for hours.' The Saturday traffic was trundling past behind her and she'd parked on the yellow line, but in her immaculate jeans and white shirt the traffic warden would melt, surely. 'I'm off to Clarke's Village. Thought I'd shop till I dropped and grab a new look, a new me.'

'There's nothing wrong with the old one.'

'Ah, but I feel a bit "end of a line". So I'm bound to find something to suit, or a seconds, or . . .'

Fran waved her silent. 'Rubbish, you're looking good. You've lost a bit of weight, I think.'

Linda patted her thighs, a satisfied smile growing. 'All those sessions at the gym.'

Fran was amazed. 'So that's where you've been. And what's it all in aid of, might I ask?'

'Absolutely nothing, just keeping fit. Like Ken.'

'Ken?'

'Yep, saw his back view the other day. Wouldn't have thought they could afford it.' Linda's look was keen.

'They can't. I expect he was just making enquiries. You know what Ken's like. Someone important probably goes so he floats along on the off chance . . .'

'Someone important does—moi.' Linda was smiling, then whispered, looking over Fran's shoulder, 'Come shopping with me. Do a bunk. I miss you. I miss our life as it was. I'm lonely.'

It was a moment before Fran shook her head, but as she did so she reached out and gripped her friend's hand, because she missed her too, but not that much, and she felt embarrassed. 'I'd like to, but there's this.' Helplessly her arm encompassed the gallery.

Linda grinned, covering the layer she had revealed. Fran said, 'Come and have some coffee, please.' Her grip tightened, as though she could stop Linda leaving. 'Come in and tell me what you're doing, how things are going. Let's just share a moment.'

Linda shook her head ruefully. 'I would, but I really need some clothes, Fran. I'd have to repark, it'd take ages.'

'Come here for lunch on Monday? It's my afternoon without the children.' Fran's voice was urgent. 'Come and let's chat, like old times.' But it wasn't old times. She said, 'We've still room for one another in our lives, surely?'

Linda smiled. 'Why not, if Sally the Rottweiler hasn't booked a lunch meeting. Do I bring my own?'

Fran laughed. 'I might actually be able to sort that out, you idiot.'

Emily suddenly erupted into the hall behind Fran, shouting, 'But why should I?'

'Emily, come back here,' Josh bellowed. Fran turned to see Emily marching towards the front door, her arms crossed, defiance in every step.

When she reached Fran she tried to bulldoze past, but Linda shook her head. 'Whoa.' Her hand was up as though she was directing traffic. Suddenly Fran was back at the church.

Josh caught up, red with irritation and frustration, reaching for his daughter. 'Emily, come on.'

Fran moved back against the wall, aware that

Emily was not about to come on and wishing she weren't involved, because anything she said would be wrong but at Josh's wordless plea and his touch on her arm she lined up with Linda, saying, 'What would you like to do, Emily? Why don't you and Dad go . . .'

'To the swings? I don't think so.' Emily tossed her hair flamboyantly.

'Shopping, I was going to say.' The thing was not to let the humongous, colossal irritation show. This is what she had always said to herself with Jane.

Josh was tight into the group now, his hand touching hers, only touching, because they had decided on no overt signs of affection in front of Emily. 'Old sex is disgusting,' she'd announced when they'd watched thirty-somethings holding hands as they walked down the street last time she'd come.

Fran continued, 'Your Dad was talking of buying you something for the launch.'

Josh looked mystified, then he recovered, nodding gallantly. Emily had stopped tapping her foot, her attention caught. But then she shook her head. 'Oh, I can't go with Dad, he hasn't got a clue and I'd end up with one of your long skirts, which is not my idea of heaven. Why don't you just give me the money and I'll go with Mum?'

Out of the mouths of babes and sucklings. Could irritation become doubly colossal? Linda pressed an elbow against her, saying to Emily in that 'let's keep this under control' voice, 'Tell you what. Come with me. I'm going anyway. They've some really good shops, almost designer level, not your Gucci, of course, but definitely worth a look.'

For a moment Emily looked Linda up and down,

and what she saw passed muster. A smile came to the child's face, for that was what she was, Fran reminded herself, a child.

Within ten minutes they were gone, with a promise from Josh that Emily could go up to £100 and he would repay Linda's credit card. The expression 'sucking a lemon' had come to Fran's mind, as Emily absorbed this piddling amount. For once, though, she said nothing.

Josh closed the front door, leaning back against it as though he had survived some long drawn-out war. 'Just a few years ago she was a biddable child.'

'Stepmothers have a bad press, so lay it at my door.'

He held out his arms. 'Please, this is not your fault.'

'Of course, in common with most girls of her age, it could simply be that she has a spring tide of hormones swilling about,' Fran muttered, kissing him. Not adding, 'As well as an appalling mother', although sorely tempted. Instead she said, 'They all have these moments. Think how sweet she used to be and cling to that life raft.'

He laughed, finding her mouth, kissing her gently.

Simon called, 'Fran, can I have your beady eye on this shelf arrangement?'

She went, still feeling his lips on hers, glad to be here, beady eye and all.

*   *   *

That evening she, Josh and Emily took home a Chinese takeaway, which attracted the neighbours even more than chips and by now Emily had

180

metamorphosed into the prepubescent version, even if the dress she had finally bought cost £120. Josh had not flinched, but said, 'Well, you can serve the canapés at the launch to make up for it.'

But would she? wondered Fran.

As they dished up, James, Paul and Gail called round to pick up their wages. They pocketed Simon's to give to him later that night at the rave. 'No,' said Josh, even before Emily had asked. There was only a token pout.

James and Gail stayed for a drink, sitting in between Stan and Cindy. Within half an hour Mark arrived back from Scouts and treated all talk of toggles and woggles with the contempt it deserved, settling himself next to Emily. They talked, heads together, like the old friends they were, while Fran brewed tea for herself and Cindy. As Stan and Josh tuned up Mark said, 'Come on, Em, get your vocal cords sorted, you're not the ruddy Lady of the Manor here, you know. You can sing for your supper; and how's that snotty school, while we're at it?'

'It had better be good, the money it costs,' Josh muttered. Fran flashed a warning, but Emily hadn't heard. Anyway, they had a couple of months to gather up the next term's fees.

Josh led Stan into a Beatles medley and Mark prodded Emily unmercifully. However, when her protests had gained the full attention of James she allowed herself to be persuaded to join her father in 'A Hard Day's Night' and if she had been stunned by Josh's voice, Fran was amazed at the exquisite maturity of Emily's.

When they were finished Fran said, 'You are absolutely marvellous, Em. Really wonderful. I'm

181

just so impressed.' Gail and James had moved to sit with Mark, so the only place was next to Fran. Emily shrugged and half smiled as she joined her. 'You sing. Let's compare.'

Fran shook her head. 'I know when I'm beaten. You and your dad carry on.'

They did, but Emily remained next to her, leaving only a token empty space, and she didn't shrink too much when, at the end of the evening, everyone linked arms and sang. Though by the end Emily was hysterical because Fran really was truly awful.

The next day Fran suggested that Emily and Josh drive to the coast.

'You can come with us,' Emily said. It wasn't gracious, but it was an offer.

Fran smiled, 'If I'm not in the way?'

They packed her clothes, including the outfit for the launch so that they could drop her at Catherine's on the way home. They did not prepare a picnic, deciding instead to splash out on a café lunch. 'When the launch is over we'll start cooking you proper meals, Em,' Fran promised.

The sun was warm, the breeze slight. Mark came too.

They drove to Hive Beach at Burton Bradstock and after they'd negotiated Fran's Factor 25 down to Emily's Factor 15 there was just the laughter of the two teenagers and disobedient Sunday papers which fluttered too much to be read easily.

'I feel as though I could breach the wicked witch of the north barrier, given time,' murmured Fran, as Emily and Mark paddled in the cold, cold waves.

'This is how the real Emily is,' Josh said, stroking the sand from her arm. 'I don't think Catherine has

182

spilled the beans or more tantrums would have been in evidence.'

Fran watched as a wave caught Mark and wondered how the light was in St Ives. 'It'll all be fine.' She caught his hand, kissing each finger. 'Catherine will run out of steam.'

CHAPTER SEVENTEEN

By mid-morning on Monday Fran suddenly could not bear the thought of yet more sandwiches at the art gallery and phoned Linda at work. 'Let's walk in the park, I'll treat you to coffee and a hot dog from the stall. It's still chaos here and too Mondayish to be bearable.'

'You're on. Where shall we meet?'

'Beneath the spreading chestnut tree.'

Linda laughed. 'What, the one with the yellow ribbon?'

'Actually, make it the pelican crossing entrance.' She was holding the receiver with her chin as she tried to staple some papers together.

'When?'

'One. If I remember right you don't have appointments then.'

'Fine.'

Fran put down the phone. Appointments were things she had once made. Suits were things she had once worn. Suddenly she didn't feel Mondayish any more, she stretched, pirouetted. Ruth called through from the coffee shop, 'Don't buy coffee. I'll brew you both a takeaway. I thought we should do that from the coffee shop anyway. You can be the guinea pigs.'

The phone rang. It was O'Reilly. 'I've sent the prints and follow in hot pursuit for the launch. It'll be nice to meet you. Tell the old devil to lay in an Australian Shiraz, a good one and lots of it. I'm coming by train.' Click.

At last. It was going to be a good week.

She met Linda at one, bearing the two coffees Ruth had produced. They found an empty bench and joined the young mothers guarding their children, or the elderly putting the world to rights, and the lovers.

This was where she and Josh had walked. Why had she taken so long to return? If St Ives was too far, this would do. Linda was easing off the plastic lid which Ruth had secured with cellotape. She said, sniffing, 'Coo, real coffee. We could do with this blend.'

Fran pictured the coffee machine in the corridor outside Mike's office. He liked proper cups. She liked mugs. He liked . . . She drank from her polystyrene container. 'How is he?' she asked.

'Fine.' Linda's voice was clipped. 'Busy. Fine.'

'How was the concert?'

Linda looked surprised. Fran smiled gently. 'Jane.'

'Ah.' Linda laughed ruefully. 'Well, you can imagine me being given tickets for Mahler. What on earth was I going to do with them? Now if it had been *Cats*.'

Across from them a child of about Lucy's age was sucking an ice lolly, which was dripping down her arm and being absorbed by her rolled-up sleeve. Her oblivious mother was talking to her friend. Good luck to her. If it brought her a few minutes' peace, well and good.

Fran would try to bring the children tomorrow afternoon. She might even push Lucy on the swings, but would Harry cry, as he seemed to an awful lot, or did they all? Was she forgetting? Or could it be colic?

'I couldn't do it.' Linda was staring at the child with the lolly. 'I could not tend a child at our age, let alone two. You're insane, Fran, and it's totally unreasonable of Ken and Jane, and you were a great wet thing to take it on. Why on earth didn't you bolt to Timbuktu? You still could, you know, or down to Jessie at least, or somewhere needing a cultural oasis. Why don't you both? It would be a fresh start, a proper fresh start.' Linda was squeezing her coffee in and out. Soon it would spill all over her skirt.

Fran took it from her. 'Hey, who's been rattling your cage? Look, it was bad enough that I bolted but to leave Jane altogether when they're in this pickle . . .' She petered out. 'I need to be here for emergencies.'

'Four afternoons of emergencies?'

Fran ignored her. 'There's Emily too and Josh had his house and there's mine to sort out. Look, what's brought this on? We're the other side of town so we're not in everyone's face, staining their existence. We're just . . .'

'On overload four afternoons a week.' Linda took back her coffee, sipping it. 'You protected her from David and never told her what a shit he was. You protect her now from her responsibilities.'

'I help her, that's all. Anyway, you were keen enough for me to take on the role when I was about to stump up the aisle with Mike.'

185

'That was different. Everything was different then.' Linda drained her coffee and looked around for a bin.

Fran pushed it inside her own finished mug. 'Come on, you crabby old thing, let's walk or it'll be mugs at ten paces.' She was laughing, but surprised. As Linda stood, Fran tucked her arm in hers and they dawdled beneath the horse-chestnuts. 'What was different?' she asked Linda quietly.

Linda stood quite still and looked up into the huge tree they were beneath. 'Oh, nothing. Everything. You threw a pebble in the pond, dratted woman that you are. You dared and you won.'

'That's because Josh helped me, pushed me and was there to catch me.'

Linda drew away from Fran, setting off towards the hot dog stand. She called back, 'Is it good, Fran? Is it really as good as it looks? Is love so wonderful that it can absorb an adolescent stepdaughter, two tinies and an art gallery?' She had turned and was walking backwards, away from Fran, and she looked so strained suddenly. 'Is it that good, Fran? Will it endure?'

Fran didn't answer, but ran to catch up, linking arms again, panting a little, concerned. 'So, you go to the gym. For whose benefit, besides your own?'

Linda shook her head. 'No one's.'

Two elderly joggers ran past in their matching tracksuits and they both watched them roar ahead, astonished. Linda muttered, 'No one knows how to behave any more.'

They both laughed, then walked together quietly. Fran said, 'Mum used to say that age should bring acceptance, equanimity.' Involuntarily she raised her eyes heavenwards, sure she was there, because her mother's few sins had been those of ignorance, of disbelief, not of intent. She had been a good, kind woman. They had reached the hot dog stand. Fran insisted, as Linda foraged for her wallet: 'My treat. The hot dogs are really good, or so James says.' She found a fiver in her bum bag.

Linda shook her head, slapping her thighs. 'Get thee behind me, Satan.'

'Oh, come on.' But Linda was adamant and walked on. Perplexed, Fran caught her up. 'You must have someone in your sights,' she insisted. 'The last time you refused a hot dog it was Samuel Bewstow. You should have married him.' They were in the shade, beneath the chestnut tree. Over to the left toddlers and their mothers were playing tag. Their small voices carried on the light breeze.

'I didn't love him enough.'

Fran felt silent. She knew what Linda meant.

Linda hesitated, stopping for a moment, toeing a daisy. 'You're right, though, I have met someone.'

'Tell me who at once, or I shall implode.' Fran was grateful for the excuse to push Mike away. It was she who was walking backwards now while Linda dawdled as though uncertain where to go. 'Let's head for the ducks,' Fran suggested, leading the way. Who was it? Would this one work? She hoped so, she wanted everyone to be as happy as she was, because she was. Funnily enough, it had helped having a difficult Emily, because the balance of obligation was better.

They had reached the pond. A slight breeze rippled the surface. A little boy was dragging a small wooden yacht with a big red sail, which

187

strained at the string leash. Linda pulled her lapels tight round her throat. 'The trouble is, I don't think this man is quite available.'

Fran groaned. 'Oh, Linda, remember that married man, Tom something or other. You can't put yourself through that again. Now, how involved are you? If there's a wife it's no go.'

The boy was lifting the dripping yacht from the water. His mother came and wiped its bottom. 'And it was ever thus,' Linda said, pointing. Both laughed, then Linda shrugged. 'It's not a wife, it's a sort of "dug deep in the soul" relationship.'

'You should have talked to me about it, Linda. We've still got one another, we really have. We must make time, we're being silly.'

'There's Josh. We haven't really still got one another, not as we had.' Linda sounded thoughtful, not angry.

Fran ached with remorse. 'Life's just hectic at the moment, but that's what a new relationship is like, I suppose, and a new career and a variety of kids. But never doubt that I'm always here for you. When you're down, just phone, please. I mean, honestly, the other night I nearly rang. I nearly walked out. Oh, I don't know what I nearly did.' Linda had swung round and was listening intently, anxiously. Fran stopped. 'But we're not discussing me. It's you and I'm here, any time, any place.'

Linda had her hand. She was shaking her. 'What's wrong, Fran?' There was too much concern. Far too much and it didn't matter now, because it had all passed.

Fran smiled. 'Linda, it's nothing. It was just a glitch, nothing like that. We're talking about you now. You're not yourself and I can't bear to think of you being hurt. Who were the concert tickets for really? Who were you going to treat? You hate Mahler, so give this guy up, and go out and buy tickets for Lloyd Webber, or Bryan Adams; something you'll enjoy. Love can't endure if there's too big a difference.' She saw Linda's face set in that way it had and grinned. 'OK, tell the fool to stop messing about and get on with it. Tell him to take up the cudgels, give you a big smacking snog. Get tickets to the show you want and see how he enjoys it.'

'Hey, hey.' Linda was laughing, holding her finger to her lips as the joggers, on their way back, ran round them, their panting audible. They bounced on their air soles, pulling away from them steadily. In the distance the clock chimed the half-hour. Linda checked her own watch. 'Got to go. I've a meeting with Bob Walker's partner. Young Rick is charming to your face and then sticks the knife in the moment your back's turned. Mrs P's husband is his client. I'll try to talk some decency into the man.'

'I remember him,' Fran said gently. 'I haven't been away that long.'

Linda kissed her. Fran ordered: 'Phone me, whenever you need to. Or why not talk to Mike? He's pure gold.'

Linda walked away towards the Leisure Centre entrance, head down. Walker's office was not far from there. Fran watched. No one could help. Not really.

*   *   *

The next morning Linda replayed Fran's words as

she pressed her jacket. Why had she almost phoned her? Why had she almost left home? Would they endure? All these disparate children were too much for them, but the only situation she could influence was that of the grandchildren. She must have a word with Jane. Yes. That's what she must do. She had barely slept, tossing and turning, feeling free to think of herself now that Fran wasn't being beaten.

She hurried into the hall, slipping into her jacket, checking herself in the mirror above the radiator. She had bags under her eyes, and at eleven o'clock she had a meeting with Mike. What about Lloyd Webber? Too light. *Les Misérables*? It was at Bristol at the moment and no one could call it a doddle.

CHAPTER EIGHTEEN

James and Simon had melted into the kitchen, Ruth was wiping down the new tables in the courtyard and Gail was finishing the weeding. Along the wall were pots of geraniums that Jessie had brought up at the weekend. Petunias, pansies and other limp and thirsty annuals were waiting to be planted. Well, they would have to be patient for rather longer.

Leaning against one of the coffee tables, Fran tried not to worry that the catalogues which had been delivered from the printers half an hour before were the wrong colour. She tried to ignore the insistent phone and to forget all that she had to do before she picked up the children, because Josh had just arrived and was pacing the floor, and she could make neither head nor tail of his fragmented raging.

'Josh, take a breath.' She grabbed him, made him stop.

He almost shook her off, but instead hugged her to him. 'She's everywhere, like an octopus.'

Fran's heart sank. Gently she asked, 'Catherine?'

Josh took a very deep breath. 'Soon to be Mrs Roger Ashley. Another licence job being hurried through.' His laugh was bitter.

Fran stood very still, encircled by his arms, feeling the warmth of him through his maroon shirt, knowing the texture of the skin beneath, knowing every contour but frightened suddenly. Very frightened. She said slowly, 'Don't you like the thought of it?'

He held her away, shaking his head at her. 'I don't give a fuck about that, Fran. It's this.' He waved the letter in the air.

What was she, a mind reader? 'What is it?' she shouted, when what she wanted to say was not another bloody demand.

Outside she could see Gail and Ruth share a look as they watered the annuals in their trays. No, it wasn't a lover's tiff, but it was damn close. 'What is it, Josh, another claim for money? That's nonsense. By marrying the pretence will stop; we can relax.'

The phone had stopped. It seemed wonderfully quiet. Josh had moved to the window and was watching the girls transplant the dripping annuals. 'She's saying they're moving to the States for two years. They want to take Emily.'

Fran watched him watching the girls. She

191

borrowed James's saying: 'Be still my beating heart'. Then, appalled at herself, she wiped away the relief. This was his daughter they were talking about, not any old adolescent bundle of difficulty, for the tantrums were still very much in existence despite the lull at Hive Beach. How would she have felt if it were Jane?

Reminded, she checked her watch. In twenty minutes she must leave to fetch the kids but how could she ask him to tailor the crisis to a time scale and one dictated by her side of the family at that? She sat down on the table, something she had just told James not to do. The phone began again. James edged out of the kitchen, looking at neither of them, hurrying through to the gallery to answer it.

Why hadn't she put the answer machine on? Why did Catherine have to keep doing what she did best: be a bloody pain? Why did Ken and Jane keep on being the same? Why didn't she and Josh tell them all to take a running jump? She hung her head, looking down at her feet, but not really seeing them.

OK, so how *would* she have felt if it were Jane at thirteen? At times it would have been as though she had won the lottery, but at others, far more often, it would have been like a death. 'If you say no, they don't go. Is that the scenario?'

Josh had dug his hands deep in his pockets, the letter lay on the windowsill. He didn't answer. Had he even heard? Where was he? With Catherine at the birth? Emily's first Christmas?

Josh still said nothing. Just stared at the girls, his breath clouding the window. In the gallery James was handling the printers. Were they going to redo

192

the catalogues, free of charge and p.d.q. as she'd asked?

She checked the time. Ten minutes. Could she ask James to fetch the children? But he wasn't insured to drive her car.

Josh said, 'Big deal, they say I can visit. Just hop on a plane to San Diego—and with what? She's going to put her in private school over there, so that'll cost as much.'

Fran came to him, linking her arm in his. 'Look, we won't have to pay Catherine's maintenance and we'll find the rest somehow, so you can take her on a good holiday over there. The gallery will be earning, especially once the workshops start.'

He pulled away, stabbing the letter with his paint-smudged forefinger. 'So, we can find money for that and not for the extra when Catherine demands it, which is why this is happening?' He was waving the paper at her.

She recoiled, then shouted back, 'No, *we* can't find anything if you speak to me like that. *You* can. *You* can pay, however you like.'

'Because your money is Jane's.'

She left him by the window, hunting in the kitchen for her handbag and car keys, ignoring Simon who was studiously polishing a gleaming kettle. She found them by the bread bin and swept through the coffee shop, her heart beating too loudly, her throat hurting. Josh caught her at the door, pulling her round. 'I have Jane's children to fetch,' she shouted. 'Yes, *my* daughter's children to collect, and I'm sorry. It's not what I intended when I ran off with you. But I don't happen to have a sunset tucked up my sleeve for us, any more than you have. There isn't one, as you damn well know.

I just wish there were.' She broke from his grasp, and ran down the steps, out to the car. He didn't follow and she longed for him to.

She picked up the children from Maisie's. On the way back to the gallery Lucy talked of the story about the wolf with fangs, in grandmother's cloak. 'Where do you keep your fangs, Grandma?'

'I don't have any, darling.' She felt tired and almost turned left to take them home, instead. But it was Josh's home. She banged the steering wheel and took them to the park. She bought a hot dog for Lucy and pushed a crying Harry backwards and forwards as they fed some of the roll to the ducks. Lucy looked up at her. 'Harry's hungry, Grandma.'

She knew he was. He should be fed too. They should go to the gallery, heat the carrots, heat the bottle. But Josh was there. Beyond the duck pond there were silver birches. They seemed dark today. In the sky there was very little cloud. In her chest something ached, something that made her voice small as she said, 'We'll go and see James and Simon, shall we?'

Lucy skipped ahead, calling back, 'Uncle Josh too. Will he stand and look at my painting again? Will he stand and say I'm like him? Will he paint with me again?'

'Perhaps.'

Josh was crouching in the courtyard finishing the planting. He must have heard them come into the coffee shop but he didn't turn. He must have heard Gail say, 'Great, now you're here, Fran, perhaps you two will sort yourselves out, because we'll all have migraines if this goes on. We're going out, so shall we take the kids?'

All four students waited, almost drooping, at the

194

entrance to the kitchen. Fran shook her head. 'We come as a parcel and besides, Harry's lunch calls.'

They waved to Harry as they went, but Lucy had rushed out into the courtyard towards Josh. Hardly breathing, Fran watched through the window as Josh was almost knocked over in the rush, as he kissed Lucy's hair, stood, then threw her into the air, laughing as she squealed. Fran loved him so much. Too much?

In the kitchen she heated Harry's carrots, testing them for temperature, spooning them into his mouth as he sat, quiet now, in his pushchair. Still Josh and Lucy remained in the courtyard.

She took Harry from the pushchair and gave him his bottle, sitting on a chair at one of the coffee tables, looking on as he played idly with the bottle, feeling the weight of his body settle against her. 'I wish we had met years and years ago and any children were *ours*. It would be so much simpler, but I'm still glad we have these.' Josh was standing at the kitchen door, Lucy on his arm. Their hands were dirty from the earth.

'What about Emily?' Fran asked carefully, watching him, seeing that he looked as tired as she felt. 'Surely she should be consulted in all this. The States might appeal, they might not. It's up to her as well.'

Josh shook his head, rubbing the drying earth from Lucy's hands. 'There's no point. I panicked, but it's a ploy again, that's all.'

Fran felt exasperation lift the tiredness. 'Ploy? What ploy?'

'Last year Catherine said she'd take her to South America if I didn't cough up.'

'Would she have done?'

Harry needed to draw breath. Fran eased the bottle from his mouth. Milk dribbled on to his bib. He started to whinge. She stuck it back quickly, feeling his pull on the teat.

'She did it straight after she'd asked for a top-up and I refused. I paid up. It's the talk of wedding bells that threw me this time. But that'll be a lie too.'

Josh came over and stroked Harry's hair with an earthy finger. Then he touched her cheek. She leant into him. 'I love you, darling Fran. I love you and I'm sorry for the baggage.'

'Don't be. Look around, I've a few colossal pieces too.' They were laughing now, quietly. Josh pulled up a chair and sat close to her. Lucy leaned against him sucking her thumb, almost asleep. The June sun had coloured her cheeks, just as it had Harry's and there was the scent of summer on them both.

'What will you do?' Fran's voice was almost a whisper as Harry's sucking grew slower, his lids heavier.

'Refuse permission and offer to pay her just a little something, like I did before.'

'So next year we'll have this again?'

Josh shrugged, 'What else can I do? She'll grizzle to Emily, who'll think I'm a selfish arse who doesn't care enough and on it will go. On and on.'

She shook her head. 'One day Emily will grow up. One day it will end.'

He looked down at Lucy, then raised an eyebrow at her. 'Grandma?' he whispered. 'So it ends, does it?' They both laughed. The phone rang again. The answer machine took it as they sat together while the children dozed. Finally Josh stirred and murmured, 'One day we'll sit in our bathchairs on Worthing front looking back and wondering what all the fuss was about.'

Fran leaned forward and kissed him, a great relief oozing through her. She had shouted at him, she had walked away and nothing dreadful had happened. Suddenly the world was full of sunshine.

*   *   *

They were drifting off to sleep late that night, their arms around one another as always, when the bedside phone rang. Fran jerked awake, groping for the receiver. The phone fell silent. Josh grunted, 'What's the time? What is it? What's wrong?'

The alarm clock showed 11.35. Fran turned on the bedside lamp and dialled 1471. 'It's Jane's number.'

Josh half sat up. 'Perhaps something's wrong. One of the kids . . .'

Fran was already dialling. She let the phone ring and ring. At least the answer machine wasn't on. The receiver was lifted. Ken spoke, 'Yes, Ken Swanton?' He sounded as though he'd been running. There was the sound of something in the background. 'It's Fran, Ken. Is something wrong?' She was shouting.

'Wrong? I'm not with you.'

Relieved, Fran half laughed. 'Thank heaven's for that. Our phone rang and then stopped and your number came up on 1471.'

There was a short pause and now the sound was clearer. Was it crying? Ken said, 'Just a moment while I shut the sitting-room door. There's some stupid film on.'

A door banged. All went quiet. Ken picked up the phone. 'Sorry to have disturbed you, Fran. I was working on a file and needed to speak to Mike, then realised the time and thought better of it. I must have pressed the wrong stored button. So sorry.' He sounded strained and tired. She wasn't surprised if these were the hours he kept. No wonder Jane felt she must work.

She said softly, 'Goodnight, Ken. Don't work too hard and do think of cutting down your . . .' She stopped. It was late at night and here she was, nagging again. 'Just goodnight. Take care of yourselves.'

She hung up, turned out the light and lay in Josh's arms, loving this small room, this small house, this terrace, this man, this life, glad she wasn't young and striving any more. 'We're getting some sort of balance, aren't we?' she said. His arms tightened around her.

His painting had been astonishing in its vigour and perfection this evening, and more and more it was of the Newlyn school, while hers had been deft, clear, calm, strong but still amateur beside his. Josh had left his own easel and said it had echoes of Chagall although standing up perfectly well as an abstract. He reminded her how to use the wide brush to pull the colour down. As his hand overlaid hers, he had whispered, 'No spirals for a while? I'm so glad.'

CHAPTER NINETEEN

It was strange to see Linda sitting where her mother should have been. Jane passed her the baby corn and French beans. She had remembered to use the Port Meirion bowl, though at first Ken had suggested the silver plate.

Linda noticed. 'So glad the bowl has come in useful. I thought it was a good size when I bought it.'

Ken glanced at Jane. They shared a smile. The scent of freesias on the sideboard was strong. It filled the room. He had kissed her gently and brought them from behind his back when he came home. 'I'm so sorry,' he'd said.

She already had the vase ready filled to an inch below the surface with half a soluble aspirin dissolved in the water.

Linda was passing the bowl across the table to Mike. 'Beautiful flowers, Jane.'

'Yes, I'm very lucky.'

Ken had held her gently, stroking her hair. She had touched his, just above his temple, her favourite place. It was going slightly grey and she thought it distinguished. 'I'm sorry too, so sorry,' she had said.

Now he was smiling at her. 'I have a smashing wife who deserves treats.'

She blushed.

Mike had trained in silver service when he was working his way through college and was helping himself to vegetables one-handed, two-spooned. 'You'll never be out of a job with skills like that,'

Linda said, laughing.

It was what her mother used to say. But her mother had always added, 'After all, you could play the spoons on Brighton Pier.'

Linda did not. Ken thought Mother frequently went too far. Mike hesitated, then passed the vegetables to Jane, saying, as though prompted as Jane had been, 'How is your mother?'

Ken stopped carving the chicken, Linda put another roast potato on her plate, Jane looked only at Mike, nowhere else. 'She's fine,' she replied. 'Would you like bread sauce?'

Linda rushed into a résumé of the weather forecast but Mike cut across: 'The gallery launch is imminent, isn't it?'

Ken put down the carving knife with a clatter. Jane stood. 'I'll pop it back in the oven if you have enough, darling.'

'Quite enough,' Ken said, his voice tightly controlled.

'Let me.' Linda was on her feet too, almost snatching the carving dish from Jane and she was gone, into the kitchen. Jane found her napkin on the floor.

Ken asked Mike, 'How's Jenkins these days? I heard that after the operation he wanted to take it easier.'

Mike was pouring gravy on his plate, catching the drip with his knife. He passed the jug to Ken. 'Yes, he's thinking of early retirement.'

'So that will leave a gap, one which needs to be filled.'

Jane felt he was a little blatant. One shouldn't criticise, but Linda, returning from the kitchen, squeezed her shoulder. For a moment the world went black with pain. 'It's keeping warm in the oven.' Linda settled herself on her chair.

'Do start,' Ken insisted, 'while it's still vaguely hot.'

It was an effort to lift her arm.

Mike smiled at her, 'Delicious, Janey. You haven't lost your touch, and I think you make your mother's interpretation of parsley and thyme stuffing even better than she does. What do you think, Linda?'

Linda's smile was hesitant. She tried the stuffing. 'Goodness, it's certainly a close-run thing.'

Mike turned to Jane. 'So, is everything all sorted for the launch? Please, let's not have awkwardness. I am interested.' His smile was genuine, his tone as gentle as always. Her mother was a fool. Ken was so right. She had been so wrong. To phone like that. Very, very wrong.

'Jane?' Mike's voice was concerned. 'Janey, are you all right?'

Jane looked at his dear face. 'I was just trying to remember if all the exhibits were hung and they are. O'Reilly's prints arrived. Not your sort of thing at all.'

Mike was nodding, as though he wasn't thinking of the prints. 'She's well?'

Linda said quietly, 'She's very well, Mike.'

Ken leaned forward. 'More than can be said for Jenkins, then. So, when will he leave?'

Linda snatched a look at Ken. He really shouldn't, Jane thought. He really shouldn't. Linda said firmly, 'Hey, this isn't a board meeting of Gilbert and Gilbert, young Kenneth. It's an after hours "let's leave work behind and enjoy some perfect food". The beans are absolutely *al dente*,

Jane. Very well done. Mine are invariably sad and limp, and utterly not as they should be.'

Mike was holding up his glass. 'A toast to the chef.'

Ken lifted his glass to her and smiled. It didn't reach his eyes.

She acknowledged the toast and deflected the conversation, asking if Linda had been to any more concerts recently. She hadn't. 'It's a problem finding someone to go with, now.'

Oh, God, back to mother. Jane mentioned that *Les Misérables* was coming to Bristol but then wished she hadn't, because it still left the problem of lonely Linda. She was so stupid. So terribly stupid. Mike took up the ball, though, and ran with it, musing over the way classics were ruined when turned into popular culture. Bless him. Dear, dear Mike.

Linda shook a finger at him. 'You shouldn't pass comment until you have seen the result.'

Mike pulled a face. 'Quite right.'

Now Ken recollected his father's visit to *Hair*. He had thought it was some avant-garde phenomenon and when everyone stripped off he hadn't dared leave in case he was yanked on to the stage.

This was the Ken Jane had first met at Mike's Christmas party, the Ken who could make a room full of people listen and laugh. Suddenly the evening clicked into a different gear, it was almost as it had been before the children.

When one and a half bottles of Chardonnay had been consumed and still no one needed a second helping, Linda helped Jane remove the plates, to-ing and fro-ing to the kitchen. Jane let her bring

202

through the cheese board, while she brought in the meringue surprise. It was from the local delicatessen, but could pass for home-made.

Mike had brought a small bottle of dessert wine. Jane wanted only a thimbleful, Linda none. 'I have to walk home and there are several lamp-posts which could just leap out and ambush me if I have even a fraction more alcohol.'

Ken drank a glass, Mike only half. Ken would sleep tonight. He would leave the debris of the evening and clasp the banister as he climbed the stairs. He would crash to the bed. Jane smiled at Mike and at Linda. He would sleep.

While the men drank port with their cheese Linda insisted on stacking the dishwasher, leaving Jane free to wash the pans. Linda said, 'Nothing worse than coming down to it in the morning, when you're rushing yourself and the children out of the house. I remember your mother's hassles.'

Jane carried the roasting pan over from the oven. It was cast iron and heavy. It slipped and fell into the bowl, splashing her. Linda looked up, 'Oops.'

Jane tried to lift it from the bowl. The pain. She let it go again. Linda stood straight, the knives in her hand forgotten. 'You must have twisted something. I hate these heavy great things.'

Jane said. as the waves of pain rolled on, 'I know, but things cook so well in them.' She didn't really know what she was saying. She felt sick. Linda bent again to the dishwasher. 'I'd go back to an aluminium one, Jane. Life's difficult enough without adding to it.'

That's what Ken had said as he grabbed her. But who could blame him? She'd been going on and on about being tired, or that's what it must have sounded like to him as he ploughed through the work he'd brought home. It was like last week when he'd had a bad day in Bristol. She should have picked up on his tension. She should not have shown him the red bill. It was her fault. She didn't think.

Linda was nudging her to one side. 'You sort out the coffee, I'll put this great monster to bed.' She picked up the scourer and plunged her hands into the bowl.

Jane poured water on to the coffee in the cafetière.

Imagine telling any man when he was still working at ten, as he was last night, that his mother-in-law had had a row with her husband. Imagine saying, 'If only she hadn't been so stupid. If only she'd married Mike.'

Imagine his glee, because he wanted the union to fail. Imagine saying, so very stupidly: 'But I gather it's made them stronger than ever.'

Of course he'd say, 'Don't add to an already bloody day, Jane.' And didn't she sometimes feel like shaking the children, smacking them? He was right. Of course she did, *and* they were less irritating than their mother, she could see that.

To then phone her mother, wanting to say, 'Mum, you've made it even more difficult for us. Please, come back. Be near me. I love you. I need you. Help me.' Was she insane? Of course he didn't want Mother upset and prying into their lives. He was a good man, a proud man, a man who wouldn't have bought this house if he hadn't thought Mike would want a son-in-law in the firm, someone to groom, to hand on to. It was all their fault, hers and her mother's. He was right.

Linda said, 'If you stare at coffee does it turn it into gold?'

Jane took a moment to focus, then she smiled. 'Now, that would be quite something. I'll take the cafetière if you take the tray. I think I really did pull a muscle, or something.'

* * *

Linda walked home, Mike at her side. She hadn't expected him to escort her, but she'd hoped. Oh, how she'd hoped. She wished it were a hundred miles instead of a hundred yards. She wished there were bright and sparkling nuggets of conversation spilling forth with which to beguile him. There was nothing. There was just the sense of him there, at her side. Touching, almost.

He said, 'Ken isn't coping too well. He's pushing a bit.' They passed the lamp-post with the flickering light which infuriated the residents. Their complaints had come to nothing, though. Perhaps it was more than a replacement bulb that was needed.

'Will Jenkins leave?' Linda asked, wanting instead to say: 'Come and see my etchings.'

'I really don't know, and if he does, will Ken fit the bill? I'd like to move him over, for Jane's sake. She's looking tired and I don't like her having to work with two small children.' He dodged round another, more steadfast lamp-post, returning to the pavement.

'It would be promotion, wouldn't it; more money?'

'Yes, but is he ready for it? He isn't handling the

Mainwaring case awfully well, in spite of working on it to excess. Or so it seems, since the file was with him when I needed some information.'

Linda could see the lights of her house. She slowed the pace, unwilling to arrive. Would it be a handshake? A peck on the cheek? She must not grab him, simply must not grab him.

They were at the gate. Her lights were on, her neighbours' were not. They were nicely tucked up in bed. Bed. I wish. She stopped. He said, 'I'll just see you in, my dear. I don't like you coming home to an empty house.'

It was what he had done with Fran, she knew. He did it with everyone, probably.

They heard the radio the moment she opened the door. He stepped back, 'Oh, you have company. I didn't realise.'

Too quickly she said, 'Oh no, it simply makes me feel less alone.' She shut her mouth. Was anything designed to make her look more neurotic? She walked into the hall.

He followed. 'You just have a look around, check the rooms, then I'll go.'

She didn't hurry. She wanted him there, in the hall. Wanted to remember the shape of him, the way he was looking at the photographs on the wall as she came quietly down the stairs again. She hesitated on the bottom step, remembering that many were of her and Fran. She stepped down. 'There we are, quite alone. No strangers, but thanks so much.'

He was nodding, his back to her, still looking at the photographs. He said, 'Until you mentioned that you had no one to accompany you to *Les Misérables* it didn't occur to me that you too had lost a companion.' He turned now, nodding towards the radio. 'You and Fran did a lot together and loneliness is a terrible thing, so why don't you throw me to the lions?'

She was confused. He walked towards her, kissed her on the cheek, then stepped out on to the porch. 'If you manage to get a couple of tickets for the musical, how about me coming, to see just what sort of a fist has been made of a very good book?'

'When?'

He laughed. 'Phone my secretary, she has control of my diary.' He walked down the path, shutting the gate carefully and waving.

She stood in the open doorway watching until he disappeared from sight. OK, so what if it was pity. So what if she was still among the ranks of 'colleagues' who approached through the dreaded Anne. Most did. It was what he did, now that his wife was dead. She removed her jacket, hung it on the bottom of the banister, hurried into the kitchen and turned off the radio. Tomorrow she would check dates with the secretary; what did she care if she and Sally gossiped about it over their Ryvita? Then she would order tickets. Did it seem too keen? Who the hell cared.

CHAPTER TWENTY

Why did the silly prat have to loom over her like that? Catherine looked up from the huge suitcase she was packing. 'Roger, darling, can't you find something useful to do?'

Roger tapped the lid, that irritating frown still

wedged between his eyes. Would he consider having those horribly close brows plucked? Probably. After this, he'd do anything for her. 'Catherine, I still think we should have given everyone more notice.'

'I've written. Josh will get the letter tomorrow and why tell Em before we have to? She's going to be furious . . .'

'Actually, I think that's the wrong word, surely she'll be distressed?'

Catherine slammed down the lid. 'That's enough, Roger. None of this is our doing. If Josh wouldn't give his permission then that's that. I can't pull miracles out of the air and what about me? What mother likes to have her child torn from her? It is no light thing, Roger, for me to choose your well-being over my own.'

Roger looked stricken and reached for her. She let him hold her for a moment, let him say, 'Darling Catherine.' She let him tighten his hold, but then he said, 'I can't let you do this. I'll phone, back out.'

That was the trouble with Roger, he took things too far. She pulled away, smiling gently. 'Please, sweetheart, let me do this for you and our baby. Anyway, thinking it through a little more I'm sure that after a few months they won't be able to get rid of her quickly enough, and she'll have had a basinful of the tatty little hovel and join us, full of sunshine and light. Imagine, a smiling Emily.'

Roger pulled her to him again. Again she allowed it for a moment, then patted him. 'Must finish packing her stuff.' There was a solitary piece of confetti caught in his hair. He'd groomed out the rest with his fingers the moment they returned from the Register Office and placed the coloured

208

hearts in his cuff-link box as though they were the Holy Grail. She picked out this last piece and rubbed it into dust.

His grip was still tight, though now he squeezed her even tighter, stroking her hair, saying, 'Won't you at least phone Josh, talk it over with him, tell him it wasn't a ploy so we don't leave on this note? Where did he get that idea from anyway?'

Catherine swallowed. She sat down suddenly on the Victorian bedroom chair, her hand to her forehead, the nausea building. It was almost four o'clock. Why was it so regular, eight and four? Soon Emily would be in, galumphing around, up in the air one minute, brutishly down the next. It wasn't fair for someone in her condition.

Roger was by her side, rubbing her back. Did he really think that helped? She bent over, her head in her hands.

They heard the front door open and slam shut. Well, the good mood of the morning, the glass of wedding champagne, the gift of a silver locket hadn't lasted very long, had it?

Catherine waved Roger away. 'Come on, she mustn't see the cases. While I go and talk to her you take this one into our room. She won't notice a few clothes missing from the wardrobe.'

'I still think . . .'

'Don't think, just do as I say.' Her voice was harsh and if she said any more she'd vomit all over him.

CHAPTER TWENTY-ONE

Emily arrived at 8 p.m on Wednesday, as the letter had said she would. It was a letter that Josh and Fran received on their late return from the gallery. Late, because the launch was the next day. Ten minutes afterwards the taxi pulled up.

Fran held open the front door as Josh paid the taxi and Emily strolled past her without a sideways glance, without a hello, carrying a Gucci shoulder bag. 'My cases are in the taxi.'

'Go in, Em. Make yourself at home while I help Josh with the cases.' Even to her own ears her voice still sounded shell-shocked, disbelieving.

This was mirrored by Josh in the way he reached for the two huge suitcases, the way he waved away the taxi driver's change. She rushed to take the remaining smaller one. Smaller it may have been, but she still needed both hands and someone else's back, or even Em. But she had seen the girl's red-rimmed eyes, the reddened nose, the top lip chafed from crying.

Bloody, bloody Catherine. Hanging was too good for her.

She staggered down the path. Stan leaned out of the window. 'I don't believe it.'

'Try,' she grunted.

'What's the cow done, dumped her and run?'

'To the States,' Fran mouthed, afraid that Em would hear, that it would make a bad situation worse.

The letter had said:

Since you've refused to allow permission and offered a pittance to buy our refusal of a crucial transfer, I am forced to give up my child, as you clearly intended. I don't understand your accusation of a ploy.

Is this how she had put it to Emily?

Fran shifted the case, her arms feeling as though they were being wrenched from their moorings. Why hadn't they talked? It was absurd, cruel. They should have followed up, perhaps she could have contacted Catherine? But Josh seemed so sure it was a ruse. Didn't he know his ex-wife at all? Suddenly she was angry, but then that passed.

Josh was in the doorway, taking the suitcase from her. Emily stood at the foot of the stairs, defiant. There were too many of them in this small hallway. There was too much unspoken pain, anger, shock, disbelief banging against the walls.

Josh took one suitcase at a time up the stairs, there was not room for two. As he passed, Emily stared after him bleakly. Fran walked into the kitchen, unable to bear the abandoned shock of the girl. What had they all done? How the hell had it come to this?

She made tea: Earl Grey. She poured three mugs and took Emily's to her, handing it over. 'Em, come into the kitchen, it's cosier there.'

'Cosy is an estate agent's equivalent of poky.' Emily clutched her mug.

Oh, bugger it. But then Fran saw the tremble in the child's hands, saw her gulp the tea and again wanted to take her in her arms. She reached out. Emily ignored her. Fran said quietly, 'Perhaps the sitting room, then? We can talk. We're so happy to

211

have you, but so sorry.'

Emily was slurping her tea as though she had found an oasis in a desert. Perhaps she should have put shock-reducing sugar in it? She could hear Josh moving around in Emily's small bedroom. She heard a bang, a muffled curse. Leaving Emily propping up the wall she found the sugar and put two heaped teaspoons into Josh's mug. She considered her own, then decided against.

She was calm now. horribly calm, floating above it all somehow, seeing it from a distance, but not sure whether to be with Emily or remain distant. She leaned back against the kitchen table. Leave the clothes and get down here, Josh. She said it three times, silently, relying on telepathy.

It must have worked because she heard him on the stairs. Not light and enthusiastic but with an 'Oh Lord, it's Catherine' tread. She heard him say, 'Come into the sitting room, Em.' She heard the girl's tears now, great gulping ones that grew out of grief and loss, and owed nothing to histrionics. She heard the click of the sitting room door as it shut.

She leant against the table while his tea went cold. Her feet were aching. She'd been on them all day, but the gallery was finished, bar the smallest of tweaks, as James called them. What would he call this? That poor, poor girl. The phone rang. She leapt to silence it before it disturbed Josh and Em. Roger spoke, 'Can't stop, flight's been called. Has she arrived safely?'

For a moment Fran was stunned, then she said, 'Yes, but please let me fetch Em, or my husband. I'm sure there are things to be said, things that should have been talked about, that could have prevented this and might even do so yet.' How

212

could she be so calm?

Roger said, 'I think we've handled it rather badly. I think . . .' There was a muffled conversation. Roger came back on the line, brisk now: 'Just as long as she has arrived safely. Her mother was worried. Please tell her that.'

Click.

Fran replaced the receiver in a civilised fashion, but actually wanted to slam it down on Catherine's head and now she was the one who was trembling. How dare that woman. How bloody dare she play games with her daughter's life. She felt sick, impotent, wanting to take the child in her arms and make it better.

She kicked her sandals across the room and padded in bare feet outside on to the patio. She could hear the murmur of Josh's voice, his words indistinct through the open window. Then silence. Night had not yet fallen properly. Soon it would be the longest day. Well, today was proving to be a pretty long trail. She gazed at the molehills. She should rake them over? She should weed the beds? There would be more time next week, now the 'setting up' was done. Next week? A light was turned on in the sitting room. It highlighted the patio table. She ought to make up Emily's bed.

Thank heavens for bedtime, for thinking time.

Still she didn't stir, just stood. Josh began to speak again. Then nothing. She must move. She must put away the paints, the easels and find sheets, pillowcases, fluff the duvet, towels too. Or had Emily brought towels? Surely those couldn't all be clothes? But you needed large suitcases for a lifetime.

A lifetime. Damn that cruel, bloody woman.

Damn her. She wanted to rush into the sitting room, tell Emily that her mother loved her and wanted her after all, that it had been a stupid mistake. A silly stupid mistake and there were tickets waiting at Heathrow, and her Dad would come out every holiday, and everything would be wonderful.

She rubbed her arms. She should have said that to Roger, for God's sake. She should have thought of all this then. She should have called Josh, or let him answer the phone. She took a few steps towards the French windows, then stopped. It was too late. Or was it? Perhaps they could put a call out at Heathrow.

There was a loud knocking at the front door. She closed her eyes. Catherine? She hurried through the house to the door. The knock came again. It was the taxi driver. He held a cat carrier, in which a tabby miaowed plaintively. 'The girl left it on the back seat,' the man said, handing it to Fran. 'Got to get on, the pubs'll be out soon and I'll be rushed off me wheels.' He was already heading back to his cab.

Fran clutched the basket to her, while the cat howled loud enough to bring out a second moon. She backed into the hallway, shutting the door with her foot as Emily burst from the sitting room. 'Big Job, you're here. I forgot you. How could I do that?' She was pulling the basket from Fran.

Fran said, 'Easily done, Em, especially . . .'

Emily hugged the basket and shouted over the howls, 'Especially when everyone else can forget about me, you mean.'

Was now the time to mention that Roger had called? Josh was with them and here they were

214

again, squashed into the hall. Fran gestured to the kitchen. 'How about taking him through into there, Em. We can find him some milk.'

Emily looked at Fran as though she was something rather nasty. 'He doesn't drink milk, only water, and he must not be allowed to leave the house tonight, or for the next few days, or he'll try and find his way home, and we all know that there's no one who wants us there.' Em bent to speak through the small window of the basket. 'It's just you and I, little Big Job. Just you and I.'

Oh, God. Fran told Josh to put the cat carrier on the kitchen table for now and suggested that Em choose linen from the airing cupboard, then Dad would be up to help make up her bed. If a meal or cocoa was required in the meantime they should just yell. Meanwhile she would find something that would do for a litter tray. As Em stamped up the stairs she beckoned Josh into the kitchen. 'That was Roger on the phone, at Heathrow. I wanted to call you, but he rang off too quickly. They wanted Em to know that they were concerned she'd arrived safely, Catherine especially. I think he felt all this was badly handled.'

Josh stared at her as though he couldn't take in any more. She held him. 'Shall we phone the airport, put out a call, try to reach . . .'

'For Catherine to turn her away once more? I don't think so, do you? Let's wait, talk things through with Em. We can always fax some sort of an offer.'

He sounded old and tired. He leant his head against hers. Em called, 'Dad, I need you here.'

In the light from the kitchen window Fran found a use for the mole earth at last, putting sufficient into a seed tray for Big Job, preferring not to dwell on the connotation of the name, hoping for huge turbulence over the Atlantic, really, really huge turbulence.

While Josh and Emily sorted things out she stayed in the kitchen, finding a tin of tuna in sunflower oil, draining it pretty thoroughly, putting just a little in a saucer, hoping it wouldn't upset the cat. At a call from Josh she popped next door to borrow more coat-hangers. Emily took them from her on the landing, shutting the bedroom door firmly in her face. From behind it Fran heard the murmur of father and daughter.

No one wanted food, or cocoa, or anything. They all just fell into bed, needing oblivion, but sleep wouldn't come to Fran or Josh, who did not lie in one another's arms as usual, but side by side listening to the intermittent sobbing.

Fran moved, sliding her arm across his chest, her leg over his. 'What has she said?'

'That her mother wanted her until we wouldn't pay what she needed to keep her. That we could pay for a gallery, but nothing for her, so what did that say about any of us?'

He turned away from her, lying motionless on his side. Fran stared at the ceiling which was busy with shadows from the plum tree's waving branches. A full moon? Well, what else on a night like this? She said eventually, 'We, or me, Josh? We wouldn't pay? Or I wouldn't pay?'

He said, 'I tried to tell her we couldn't afford it, but what will she think when she sees your launch tomorrow? What will she think? We should have found the money, or I should have talked it through with Catherine. I should have taken her

216

seriously, discussed the move.'

'Instead we'll have to talk it through with Emily in the morning as we've already said, when the shock has worn off a little.' Did her voice sound as hollow to him, as it did to her? *Your* launch. But her own hurt was as nothing to that child's.

Emily's crying had begun again. Fran threw back the duvet and started to go to her. Josh called, 'It isn't your problem, I'll go.'

He shrugged into his dressing gown, shutting the door firmly behind him, and again there was the murmur of indistinct voices. Then silence. Then the creaking of the floor, the shutting of the door. Then a high-pitched shout: 'Anyway it's all your fault, you and *her*. I could be there in the sun, in a beautiful house. I hate you, I hate you both.'

When he returned he lay on his side, his back to her. 'Try to sleep, Fran.'

After a few fitful hours Fran woke early, to that same back. Tentatively she reached out a hand, touching his warm skin. He didn't move, he didn't turn to hold her close. Perhaps he was asleep. Perhaps. But obviously not, for the next second he slipped from the bed, not looking at her. Instead, he took his clothes to the bathroom.

The room seemed so quiet and each breath she drew seemed too deep. She heard the creak of the stairs, the miaow of the cat as Josh opened the kitchen door. 'Don't let him out,' she said aloud. Anything to break the loneliness of the room.

She dressed hurriedly, washed and crept quietly down the stairs, conscious of Emily: desperately, painfully conscious of the child. She opened the kitchen door quietly. Josh was making coffee, two mugs. One for her? Or Emily? She rubbed her

217

forehead uncertainly.

Catherine's letter was on the kitchen table. Josh walked towards her, a mug in his hand. Was he going past her? No. He stood close, bent and kissed her mouth. 'I love you.' They stood together like two castaways. He smiled briefly. There were deep circles under his eyes and he was pale. She took the mug of coffee. He returned for his, leaning back against the sink, one arm crossed over his chest.

He nodded towards the letter as he took a sip. 'I read it again. She says her decision is final and that it's no good chasing her to the States arguing about it. It would only make Em think that no one wanted her. Emily is to go for the *Christmas* holidays.' His voice was bleak.

Fran said, holding her mug with two hands, watching the cat pushing the tuna with its nose, 'It's not my fault.' Was she whining?

He shook his head. 'I know. You don't need to tell me it's mine.'

Fran's voice was loud and strong, this time. 'It's Catherine's, she's manipulated the situation. She didn't give us the chance to . . .'

Emily pushed open the door, shouting, 'No, it isn't. It's yours, Fran. You're the one who made it too difficult for her. Do you think she wanted to leave me? Do you think I want to be here, with you, in this poky little hole where there's not enough room. Don't you dare blame my mother, when you're the one who decides where the money goes. You got the courtyard tables I bet. You got those, but you wouldn't let Dad give Mum a decent amount. And Dad's just a woose to let you get away with it.'

Fran had spun round. Now she put up her hand,

218

but what could she say? How about, I think we should all have asked you. I think your mother had loads of money, far more than her entitlement. She was a liar. She was greedy. Perhaps she just didn't want you, or wanted to damage us. Because, in the clear light of day, that's what Fran realised half of her thought. The rest firmly believed Emily. She let her hand fall to her side.

Josh came to Emily. 'That's not the case. I don't want you talking of Fran like . . .'

'Josh,' Fran's voice was sharp. She shook her head. 'Not now,' she murmured as the child hurled out of the room. 'Nothing we say will change what she needs to think. Just go after her.' Josh shook his head helplessly. 'Go on,' she insisted, making her way to the sink as he followed Emily. She poured her coffee away as the cat wound round and round her legs. 'You and me, Big Job,' she said. 'We're out here, looking in.' She felt an outsider, an exhausted outsider, a bruised and battered outsider who should have prevented this.

The sun was casting long shadows in the garden. Another day. She heard the slamming of a drawer from Emily's room and made her mind work. Another day and what were they to do with her for that day? Something smacking of normality. Just anything. Thursday, a school day. School?

She snatched up Catherine's letter, reading it through once, then twice, then let it drop. Of course the damn woman had withdrawn Emily from her independent school, what else? When the obvious thing would have been to keep her on as a boarder until the end of term. Had she really been thinking of all the ways in which Josh's life could be made difficult, at the expense of Emily? What sort

219

of woman was this?

She traced the words with her finger, *but decided against it, because you, darling, Josh, would doubtless have refused to pay the extra.*

Fine. So if they now tried to reinstate the child as a boarder, or even suggest it, it would reek of rejection. Emily must somehow be given the option because it might be what she wanted. Otherwise, one of James's tweaks was coming up, unless of course she could remain a day pupil. Just how far was the school?

Fran sought relief in the form of action, rummaging for the road map, finding Dorchester, then the school. It was miles. It would take nearly two hours round trip if she were to drive. But if Emily wanted to go . . . She tossed the map back on the shelf, dragging a chair from the table, sitting down, trying to think. The clock chimed in the hall. It was eight o'clock. Today she already needed more than the hours there were in the day. Josh had lectures . . . but for Emily's sake, some sort of routine should be instigated, some sense of permanence, of them wanting her to stay. It must be offered.

She reached for the phone. She dialled Jessie's number. That warm, robust voice shouted, 'Potty Pots, but we're not really up and running yet. Try again at . . .'

'It's me, Fran,' she interrupted.

'Darling, what's wrong. We're so sorry we can't come tonight, but if there's a real emergency we could delay our own opening this evening.'

'Don't you dare. I just want your wise old ears for a moment.' Fran spoke quietly, frightened that Emily would hear.

She told the tale. There was a stunned silence. Fran could picture Jessie at the Aga, leaning back against its warmth, Hercules at her feet. It grounded her, as nothing else could. 'She's a sad woman,' Jessie said at last. 'She's offloading an adolescent cauldron, hoping it will cause maximum damage regardless of the effect. What a cruel bloody witch.'

'We should have talked it through.'

'How, when it's the last thing she wanted. She had her own agenda. Josh would have known that, so remind him if he's spinning into a flagellation session. Last year she was rushing off somewhere distant with her, the year before it was somewhere else.'

Fran could hear the stairs creaking. She whispered, 'I have to go.'

She replaced the receiver and was back at the kitchen table as Josh entered, conscious that she hadn't asked Jessie the question: 'If we'd have given her enough money as he had before, this wouldn't have happened, would it?'

The clock chimed again. She was going to be late. Gail and James would be waiting on the doorstep because Ruth, the other keyholder, was at the Cash and Carry. Well, they'd just have to wait.

She heard Emily shouting. Josh returned to the foot of the stairs. Emily said, 'But I'm telling you, I don't want to go to school here, with all these sad gits.'

Josh called up, 'Just get dressed and we'll sort it out while you're having breakfast.'

'Orange juice, then coffee and toast. By the way, I've changed to ginger marmalade.' Emily's voice was imperious but still there was the tremble.

The cat was winding itself around Fran's legs again. She felt suddenly suffocated and grabbed her purse, slipping out of the back door, shutting it quietly behind her, hurrying along behind the cottages. Stan was sitting outside, smoking his breakfast. 'The corner shop has it,' he whispered. 'But what she really needs is a smacked backside. Or her mother does, with one of those coat-hangers. Trouble is, she'd enjoy it. Fine old mess she's left you with.'

Fran smiled. It seemed strange that outside the house the world was just the same. She heard a phone ringing. Was it theirs? Was it Catherine saying she'd changed her mind? Even so, it was still feeding time at the zoo. She said to Stan, quietly, 'She needs her mother.'

'Well, she's not going to get her and if you ask me, she's better off without her.' Fran put her finger to her lips. Stan shrugged. 'She can walk to school with Mark, he won't mind being classed as a sad git. I'll fill them in at college if Josh is late.'

Fran found ginger marmalade at the corner shop as Stan had promised. She also found two varieties of cat food and bought them both, and a carton of fresh orange.

She fumbled at the back door, her arms full. It was opened for her and Josh pulled her in, his arms tight around her. The tins pressed into her breasts, 'Hey.' She half laughed.

His voice was urgent: 'Oh, God, Fran, I thought you'd gone, just walked out. I hate that bloody woman for what she's done to her and to us. How the hell are we going to cope?'

The tins were hurting and she didn't know the answer, just didn't know; but then she saw Emily enter the kitchen, her movements lethargic, her face puffy. Fran said, easing away from Josh, placing the marmalade and cat food on the table, 'We're going to have a wonderful time really getting to know one another. Mark's looking forward to walking to school with Emily unless you want us to try and reinstate you in your old school?'

Her eyes asked Josh the question. He nodded.

Emily stared at her as though she were a cretin. 'And have everyone there sniggering because Mum and Roger have gone without me and left me in this hole . . .' Emily's voice broke. She sat down, her shoulders slumped. She pushed the marmalade around with her ringed forefinger. 'Are girls allowed to wear rings at Mark's crummy school?'

Josh and Fran exchanged a carefully neutral look. Fran put bread in the toaster, leaving Josh to say, 'Not sure about rings. The new head is strict about uniform and so on. We'll have to settle the minutiae.'

Oops, Fran thought and wasn't surprised at the snort from Emily. Josh had come close and murmured, 'Gail phoned. They're camped on the doorstep. I explained, said go away and have some coffee. Be back in an hour.'

Fran checked her watch, saying, 'There's a spare key at the newsagents, they really need to get on. Time's short enough without . . .'

There was a crash. They spun round. The marmalade had smashed on to the floor and lay, a heap of sharded glass, peel, the works. The toast popped up. Bugger, bugger, Fran thought, but said calmly, 'There's a cloth under the sink, Emily. Josh, how about phoning the school?'

Josh headed for the hall phone, his jaw muscle

working. Emily just sat there, twisting the ring on her finger while the cat showed an interest in the marmalade. Fran put on the radio, needing Wogan's soothing touch, not knowing whether to plunge straight into a disciplinary crisis. Josh reappeared at the door, eyeing the marmalade, the same doubt in his eyes. He said, 'They can interview her at eleven. It'll just be a formality, then they'll take her for the rest of the day.'

'Hello, I'm here,' Emily shouted. 'Try telling me, not talking over me.' She scooped up Big Job and ran from the room, pounding up the stairs and slamming shut her bedroom door.

Fran put the toast on a plate and the plate on the table. 'You've a free day, have you?'

'No. It'll be difficult to take much time after St Ives. How about you?'

'Josh, I'm not her mother, I'm not *in loco parentis*, and she needs to know you care.'

Josh snapped, 'Are you suggesting I don't?'

'For God's sake, Josh.'

He put up his hands, stepped towards her, crunched on to the marmalade. 'Oh shit, where's that damned cloth?'

She said quietly, 'Shouldn't we make her clear it up?'

Josh was wiping the sole of his boot with kitchen roll. 'We're never going to get anywhere if we start off on the wrong foot.'

Fran grinned suddenly. 'As it were.'

Josh looked up and he too was grinning, and now they laughed, and she went to him and kissed his face again and again, until Emily called down from the bedroom, 'Anyway, I can't start without a uniform.'

224

Josh murmured into her neck, 'I think that is teenage speak for "OK, I'll go, but I'm not surrendering easily; there are a few more rounds I can fight".'

Fran groaned, 'Who's going to do the uniform bit?'

He looked at her. 'If I promise to cover you in chocolate . . .'

'You do the interview, I'll do the clothes. Bring her to the gallery after the interview, I'll dash her to Denners, then into school. How's that?' She held out her hand.

He slapped it, 'Done.'

They both looked at the marmalade again. Josh dug beneath the sink for the cloth. 'You get off. I'll do the worst of it, she can finish and make do with ordinary on her toast.'

*   *   *

At the gallery it was organised chaos, the highlight being the delivery of the correctly coloured catalogues and the samples of Ruth's canapés that Fran and the gang had to test. James found them not quite right and felt the need to try many more to feel truly confident. Fran told him to take a runner. He said he thought comments like that not conducive to proper employer-employee relationships. She said, 'My heart is broken, now get to work.' He called her a hard woman.

At 1.30 Josh delivered Emily. Fran had created a window in her day by overloading on to the others, a fact that James shared in the coffee shop with Emily. Aghast, Fran stood by for the fallout. Emily merely put her shoulders back and chest out, saying, 'Uniforms make me feel absurdly young, but if I have to, I have to.'

Josh shrugged and fled. Emily half turned, calling after him, 'Dad, can't *you* take me shopping?'

Fran ignored the meaning, and pointed her towards a coffee table and the sandwiches Ruth had provided. 'Eat, then we'll shop. There's tuna, or egg.'

James took the press releases through to the gallery. Emily's shoulder slumped. 'I don't like tuna, or egg.'

'Then pick those bits out and turn them into salad sandwiches.'

'Then I won't have any protein.'

Gail came from the kitchen, bearing piles of paper plates which she set down on the desk at the entrance to the coffee shop, whispering behind Fran's back, 'Then she must shut her mouth and preserve her strength.'

The doorbell rang, the front door opened, Lucy called, 'Hello Grandma.' Fran's jaw dropped. Surely she'd said not today. Surely. Jane called, 'Honestly, Mother. Maisie rang to say you hadn't picked them up.' She rushed in behind Harry's pushchair, her face flushed and angry. Harry was crying, but then, what was new?

At the sight of Emily, Lucy ran to her, arms outstretched. Emily caught her up, sat her on the sandwich table. Jane thought she took in the situation at a glance. 'So, Emily's here for the launch too.' If only . . .

Automatically Fran took Harry's bag as Jane turned on her heel and was already making for the door before Fran had gathered her wits together.

Frantically she called, 'Wait, Jane. I said I couldn't manage, not today.'

Jane was rushing into the street. 'But then you agreed, I'm sure you did, because we can't mess Maisie around. She just can't produce two vacancies out of a hat because we're in trouble.'

'Then you should have taken time off.' But Jane was gone.

'When are we shopping for this dorky uniform?' Emily called over the shutting of the front door, feeding a tuna sandwich to Lucy.

'it's not dorky, for goodness sake,' Fran shouted. Suddenly silence fell and even Harry in his pushchair stared in surprise. Fran said, her voice quieter, 'Its no more dorky than other uniforms and we will shop for it in ten minutes flat, when everyone is changed and watered.'

*   *   *

The launch kicked off on time and though the punters weren't actually queuing at the door they trickled in in a steady stream and by eight the gallery was heaving. Stan and Cindy had taken up root behind the bar, and were topping up glasses and talking up the gallery as they did so. Linda loved O'Reilly's prints; his pen and ink were good, but his screen prints were just fantastic, she raved, especially the one of the sky-diving granny.

O'Reilly, already on his third glass of wine as any self-respecting Irishman should be, was delighted. He linked arms with Linda. 'Come, let me lead you away from these heathens and I'll talk you through my favourites, and we will stand before those that are not my work and criticise.'

Linda laughed, winked at Fran and together artist and admirer circled the gallery including Emily in their circle on the third circuit, and picking up Fran on their fourth. Emily immediately found a pressing need to talk to James and disappeared, and the glance Linda and Fran exchanged was one of resignation, while O'Reilly, expansively enthusiastic, said, 'Wonderful exhibition, wonderful couple. I'm so pleased for you and Josh. You're just what he needs, my dear. Someone who understands him and stands by him, through thick and thin. He's a bundle of uncertainties after that doleful bitch.' He was looking at Emily now, his face sad.

Linda leaned across, tidying Fran's necklace, which had become tangled. 'They make a good team, because Josh understands Fran too. He's let you fly with it, hasn't he, Fran. But you should see her paintings, Liam. This is a woman of many talents.'

O'Reilly looked interested and Fran grinned at Linda, who had not seen anything she had painted since she had been struck speechless with something close to horror the first time.

Linda looked over her shoulder, calling, 'Josh, come and join us.'

He squeezed through, slipping his arm around Fran as she said, 'They're saying nice things about us and they're all true.' He pulled her close, kissing the hair above her ear. Emily's voice rose above the murmur: 'Must they?' James shook his head though others laughed: they thought she was joking.

Josh stiffened but did not relinquish Fran, who kissed him back, her eyes holding his. Beleaguered they might be, but tonight was theirs. She said this to him fiercely, so only he could hear, so that she would remind herself of that fact. His answering squeeze was all she needed.

O'Reilly continued to circle, accompanied by Linda, and within five minutes the press had arrived and were taking photographs of the new gallery owners, staff and O'Reilly in the courtyard. Emily was there, still attached to James. Her launch clothes clashed with his cords, polo neck and scarf—launch clothes which had been bought before . . . Fran wouldn't think of it.

She saw Jane and beckoned her forward, pleased and relieved that her daughter had come. Jane's pink dress had always suited her, but now she seemed even thinner. Fran felt a flicker of concern as she placed her next to O'Reilly. 'Where's Ken?' Josh asked as the photographers flashed.

Jane turned to him. 'One of us had to babysit. The children were far too tired after being dragged round the shops all lunchtime.'

'To me,' called a photographer. 'To me, the lady in pink.'

I do wish you would, Fran thought. Go to him, run away, just for tonight. I really have more than enough to deal with. Josh pressed his arm against hers. She drew patience from it.

O'Reilly was interviewed, Fran was, again, Josh too and now excitement took the place of patience. It was happening, their gallery would be in the papers. They had really begun. She saw the same feelings in Josh.

To their left, sitting on the courtyard table, Emily ignored Mark, who had just brought her a Coke, and fluttered her eyelashes at James. She had somehow filched a glass of wine, but neither Josh nor Fran had any intention of taking it from her at this precise moment they valued the atmosphere too much. Stan and Cindy had left the bar in Gail's tender care and now joined them.

The reporter for the *Western Daily Press* was asking Josh, 'So, what is the ethos of the gallery, Mr Benton?'

Josh explained their determination to promote not just local art, but all fresh, unique work. As he slid into an in-depth discussion of the difference between avant-garde and traditional, Stan poured half his glass of wine into Fran's. 'Have a top-up, I'm driving.' So was she, so she put her glass on one of the tables.

At that moment Mark slid up to Cindy, his voice choked with humiliation but loud enough for Fran to hear, 'Em says I'm just a kid, and to go away and play with my balls, if I have any.'

Fran's glance flickered from Emily to Mark. Stan was pulling his son to him, but such a display of support did not improve the situation for the thirteen-year-old and Mark shrugged away. Instead, Stan stood between his son and Emily, his smile steady. 'Girls are like that when they're this age. Ignore it. She'll come round.' Stan's smile might have been steady, but Fran's was not. Josh had not heard and was pointing the reporter to the gallery, suggesting that she come with him and take a look at their youngest contributor's work.

As he moved to the gallery, Fran stayed with the reporter from the *Western Gazette*, talking him through a similar spiel, sending him and the photographer through to the gallery, taking a moment to catch her breath, to wonder what to do about Emily's unkindness, but now Jane caught at her arm. 'She's been dumped, I hear, on you. Well, I don't know what to say . . . and is that wine she's drinking? She's far too young and if someone should see . . .' She left the consequences to speak for themselves.

Fran longed for Jane to talk of paintings, screen prints, anything other than all this. She said quietly, 'For someone who doesn't know what to say you're doing rather well.' She tried to make her tone light, to deflect what she feared was on its way.

Jane squared up to her, as she did when she had a 'this is for your own good' opinion. 'Honestly, Mother, it just isn't right. She should be on orange, or something like that.'

Behind her Stan was still talking to Mark. Around her guests were circling, enthusing. Ruth and Simon were flirting near the largest O'Reilly screen print. Jane moved even closer. 'Mother, you should do something about that child. It could upset the evening.' She was quite right, of course, and suddenly Fran snatched Jane's glass of orange juice and carried it to Emily, grabbing her wine from her, replacing it with the orange. 'You are too young and I won't have it, and you will not be unpleasant to Mark, who has been a good friend to you for two years. Is that clear?'

She didn't wait for a response but turned on her heel and marched to Jane who was smirking. At her age she was smirking. She pushed the wineglass into Jane's hand, whispering fiercely, 'You drink that and stop being so bloody mealy-mouthed, and put on some weight. You're not the girl Ken married, you're the mother of his children and you owe yourself a few extra pounds, and what's more

231

you can tell him I said that. Now for goodness sake go and look at this wonderful work, including your own daughter's painting.'

For a moment Jane stared, then turned on her heel, pushing a way through the chattering guests. Stan tapped Fran's shoulder and gave her a thumbs-up. She snapped, 'And don't you even think of producing a roll-up.' But now she was joking, her frustration evaporating as quickly as it had come.

His hands were up in surrender. 'I run when the cavalry approaches. Good one, Fran.'

Jane had stopped and was looking back, vulnerable all of a sudden and Fran's heart twisted. She blew a kiss and went to her quickly. 'I love you and I love it that you came, and I want you to love this.' She waved her arm at the gallery. 'Goodness, you've seen it develop from its early chaos, after all. Now please go and talk to O'Reilly about his work, or have some of Ruth's wonderful canapés. I want my daughter to share in this evening properly. I want you to be proud of me, darling. Just as I am of you.'

Jane bit the inside of her mouth, saying nothing. She turned quickly, heading towards the coffee room. Fran watched her until she was swallowed up in the crush, but now she remembered Mark and found him sitting on the low wall, next to Simon. She tapped the top of his head. 'Come into the gallery with me. I need someone with an ounce of nous to be in charge of the catalogues.' Mark grinned and together they wound their way through groups of people, some of whom she recognised, some of whom must have responded to the newspaper previews.

She dropped Mark off at the gallery desk, but

before she could return to the fray he said, 'Fran, those new platform shoes Em's wearing won't be allowed in school. She'll get into trouble. It might upset her. She's obviously already in a hell of a state.'

She smiled because she'd done her dusting down for this evening, she really had, but when she turned she grimaced. Damn and blast. But not now. Now it was the gallery's turn and she forced herself to drift, seeing the first of the red dots on the prints, nodding as Gail wrote six in the air. 'Good girl,' she mouthed.

Linda's voice was warm in her ear: 'You're the good girl. This is incredible and after a day shoe shopping I can't believe you still have the energy to push-start your baby into being. Did I hear that platforms were the result?'

'My, what big ears you have, Grandma.' Fran grabbed a glass of orange from the tray Ruth had replenished. Linda stood shoulder to shoulder with her as they watched the rest of the room, 'You're the grandmother, honey pie. Platforms, eh, so you lost the sensible-shoe battle. Ah, I remember those Saturdays with Jane and how you rushed back to work on Monday, seeking sanctuary.'

Fran was shaking her head. 'I gather from Mark they really are a no-no. Damn and bloody blast.' But now she was repeating herself. She shrugged. 'It was just at the time Lucy pulled down the rack and Harry bawled, and I would have agreed to anything.'

Linda laughed aloud, but no one turned, no one heard over the hubbub, no one but Jane who had found them again and had caught the gist, for now she said to Linda, 'You see, she's being taken advantage of. Look around, who are these people? None of our neighbours are here, none of our old friends. Were they even invited? They're all his friends, or Joe Public, and just who's getting the credit? Mr Josh "I'm the local artist" over there, busily being interviewed. Mum just can't see what's happening.' Her voice was strained, almost distraught. 'Its got to end in tears if it goes on like this. I mean, who's having to do the chasing around for the girl? My mother, who's been kind and had her own grandchildren, though not in the peace of her own home, in this madhouse. It simply isn't fair on her. A stepdaughter. Another child to bring up.' She turned to Fran, who could smell wine on her breath. 'Look, Mother, Mike's still keen, Ken knows he is. Cut your losses, leave this lot to their own devices, think of yourself.'

Fran held on to her daughter's flaying hands. 'Hey, calm down.' Now people were looking. Fran lowered her voice, striving to present an 'everyday story of country folk' front, but in reality seething. 'Look, I'm so touched that you care, but really . . . Linda, tell her.'

Linda was looking amazed, as though she could hardly believe her ears. 'Ken said? What on earth does he know about anything?'

Fran still held Jane's hands, but now her daughter pulled free, her voice uncertain. 'Well, maybe he's guessing; but either way, he just wants what's best for Mother. For heaven's sake, we're only thinking of her good. Look at her, she's got bags under her eyes, she looks years older and it should all be so different. It could still be, I'm sure it could.'

Fran snatched a glance at Linda. Bags, years

older? Well. Then the real anger got going and she was confused, startled, almost numb. Jane was the one to reach for her hand, now, and Fran the one to pull away. Jane said, 'Mum, think about it, about this, these people, this life, it's all so . . . Oh, I don't know.'

Fran did look, as though from a great distance, and she liked what she saw, she bloody well liked it, which was more than could be said when she looked at her daughter, with her disapproving . . . No. No. This was not the time. She struggled to smile for those who might be watching, to keep her voice level and to choose words she really meant. 'If they're so . . . Then so am I. It's who I am now. It's what I am. It's as I choose to be. I love Josh. I can come to love his daughter. And I love you. Most of all, I love you.'

Jane seemed to wilt with each word, looking confused, running her fingers over her lips almost as though she were not sure where she was. She whispered, 'This is so wrong.' Then she left, stumbling, almost running, forcing her way to the hall.

Fran watched her go and now Mark was tugging at her sleeve. 'Josh says they want a photo of you beside Lucy's masterpiece.'

Linda's arm was around her. 'She's pissed. Ken's probably been jabbering in her ear, though what it's got to do with him I don't know.'

'Then she mustn't drive.' Fran's anxiety was automatic, because she was still reeling from the outburst and now Josh was beckoning and Mark was still waiting. Linda was kissing her. Fran caught at her sleeve. 'Catch her up, give her a lift. She's obviously not coping, she's not herself, hasn't been

235

for a long time.'

Linda was already turning. 'We'll talk. I'll rush. Phone me?' She was gone.

Fran followed Mark remembering to smile at the guests, reaching Josh at the same time as Emily, who wrapped herself around her father. Josh's art students were gathering and a few of her old evening class. She felt tired, so terribly tired, and she was sick of smiling, and she hadn't invited her old friends and neighbours because she had forgotten. Bags? Old? Not coping? Oh, Jane.

The launch ended late. Josh took Emily straight back in his Fiesta so she could be bushy-tailed for school in the morning, while Fran helped Ruth and the gang clear up. It didn't take long and, what was more, they had sold ten prints.

She deposited James and then Gail on their doorsteps, and on her return she diverted to Mike's territory. The hall and sitting-room lights were on. She slowed, stopped. In the sitting room he would be sipping cocoa, sitting back in that comfortable old armchair. The standard lamps would be on. There would be bourbon biscuits. If it had been this time last year Mike's voice would be level, interested, reasonable. He would have listened. It would be quiet, easy.

She reached for the door handle. She could rest her head back against the chair, let the tension drain away. She let her hand drop. What the hell was she thinking of? She drove away instead.

Emily was tucked up and Josh too, but he had cocoa in mugs by the bed. She stripped, slid beneath the duvet. The cocoa was still hot. 'How did you know how to time it?' she whispered.

Josh said, 'I rang Gail, but you took longer than

I thought.' They were both sitting up against pillows, bare shoulder to shoulder.

Emily called, 'I'm trying to sleep and how can I when all I can hear are your voices.'

They drank their cocoa in silence and Fran wanted to talk of the evening, of the day, of other things, difficult things. They lay down, seeking sanctuary in one another's arms. He ran his hands down her back whispering, 'I forgot the chocolate.' The bed creaked. They both tensed. Josh half laughed. 'I need to sort out an oil can.'

They lay together but that was all. He slept. She couldn't.

CHAPTER TWENTY-TWO

Linda had caught up with Jane as she reached her car. 'Come on, my girl, you're not driving anywhere, you're coming in my car.'

Jane had protested, saying she needed the car for the morning. 'Fine,' Linda said, hauling her along to her Peugeot. 'I'll drop you, and then the great and glorious Ken can come back with me and drive it home.'

Jane shook her head. 'Please, he's work to do. Please, I'll drive.'

Linda had the passenger door open and was pushing Jane in. 'Clunk, click, there's a good girl. He won't mind and too much work makes anyone a dull boy. Heavens, it'll only take two ticks.' She slammed the door on Jane and made her way round to the driver's seat, settling herself in, starting the engine.

'Please,' Jane said again. 'I'm sure I can manage to drive.'

Linda drove out of the car park. 'I'm a lawyer, don't argue with me. Imagine how Ken would feel if you were stopped over the limit. Not that you are, you're just tired and you too have bags, my girl. I don't think that outburst was funny, neither do I think it was kind.'

She waited at traffic lights, in silence, for Jane said nothing. Linda tapped the steering wheel. Where had the time gone? Once Jane had been a bright-eyed kid into school dramatics, then a difficult adolescent who had blossomed into a delight, and now she was an uptight aggressive prune. Linda sighed. Life was swings and roundabouts, ups and downs, and they said small children could be the biggest down.

Well, these two Swantons were making a ruddy meal of it, weren't they. Perhaps she'd been lucky not to have children? Perhaps, and anyway, she'd always felt she'd shared Jane. Now she put her hand on the girl's knee, flashing a glance. Jane was staring ahead as though going to her own funeral. The headache had obviously set in and probably the guilt. Linda said gently, 'Take it easy when you can, Janey, and let sleeping dogs lie. Your mother has her own life to lead. She's married, committed, in love. Concentrate on your own little family, eh?'

They were there, at Jane's house. Linda switched off the engine. 'Come on, I'll help you in.'

Jane was grappling for the door handle. 'I can manage, Aunt Linda. Really I can. You go home. You've a busy day tomorrow. I remember what Fridays are like. I'm sorry I made a fool of myself, but I love her, you know, and Mike would have

238

been . . .' She trailed off, opening the door in a rush, shutting it quietly behind her, waiting on the pavement for Linda to drive away.

Linda watched through her rear-view mirror. Mike would have been? Well, yes, and as far as she was concerned, Fran had said loudly and clearly that it really was completely in the past. She watched as Jane walked down her drive, slowing until she saw the door open. Ken was a controlling devil with that key business, though she had to admit it used to drive her mad when Fran never seemed to put hers in the same place twice.

She smiled as she drove round the corner and into her own road. Aunt Linda: gosh it was years since Jane had called her that. Silly girl, she must ease up. Fran was right, she wasn't coping. Perhaps she was heading for some sort of a crack-up, though what more could anyone do? Fran was having the kids as much as any saint could. But that was Fran.

Linda gave up, then wondered whether to talk to Ken about it, but the thumbscrews were on him enough as it was at the moment. He wasn't holding up his end on the Mainwaring case and seemed to be procrastinating. Hadn't turned up at a few meetings, wouldn't relinquish the file because he always seemed to be working on it. Mike had wondered just how competent he was, right from the start, and said there was a lot of gloss, but he wasn't sure about the substance and only time would tell.

Perhaps that time was here. They really should not have bought that house. Fran had tried to dissuade them but oh no, she was kicked into touch over it. Jane had such a tongue on her now, such a bloody tongue, and not for the first time Linda wondered who wore the pants in that particular family. Maybe Ken's bit about the key was his way of putting his foot down? As she turned into her road she was struck by a thought. David + Fran = Jane. Could Jane have more of David's genes than was desirable? Surely not.

She parked the car in the drive, staring at her brightly lit house, deciding that she was utterly sick of coming home to no one, especially when her mind began to take off down dark alleys. She took herself in hand, wiping such ridiculous notions from her database, thinking instead of Mike.

* * *

Ten minutes later she had stood in Mike's sitting room, repeating, 'So sorry to call so late.' She had marched on Mike's house as though he were the enemy and now she was here she couldn't think of anything to say. 'I didn't want to think you were forgotten on this night of nights.'

Mike took her jacket. It was linen and had creased unforgivably. Good God, she must look as though she'd slept in it. She said, 'It creases in the car. I should have taken it off, how silly . . .'

He cut across: 'How about a nightcap, or I could do cocoa? But I've gone off it. I thought it summed me up rather.' He was gesturing to the armchair to the left of the fireplace, the big comfortable one which Fran said supported your neck and let the tension drain from you. Mike picked up his glass from the small table at the side of his armchair and waggled it at her. 'I'm on Scotch,' he said. 'Cocoa equals comfortable. Comfortable is what Jane

240

called me a few weeks ago. It made me feel like a pair of well-worn slippers.'

'Scotch, then. It brings to mind a stiletto image.' How could she be this slick when her stomach was doing its Michael flip?

He laughed. 'Now that's a thought. Would I need a skirt as well? Please sit, while I sort out the drinks.'

The armchair was as comfortable as Fran had said. She called through the arch to the dining end where Mike was clinking glasses on the sideboard, 'I can see you in Gucci, that lovely sort of soft leather, with a dull shine.'

Mike reappeared with a glass in each hand. 'Dull is a word I have struck from my vocabulary. Dull is what I have been, so no wonder she did a bunk.'

Linda kept her smile somehow, held her hand steady as she took the glass he offered and her stomach did its usual post-flip sag. So he was trying to change. To entice Fran back? Damn and bloody sodding blast. But she wasn't angry, not really, it was just that she needed the pretence of rage to keep her steady, to help the Scotch to go down and the appropriate conversation to flow. For Fran had said . . . And love couldn't endure without nurturing. She relaxed. Hers had. That was different.

Mike was at the gramophone, turning over an LP. He rested the arm gently on the vinyl, adjusting the sound. She braced herself for Mahler but it was jazz, Erroll Garner. He brought the sleeve to her, then settled himself. She said, 'I adore Garner, especially playing "She's funny that way".' Her voice sounded fine.

Mike raised his glass. 'Cheers, my dear. I'm glad

241

you like him too. It's years since I played these records. I'd quite forgotten I liked them. Muriel didn't, you see. It gets difficult when the pattern you have woven for yourself is no longer valid. By then you have forgotten who you *really* are.'

She sipped her Scotch. Mike was slightly pissed. He was slurring his words. He said, 'Of course, you do not have this problem. You have always been exactly Linda. No partner. No accommodation.'

She shrugged. 'There's always accommodation. You blend into friends, into the pattern of a life, surely.' She didn't know what she was talking about and even less did she know if he was listening, because his eyes were shut, his foot was tapping and his glass was against his cheek, just where she would like to kiss him, near his eye.

She took another sip. Get a grip. She said, 'I wonder if they've remixed Garner for CD.'

Mike opened lazy eyes, smiling slightly, pointing a heavy finger. 'There you are, I'm playing records when CDs are the thing. Where the hell have I been?'

'Working, living. The usual things.'

He put his unfinished drink down carefully on the table. He pushed himself to his feet, patently steadying himself before navigating a path to the door. 'I'm going to find olives and bugger the digestion.'

Linda watched, fascinated, and heard herself say, just as he found the door handle, 'Olives bring the sun to mind. Sun, sex and . . .' She stopped, appalled.

'Sangria.' He laughed, opening the door. She heard his heels on the tiled floor. He wasn't wearing slippers. The new Mike? Would the new

Mike like *Les Misérables*? Did he still want the tickets? But she couldn't just allow herself to be a fill-in. She took another sip. Of course she damn well could. A little fleeting piece of him could grow into something else.

He returned with the olives, black and pitted, a small bowl each. 'I'm slightly drunk,' he confided in her, leaning down, placing her bowl within reach and returning very, very carefully to his chair. 'Tonight is a sort of watershed. Tonight I wasn't there at the gallery. But then I wasn't at the wedding. Hers, I mean. It's all been a bit of a blur, too much pain to plan. I've thought a lot, though, recently. Ruts are dangerous things, my dear Linda.' He lifted his glass. 'So tonight I'm a little drunk.'

She lifted her glass to him. What the hell was he talking about? Had his pain gone? If so, why? Had ruddy Ken been round with talk of another try at goal? She asked the question, or half of it: 'Has Ken been round?' It sounded too bald, like a bright light in the eyes, a rubber truncheon job.

He dug into his olives, popping one into his delectable mouth, then said, 'Dear Ken and Jane, they're so concerned.'

That was no answer. Erroll Garner played 'I'm in the mood for love'. Well, quite. Mike tapped his foot, holding his glass to his cheek again, his wonderful cheek. His shirt was unbuttoned at the neck. His throat was kissable. His sleeves were rolled up. She'd never seen his arms before. She wanted to see the rest of him.

Erroll Garner played 'I surrender dear'. Oh, yes, absolutely. Across from her Mike had ceased to tap his foot, his eyes had shut. To whom was he

243

surrendering? She couldn't bear to look any longer and shut her eyes, leaning back, drifting, moving in time to 'This can't be love', knowing that it was, always had been and always would be, and that life was a bitch.

Slowly the noise of the gallery left her head, even the echoes of Jane advocating Mike. She was here with him and that was enough. Suddenly it really was enough. She, Mike and Erroll tickling the ivories. On and on he played and the glass grew heavy in her hand. She rested it on the arm of the chair, the wonderfully comfortable chair. Her jaw grew slack, and her mind soaked up the sound and became part of it, and when it ended it didn't matter. She just sat on, the click, click, click of the record gentle, soft, soothing, but then she jerked, came to, opened her eyes, her mouth dry. She'd slept.

She put the glass down on the table. She hadn't touched her olives. Across from her Mike's empty glass was on the table, his eyes were shut, his hands limp. She said softly, 'Mike?'

Should she wake him to attend to the click, click, click? She did nothing for a moment, just watched how he rested against the pillow, half turned towards the fireplace. On the the breast was a picture of the Lake District. Once Fran's painting was to have hung there but it was on the landing at Hamdon Terrace. She dragged her gaze back to him. Tell me if I have a chance, she wanted to ask him. Perhaps from the shades of sleep the truth would come. Don't be a pillock, she told herself. You'll be writing purple poetry next.

Quietly, she crossed to the gramophone, lifted the needle arm from the record, tucked it on to its rest, switched off the turntable. She looked back at him. He was so beautiful and she wasn't bad. On impulse she crept to him, touched his shoulder whispering, 'Thanks for the drink.'

His eyes opened, he caught her hand. 'You're kind to think of coming. So kind. I wasn't asleep, not deeply.'

'Don't get up.'

He did anyway, collecting her jacket and herding her to the front door. It was still quite warm outside. It had been a good month. 'Hope July is as good as June,' she said. Why did the British drag the weather into everything?

He pulled his hand through his hair. 'Are you safe to drive?'

'I left the car at home and anyway I've had a very little to drink.' Why did it always come down to *her* drinking?

His smile was rueful. 'Sorry, I'm a nag. I'm the one who would fail a white line. I should walk you but . . . Have you your mobile? Keep it in your hand. Dial me if you need me.' He touched her arm. Would he kiss her cheek? Usually he did.

He didn't.

She hesitated. '*Les Misérables* is next week. Are you still on?'

He smiled, rocking back on his heels slightly, grabbing hold of the door. 'I look forward to it very much, my dear.'

He shut the door in her face.

CHAPTER TWENTY-THREE

Jane lay quiet and unmoving at Ken's side, thinking of Emily in the bedroom next to her mother. In the morning, on the dot of 7.30, her mother would call, 'Come on, rise and shine, another day awaits your glorious presence.' Or would she? Was that reserved for a proper daughter?

Would toast be popping up from the toaster as Emily entered the kitchen, just as it had done for her? How had her mother managed that? She couldn't quite time it correctly for Ken.

Would her mother have Radio 2 on? Would she switch it to Radio 1 for Emily on the grounds that everyone needed a touch of what they fancied to start the day?

Yes, she did that. She had Wogan on until she heard Ken's tread. Then she flicked on to Radio 4. She'd managed to get that right, so why couldn't she do the toast?

Would they leave the house together as she and her mother had done, her mother going on to Mike's office after she'd dropped her at school? Mike? Jane had called on Mike the evening before this ghastly launch, but he had a glass in his hand. He no longer drank cocoa last thing, but had a nip of something stronger. She had smelt Scotch.

The thought of it made her feel sick, made an awful sort of panic come. She turned carefully on to her side and stared at the digital alarm clock, watching it change, until she had calmed, not understanding herself.

She had meant to say, 'Mother's not looking too

good. Emily's with them, the pressure is building. I think she's going to need you.' She had said none of these things. Just that she had wanted him to know that he wasn't forgotten. He had smiled, asked her to come in. She couldn't, not with that smell. She watched the numbers on the clock face re-form again and again.

Beside her Ken stirred. She froze. Ken drank gin. She did not mind gin, the smell of it. She never drank it herself, not now. It made you careless. You might let something slip. She shouldn't have drunk that glass of wine tonight, and the others, then she would have handled it better. Then he wouldn't have taken a taxi and fetched the car. It was so stupid of her. So stupid. It was a song, now, that kept beating inside her head and she wished it would stop.

If only Mother and Mike . . . Ken would have been so pleased. She'd almost given up hope, but perhaps . . . If Mike was drinking. If Emily was there. Her mother might say she had changed but she could change back.

She watched the numbers. What mother would dump a child? Of course her mother would pity the girl. Would she make her a walnut cake tomorrow? Would she be home in time from the gallery, as she had been from the office, to greet Emily, calling, 'Hey, tell me about it; the good, the bad and the ugly'? Is that what she'd say to a stepdaughter, or was that reserved for her only?

Ken flung his arms wide. One caught her and she winced. She closed her eyes very tight. She waited and waited until he turned on his side. She began to breathe properly again, wanting to be Emily, to sort out her head, do things right. For

247

God's sake, why couldn't she start doing things right?

A car drove past. The sound of its engine was friendly, its lights too, sliding across the curtains on to the ceiling. It made her feel there were people out there. She wasn't alone.

CHAPTER TWENTY-FOUR

The early part of the following week was hectic. O'Reilly's prints sold well, which encouraged other artists to approach Fran, rather than the other way round. Several were keen to hold workshops, a few immediately. The boys had started to decorate the rooms above and classes could begin in two weeks. This afternoon she would draw up a flyer to be sent out to schools.

The Jessie–Fred brigade offered a pottery week in September, but only if Fran could put them up on the sofa. She couldn't wait. Jessie rang again, catching Fran at the Gallery desk rather than at home. The frequent update à la Emily was depressing. From miserable, angry and difficult she had escalated to miserable, very angry and difficult.

'All this will pass.' Jessie said by way of farewell. Fran's raspberry produced a laugh.

Busy though it was, Fran had organised enough of a routine at the gallery by Wednesday to be able to have the children at Hamdon Terrace in the afternoons, for she had decided that it would be far better for them and thus had been reinforced by Linda's mid-week phone call regarding Jane.

'It's probably stating the obvious but that girl of

248

ours is in a pickle. She hasn't got used to this juggling act that's called being a working mother and everything's assuming monstrous proportions. We don't want her cracking up.'

Fran had fiddled with a paperclip at the reception desk of the gallery. 'I know, I've seen it coming so I'm having the kids at the house rather than the gallery, since its very existence seems to wind Jane up. It's far more suitable anyway, and possible now that the main renovations are complete. The boys are fine on their own with the upstairs rooms. Josh is happy with it since it means someone will be there when Em comes home from school. It's the "three birds with one stone" scenario.' Linda laughed along with her. 'I'm going to have them until six, so she doesn't have to rush quite so. It was just that with the pressure of setting up the gallery . . .'

'Hey, don't explain. You're doing more than most as it is, you old fool.'

'Less of the old. I'm slapping cucumber on my bags. I'll keep an eye on her as much as I can, and you too, eh?'

Linda agreed. 'Count on it and we'll do lunch.' But then Fran heard Sally bring something into the office, or was it someone? Either way, Linda assumed her legal voice. 'I'll get back to you on that.'

Fran grinned. 'OK, boss.'

Linda laughed. But Fran had no boss now and it made the sun come out from the cloud when she remembered to think of it.

From the first the new arrangement worked well, with the urgent calls being rerouted to the Terrace. Even Harry seemed more content and lazed on the old duvet Fran positioned in the sitting room, or in his chair, and Emily could not now add latchkey kid to the litany of their faults. When Josh came in at the end of the first day he wondered if they should erect mobiles all over the place.

Fran felt the whole place resembled a mobile. 'Just look at the colours, darling.'

Emily, who had trailed in, her backpack hanging off one shoulder, sniffed and said it was a madhouse, and how was she supposed to settle when the goalposts kept moving.

It was Josh who said, 'We did ask you. You did say it didn't matter to you as you'd be at school most of the time.'

'Most,' Emily said before flouncing up the stairs. 'That still leaves the overlap. I mean, the reality is often worse than the imagined, isn't it.'

Fran had slammed the kettle down more than was necessary and called after her, 'Don't worry, I'll keep the lid on them. Maybe you could do your homework up there until they're gone.'

'Right,' Emily had yelled down the stairs. 'Up in my room, exiled: the outsider.'

Josh raised his eyebrows and poured them both a cup of tea which they took into the garden, walking to the end of the lawn, now devoid of molehills. Fran pointed at the bare patches. 'A wise man said every obstacle is designed to provide a benefit and he was right. We have a happy cat, no puddles . . .'

Josh sipped his tea. His fingernails held the traces of oil paint. On Fran's there was none. He had taken his easel to college, but there was no time for that in her life any more, not for the moment. She must be seen to be alert to Emily once the children had left.

By Thursday Jane seemed calmer. She said, 'Thanks, Mother.'

Josh raised his eyebrows. 'Can we be winning?' he said when she'd taken the children and they'd restored the breakables to their original height.

'You're a good man, Josh Benton.'

'You're a star, Fran Benton.' He held her and they clung together for a precious moment.

'I'm sorry about all this,' she murmured. 'The kids, the chaos.'

'I'm sorry,' he replied. 'The kid, the chaos.'

They laughed. It would be fine and they repeated the mantra they had devised, and one day it might even be easy. Hey, and one day Jane would even be on top of things, and Emily would pass her A levels, and until then they must just take one day at a time.

*   *   *

On Friday, to celebrate the end of the week, she and Lucy mixed up a walnut cake, licked the bowl, and put the tin in the oven while Harry slept in the camping cot in Fran's and Josh's room, his comfort blanket tucked under his chin. Cindy had lent them the cot. It had been Mark's and had never been sold on, since that family could hoard for England.

Fran washed up the bowl and mixer paddles while Lucy coloured another masterpiece for Uncle Josh in the sitting room. She checked the clock; Emily should be back by now, but perhaps she was still sulky and had dropped in to Mark's. She called through to the sitting room, 'Lucy, leave the drawing now, darling. I'm going to take the cake out.'

After a moment Lucy ran in and Fran sat the child on the table, dodging back from the blast of heat as she opened the oven door, pulling out the baking tin. The cake had sunk in the middle, just as it always had with Jane, but that was the preferred texture then and with luck would be now.

Lucy liked the smell and reached forward as Fran tipped it on to the wire tray. Fran put up a hand. 'Just wait, it'll burn you.'

It was only then she noticed the nail varnish on Lucy's hand. A pale, shimmering pink, last seen on Emily's nails just before Josh had ordered its removal for school. For a moment Fran didn't grasp the point, but then she feared she did and scooped up the child, dumping the cake tin in the washing-up bowl, wondering just how much of Josh's carpet was ruined.

In the sitting room, on the floor were the shoes, *the* school shoes which had been given until today to be discarded, or so Weston, the head teacher, had explained on the phone last night. He had also explained that he was phoning because he had not received Josh's acknowledgement of his letter referring to said shoes. It was a letter Josh had not received. Weston had merely sighed. 'Well, that is not unusual, hence the phone call.' Emily had been defiant.

This morning Nikes had been worn and a note sent explaining that new shoes, sensible shoes, would be in existence by Monday. 'Over my dead body,' Emily had grumbled.

'Don't tempt me,' Josh had muttered quietly.

On the right shoe was a great splash of pink. Beside it was the topless nail varnish. There was nothing on the carpet. Fran should be relieved, but as Linda would have said, the timing was crap. Still on Fran's hip, Lucy put her thumb in her mouth and leant into her grandmother. 'Didn't do it. Not really. I wanted to look at it, smell it. It smells different. Then it fell.'

The colouring book was on the coffee table. Beside it was the dried nail varnish brush. Holding the child tighter, Fran picked up the nail varnish. She should have checked, of course. She thought they'd made the room safe. You can relax, she'd told Lucy. There's nothing you can hurt, just don't colour anywhere but on the book. It had been a gamble, but you had to trust a child some time, or that was the path she'd taken with Jane.

Now she said gently, 'Yes, I can see that. Emily must have forgotten to put the top on. It's just a shame that the varnish didn't dry as efficiently as the brush.' She didn't feel gentle. She felt: damn— now what? Another round with Ms Emily Benton?

The back door slammed. Emily called, 'Lucy, I'm back.' Would Ms Emily Benton ever have the courtesy to include Fran in her greeting? Would she, hell. She braced herself, but then softened, for at least Lucy had breached the barrier of Emily's resentment, which had been good for them both.

Fran called, 'We've baked you a cake. Tell me everything; the good, the bad and the ugly.' She held the nail varnish in the palm of her hand and looked at that, not at the door. So Jane's habit of watch-checking was hers: a genetic predilection for avoiding issues? How damned profound and useless that little gem was, and even as she thought this Emily was raging at the doorway: 'What the bloody hell have you done to my shoe?' Fran

253

continued to examine the varnish as she turned it and turned it in her hand, feeling Lucy bury her face in her neck. She snapped, 'Don't use language like that to me.'

'Why not?'

Fran looked up reluctantly and saw Emily, and the tone of voice her grandmother now used caused Lucy to bury her face even deeper. 'What the hell have you done to your face?'

Emily was defiant. 'Don't you use language like that to me. I'll tell my mum.'

'Never mind your mother, what do you think your father will say?'

Fran was aware that she was shaking the varnish at Emily, or was it at the ring through her eyebrow and two in her ear, and her red highlighted hair. Lucy had turned to peep but now Emily was pointing to the shoe. 'You've done that deliberately. You never wanted me to have them.'

Fran was tempted to throw the varnish across the room, but instead replaced it gently, holding Lucy tighter again, patting her as the child huddled into her. Striving to control her voice she said, 'Emily, stop being so difficult and so absurd. Lucy knocked over the nail varnish which shouldn't have been here in the first place.' She stopped, taking a hard look at Emily's face. 'That's not the real problem, though, is it? First it's the wrong shoes, now it's this. Has everything got to be an issue?'

Emily stormed across and recovered the shoe. As she examined it she muttered, 'Oh, so it's my fault, is it, when I'm stuck in that cupboard upstairs with no room to do anything. I was only doing as Dad told me. It was his fault. If he'd let me wear nail varnish this wouldn't have happened. He's an anal retentive, that's what he is.' She was shaking the shoe right under Fran's nose. Lucy flinched.

Fran struggled hard for calm. She snatched the shoe, put it on the table. Emily grabbed for it. Fran blocked her. 'Emily, that is enough. Quite enough.' Somehow her voice was still quiet.

Emily hesitated, then flounced out of the room, yelling, 'There's no peace in this dump with kids always cluttering up the place.'

Fran was trembling, for goodness sake. She held out her hand. How ridiculous. Emily was a child, not a great looming . . . She soothed Lucy who was whimpering, knowing she should also go to Emily, and to Harry who had begun crying. She took Lucy to the kitchen, hearing Emily barging about the bedroom making her point, and then the music started: Bryan Adams, 'Waking tip the neighbours'. How apt. She could have screamed.

She said to Lucy, 'Golly, these bigger girls, they like acting all sorts of parts, don't they? Silly things.'

Lucy smiled uncertainly as Josh flung open the back door, his art bag on his shoulder, pointing upwards. 'How many times have I told her?'

He looked more closely at Fran and Lucy. 'What now?' Could neither of them think of anything else to say?

He flung his bag on the table and started for the stairs. Fran said, 'Leave it for a moment.'

Josh shook his head. 'I've had just about enough. Look at Lucy and you're worn out.' Had she put on even more years?

He pounded up the stairs in his turn and knocked on Emily's door. 'Turn it down. Harry's crying and we have neighbours to consider.'

The music stopped dead. Emily's shout was clear: 'Oh, so it's Harry and the neighbours and their sensibilities we must consider. But what about the cannabis they all smoke? That's all right, is it?'

'Open this door and stop shouting.' Josh's voice was ominously deliberate.

'Well, pardon me for living.'

'Open this door.'

Fran waited for the door to open, for Josh to see the ringscape, crooning to Lucy, hoping that Jane wouldn't come, not yet, while all this was going on. Hoping that Josh did not explode and that there would be no more shouting. She called up, 'Please, Josh, when you see it, don't shout. It'll make things worse with Em and it's bad for the children.'

'See what?'

She walked into the garden, but still she heard the door open, heard the shout. 'What on earth have you done? You silly, stupid girl. Get downstairs at once. I won't have it. I won't have you defacing yourself. You're only thirteen, for God's sake, and what about the school when they've bent over backwards to accommodate you? It's because I said no to the shoes, isn't it. Well, rules are rules. I'm speechless, Emily.'

'You could have fooled me.'

'Down those stairs, now. I've had enough. That rubbish is coming straight out, do you understand. We'll go straight away and get them cut off, or whatever happens.'

Lucy and Fran were standing in the garden. Harry was no longer crying. Was he also caught up in the drama?

But he was in Josh's arms, Josh, who marched his daughter out to Fran, who was scarlet with

256

outrage and who handed an equally scarlet Harry to her. 'Just look,' he said.

Did he think she hadn't seen? Why else had she said don't shout? She said it again: 'Don't shout, Josh. Let's keep it in perspective.'

Beyond him she saw Jane, who was standing, as though rooted to the spot, almost outside Stan's back door, her expression one of outrage, curiosity and could it be satisfaction? How long had she been there? Long enough, obviously.

Fran called, 'Hang on Jane, I'll bring them to you.'

Jane took no notice and instead hurried towards her. 'What's going on? You can hear you all right down the street.'

'Don't exaggerate,' Fran snapped.

'Mother, don't use that tone to me. I knocked, you were all too busy yelling, so I came round the back.'

Fran said, 'Their bag is on the kitchen chair. There's a walnut cake. Take it.' Harry was rubbing his eyes. Emily had stormed down to the bottom of the garden, Josh right behind her.

Fran followed Jane and Lucy into the kitchen. Harry was pressing his face to Fran's. She kissed his cheek, scooped up his sunhat from the hook on the back of the door. His buggy was in the hallway, and she carried it out of the front door and into the boot of the hatchback. She put Harry in his baby seat.

Jane and Lucy were just behind. Lucy clambered on to the back seat and Fran clunk clicked her, whispering, 'I'm sorry we all got so cross. Emily's just a bit unhappy and that makes her naughty sometimes. She doesn't mean it. She likes you

257

really. She likes us all. She's just missing her mummy.'

Jane was putting the bag on to the passenger seat and as Fran straightened she said, 'It won't do, Mother. It isn't good for the children.'

'Shut up, Jane. I don't want to hear another word. Make alternative arrangements if it causes you that much anguish. Believe it or not, I had more than one crisis with you when you were thirteen and I pray I will live long enough to see Lucy do the same to you. Tomorrow your children will see that all is well, that Emily is fine, that the sky hasn't fallen. Now, go home.'

Jane eased into the seat, starting the engine, saying, 'Not tomorrow, actually. Tomorrow is Saturday. Tuesday is when I will bring them next.'

Fran waved to the children and turned her back, walking to Mark's house, not her own. She tapped on the door. Mark opened it quickly. He'd already changed from his uniform into T-shirt and jeans. He was grinning. 'Hey, that was some show.'

Fran laughed and almost meant it. 'Never mind the entertainment value, where did she get it done? A proper place, I hope.'

Mark looked anywhere but at her. 'I can't say.' So perhaps avoiding eye contact wasn't a genetic flaw after all. It was oddly comforting, but only distracted her for a moment. She said, leaning forward, picking at a piece of fluff on his T-shirt, 'You'd better say, my young friend, if you have any sense of self-preservation.'

Mark looked left and right, then over his shoulder, before whispering, 'On the corner of Mallard Street, but don't say I said or she'll have one of her "hates" again. Actually, I told her to wait until the holidays, but there you go. I reckon she wants attention. You know, after everything that has happened.'

'Thank you, Dr Freud.' It was nothing that Fran didn't already know and she took the long way round, dawdling along the back right of way, bracing herself, finding Josh and Emily ranged against one another either side of the kitchen table, silently glaring. As she entered Emily spun round. 'Mum said I could have it done when I got down here. She gave me the money; for my hair too. All the girls at my proper school were going to. It's not as though it's a crime.'

Josh slammed the table with the flat of his hand. 'God Almighty, she had no right. First she dumps . . .'

Fran cut in, 'Josh, we're pleased to death Emily's here and we just need to talk this through.'

She sat at the end of the table, pressing her knee against his. He sat back, shaking his head tiredly, but at last returning the pressure of her touch. Emily picked at the grain of the pine table, saying sullenly, 'Talk what through, my ruined shoes, perhaps?'

Josh looked at Fran. She explained about the nail varnish. Josh said, 'Suddenly the sun has come out. We've stopped the monsters in their tracks. Give Lucy a medal.'

Fran laughed and Emily almost did. At this slight thaw Fran took the opportunity to ask, 'Are you sore? We must keep the pierced areas clean with salt water until we decide how many you can keep.'

Josh turned to her, aghast. 'How many?'

Fran kept the pressure on his knee. 'Yes, I think a little compromise is usually best. While I sort out

259

some salt water why don't you try to catch the head teacher before he disappears for the weekend, and establish the policy on piercing and dyeing. I expect ears are allowed. Eyes probably not. We might have to do something about the highlights.'

Reluctantly Emily touched her hair. 'It's only mousse. A girl at school did it.' Her voice was unsure and small suddenly: 'I'll wash it.'

Josh checked his watch. 'Weston should still be there.' His chair scraped as he almost leapt up. He used the phone in the sitting room while Fran made up a saline solution and found cotton wool in the First Aid box under the sink. As she looked up she saw Emily touching her eyebrow and wincing, her eyes filling with tears. Fran said gently, passing a saline swab, 'You do the eyebrow, I'll do the ears. If that's all right?'

It was.

'You need to keep turning the rings,' Fran ventured as she swabbed gently. 'But I expect he told you that.'

'Of course.' The cockiness was back. Well, it would be, but she'd never been allowed this close to the child since she'd come to live with them. Hope sprang eternal . . .

CHAPTER TWENTY-FIVE

Lucy banged on the back door again. 'Mummy, I want to come in. I don't want to be out here alone.'

Jane was on her way when Ken appeared. 'For heaven's sake, I'm trying to work. What the hell's the matter with the child?' He ripped the door from her grasp and glared down at his daughter. 'You've got a sandpit, so play in it.'

Lucy shrank back a pace. Jane slipped past him, catching up her daughter, holding her very tightly, saying, 'She's unsettled, there was a sort of row at Mum's. She doesn't like rows. They frighten her, they frighten me . . .' She trailed off, glad they were here on the path, that Mike overlooked their garden.

Ken stood, blocking the entrance to the kitchen, but his knuckles were white where he gripped the door. He had big hands. He didn't know his own strength, how powerful his fingers were when they gripped like that. He really didn't.

He shook his head, more in sorrow than in anger. Where had she read that? 'Look, Jane, darling. I really have to work.' He looked beyond her, raising his hand. 'Morning Mike.'

She turned, relieved. Mike had opened his bedroom window. He was wearing what looked like overalls, and he waved back with a paintbrush. Well, that was a positive sign. Mother had never liked the decor, because it was his wife's.

Ken's hoarse whisper was heavy with sarcasm, though he kept his hearty smile. 'Can I assume I have at least an iota of your attention, Jane, because if I don't sort out this Mainwaring thing I doubt we'll have a roof over our heads come next week. For the last time, keep the kids quiet.'

It was what he seemed to be saying every week now, but with Mike up there she was able to find a coherent thought for once. 'Is it rumbling on?'

His knuckles were still white, his face still set in that ghastly sort of hearty rictus smile. 'The bastard's saying I should have lodged some papers

261

at court, when of course I never received the necessary details from him in the first place. Difficult to check when a file's gone astray. I just can't think where it's gone and my damned secretary swears she hasn't misfiled it. I bet she bloody has. Either way, the customer's always right. Or so he'll say. So keep your mouth shut about it. I don't want him knowing before he has to.' He jutted with his chin towards Mike. 'Why don't you take the damn kids for a walk, do something useful for a change?'

She didn't want to squeeze past him. 'Where's your little bucket?' she asked Lucy who was gripping her as though she'd never let go. She repeated, gently this time, 'Let's tidy up the sandpit, then take Harry for a walk and wave again to Uncle Mike.'

She carried her child gingerly, her warm, soft child, back to the sandpit. Together they sat on the edge and while Lucy found all the moulds and fitted them into the lid of the bucket she let the sand trickle through her fingers. She liked to do this. To think of herself as a tiny grain, in among millions and millions of others, and it sometimes made her feel better, made her feel that she was of no consequence, that life would go on, no matter what. That there was a huge scheme in which she played just a tiny part.

Around her the birds were twittering and somewhere someone was mowing a lawn with what sounded like a hover mower. It was normal, it was comforting. In that garden there would be the smell of grass cuttings. Her mother had cut her small lawn with a hand mower, because she had a thing about noise. More than that, she'd liked the rhythmic backwards and forwards sound. It was patient and traditional somehow.

Jane would help her rake up the cuttings and the smell would be with her until bedtime. She wanted to go along to that garden where the hover mower was working. She wanted to dip her hands into the cuttings and hold them to her face and breathe in the past.

She looked up at the sky, at the scudding clouds. Was she going mad as Ken said? She thought she might be because her mind was a jumble and words came out too sharp, words that she didn't mean cut into people. But they mustn't get too close, that was the thing. No one must get too close or she might tell and that wouldn't be fair, because this wasn't the real Ken. But the trouble was she really, really wanted someone near, someone just to be there, within call. Someone who loved her, that was all. She bit her knuckle.

'Mummy?' Lucy was leaning against her knee, the completed bucket in one hand, the spade in the other.

Jane bit harder and harder until her head had calmed, until the waves of stupidity had settled, until she could dust off her child's hands, then her bare feet, tweaking all the little piggies, making Lucy laugh, making her forget the shouting at her mother's. Now the waves were starting again and how dare her mother make things worse? How dare they row in front of her child and make her restless, make her call out at eight and upset her father who hadn't meant . . .

How dare she get caught up in such a family: one whose abandoned daughter seemed to take all the space? How dare she desert her?

263

She lifted Lucy carefully and the pain cleared the waves, but Ken hadn't realised she was so close to the chest of drawers, that was all. He was only half awake, driven to distraction by Lucy's call, and just didn't know his own strength.

She put her fingers to her lips and made for the house. The back door was shut. She flashed a look backwards. Mike had gone. 'Let's play mice. We'll creep upstairs and get Harry and take him round the block, maybe even to the see-saw.'

Lucy nodded, her own finger to her lips.

The park was busy and Lucy tried the see-saw, but there was no one on the other end so she wanted to move on to the swings. They had to queue. It was hot. Marienne was there, with little Yvonne who attended Maisie's three days a week. She was slapping Factor 15 on her arms and on Yvonne's, and offered it to Jane, who had forgotten her child's well-being. Just forgotten. She was so stupid. She rubbed it on Harry, then Lucy.

Marienne nudged her. She didn't wince. She knew she must not do that. Marienne said, 'Go on, roll your sleeves up, get a tan. Live a little.'

Jane screwed the top back on the tube and returned it. 'We'll try the slide, Lucy.' That was the trouble with people, they asked too many questions, they assumed too much. They didn't leave you in peace. Her head was almost spinning. She grasped the handle of the pushchair. There, you see, her knuckles were white. She hadn't realised she was gripping so hard. It was so easily done.

Lucy clambered up the ladder, her little dungarees spotless, the red and white stripes almost too bright. She waved to Jane, who smiled and directed Harry's gaze. Harry's movements were even more co-ordinated than last week. She found his teething ring which had slipped from his lap to become wedged between his thigh and the side of the pushchair.

'Watch me, Mummy,' Lucy called.

She watched her daughter whoosh down the slide, but the home straight was too long and Lucy slid, slid, slid off. She lay. Oh, God. I should have been there. Stupid woman, I should have been there.

She ran with the pushchair, but then Lucy scrambled to her feet. 'Again, Mummy.' Beneath Jane the ground was squashy rubber. Lucy was running full tilt. Jane caught her and whirled her through the air. It hurt, but her daughter was all right. It hurt but she would heal. It would pass. All this would pass if she could only get on top of things.

Panting, she lowered Lucy to the ground. 'Go on, then. Have another go, but Harry and I will stay here on guard.' Lucy ran, blending in with the other children, taking her turn nicely. But then an older boy barged in front, yelling 'Make way for Batman'. Lucy stopped dead before dropping back and letting the other children take her place. She stood with her thumb in her mouth, just watching.

Then she rushed at him as he was putting his foot on the ladder. She rushed and grabbed him. 'Naughty boy,' she shouted. 'Naughty boy.' She shook him. A little girl was knocked and fell, and began to cry, but her mother was already running from the bench where she'd been sitting.

Jane ran too, scooping Lucy out of the mêlée. 'You should sort out your girl,' screeched the

265

mother of the fallen child.

Lucy was crying now, sobbing into her mother's neck, 'Naughty boy, naughty boy.'

'You mustn't do that,' Jane said frantically, patting her shoulder, rushing back to Harry.

'He shouted, Mummy. He shouted.'

She released the brake of the pushchair and walked away quickly. Lucy was too heavy. She pressed against her ribs. Her head was still spinning. She couldn't think. The pushchair was too heavy, the wheels wouldn't work properly on the grass. Why didn't they keep it cut? It was almost July, for heaven's sake, they paid enough rates. But they weren't called rates, were they? God, she was so stupid. She stopped, let Lucy slide to the ground. 'Carry me, carry me.'

'I can't carry you, you silly girl.' She leant over the pushchair, feeling sick. The sweat was pouring down her back.

Lucy banged her leg. 'Mummy, Mummy.'

Lucy must stop it. She must stop hurting her. She must stop shouting. She felt sick. Very sick. 'Mummy, Mummy.'

The grass was very green, very cool. She sat down, her head in her hands. It was dark in here. Nice. Dark. But not cool. Not quiet because Lucy was still saying, 'Mummy. Mummy?' If she didn't stop she'd scream.

'Jane, my dear. Are you quite well?'

Lucy fell silent. The voice made the spinning stop. Jane breathed down the nausea, the clammy, awful panic. She found a smile and looked up. 'Mrs Thomas, how nice. Yes, I'm fine. Just playing a game with Lucy.'

She scrambled to her feet, dusting off her skirt.

Mrs Thomas, who had the other side of Fran's semi, whom Fran had recently christened 'Thomas the Teasmaid', was handing her Harry's rattle. 'You dropped it when you ran towards the slide. What a to-do that was. It'll need a wash. I know they say poop scoops must be used, but it's on the ground before it's popped into one of those bags, isn't it. I saw your little Lucy. It's not right, you know, pushing and shoving like that. Where has she learnt that?'

Jane took the rattle, propping it on the hood of the pushchair. 'From children like that boy.' Yes, that was it, because Lucy had only seen her daddy just once, last night, and then she had been almost asleep.

Mrs Thomas had planted her legs as though she was going to block her way for ever. 'Well, of course that's so. But his mother works too, you see. Farms him out and what do you get? Pushing and shoving. If your mother were still living in the street I'd tell her to her face and she'd tell you. I don't mean to intrude, but advice from those who have brought up three children can't be a bad thing. Or that's what I used to tell your mother.'

The spinning was back. She'd forgotten Mrs Thomas and her tongue, how she'd only allow her to retrieve her ball once a day. After that it went in the box until the following morning. Her mother had said that some people had their funny little ways and underneath there must be some gold, if anyone cared to dig for it. Her mother was too easy to please.

Lucy was sitting on the grass, picking daisies. There wouldn't be daisies if the grass had been cut. There would be cuttings, the soft rich smell, the . . .

Mrs Thomas chided, 'I wouldn't let her do that. Remember the dogs.'

Lucy looked up at the woman and reached for Jane's hand. Mrs Thomas sniffed. 'Insecure. Working mothers make children insecure. Your mother's against you working, I know that much. She had to, you don't. What's that husband of yours thinking of.'

The spinning grew worse. Jane said, 'My mother's not in a position to cast stones, or give advice any more than . . .'

Mrs Thomas said, leaning forward, 'I know, dear. A shock to us all. But I repeat, I would have thought that with a husband at Gilbert and Gilbert you could afford to stay at home. Just take my advice, don't let this get any worse.' She pointed to Lucy who was clutching Jane's leg and grizzling. Jane wanted to shake the child off, to tell her to smile, for heaven's sake, or this silly woman was going to make her go mad.

Harry started to cry. Jane pulled Lucy away from her leg. Lucy's grizzles became tears. Mrs Thomas said, 'There you are, you see. Working mothers equal miserable children.'

Lucy was swinging on her hand, her cries louder. Jane shouted, 'Mrs Thomas, I wasn't miserable when Mother worked and my daughter is perfectly fine. She's just upset. There was a row, that's all, when Emily turned up with rings through her ears, her eyebrows and goodness knows where else, shouting about drugs . . .' Jane stopped. God, what had she said? She continued, 'Lucy doesn't like rows.'

Mrs Thomas was staring at her. 'Drugs? Oh, my word.'

Jane shook her head. 'No, not drugs. I don't know why I said that. It was just that I get confused. You know how these teenagers rebel.' But Emily had said that, so why should she lie? Why the hell should she lie for people who heedlessly upset a small child, leading to so much else?

Mrs Thomas's face was grim, her shoulders hunched. 'Oh, well, I can't say I'm surprised, I was rather waiting for it. Josh Benton's been cautioned for possession and the police thought they could get that Stan for dealing, and him with a child. Old Fred knows all about that little lot, or so he told me at the bowls. He was a detective sergeant, you know, or you would if you played bowls. He's a bit senile, I reckon, because he rambles and you can't get a word in edgeways, but if you ever need anything doing, ask him. He's still got his contacts. Now, should I tell your mother, you know, about Josh? That's been my dilemma, but from what you say she knows so I shan't bother. Though it's all a bit of a worry now Emily's there. I'm just glad your mother has your children at the gallery. But that's not perfect, is it, not by a long . . .'

Lucy was dragging at Jane's hand. 'Mummy, I'm hungry.'

Mrs Thomas smiled down at her. 'Then you shall have an ice cream.' She began to dig in her string bag for her purse.

Jane shook her head. 'Please, I wouldn't dream of it. I'll take her home instead. We can find a Penguin in the cupboard.' Harry was still crying. 'And a bottle for Harry.'

Mrs Thomas smiled as though with satisfaction, opening her hands to the sky. 'There you are, you see. Bottle-fed. I'm not surprised, it's the bonding, you see. It goes out of the window. They need their mother's milk, just as they need . . .'

Shut up, you old hag. Just shut the fuck up. For a moment Jane's head cleared with the horror of her words. Had she said them aloud? But Mrs Thomas was still smiling. 'I've got to go,' Jane muttered, letting Lucy lead her away.

Mrs Thomas called after her, 'You should always lead them, my dear. Not the other way round. It's the road to ruin, you mark my words.'

Shut up, Jane repeated silently, flinching as she put her weight behind the pushchair, trying to steer through the spinning.

CHAPTER TWENTY-SIX

Linda and Mike clutched their hard-won interval gins in the Bristol Hippodrome bar, leaning up against the wall they'd been backed into, Mike in his new moleskins and shiny Gucci-type shoes. 'I should have placed an order before the show.' Mike grimaced. 'I'm just not with it at all.'

'We managed in the end, so don't worry,' Linda reassured him. 'Anyway, what do you think? Would you rather be listening to Mahler?'

'Emphatically not.' Mike protected his drink from a hand-waving youth who was waxing lyrical to his girlfriend. 'I mean, the power of the voices, the music, the sets.'

'It does get to you, doesn't it?' shouted Linda over the bell which was already ringing to summon them back to their seats. Mike looked around in disbelief. 'I've cocked it up a bit, haven't I, and I so wanted to make amends for the Scotch débâcle.'

Linda downed her gin in one, then laughed. 'Hey, don't bring it up again. I think the chocolates on Monday were *mea culpa* enough and unnecessary anyway. Have you any idea how that box of Belgian delights got in the way of Sally's and Frances's Ryvita chomping? What were they to think?'

Why did she say that? She followed Mike as he squeezed his way through the harassed 'quick let's drink up' crowd. At last they were at the bar and he was wedging their glasses into a space, before leading the way to the Gods. She felt like a child again, trotting along in the wake of her father.

They settled themselves on to the benches which were as hard as charity and miles above the stage, and she should have realised that when she booked but they were all that were available. She apologised again as they wriggled but Mike reached for her hand and squeezed. 'No more of that. I'm enjoying this, it makes me feel young again. It's all I could afford when I was a student. Not that I think it's all you can afford. I mean, I know it isn't.' He stopped, drew a breath. 'Oh, shit.'

She laughed. She'd never heard him like this before, never seen him blush. Never felt him squeeze her hand. The curtain rose. Now he would release her, but he didn't, or not until the barricades were strewn with dead young men. Then he needed his hand to grope for his handkerchief in unison with the rest of the auditorium and again when Valjean sang 'Bring him home'. As the final curtain fell they sprang to their feet and he stamped along with the rest of the audience and hollered, turning to her, his face alight: 'Wow.' That was all. It was enough.

They didn't try to find a post-show bar afterwards, but joined the throng making for the multi-storey car park. They stopped at the kerb, looking right and left, and right again. 'Like good girls and boys,' she said. Why didn't she shut up?

They began to cross. He took her hand. Was she that infirm, or . . . ?

He kept hold of it once they had reached safety. He kept hold of it as they climbed the steps. Which floor was it? The highest she now wished. It wasn't. He released her when they spotted his car, unlocking it from a distance of four feet, holding her door open as she arranged herself. She felt absurd. She felt his hand, his fingers on her skin still. She *was* absurd.

They drove back with Classic FM playing and it took just over an hour, as it always did, but it seemed only five minutes. Why did time fly when you were enjoying yourself? He pulled up outside her house. The light was still on. He hurried round to open her door, but she, unused to such things, had already decamped. Should she ask him in for coffee? Is that what one did when you actually wanted to strip every vestige of clothing from someone and eat them as though they were a Cornetto?

He came to her. 'Let me just see you in and you can check around, but I dare say your radio has kept all predators at bay.' His laugh was gentle.

Was he mocking? She led the way, trying to find her key in her handbag, feeling like Fran. So, don't bring her into it. She continued to grope in the light of the porch, finding it at last. He stood by the photographs as before while she pounded up the stairs, checking the rooms as he suggested. She returned downstairs. He was still looking at damned photographs. When he'd gone she'd take them down and replace them with something else, something that evoked nothing at all.

She checked the sitting room and kitchen, and made her way back to him. He said, 'I've had a wonderful evening, Linda. Thank you so much.' It was she who looked at the photographs now, quickly. Then away. He said, 'It was a bit of a tear jerker. Just imagine all those grown men snivelling. I needed that. Men don't, you know.'

Damn. They were back to Fran. 'Perhaps they should, more often,' she said, not knowing what the hell she really meant.

He reached out his hand. Did he want to shake? Well, what could she expect after numb bums in the Gods? Would choice seats have meant tongues? Why didn't she shut up? She shook his hand. He looked surprised, then lifted it to his mouth, kissing it, pulling her to him, enfolding her in his arms, kissing her and she discovered that tongues came with cheap seats too. Tongues that reached parts physiologically impossible. He released her. Her legs nearly let her down. 'Thank you, dear Linda.'

His dear, dear face was so close. His eyes so grey, his lashes so long.

She steadied herself on the radiator beneath the photographs. 'Just sorry that the seats were a little . . .' His finger was on her mouth. She wanted to lick it.

'Thank you for everything,' he said. That's everything? she wanted to shout. A kiss is everything? There's a body here, a heart, a whole

273

lifetime of waiting. He stepped on to the porch and walked back to his car.

The moths were fluttering around the light. There were cobwebs. She must do something about them. She watched until he drove away, but before he did he blew a kiss. She hugged it and every second of the evening to her all night, but dwelling in an unseemly fashion on the kiss, the real kiss, the one that had delivered the promise of him, or so she prayed, hoped, longed for.

CHAPTER TWENTY-SEVEN

The small group standing on the doorstep were very polite. Somehow you wouldn't have guessed that two were policemen and one a social worker. DC Brown was almost apologetic as he informed Fran that they'd had a couple of complaints about drug use at this address. 'May we come in?'

Josh put an unsteady hand on her shoulder. 'Drug use here? What complaints? Who? Are you insane?'

DC Brown looked ridiculously young, but the man standing to one side did not. He looked tougher, harder. Quite right too, Fran thought with the rational part of her mind, the part which hadn't been plunged into shocked numbness. Quite right if he was trying to sort out misuse, but here? Stan smoked, but only outside and never in front of the children.

It was the older man who stepped into the frame now, showing them his ID. 'We're not at liberty to give you names, sir. May we come in? We don't want a seminar on the doorstep for everyone to hear, especially when you have a thirteen-year-old girl under your roof.' The social worker was now introduced. Fran forgot the name as soon as she heard it, but the woman had a nice face. Behind, in the street, a car passed. The sunlight caught the wing mirror.

Fran felt Josh's hand tighten. Especially when you have a thirteen-year-old. Especially . . . She stepped back. They knew there was a thirteen-year-old, a minor at risk, in her care? 'Do come in.' Her voice was unsteady. Josh led the way into the kitchen, looking up at the ceiling. 'My daughter is upstairs, getting ready to "do" the shops. Perhaps you want to check her purse, make sure she's not embarking on a buying trip this very minute, or maybe we're sending her out dealing?'

'Josh,' Fran said quietly, 'that's not necessary.' Her voice was still unsteady. Or perhaps she was wrong and it was necessary? Would they search Emily's bag? What would they find? She went hot, then cold, standing aside as they passed her, no one quite meeting her eyes. So gaze evasion was normal. Surely she must have noticed that long before she reached the ripe old age she now was? Shut up.

Josh led the way into the kitchen. She wanted to stay out here, by the front door, just for a moment, to catch up. Every day it was something. Every day and it was all getting too much.

Josh called, 'Come in, darling, please.'

Somehow she did. The social worker was sitting at the table, the policemen stood, blocking the light from the window. Mrs Jennings, that was the name. Mrs Jennings smiled slightly. She looked almost bored. How could anyone be bored when they had come into her house to ask about drugs? No, his house, the man she loved, the man with whom she had run away.

'Fran, are you all right?' Josh tossed his toast into the flip-top bin, releasing the stale smell of last night's stubs, smoked by Stan and Josh when the Terrace had been round to view the pierced, newly hair-washed wanton. They had applauded the two in her ear and given a no-no to the eyebrow job. It reinforced the headmaster's ruling. That's where they'd been going today, to Mallard Street for the great removal, because Emily would not allow Fran to do the job. Perhaps she thought she would be able to flog the ring back. A no-no, Fran knew, but nonetheless they were going, an accommodation had been reached, a basis for going forward, or so she had thought.

DS Davies glanced at the bin. She felt her shoulders tighten. Had Stan smoked reefers here after all? Josh? But no, never here. Two calls? Complaining about *her*. How had she failed this badly?

Above, they heard the creaking of Emily's floorboards, the rasping of her drawers. The clothes would be coming out, decided against, tossed on the bed or the floor. Another 'tidy-up' battle in the making and soon the phone would ring. Soon it would be time for Catherine's weekly call, or so it had become. Soon, while the police and a social worker . . .

Josh's raised voice brought her back. 'But whoever would say something like that? We have nothing to hide.'

'Then that's fine, isn't it, sir?' DS Davies had

276

moved closer to the bin.

Fran stirred herself at last. Josh was shrugging helplessly, as confused and panic-stricken as she. Emily? Surely not. Josh would know, he could recognise it a mile off. But she'd been so . . . 'Tea?' she said, moving to the kettle. It sounded pathetic.

Emily called down, 'Who's that? When are we going?'

'The police,' Josh replied almost inaudibly. He repeated it, more clearly this time, adding, 'Emily, come down a minute, please.'

'Oh, p-l-e-a-s-e,' Emily called back. 'Do you think I'll fall for that? I'm going to have the damned ring out, so why can't we stop the messing about?'

'Why don't you ask her to join us, sir?' DS Davies suggested. Only it wasn't a suggestion. The social worker nodded. Fran thought of St Ives, the light, the love, the peace. It would come back. The peace. The love was rock-solid. It must be to endure all this.

'Just come down,' Josh yelled. 'Now.' His voice was too fierce, too frightened.

She came, flipping her hair over to one side of her head, astonished. Fran's mind moved on. Or was she? Two calls? The result a possible removal to mother in the States after all? Fran wiped the draining board. There were far too many of them in this small room and now the cat clattered in through the cat flap Josh had installed. It wound itself around her legs. Breakfast, please.

The police sat down at the table, introducing themselves, introducing the problem, pulling out a chair for Emily. 'I don't know what you're talking about.'

'Do you know a Stan Manning?'

'Of course I do, he's Dad's friend. He was here last night.'

'Do you know a Sandy Wentworth.'

Emily examined her nails. 'Yes, he gave me a lift home yesterday. I met him after . . .' She touched her earrings. DS Davies already knew this, Fran realised. Josh flushed and snatched a look at Fran. Sandy Wentworth was not a stranger, she realised. The cat still wound around her legs.

'Where did you meet Sandy Wentworth, Emily?' It was the social worker. She had freckles, pale skin and red hair. Her smile was gentle. She still looked nice, and bored. Maybe she'd seen this a million times but Fran had not. Not this. Not concern about a child in her care. Women protected children. She had tried, always she had tried, even after he died. She shook her head, trying to clear it.

'I told you, after I'd had my rings put in.' She was touching them.

'Don't, they'll go septic,' Fran said automatically.

Mrs Jennings smiled understandingly at Fran, then repeated, 'Where did you meet him,' adding, 'originally?'

'At my dad's party last year.'

'This Sandy, he didn't give you anything then, or yesterday? Didn't suggest you might like to try anything?'

Emily shook her head. 'I know he likes a bit of this and that, but I don't and I won't. I'm not daft.' DC Brown was staring at her earrings and her eyebrow.

Did Emily look as though she liked a bit of this and that? Did she? Should a stepmother have known? Suddenly Emily tipped up her bag, all over the table. 'Look at this lot if you don't believe me and search my room, and I know Dad doesn't, but I don't know about her. Or rather, perhaps I do. You should go through her stuff and don't forget the bathroom cabinet; her side, mind you.'

Fran heard the words, she almost saw them drop from the child's mouth, but for a moment she couldn't place them into a pattern that made sense. Josh was saying something, she felt his arm round her, the kettle beneath her hand, the cat. Emily was glaring. Josh ended: ' . . . so, you see, we're having a settling-down period. It's not easy. But please, search wherever you like, even us.'

Now the phone was ringing. The damn phone. The damn cat. Why didn't they all leave her be? The police nodded as Emily said, 'It's my *real* mum, from America.' She slouched from the kitchen into the sitting room.

The policemen looked questioningly at Josh. 'Would you like to lead on, sir.'

As they left the social worker was studying Fran. 'How about that cup of tea?' Mrs Jennings said. As Fran put tea bags into mugs and waited for the kettle to boil she heard them above, the creaking of the floorboards, the rasping of the drawers.

Oh, so some had been pushed back in. Yes, she thought they were making a little progress. She pushed herself away from the sink, moving into the hall, away from the creaks. Josh was on the small landing, looking down at her blankly, as though in shock. She leaned against the wall. Emily laughed on the phone. 'Yes, I did and you were right, it's caused a bit of a tizz.'

The police were in the bathroom now, lifting the cistern lid, from the sounds of it.

279

A tizz? Fran dragged her fingers through her hair. 'Mum, you really should come and get me. You were right, it's not a safe place to be.'

The kettle must have boiled because Mrs Jennings was pouring water into her mug. She waved the kettle at Fran from the kitchen doorway. Fran shook her head. 'Come in and sit down,' Mrs Jennings suggested, although it wasn't a suggestion, not really.

Fran looked at Josh, who was standing helplessly halfway down the stairs. The police entered their bedroom now.

Emily had lowered her voice. Fran wanted to hear every word, because anger was taking over, a real, deep, bubbling rage, for this child did not take drugs she was sure, but she could lift a phone, she could make complaints, cause a bit of a tizz. She took a step forward, but now Emily came to the doorway. 'Dad, Mum wants to talk to you.'

'Not now, Em.' Josh was craning his head to see what the police were doing.

'Yes, now, she says. She wants to talk to you about the situation you've placed me in.' Emily stood with her arms crossed, a satisfied smile all over her face, a smile Fran itched to remove. She was glad now that the eyebrow looked red and sore, that the damn thing would hurt to remove. She watched Josh tear himself away and come, leaden-footed, down the stairs. He grabbed her hand and pulled her to the phone with him, saying into her hair, 'I can't take much more of this.'

He couldn't?

He picked up the receiver, then saw Emily standing in the doorway. 'Just go into the kitchen and why did you have to . . .?' He clamped his mouth shut.

Open your big gob, Fran wanted to finish for him. Emily flounced into the kitchen. No doubt Mrs Jennings would make tea for her. Tea and sympathy. Whatever would the child say?

'Yes, Catherine?' Josh said, holding the receiver so that Fran could hear.

There was the usual transatlantic time lag, then a shrill Catherine shouted, 'How dare you jeopardise our child, when you have a duty of care. Not content with depriving her of her mother, you have her in a house which is raided by the police, you stuff her into a totally tiny room, you inundate her with screaming toddlers, you . . .'

Josh cut in: 'It's the best we can do.'

'What is, having a raid?'

Josh yelled, 'No, the rest. The raid's a mistake. And it's not a raid, it's a misunderstanding. I know Emily doesn't take anything; I can tell.' Outside it was clouding over.

'So that leaves the adults. I remember how you used to . . .'

'That was then. We were young. I am not any more.'

'Nonetheless you are *in loco parentis* and what about *her.* I wouldn't be surprised . . .'

'Why don't you shut up, Catherine.'

The floorboards were still creaking above them. The murmur of voices came from the kitchen.

Josh tightened his hold on Fran, kissing her forehead, but the police were in the doorway. Fran gestured them in, watched them lift and look, lift and look, much as Lucy had done last week. But not like her, really. She pulled free, moving into the hall, watching Mrs Jennings watching Emily as she

281

touched her eyebrow and then her ear. Please, God, let Catherine want her back. At least for a while. Please let Jane settle and take the children to Maisie's, just for a bit so she and Josh could catch their breath.

Emily was brushing back her hair and there were dark shadows under her eyes. Was it drugs? Or just a kid desperate to go to her mother? Please want her back for her sake, if not ours. One of the police dropped a book. Fran turned. They were flicking through the pages, shaking the book by the spine. Josh was saying grimly into the receiver, 'We've been through this and I know it's bigger, but it's Fran's.'

The police were gesturing to the kitchen now. Fran followed them. 'Come on, Em, let's wait in the garden.' She opened the back door and led the way. She examined the roses for black fly as there were no more molehills to kick while Emily flipped her hair over her head again and flung herself down on the garden bench.

Then the police were in the garden. DC Brown investigated the shed while DS Davies plodded down to the bottom. Emily said, 'He's looking for fairies, but they're next door.'

Fran sat down opposite, glad that the French windows were closed and she couldn't hear the phone conversation, because Josh was waving his hand, stabbing a finger. She said gently, 'Don't be unkind about Tom and Edward, and I don't take drugs. You know I don't. I think I know you don't. Have you any idea who could be responsible for this?'

Emily looked at her and flushed uncomfortably, but then smirked. 'But I don't know anything, dear

Fran, about you. I can only vouch for my father and myself.' She stood up, watching the police, then spun round. 'Hang on, what do you mean, do I know who's responsible?' Realisation was dawning. 'Oh, yes, Fran, that's neat. You think I phoned. You really think that?' She was scarlet, outraged. 'It's more likely to be that stuck-up snot of a daughter of yours, so go and crap all over her, why don't you, and what's more you can keep your stupid salt water wipes.'

She tore inside and Fran could hear her pounding up the stairs. Even out here, she could hear. Oh, well done, dear. Well done. Why on earth did you say anything? She saw Mrs Jennings watching through the kitchen window.

Fran put her elbows on the table and covered her eyes. When she was a child this had made her feel invisible. Later, much later, she had made herself invisible, acquiescent, and now she realised that she had increasingly forgotten all about that, which was a mistake, a terrible mistake. She heard a cough. It was DS Davies with Mrs Jennings.

She stood up. He said, 'We have to follow these things up, or we try to, if we have the time. Especially if they're from someone it's hard to ignore. Our superintendent feels strongly about this sort of thing. Thank you for your co-operation and best if Emily doesn't spend too much time with people like Wentworth. He's the real problem.'

Mrs Jennings held out her hand. Fran shook it. The woman's smile was patient. 'We do really follow these things up, especially if it's two separate sources.'

'Who?'

'Oh, I shouldn't worry about that. Hang in there.

283

You're doing fine. I'm pretty sure she's on the straight and narrow.'

Fran led them through the house rather than along the back past Stan's. She showed them to the front gate, holding out her hand. She supposed she should feel relieved, but she did not. She just felt exhausted, embarrassed, devastated. DS Davies shook it. Perhaps it would look to the neighbours as though they had come to give security advice. He said, 'I've got one of those,' raising his eyebrows towards the house. 'He's fifteen. It's a minefield. Although, come to think of it, I'd rather cross one of those than go through the last year again.'

Fran's smile became real. She waited for them to draw away, then returned to the house, looking neither to left nor right, feeling as though the eyes of the world were on her.

Josh was sitting by the phone, his head back, his eyes shut, taking deep breaths. Catherine must be responsible for vastly improved lung capacity in everyone who was unfortunate enough to know her. Fran touched his knee. 'Still with us?' she asked softly.

Josh half opened his eyes and tried a smile. 'Just about and so is Emily.'

Fran tried not to show her disappointment.

Josh had shut his eyes again and now rubbed them with the back of his hand. 'What a start to the day.'

Quite.

'The thing is,' he whispered, leaning forward now and checking the open doorway. 'The thing is, Fran, she's pregnant and she wants me to break the news. Now just how do I do that in a way that doesn't make it seem as though Em's been turned out of the nest in order for another to take her place?'

'Oh, dear,' said Fran, because she must try to be careful. She must start all over again being careful.

*   *   *

That night, as they lay in their bed, which still squeaked in spite of liberal oiling, Fran said, stroking his arm, 'I could see if the tenants can be persuaded to move out of Eastbourne Avenue, then we can let this.'

He hugged her. 'No, it's yours. You were banking on the income until the gallery's properly viable and there's Jane. What would she think if we all moved in?'

The feel of his naked body against hers brought her to life for a moment and as she ran her hands down his back she said, 'You've cancelled the maintenance payments, haven't you, and there's the slack now you're free of school fees? All that will make up the shortfall. It would show Emily that we take our role seriously.'

His hug tightened even more. 'You really are the tops.'

She wasn't. Because she still thought his daughter had phoned the police and probably arranged for a second call, and the unforgivable part was that she had let the child know. A child who had been excluded by her mother, whom she was fighting a losing battle to like. Josh's child, who had gone to such terrible lengths to gain attention, to return to her mother, to hurt the woman who somehow wasn't giving her what she needed, and Fran had had enough of pain.

285

He was kissing her mouth. She wanted him. She couldn't have him because the bed squeaked. He said, 'This isn't what I'd planned.'

She said, 'We didn't plan.'

They rolled over on to their backs. She stared at the ceiling. The only answer was to move but she'd be returning to her world and it would be seen as failure. Mrs Thomas wouldn't let Lucy have her ball back more than once a day. She should have handled it all so much better.

She turned on her side, away from Josh, from his wonderful body, the touch of his hands.

CHAPTER TWENTY-EIGHT

Sally's voice on the intercom was as tinny as usual: 'Mrs Benton on the line. She says it's urgent.'

'I'll take it,' Linda said. 'Fran, how lovely.'

Outside the sky was blue. Last night Mike had rung to suggest a pub supper mid-week. All was well with the world.

'How are you, Linda? Is this a typical Monday?'

Fran sounded tired. Linda said, 'Yes, a typical Monday,' when what she wanted to say was: actually I feel as though I'm floating because I'm to share scampi and chips with the man who loved you. Loved being the past tense, please, please, God. In the background Linda could hear the sounds of the gallery. 'How's biz?'

'Fine, but other things are not so sparkling.'

Linda felt her face set into the non-committal mask she wore when a client told her he'd been photographed in flagrante with his mistress and did it matter, since it was a quickie in the lee of a sand dune and not a 'stay the night' job?

She didn't want to know that Fran's life was not sparkling, that this particular frigate might be back in circulation, right under Mike's gun turrets. But then, it might be nothing like that. Why should it be, for heaven's sake?

'Linda, are you still there?'

Linda said, 'Of course, I was just getting comfortable. Go on, what's the problem?'

'My house. Do you think the tenants might be persuaded to go? They're friends of friends of yours, aren't they? I'm so hassled I can't even remember their names.'

Hassled? 'Sidebottom.'

'How could I forget. But would they?'

'I'll make a call.' Linda was already leafing through her address book, knowing Fran wanted her to ask why, knowing from the texture of her voice that something was wrong, because that's what friends did—ask. It's what Fran always did. But nothing must be wrong if Linda was to have a chance of getting things right. She capitulated. 'What's going on?'

'Bit of a do on Saturday. The police called. They've had two tip-offs that we are operating as a druggies' den or something just as absurd. Fancy Pants called from the States just as they were having a poke about. Big Mouth told her. Fancy Pants got on her high horse to the effect that the house and its environs were unsuitable, that things could not go on as they are, that my house would be just about OK.'

'Bollocks, Fran. Don't let her intimidate you. When will you start standing up for yourself? You

287

made a good start by doing a bolt and marrying Josh so keep it up, for goodness sake.' Don't come any nearer to us, she meant. Don't return to our world. Do not jeopardise what I'm hoping to have, what every fibre in my being is on full-scale alert to receive.

Fran snapped, 'It's not intimidation, Linda. It's a fact of life. We need somewhere bigger. We need to move back, failure though it is.'

Linda shut her address book. 'Look, it's not a failure but it shouldn't be necessary anyway. Just say it can't be done and then Emily will have to put up with things as they are.'

'It's not that simple. Apart from anything else, Stan's fed up that his past has been resurrected so a cooling-off period would be a good idea, and Emily's got problems which I've been ignoring and a fresh start might wipe the slate clean. We'll make it clear it's for her sake and willingly done. We've a pregnant Catherine in the picture now.'

'What?'

'Exactly and we have to find a way of breaking it to her, and on top of all that I all but accused the child of making the phone calls herself.'

'Did she?'

'I think so and if she did it's a cry for help. As I've said, it's a bloody mess and whatever was I thinking of?'

Linda was instantly wary. 'Thinking of?'

'Rushing off like that, thinking I could outrun the baggage, the old, that awful stuff, and the new, but I didn't dream there'd be so much of that, I really didn't, Lin. I'm sitting here wondering which way to turn.' Her voice broke.

Linda felt sweat break out all the way down her

back. 'Fran, come on, darling. You're just very tired. It's darkest before the dawn.' What! She made other soothing noises as Fran cried, really cried, and Linda was split between wanting to hug her friend and take a bull whip to drive her back into the bed she had made for herself. She said, as Fran quietened, 'Do you still love Josh?'

The silence was terrifying. At last Fran said, half laughing, 'What the hell has love got to do with it?'

'Everything, I would have thought.' Linda couldn't laugh, couldn't pretend to be anything other than serious.

'Of course I love him,' Fran said slowly. 'Of course.' Did it need thinking about? Was she unsure? Fran went on hesitantly, 'I love him but we can't even make love. The walls are too thin and I miss him, and he misses me and I could scream, and I'm frightened that everything that is being thrown at us will pull us apart.'

Linda opened up her address book immediately. 'Of course you need to get out, and fast. I'll call them. How about if I can arrange a swap? You to them. They to you. They're a couple with no kids so thin walls are immaterial unless they're into a noise fetish.'

Fran was laughing a bit now. Linda could still feel the sweat on her back. Yes, Fran would be closer but better now than later, sans husband, on the market.

'Or', Linda continued, 'we could hunt down something else a bit bigger for you.'

'I just think something's got to happen quickly, Linda, or . . .'

'Fine, fine. The Sidebottoms are nice, not stuffy. They're trainees in retail management, so might

289

quite like a lower rent.'

'Are you OK to do it? I'll phone if you'd prefer. I just thought that as you knew them, it could be done quickly, though I suppose I should ask Mike to redraft the contract, as I think you said he handled that, though . . .'

'No need to bother him. Leave it to me, Fran. I'll call Sidebottom at work and get back to you as soon as possible. Try not to worry.'

Fran sounded almost light-hearted as she said, 'You're a good and kind girl, Lin.'

'No, I'm not.' Because it was for her own sake.

'Yes, you are.'

Well, perhaps it was a little for Fran, because she did love her. 'OK, yes, I am. I'll call you. Hang in there. Don't do anything rash.' Please. Please.

*   *   *

The Sidebottoms were delighted. They were raw from the weekly run-in they'd been having with Anne Thomas over hanging washing out on a Sunday. It was making Rottweilers of them. 'We'll take the afternoon off and move today, if it will help?'

Linda laughed. The sun was out again, the scampi was looking promising. Please, please. 'Let's make it tomorrow, first thing. You're sure about taking on the Terrace?'

'Absolutely, but it will have to be Wednesday. Tuesday is impossible. We'll call round and look through the window at lunchtime, shall we?'

'Phone Fran at the gallery. She'll meet you there and give you the guided tour. Just let her know what breakages there have been at the house and

I'll get her to sort an inventory for the Terrace.'

'Can you draw up a lease in time?'

'Anything's possible it the spirit is willing.'

Fran promised her all the fruits of the earth as a reward. Linda forbore to tell her what she really wanted. Sally knocked on the door. Linda checked her watch. It was teatime. Would it be digestives or bourbons? Suddenly she felt she could eat a horse.

CHAPTER TWENTY-NINE

That same day the children were bathed and in bed on time, and positively gleaming. Tonight's story book was neatly stacked on the shelf; tomorrow's clothes on the one below. Jane straightened the duvet on Lucy's bed. She checked Harry's, but he had squirrelled out and on to the top again. If she moved him he might wake and cry.

A man on the radio had said a child cried because it picked up on his mother's tension. Ken said she must relax, because obviously it wasn't just him she was driving insane. She touched her son's head. His hair was so soft, his head so round and Joyce said he was the spit of Ken at that age.

It had been a quick and easy birth. Her mother had come to stay while she had been in hospital and apparently she had cooked the most delicious meals. According to Ken she'd also had Lucy in bed and asleep by 6.30, and his meals were on the table at 8 p.m. on the dot.

She had asked her mother how she managed it. Her mother had laughed and said she did not remember it as the same slick operation, and besides, two children were more than double the trouble. Just don't make it three. As she said it she had looked so sad.

Jane moved to the window, peering out between the crack in the curtains at Mike's house. Her mother had never said if she'd wanted more children, just that something had happened that had made it impossible. Outside it was still daylight and warm, and the sandpit cover must be put on or next door's cat would pay a visit. Soon Harry would be old enough to build sand castles, she had told Lucy this afternoon.

What would it have been like with a sibling? If it was a sister, would they have been on the phone to one another every day? If it had been a brother would he have been strong and tall like her father in the photograph? Would he have looked after her? Would she have known better what a man liked?

The lights were on in Mike's bedroom. He had finished the ceiling and had begun the walls. It looked as though he had chosen a soft yellow. She could have confirmed it yesterday when they chatted over the fence. He had been picking runner beans and had given her some. He knew she liked them young and without the stringy bits.

Yes, she could have asked him but somehow it seemed awkward. 'What colour is your bedroom, Mike?' It was too personal. Of course, if her mother had still . . . No, she really must not start or her head would spin, she would become confused, she would want to cry.

She drew back, pulling the curtains tight shut, switching on the night light that Lucy liked. It was a dull glow within a toadstool with little elves around a table. She had had a similar one at home, when she was growing up. It was still there, on her bedside table, or had been until her mother had let the house. Perhaps it was in a box in the loft.

When they'd moved back in she could go up there and bring everything down that was hers. She could set up the light in their room. No, no. Ken wouldn't like it, so she'd place all her things carefully in her old room, at her mother's. Just for now, as a sort of talisman: happy times remembered, times which would come again here, for her own family.

Gently she sat on her daughter's bed, reaching out, stroking Lucy's hair, those sweet, glorious curls. The thought of her old bedroom helped, just as the thought of her mother being closer did. It would stop all this rambling, it would help her get sorted. It would just help. She must be quiet. She must stop her mind going round and round and getting nowhere.

Lucy stirred. Jane sat quite still. Tonight the children had settled very easily and she could kiss Thomas the Teasmaid, she could absolutely kiss her, for creating a climate which had encouraged the Sidebottoms to agree to the exchange.

She crossed her arms carefully, moving her neck from side to side. There, it barely hurt any more, or only when she laughed. She smiled at her small joke, then sobered. Or *was* the police visit to be laid at Mrs Thomas's door? Perhaps it was that Emily, or her crazy mother. Heaven knows, that sort of person was capable of anything if it helped her own cause, or so she had said to her mother. 'And what do you think that is?' her mother had asked. 'Why should she want to phone the police if she doesn't want her daughter back? It hardly makes sense, or not from that angle, anyway.'

Jane had said, 'Perhaps it was so that you would move house.' Her mother had sounded tired on the phone and Jane's heart had twisted.

'Whatever the reason, she's coming home. At least she's coming home,' Jane had said to Linda when she'd walked Lucy and Harry round the block, and seen Linda cleaning the cobwebs from her porch with a broom. 'The cracks are beginning to show, as we all knew they would.'

Linda had said nothing, but she was getting very buttoned up these days. Perhaps it was the menopause. Maybe that's what it had been with her mother. Hormones had a lot to answer for. That's what Ken said. She twisted her fingers. He'd be home soon and she should be pleased.

CHAPTER THIRTY

Fran took time out of her Tuesday morning to catch up on work at the gallery and phone Brian Lutter, the drama teacher at the comprehensive Emily was still so extravagantly reluctant to attend morning after morning. He was a friend of Josh's and took an evening class in Theatre Studies at the college, more for love than money, it seemed. He was from a well-to-do family, who positively adored anything connected with the arts. Brian had promised that when his parents returned from their walkabout in Australia he'd send them hotfoot to the gallery with their bulging wallets.

'Brian's teaching,' the school secretary said, 'but

I'll ask him to return the call between classes.'

Ruth had ginger flapjacks as a special and Fran had promised her thighs she simply would not succumb, but in celebration at the Sidebottoms' delighted response to Josh's house she overrode decency and had two. James was appalled when he trotted through from his custodian's perch in the gallery.

'One for each leg,' Fran told him, wiping her fingers on a tissue. 'Not up for debate.' She felt better for a moment, calmer.

James sat on the edge of her desk, which was at an angle to the entrance to the coffee shop. 'So, it sounds a bit of a bummer all round, really. Could it truly have been Emily?'

Fran tensed. He pointed at the phone. 'I was on yesterday, remember. Exams are over. These ears are meant for listening.'

'I hope your lips are sealed.' Fran was horribly serious.

He put up his hands in surrender. 'Absolutely. No one else was in. It's between you and me, and whoever it was you were talking to.'

Fran felt bleak. 'Emily will tell Josh that I have doubts about her, of course.'

'Not necessarily. She's not speaking to him either, is she. She's a gifted sulker who can maintain silence indefinitely. What *did* you say, actually?' He was concerned.

She repeated it, remembering all too clearly. 'She told the police that I might be taking drugs. I asked, "Have you any idea who could be responsible?"'

'I don't call that an accusation and she needs a kick up the arse for trying to drop you in it. I

295

should let her get on with it.'

James was excellent for her, she decided, as the phone rang and he disappeared to talk Ruth into a second free cup of coffee. But nonetheless her intent had been there and subsequently the guilt, and now she did not feel good any more as she told the caller the dates of Jessie's workshop, and of the watercolour class that was taking place in the finished first-floor art room this afternoon.

Brian rang within the hour. He had to be reminded just who she was. That cleared up, Fran asked if he had any end-of-term productions under way. He had: a Summer Show comprising an all-singing, all-dancing jamboree, with a few skits and so on.

Fran said, tapping her pencil, smiling at a visitor who was leafing through the schedule of events he'd picked up from the stack on her desk, 'We have some unwelcome baby news for Emily.'

Brian was surprised all over again. 'Hey, congratulations.'

'Not us, Catherine.'

'Ah.'

'Exactly. We have to break this news to Emily and it won't go down a bomb. She's very talented . . .'

'She's a prima donna.'

'That too. But, Brian, I'm pretty sure she's lonely and adrift. I would be if I'd been chucked out and into the deep end as she has and I'd want something to hang on to. Drama could swing it. She'd be part of something and have a chance to shine, to create some feeling of self-worth. She has a great singing voice, you know, just as Josh has, though I agree she's not easy. I won't pretend otherwise.'

The visitor was miming a request to take the schedule with him. Fran nodded. 'Of course.'

Brian said, 'What?'

'Not you,' she replied as the visitor left. 'I was talking to someone else. So how about it?'

He was awfully quiet. Another visitor picked up a leaflet on O'Reilly's work from Fran's desk. Fran put her hand over the mouthpiece. 'We're using a couple of prints for greetings cards. They should be ready in a week.'

She turned her attention back to Brian. 'In return, Josh would help with the scenery, maybe give the kids a few tips.'

He was laughing now. 'You'd got me with the good voice but as we're desperate for scenery painters, tell Josh—bad luck—he's part of the deal.'

'He'll be delighted.'

'No, he won't, he'll be pissed off. Now I'll try to track down the little madam before she leaves school and tell her we can't function without her.'

Fran said quickly, 'Don't . . .'

'Tell her you set it up?' he finished for her. 'Of course not.'

*　　　*　　　*

Fran was at home and the inventory completed by the time Emily arrived. She had brought a ginger flapjack for father and daughter as there had been no time to bake.

Unusually, Emily had let herself in by the front door, letting her small rucksack drop from her shoulder on to the bottom of the stairs, ripe for tripping over. 'Mark's still pissed off with us. Us, not me, so I was blowed if I was going to pass his open back door,' she said as she stepped over the rucksack and up to her room. Above Fran there was the usual opening and slamming shut of drawers, the creaking. But tomorrow evening this would not be the case.

Josh was home within half an hour of Emily, by which time Fran had finished packing the contents of the pantry and had the kettle on. She and the Sidebottoms had decided to leave the under-sink cleaning materials for one another, and the toilet rolls, light bulbs and so on.

Josh pounced on a flapjack, kissed her and left crumbs on her cheek. She whispered, 'On the sly I've arranged with Brian that in return for your help with scenery Emily will have a part in the end of term "do".'

Josh stopped with the remains of the flapjack halfway to his mouth. He looked carefully at his hands, saying slowly, 'How many have I?'

'Enough.' Fran tried hard not to snap.

He gently rubbed his face against hers. 'Only joking, darling. What a good idea. How has she taken it?'

'Nothing has been said yet.' Music was thudding above.

Fran and Josh took their tea to their bedroom and made a start on their packing, secure in the knowledge that nothing they said could be heard above Bryan Adams's 'Waking up the neighbours'. At one stage Josh pulled her on to the bed, kissing her neck, running his hand down her body but it didn't work. They were on the starter's block to break away at the first signs from the next bedroom

298

and with a sigh Josh flung himself on to his back. 'There are solid walls in our suburban heaven, aren't there? Can we comfort ourselves with that?'

That was her home he was talking about, her suburban home. What did he mean, can we comfort ourselves? Wasn't she doing the best she could? She rolled from him and on to her feet, groping for shoes, dropping them into the bin bag, labelling it; moving on to the drawers, knowing she was tired and overreacting.

Over a kitchen meal of spaghetti bolognese, which was that unforgettable old favourite of Emily's, they informed her of the imminent change of address.

'We really do want you to be comfortable,' Fran said.

Emily didn't stop sucking the long strand of spaghetti, but there seemed to be the beginnings of a smile. She wound the next strands around her fork, looking at Josh, not at Fran as she said, 'Well, I suppose a bigger room will be nice and I can do my homework in the dining room, spread out a bit.'

Could they be about to have a normal conversation, Fran wondered, realising that she was holding her breath?

'The bad is that I've been volunteered for the drama. Apparently they need a voice.' For a moment she seemed to be coyly pleased, then her shoulders drooped. 'But who wants to be in their crabby show? It's going to be awful because Mark'll walk out when he knows I'm in it. I just bet he does.'

Josh shook his head, pushing his chair back from the table, spooning Whiskas into Big Job's bowl. 'Of course he won't. Stan and Cindy are

299

discomfited, that's all. Poor old Stan's a bit touchy about his past.'

'Some of us don't understand about feelings and how they can be hurt.' Emily was bristling, suddenly, gloom turning to anger and she glared at Fran behind her father's back, then took a great mouthful of wound-up spaghetti, sucking in the tails, splashing bolognese on her chin.

Fran tried to ignore her, saying, 'I'm going to finish packing, then I'll help you, Emily, shall I? Josh, lock the cat flap, let's try and keep Big Job in tonight so we can get straight off in the morning.'

She left the room. What Josh had next to tell Emily was best shared between the two of them, but her stomach had started fluttering.

Fran heard the kitchen door slam five minutes later and feet pounding on the stairs. She sighed and waited, sitting on the bed, stuffing a carrier bag with her tights, unsure whether to intrude or not. Then her bedroom door was flung open and Emily stood there, shouting, 'That's why she wanted me out of the way, isn't it.'

It wasn't a question, but Fran treated it as one. 'No, that isn't the reason.' Fran stopped, her hands full of tights. 'We were all very stupid and didn't discuss things together, the four of us, as we should have done. The wrong tone was set. Your mother panicked because we wouldn't pay more. Your father didn't want to lose you for so long and said no to you going. He didn't realise it was a real possibility or he would have talked it through to sort out what was best for *you*. It was a thoroughly idiotic sequence of events, based on a total miscalculation by everyone. Your mother, I'm convinced, had no idea that she was pregnant at

300

that stage.'

It was what she had been rehearsing all day. Did it sound right?

Emily said, still coiled as though she were about to spring, 'Dad says the baby's due in under six months. So she must have known.' Her hands were bunched.

'Not necessarily.'

'Oh, p-l-e-a-s-e.'

Fran hated it when she said that. A-b-s-o-l-u-t-e-l-y hated it. Pushing the carrier bag from her lap and dropping the last of the tights on the bed, she held out her hands to Emily, trying for eye-to-eye contact. 'Emily, your mother loves you very much; after all, she wants you with her at Christmas.'

'But not this long holiday, so why's that? Because she wants to sit there with a big belly while Roger dribbles all over her.'

Fran couldn't bear the hurt behind the surly bravado. 'No, so that you can settle, and they can settle and everything will be wonderful when you do go out for Christmas. Think about it, Em. We have needed time, haven't we, to see that this house is too small, for the drama teacher to notice your talent, for lots of things.'

Emily was still staring at the floor and now she shrugged. 'For you to learn that you don't trust me.'

Fran let her hands drop to her knees and tried to find the right note. 'Nonsense, I was just trying to sort things out in my head. I was shocked. I honestly did think that you might have overheard something that someone had said to indicate who could have done such a thing. That boy who gave you a lift, perhaps?'

301

Emily was rubbing her bare foot along the pattern of the carpet. Abruptly she stopped, lifting her head. 'Anyway, who the hell cares about any of it.'

She left the room, but stopped just outside and said without turning, 'So, sometimes you don't know if you're pregnant?'

'Sometimes.'

'Did you?'

'No.' What was another lie? 'Shall I help you pack, Em?' Fran stood up, and a pair of beige tights fell at her feet.

'You're not my mother. I can do it myself.'

Emily disappeared into her room and Fran braced herself for the slam, which didn't come. Slowly she sat on the bed, rubbing her hands together as though she were cold. But the child had come to her. That was a good sign, wasn't it?

*   *   *

By seven the next morning they were loading both boots with bin bags, cases and cardboard boxes when Stan, who had not spoken since the police called, emerged from his house, jangling his car keys, saying, 'With my car as well it will take half the time.'

Fran straightened, saying quietly, trying for humour, 'Are you that eager to be rid of us?'

Stan chucked her under the chin in that way of his. 'Never. I was just in a nark, but it's gone and one day you'll be back, or close by. The end one has three bedrooms, you know. Tom was saying there's talk of old Briars selling it. He's looking for sheltered accommodation.'

302

Josh came out of the house with more cases. 'Is that so? Hey, that's a thought to keep us going.'

'You're not a million miles away, anyway.'

Josh grunted as he heaved the cases into the boot, 'It's another planet, mate.'

Emily was whistling now and Stan sang along as they completed loading. When he started his engine she planted herself firmly in his car for the trip to Fran's house. Fran led the convoy, passing the Sidebottoms on the way. They had borrowed a friend's trailer and obviously packed up the previous night as they had said they would, for the house was pristine and empty.

It seemed strange to be opening the door to her old home, strange and unsettling. The bleach smell was unfamiliar and their footsteps echoed hollowly as they traipsed into the hall, which appeared huge and light. Josh hesitated at the foot of the stairs, heavy suitcases in either hand. Em stood uncertainly with Big Job in his carrier. No one but Fran knew where to go. She directed Em to the kitchen with the cat, and led Stan and Josh upstairs.

She opened the door to the main bedroom, with its MFI built-in wardrobes, its bay window, its beige carpet, its magnolia walls. Josh almost tiptoed to the bed with the cases. Stan did likewise. 'The carpet won't mark, or if it does, it can be dealt with,' Fran said.

Stan glanced at Josh. 'You remember to wear your slippers, that's all I can say,' he told him. The two men laughed.

Emily called from the landing, 'Which is my room?'

Fran showed her the bedroom which had

303

doubled as her art room. There was not even the merest scent of turps or linseed oil, only the ungarnished bed, with its sprung mattress.

Josh and Stan were on their way down for more cases. Josh said quietly, but not quietly enough, 'We could put a trio of flying ducks here to complete the picture.' Stan laughed.

Fran followed them to the car and carried in the contents of the pantry. The kitchen seemed spotless, large, convenient. The garden had no molehills, but no fragrant roses in pots either. And here there would be no raucous evenings spent listening to music, or playing music, or talking of things that stirred the blood, for Anne Thomas would want to know the reason why, so perhaps the men were right. Perhaps, but what a bloody cheek, what bloody, bloody cheek! She checked her anger.

Upstairs Emily played Bryan Adams. Josh called as he panted up the stairs, 'Neighbours exist here too, Em. Keep it down. We're in Fran's home, remember that.'

'It's *our* home,' Fran corrected him calmly as she decanted their clothes into drawers. He was uncertain, that was all. He needed to become accustomed.

There was no reply. Josh helped Stan with more supplies.

When the men drove back to the Terrace to top up, Emily came to Fran as she brought the personal bits and pieces down from the loft. 'I might just as well have stayed in the other house, when you consider that poky little room. What's wrong with the bigger one at the back?' She pointed to Jane's room. Jane, who was on edge and whom Linda and Fran were trying to keep calm, on track.

Fran balanced the boxes precariously on the corner of the banister and shoved the loft ladder up, choosing her words carefully: 'That's the spare room.' She carted the boxes in there and left them by the wardrobe.

Emily had followed and stood behind her. 'Well, I can move to the small one if we have people to stay.' She went to the window. 'Anyway, I thought you said it was *our* house. After all, you've been made welcome at Dad's. Why're you being so poky?'

If this child didn't go to school right this minute, Fran would swing for her. Now Emily was flouncing back to her small bedroom. She shut the door savagely. But damn it, she was right. The larger room was available and Jane had left, and she'd just have to talk to her daughter if it became a problem. *If.* Fran rubbed her forehead, trying to get things in perspective and failing, because somehow the goalposts kept moving; too fast and too far. *If.* Yes, there was an *if* involved with Jane, whereas Emily was a definite thorn. She shook her head. No, not thorn. This was a new start, that's what she had to focus on.

She called out, as she heaved a suitcase along the landing, 'Move your stuff then, Em, but do not ever call me poky again. I will not have that attitude from anyone, do you understand?' It was too heavy. She lowered the case to the floor. It caught her leg and hurt. She was on a level with Em's closed door. There was no reply. A new start? Well, didn't that mean the child as well? Her leg was smarting and suddenly anger outstripped Fran's control and she hammered on Em's door. 'Do you understand?'

305

She was shaking and let her hand fall, but by then the front door had opened and Josh was looking up at her over a bin bag full of linen, taken aback. Fran flushed. 'Just sorting out a few ground rules.'

Emily opened the door and swept past Fran as though she didn't exist, busily transferring her suitcases to Jane's room, smiling sweetly at her father as he tiptoed up and dumped the linen on the landing at Fran's feet. Emily said, 'Yes, I understand. Just so long as you understand that I really did not report any drug problem to the police in spite of what you said to me.' She shut the door of the bedroom.

Fran watched Josh's confusion with a sinking heart and dragged the case into the main bedroom. 'I've already told you, Emily, I was just trying to see if you had any thoughts on who might have done.'

Josh could read her, could feel what she was feeling. He would know she was lying. She wouldn't look at him, but she did as he stood in the doorway and she saw the doubt in his eyes. Stan was just behind and he broke the silence by calling Em. 'Come on, you little baggage. Let's get you to school.'

No one spoke, they just fiddled with whatever it was they were carrying. At last the girl emerged in her uniform, carefully closing the bedroom door behind her. She kissed her father but just looked at Fran. The eyebrow had settled nicely. The salt water bathing had calmed down the ear. It was this that Fran made herself notice as Josh hesitated, caught between the two of them.

Stan started down the stairs. 'Move your jalopy for God's sake, Josh.'

Fran waited as Josh turned on his heel, following Emily. She leaned over the banister, fishing the spare key from her pocket. 'Emily, take this, then you can let yourself in whenever you need to. It's your home now.'

Emily caught it and looked up at Fran for a long moment. Then she sort of smiled, before saying, 'What about Dad?'

Josh smiled bleakly up at Fran. 'I've already been given one.'

They headed on out of the house. What was that supposed to mean? Did he feel patronised? Fran ripped open the bin bag and found satisfaction in the action. She began to pile the linen into the airing cupboard.

Josh made one more trip, depositing the boxes in the hall. Mrs Thomas remained in her house. Josh called up, 'Got to go, see you later.'

He didn't kiss her. He'd never left without kissing her.

It was a relief to arrive at the gallery, to collect her grandchildren from Maisie's and instead of taking them to the house staying at the gallery, wanting to remain in its vibrant atmosphere. She gave Harry his bottle, holding him close while Lucy coloured on her desk and showed visitors her latest work of art. It was so simple, at this age. She kissed his hair, rubbed her cheek against his warm head. What was Josh thinking?

At 2.30 she packed the children into the car and was home early enough to make a walnut cake with Lucy. She was also in time to compose herself and at four she called out as Emily let herself in through the front door, 'Tell me about it, the good, the bad and the ugly.'

307

Lucy ran to Emily, dragging her into the kitchen. 'Me make cake.'

'Then I shall have a slice,' Emily said, sitting Lucy on the table, handing her the knife, but guiding her hand as they cut one slice. Then Emily looked up. 'I expect you need one?'

Fran sat down suddenly, feeling much as the troops must have when they broke the siege of Mafeking, because this child had never offered her anything before. Guardedly, as though feeling for a trip wire, she answered, 'Yes, I'm rather hungry.' She couldn't understand, she hardly dared believe, she didn't know what more to say, or do, so she made a pot of tea instead, handing the mug to Emily who was dandling Harry on her knee. He was smiling. He usually smiled for Emily. 'They love you,' Fran said, touching Emily's shoulder.

The child did not shrink as dramatically as usual. There was just a little twitch, and Fran went one mile further and squeezed gently. 'They really do.'

Emily said to Lucy, 'Well, I think you're both pretty cute, too, don't I. Now come and look at my room. It's really nice and it will be good to have some space. I suppose I'm quite lucky. Stan thinks so.' She shot a look at Fran, then away again.

Could a bit more space make this difference, and Stan, wonderful Stan? Fran shook her head, not sure what to say, where to put her foot, as it were.

Emily settled Harry more firmly on her hip and led Lucy from the room, saying, 'I've been singing today and the man said he'd never heard anything quite so good. The other kids liked it too. One wants to come round for tea. Now come and see this funny little light which was in the box of things

308

from the loft. I've put it on the windowsill. We'll put the rest of the stuff Grandma brought down from the loft into the small bedroom, shall we, and you can help me put my own stuff out. You can even choose where it goes. How about that?'

'What about your tea?' Fran followed them into the hall. Jane was an *if* at the moment, she must keep reminding herself.

Emily turned, a foot on the bottom step. 'May we have it in a minute?'

A real question. Fran smiled. 'Why not.'

As Emily climbed the stairs she called down, 'Whose light is it anyway?'

'Jane's. It's usually kept on the windowsill, along with her other things. She seems to quite like seeing them there.' Fran's voice was tentative.

But in reply, Emily's voice was incredulous: 'Well, she should have taken them then.'

Fran sighed. 'Perhaps, but I think she still considers this her home. In some ways.' Would this set Emily off again, would she feel that she had no place, would they be back to square one?

'Oh, that'd be right. *Her* home. *Her* room. So it wasn't a guest room. You should try to keep your story straight, Fran.' Emily had stopped halfway and Lucy was clambering up and down the middle stair, almost swinging on Emily's arm.

Fran closed her eyes, not because of Lucy, but because every damn thing was so difficult, and she wondered why someone hadn't developed a pill which would take kids all the way from Lucy's age right up to the age of reason in a split second. But when was that age of reason with a mother like Catherine? Just shut up, she told herself, opening her eyes again and smiling, trying to keep the

309

frustration from her voice. 'Oh, Emily, you're probably right, just put them in the small bedroom. Jane will be fine about it.'

It wasn't for long. Once the end of term came they could sort out these damned houses, sort out everything and find some sort of an even keel.

When she returned to the kitchen Josh was there. He had not called out to her as he always did. He had poured himself a mug of tea and was standing against the sink. He didn't smile at her, didn't approach. She said, 'Look, can we think about sorting out the houses? Maybe selling up both and starting afresh . . .'

'I thought this was Jane's inheritance? I thought she considered it hers? Isn't that why she's left her possessions here?'

He'd heard. 'Then she'll have to rethink. Emily's right, it's daft.'

He smiled tiredly. 'She's impossible, I'm impossible. This whole thing . . .' He waved his arm around.

Fran said, frightened, 'Is not impossible.' She kissed his cheek and the area she loved by his temple. 'It's not impossible.' But things were shifting and sliding from beneath her, and he had no right to say that, because she needed something solid to hang on to while she tried to sort out his daughter, and to ignore his stupid comments about flying ducks and slippers.

The phone rang. Fran sprang to answer it, wanting a diversion, wishing it to be Linda cracking jokes, checking all was well. It was Jane instead, but she too was checking all was well and that the children could stay until six even though they'd just moved in, and wanting a word with Lucy who had

had a sniffle that morning.

'She's fine now,' Fran reassured her.

'I would just like a word, Mum. I do worry about her.'

Emily brought Lucy down, passing her to Fran on the bottom step. 'I've left Harry on the floor, not the bed, so don't worry,' she said, running back up, with no smile, but then again, no snarl. Fran handed Lucy the receiver.

It seemed so big in her little hands. Fran crouched at her side, helping her. 'Yes, Mummy. I was a good girl, Mummy. I don't mind. I'll tell Harry. I'm helping Emily. But can we have them? The things we've put in the little room. The things Emily says are yours. The things Emily says you should have taken when you went because you've got your own home, and you're a very big girl and you don't belong in this house any more.'

Josh groaned behind her, and made for the stairs. 'I'll have a word with her.'

Fran called him back. 'Don't say anything, not yet.'

She let Lucy finish the conversation and took the receiver when the child said, 'Mummy wants to talk to you.' Lucy clambered back up the stairs, Josh dogging her footsteps nervously, Fran watching them both, but Lucy was sure-footed and eager to be back up in Aladdin's cave.

All the time she watched she listened to Jane and wasn't surprised, because Jane had always been territorial at the best of times and these were definitely not those, and if the shit was hitting every other fan, why shouldn't it hit this one. At last Jane paused to draw breath.

Fran said, 'Jane, put yourself in Emily's place.

311

Just for now she needs a great deal of attention in spite of the fact that she's going about it the wrong way. You're an adult. Forgive her words, they're not what she means. This is always your home. Or if not this, then wherever I choose to live. I love you, Jane, and if this is so important, perhaps we need to talk. You're doing too much, darling. I'm worried about you.'

'What do you mean by that? Do you think I'm a nutter?'

Fran pressed her hand to her eyes. 'Of course not, I just know how I felt when I was overloaded. Things got out of perspective, I jumped at shadows, I couldn't . . .'

'Cope? Is that what you're saying? I assure you I'm perfectly fine, Mother, I'm just trying to find a balance. Surely even you can understand that?' Fran pressed her eyes harder. 'Besides, Mother, what do you mean, wherever you choose to live?'

For a moment Fran lost the thread, then remembered. 'Oh, nothing. Just like you, we're trying to find a balance. Surely even you can understand that?' She found she was shouting. Quieter now, she said, 'I'll see you at six. I'll feed the kids.' She hung up. That was the only word for it, but she couldn't think of anything better to do.

Josh was carrying empty cardboard boxes through from the hall. He opened the back door and now Big Job took his chance and fled. 'For God's sake, Josh,' Fran yelled, because she really could take no more.

Josh dropped the boxes and rushed out, slamming the door behind him. Fran whispered, 'Just leave me to cope, why don't you. Just leave me to bloody well cope.'

312

The door opened again and Josh stepped back in, holding the cat in his arms like a trophy. Fran laughed, but it was ragged. Josh said, shaking his head at her, 'Roll on, bedtime, then we can talk about this properly, for the first time for centuries.' He put the cat in the larder and shut the door. 'It's just for now, mutt, or we'll lose you and if we do we'll both have a breakdown because we're only hanging on by a thread.' His eyes were on Fran. 'It's all been so difficult,' he murmured. 'It's as though everything's roared away from us and we haven't been able to do a thing about it, and just when it feels as though it's subsiding, something else sparks it off.'

Quite. She said, 'But now we are doing something and it will improve, it is improving.' It had to.

Emily called down, 'I need someone to go over my lines with me.'

Josh shook his head, then laughed and pulled out a fifty-pence piece. He tossed, covered the coin with his hand, saying 'Let's go with the flow.'

'I don't care if it's heads or tails, father of the star,' Fran said. 'She needs you to show interest right now, don't you think?'

So it was Fran who kicked a lovely red ball over the fence into Thomas the Teasmaid's garden as she played with Lucy, and it was like being on a helter-skelter, for Anne Thomas wasn't in, and Fran felt so elated she could have whooped and hollered as she let herself in by the side gate, found the ball and scurried back.

From then on they threw the ball to one another, rather than risk a wayward kick. Lucy laughed as she dropped the ball and chased it. She squealed as

313

she caught it and rushed to show Harry, whom Josh had plonked in his buggy on the patio, before returning inside to pore over the script. Through the kitchen window Fran could hear Emily and Josh fight their way through the lines, and she gained a secret satisfaction and reassurance that Emily's angst was not reserved solely for her.

She and Lucy dribbled the ball now and she had done the same with Jane. Poor Jane. This evening she'd talk to her calmly, sensibly, as her own mother had done when Fran had found the job and single parenthood confusing. She would help her with a schedule, something, anything to help her find her own balance.

After ten minutes Lucy was tired and walked round the garden with Fran, clinging to her forefinger. It was strange to see the plants she had nurtured still in existence, odd to hear the muted sounds of the neighbourhood: the occasional car, a few children calling. It seemed a million years since she had lived here. It was like a foreign land: larger and colder, not hers any more. This was how Josh and Emily must feel also?

At that moment, from the kitchen came the sounds of Emily singing and it was beautiful, staggeringly beautiful, and when Emily finished and silence fell, Lucy started clapping, a tiny sound, and Fran wanted it huge and she clapped too, and cheered until the whole garden rang with it, until it rolled in waves across Thomas the Teasmaid's garden and beyond. This was theirs for now. Theirs.

But now Lucy was pulling at her skirt and pointing to Josh, who was laughing at the window, beckoning them to him. Emily came to the door.

'We're going to the park. Dad says you obviously need to let off steam.'

Lucy ran to Emily, who picked her up and twirled her. Fran said, 'Let's pick up fish'n'chips on our way back. Would you like that?'

As they walked Josh whispered, 'Apparently Stan explained that madam should view the move as a gesture of commitment to her. He said he and Cindy would have slapped her backside and strung her up by her thumbs long ago. Not that she told me that little bit, he gave me a bell at work.'

It was in the park that they met Anne Thomas, on her way back from the bowls match. She was dressed in her whites and still wore her panama hat. Fran glimpsed Emily's expression and prayed that she would not comment.

She did not, but that was probably because Anne was in full flow, talking of the suitability of Fran's house over the Terrace, so long as the difference in neighbourhood was respected; so long as the communal nature of their previous existence did not transfer to the close; so long as no hint of the drug culture endemic in that sort of area was transported to this fresh start. The police are usually happy to warn, the first time.

Josh had just been on the point of allowing Lucy to drag him off to the swings but at this he paused, attentive but silent. Emily had been pushing Harry's pushchair backwards and forwards, twitching her mouth, but now she was similarly quiet. Fran longed for the woman to go, to remember an important appointment, to gush herself away but Mrs Thomas wasn't done yet. Now she flicked a finger towards Emily's eyebrow. 'Oh, I thought you had one in your eyebrow as well? So good sense has prevailed there too. Must go, tea to make.'

'We're having fish'n'chips,' Lucy told her proudly.

'Rather greasy, don't you think?' Mrs Thomas said. But Emily had begun pushing Harry towards the slide, and Josh had dropped Lucy's hand and was walking alongside his daughter, his hands deep in his pockets. Fran followed, snatching up Lucy who stood looking after Josh. Mrs Thomas called, 'Oh, well. Don't feel you have to make polite conversation, whatever you do.'

Lucy was heavy but still Fran managed to run and catch up. Josh was watching Emily put Harry on the very bottom of the slide and run him just a few feet. Lucy wanted to go up the ladder. Fran let her, standing beneath, calling across to Emily, 'Em, it was Mrs Thomas who made the call. She would have asked her friend Mrs Marlow to make the other. They consider themselves guardians of the moral right. They know the police superintendent. It is Jane who would have told her. She must have heard what you said.'

Emily smirked. 'So now you believe me?'

'I'm sorry. I've said it once, that's twice. Josh?'

Josh was watching Emily with Harry. He said quietly, almost gently, 'Let's get those fish'n'chips.'

He walked with Emily, not with her. He waited with Emily while Fran and Lucy queued in the Flying Fish. He walked with Emily back to the house, and ate a few chips and half his fish in the kitchen, then settled in the dining room, where he assessed some work. Fran was glad he was there and Emily was upstairs when Jane came to collect the children. She was glad that he couldn't hear her

316

low-voiced tirade to Jane, insisting that she said nothing about their business ever again, to anyone, particularly Mrs Thomas. That the difficulties she had caused could have taken a long time to iron out, without Stan's help. Perhaps they still would. That she had to start growing up, really leaving the nest, and stop being so stupid. That they both had to stop that. That she might be under strain but nothing excused what she had done.

Jane gathered up the children and left, then called back, 'Does this mean you won't have your grandchildren again?'

'It means I will, until you can sort out your finances properly. Why not start by cancelling your husband's gym membership and suggesting he sorts out his priorities once and for all? You sort out a schedule for yourself. It helped me when I was in your position.'

She shut the door behind her daughter and leant back against it. Josh came out into the hall, the artwork in a folder under his arm. He said, 'I'm going out.'

'Where?'

'Anywhere but here. How bloody dare she try to ruin our life and then bring her kids round here? How dare you say she can continue to bring them? For God's sake, woman, get some backbone or you'll have us all dragging round on her coat-tails.'

He was pale with rage. A rage that Fran had only seen with regard to Catherine. She put her hand out to him. 'She's not herself, she's under pressure.'

'So you keep saying, but she's an adult and you should damn well let her sort out her own life. She's rude, aggressive and a bloody pain in the neck, and you let her walk all over you, us. Us for

317

God's sake. Why do you do it?'

'It's what mothers do and I'm worried about her.'

He shouldered his way into the kitchen. Big Job was yowling in the larder. Josh opened the back door. Fran couldn't bear him to go, she couldn't bear that this was happening. She couldn't bear anything about this whole bloody, sodding mess that she had allowed to happen. She whispered, as he walked out, 'That's right, leave me to look after the bloody cat, not to mention your daughter.' Whispered it because if he heard he might not come back.

In her other life she would have kept the words in her head, a head that was running riot, a head she squeezed now until the riot was subdued, beaten down. Until *she* had beaten it down and her head was clear, and she recognised the whisper for what it was. A backbone, damn you. She *had* a backbone. She had a *backbone*.

She ran upstairs, dragged out her paints from the cardboard box, and the easel, taking them through into her old art room. 'Just be. Let it all just happen,' she told herself, squeezing out paint on to the palette, taking up her palette knife, heedless of Bon Jovi roaring out from Em's room, because nothing could touch her, or if it did she would defend *herself*. She had that right. She dipped the knife into the colour and she painted herself, her life, her backbone, and there it was in the slashes and daubs, and though there was darkness it was not so deep, it did not claw up, up, to the light.

CHAPTER THIRTY-ONE

Josh did not come home until the early hours. Fran heard him stumbling about and waited for his tread on the stairs, wanting to rush and help, wanting to break his neck. She did not do either, because just then there was the slam of the sitting-room door, a muffled curse and silence. She lay in her double bed, the one she had slept in alone for over twenty years.

In the morning she did not need the radio alarm to ease her into the day. She was already dressed, making the bed. Her head ached, she was tired, she was frightened, but she still heard that whisper.

There was no sound from the sitting room. She should coax him upstairs before Emily woke, or there would be questions. She reached for the handle, then turned away for this was not what she'd signed up for. She made tea and toast. It tasted dry and unappetising but she'd eat it. She'd sit at the table, her table, in her suburban house with its bay windows and ghastly neighbour, and eat it if it killed her.

She heard Emily's alarm. Would Josh be up to take her to school as promised? If not, who would be the one explaining? She finished her toast, drank her tea, checked the clock. She'd have to wake him. She must keep her voice steady. She must not shrink, or tremble.

She opened the sitting-room door to the smell of stale Scotch. The tremble began. She clenched her hands, forcing them to be still. She made herself walk over to the settee where he lay face down, moaning softly. She stood over him, but out of reach, always out of reach. 'I expect you feel extremely ill.' How strong her voice was.

He rolled slowly on to his back, flinging one arm over his eyes. 'Bloody hell.'

'Exactly.'

He peered beneath his arm. 'Fran, I'm just so sorry.'

He needed a shave. His blue shirt was booze-stained. She felt calm and cold. There was no fear, even though he had just said what David used to say, smelt as David used to smell. 'You have a daughter to run to school, but you'll still be over the limit so I'll do it. I suggest you get yourself up to bed while she's in the bathroom, unless you are a glutton for explaining this to a child whose bedrock has already been severely shaken.'

He struggled to an upright position. She moved back a pace. He held out his hand. 'Fran, I'm such a pillock, such a fool.'

She walked away from him and shut the door firmly. She strolled in the garden, her garden where David had never been. She looked at her house, where David had never been, where there had never been the thud of his fists, the kicks, her muffled groans, her blood, the need to hide the secret from her daughter.

Was Josh in the bedroom now? Safely tucked away? Was Emily going to eat breakfast unaware? Go to school unaware?

After a snatched mouthful of toast Emily hoisted her small rucksack over her shoulder and looked up at Fran. 'I expect it was all the fuss yesterday that's given him the headache.'

'Probably,' Fran said, sounding calm and

reasonable. She dropped Emily at school, parked at the gallery, grabbed some coffee from Ruth, sorted the mail and the e-mails, confirmed a lithograph exhibition to run from January to February, worked out the rota for the following week, pencilling in time to interview Simon's replacement for late September when he would be ensconced in art school.

Visitors were signing in all the time. Two bought O'Reillys. It could well be a sell-out. This was hers. She was good. She could do it. She didn't need him. She didn't need any of it. Ever again.

The trembling began.

She phoned Linda, needing her voice, just for a moment. Sally told her that Linda was in court. Fran said, 'Put me through to Mr Wells.'

'Who may I say is calling?'

'Fran. Just Fran.'

His voice was so sane, so the same. The trembling stopped. Sometimes whispers needed support. 'Fran, this is a welcome surprise.'

He always said the right thing.

'It seemed about time I touched base. I should have done it ages ago, but I didn't know how I would be received.' She sounded normal too.

'What's wrong?'

How could he know? She said, 'Nothing. I just felt like looking up old friends, seeing how you are. It's being back in my house that's done it.'

'Yes, I heard.'

From Jane? Or maybe Linda? It didn't matter.

He said, 'Let's lunch. It's been so long.' Did he sound wistful? She couldn't be sure. Did she want him to be? She was surprised at the thought. Did she?

They arranged to meet early at that old favourite watering stop Luigi's. Did he hope it would revive old feelings? Perhaps it would.

She rang Maisie. 'Could I bump the "kid collection" until two? I'll pay.'

'Why not. I'll see you then.'

Fran left Ruth coping and drove home, letting herself in. The sitting room still smelt. She crept upstairs. The duvet was creased and flattened from where he'd lain on top of it, as David used to. She searched through her clothes but all her proper skirts were in the loft. She retrieved them, pressed a neat, straight black skirt, and wore a bosom-clinging cream top and a lightweight charcoal-grey jacket. She had one pair of black tights. She squeezed her feet into her black slingbacks feeling like an ugly sister.

By the time she drove away her feet were aching, as they had on the way to the wedding.

She parked behind Luigi's, where they had not had her hen night, and went in through the rear entrance. Mike was already at the table. Their table. He was on the alert and came towards her, his smile steady. His hands were too, as they took both of hers. 'Fran, you look wonderful.' He kissed her cheeks. She didn't recognise his aftershave. So she did not have bags, did not look old.

He led her to the table. 'I took the liberty.' He gestured to a gin and tonic in which the ice had barely melted while his was merely a tonic, disguised as gin and tonic, as usual. He pointed to the garlic mushrooms on the menu. 'Your favourite.'

Garlic? No, for Josh would know. Did she care?

She said, 'I'd rather have the Greek salad and

322

another starter to follow—perhaps the risotto.'

He slapped shut the menu and smiled. 'Like we used to.' The waiter was hovering and took the order. 'Nice to see you again, sir, madam.'

So he hadn't been back without her. He raised his glass. 'Cheers, Fran. To you.'

'To you,' she corrected him. The gin was cool. She'd forgotten how much she liked it. Forgotten so much. He straightened his tie. It was a mass of purple and red. How strange. His shirt was a deep-blue, almost like Josh's. He always wore white. In his cuffs were links of silver and malachite. They were new to her.

The starter arrived.

'Lord, what about wine?' he asked.

Fran shook her head. 'We both have to work.' Their eyes met. It was the same old routine.

He grinned. 'Some things never change.'

She wanted to say, he drank himself senseless, his daughter is tough going, Jane is not coping and is appalling. But I have changed. I have a backbone. After all these years, I have a backbone. Surely I have.

She said, 'Other things do change.' She nodded towards his clothes.

He patted his tie self-consciously. 'I realised I was a boring old fart.'

She didn't ask why. Being left at the altar must change your perception of your self-worth. She said, 'Never think that.'

He shook his head, pointing to her salad. 'Tuck in, my dear. Of course I should think of it. It's true. I haven't moved on in a thousand years. It took you to show me that. I thank you for it.' Again he raised his glass. There was no malice in the gesture, in the tone of voice, in the look in his eyes. 'Now, how's it going with young Emily, and Jane, and the whole bag of beans. It sounds pretty much as though it's a recipe for fraught and fiery.'

And the rest. She said, willing herself to talk of it, 'It's not too bad. It will just take time; Emily in particular. Imagine being dumped . . .' Had she really said that?

He laughed gently. 'Let's try another tack. How do you think Jane is? I'm concerned.'

I don't want to talk about it, Fran wanted to say. Instead, she said, 'She does too much and Ken doesn't help.'

Mike's glance was sharp as he interrupted. 'Ah, why do you say that?'

Fran toyed with her fork. All such old ground and how much did you say to someone's boss? Everything, why not. 'For one thing he joined the gym, so *Jane* had to find the money, which means I have to have the children more often. A small thing and probably better for the children, but quite frankly, his biceps aren't top priority.'

Mike finished his tomato salad. He dabbed his mouth with his napkin. 'I'm worried. I was so glad when you called because I've been wanting to talk to you about them,' he said.

He'd been wanting to talk about *them*.

She replaced her fork, her salad only half eaten. The waiter had been about to take her plate and now backed off. She called him back. 'Just too much.'

She wanted to be gone now. Instead she asked Mike, as he drew with his finger on the cloth, 'Why?'

He shrugged. 'Just a feeling. Ken's not on top of

324

things at work. He's made a real mess of the Mainwaring case, lost a file—can you imagine?—and as a result I think Bob may change horses in mid-race. So very bad for business.'

So this was all about work? Of course. That's how it had so often been. She had forgotten.

Mike sipped his drink, then resumed finger writing. It had always annoyed her. His hands were soft and white, his nails clean and pared. He said, 'You don't think they're in trouble. You know, *your* sort of trouble?'

She stared at him, stunned. 'What have you seen?' No, this was not about work.

'Nothing. They're both just so tense.'

'He doesn't drink. He's there most evenings. Yes, he's a prig but so is she now.' She sounded so hard. Mike was looking at her curiously. She defended herself. 'Well, she is. I mean, I was pathetic, I wouldn't say boo to a goose. She does the equivalent of laying in with bovver boots, which says a great deal, don't you think.' Her voice was crisp and it was not a question. 'Linda's not noticed anything either. It's not the same at all.'

Fran leant back as the waiter placed a dish of risotto in front of her. Mike picked up a fork, studying it. The waiter laid his risotto in front of him, looking anxious. But it wasn't the fork Mike was studying, Fran knew. It was the problem that needed solving, the same one her mind was also beginning to study again. But not Jane . . . it couldn't be. It didn't happen twice. There had been no clue.

Now Mike was smiling at her, digging his fork into the risotto. The waiter backed, relieved. Mike said, 'Sometimes I leap at shadows after all that

325

you went through. But you're right, it's not the same at all. I'm sorry to wind you up, Fran. After the move and trying to settle a wobbly teenager it must be the last thing you need. Forget I ever raised it. After all, I'd see or hear a fracas, or pick up on something Lucy says. I've been working on this case, you see. A bit like yours. It makes you look at everything and wonder.'

Fran absorbed his words, rearranging them, looking at them this way and that until they made a sensible picture and she understood exactly what he meant. After all, hadn't she spent most of her years wondering about other couples? Weighing them up, reading too much into the smallest thing. Always reading so much into everything. She realized she'd done that this morning, because David had always smelt of stale Scotch when he said sorry. But then he had said, 'You shouldn't drive me to it.' He had never called himself a prat. He never played with other people's children or his own. His charm was reserved for others. Josh's charm was for her first and he had snapped under pressure. Well, hadn't she? And never a blow had been struck. But all the time she was thinking: Jane? Lucy and Harry?

She wanted to be away from here, to talk to Lucy.

Mike was stuffing himself with risotto. The way he chewed had always irritated her. It did still. He said, 'Anyway, I'll have to speak to Ken soon. There's a move to Head Office coming up and I know he's desperate to join us here. But I don't think I can give it to him as things are, Fran. He really hasn't the mileage; a general attitude problem, the carelessness. Have a word, see if you

326

can kick-start him into making up lost ground, there's a good girl.'

Fran made pretence of looking at her watch. 'Heavens. I'll have to cut and run. The children, an artist. So much to do, so little time.' She was up. She blew him a kiss and wound her way between tables which were steadily filling as business lunchers arrived. Do your own dirty work, you self-satisfied shit, she wanted to say. Tell him yourself, don't try and get me all wound up and then dump that on me. Her feet were killing her by the time she reached the car.

She made time to change before collecting the children. She made time to walk them in the park remembering her first meeting with Josh; his warmth, his paint-smudged, lean, strong, tanned hands, the way he read her like a book. 'I'll make it work,' she said to Lucy. 'I love him so much, just as much as I love you.' Lucy looked puzzled. 'Don't take any notice of your silly grandma, she's thinking aloud.'

'My daddy does that, my mummy says.'

'What does Daddy say, when he thinks aloud?'

'I don't remember.'

Fran picked up the child and showed her the squirrel high in the branches of the oak. As Lucy followed her finger she said, 'Lucy, darling, is Daddy nice to you and Mummy?'

Lucy looked at her, then tried to find the squirrel again. 'Where, where?' she said.

Once the child had found the squirrel Fran repeated, 'Is Daddy nice to Mummy? Some aren't, you know.'

Lucy wriggled to get down. 'Daddy's a nice daddy. He's going to take us on holiday with our

327

spades, when he's got a new job. He said he'd buy Mummy a pretty dress. Mummy says he loves us. She says he's too tired to find the words. Can we go to the swings?'

They spent an hour in the park, and Fran watched and listened like a hawk but there was nothing untoward, only the preoccupation of a busy father. They decamped for the house. It was deserted. Emily would not be home until six as there was a rehearsal. Josh usually stayed at college and brought her home. Lucy was sorry, but ate a slice of cake and drank her juice, and chatted about her morning and the ducks she had played with in the bath.

'Does Daddy play ducks with you?'

'Daddy's at work.'

Of course he was.

So was Josh. She phoned the staff room but he was teaching. She didn't leave a message because all she wanted to do was send her love.

Jane phoned. She was so sorry and would pick up the children early. She had worked through her lunch hour and would be there at four. When she arrived she brought flowers and was awkward, standing in the hallway, calling the children to her. Fran couldn't bear it and took her daughter in her arms. 'Darling Jane, you'll never be out of my life, no matter what. *You* are my daughter. I love you.'

Slowly her daughter's arms came round her and her head rested on Fran's. 'I'm sorry, Mum. We need a holiday just to draw breath, really, and try and get a handle on everything. I don't know, two children are so much more than one and we're so hoping for this transfer. It's rather taken over, made everything build up.'

Fran held on to her, saying, 'Did you talk to Ken about the gym?'

There was no tensing from her daughter, no snapping. 'I will tonight. He's been working until the small hours on this case. He deserves a holiday.'

Fran let her go, smiling at her, rubbing her daughter's arms lightly, then shaking her, watching. Always watching. There was no sign of pain. Fran couldn't let it go, though, not quite yet. 'Are you and Ken all right? It's such a difficult time for young parents, so many pressures.'

Lucy ran out from the sitting room. 'Mummy, we went to the park.'

Together Fran and Jane collected Harry who was asleep in his chair. Lucy held Fran's hand and dragged her with them to the car. 'When are we going on holiday with our spades, Mummy?'

Jane laughed as she settled a sleepy Harry in his seat. 'When Daddy has this new job, though even if he hasn't we'll go for a little while. And yes, Mum, Ken and I are fine. It's been tiring, that's all. I feel far better today. I'm sorry I've been such a pain, so unreasonable. I'm just so sorry.'

Fran remembered Mainwaring. She said, 'I gather there are problems with a case? Bring the kids here, if it will help Ken get to grips at the weekend. I think Mike's a bit rattled. He doesn't want to lose a client.'

'Linda's rung, has she?'

'Just let Ken have some time to sort it. I want the best for you both. Remember I'm always here for you. You can talk to me about anything. Do you understand?' Was her voice too urgent?

Jane patted her arm. 'I'm a big girl remember,

Emily was quite right. Perhaps I just needed to be reminded. But of course I would talk to you if I needed to.'

Fran waved them away, relieved beyond anything she had known. Jane did seem better. Amazingly better and perhaps all that had been needed was the jolt they'd all given one another yesterday. It was just as though a storm had raged over them all and left the air quite clear, joyously, wonderfully clear.

*   *   *

Jane parked in the drive. It had taken all her self-control not to tense, not to wince but she was trying not to annoy anyone. So stupid, her mother had said yesterday, so stupid. She really must not be and she would take the children out on Saturday and Sunday, though not to her mother. Neither would she tell Ken what her mother had said about his work. He didn't like her discussing him with anyone.

CHAPTER THIRTY-TWO

Sally was bursting, Linda could tell, simply bursting to confide some great excitement, but court had been long, hot and she wasn't in the mood, and she longed for 5.30. Only an hour and a half to go. She wished she were back in the pub, and it were evening and the shadows were soft, as soft as Mike's voice, as soft as his lips as he kissed her goodnight.

That was all, again, a kiss, but it was longer and deeper, and her toes had curled, her stomach had flipped and if he didn't get a shove on she also would burst.

Linda swept past Sally's desk. 'Mail on the table?'

She didn't wait for Sally's reply, because of course it was. Linda sank into her chair and kicked off her shoes, her psyche bruised from this morning. Why the hell couldn't naughty husbands realise that if they strayed and started marking another's territory they were in danger of losing half their own patch? What a kicking and screaming went on over property and policies. What a damned waste of time and money. What a horrible dance, which ignored children and memories. She needed a shower.

The door opened. She groaned, for what she was going to get was Sally.

Sally carried a tray of coffee and digestives, and laid it carefully on Linda's desk. There were two cups. Oh, dear. Linda smiled. 'Yes, sit down for a moment, but then I must get on.'

Sally was wearing a red jacket today. She really shouldn't with her new hair colour. Her bracelet jangled alarmingly as she reached forward and took one of the cups and no biscuit. She was slimming, getting in trim for a late holiday, or so she had said yesterday and the day before. Linda took up her own cup, glancing out of the window and back at Sally encouragingly, for the sooner the gossiping began, the sooner it would end. 'Sally, tell all. You're obviously in the grip of something good.' She smiled, because there had been enough unpleasantness this morning to last until the next time.

Sally leaned forward. 'You had this call while you were at court. From Fran, my predecessor, I believe. Well, in your absence she asked to be put through to Mike. I mean Mr Wells. Anne tells me this Fran left him at the altar and maybe they're heading that way again, because they went for lunch.' Sally sat back, deeply satisfied. She hadn't drawn a breath throughout, Linda noted, but then neither had she.

Linda tried to eat her biscuit. She should say something. 'Goodness. How did Mike seem?'

'Lighter of foot on his return, were Anne's words.'

'Goodness.' The biscuit tasted of sawdust. She tried the coffee. Bilge water. 'Lighter of foot, eh?'

God was good, because the phone rang. Sally leapt to her feet and hurried out to take up her role as guardian of the exchange. Linda thought of the tuna and mayonnaise sandwich she had grabbed at lunchtime when her stomach was still riotous from the acrimonious exchanges, the poisoned glances, the tears of the morning.

While she had been wondering where to put her crusts, Mike and bloody Fran had been eating lunch together. Where? Had they played footsie? How bloody dare Fran? She had her own territory now, her own problems, her own man. No. It wasn't going to happen even if she was back in her old house. It just wasn't going to happen because old house didn't mean old world.

She finished her biscuit and her coffee, then flashed for Sally. Sally said, 'It was just a client phoning for a progress report.'

'What was?'

'The call I've just had.'

'Never mind that. Get me the number of the college and then would you, could you, slip out and pick me up a doughnut? Bring one back for yourself.' She didn't want to add to Sally's excitement by handing her some juicy eavesdropping.

She hurriedly dialled the number herself. Please be there. When did he head off home? The office put her through to the staff room. She spoke to Josh. 'Hi, Josh, it's Linda.'

'Linda? What's wrong, is it Fran?' She could picture him, all paint-stained fingers and a smock. Did he wear a smock? What did it bloody well matter for he should attend to his affairs and keep them out of her life.

Linda forced a laugh. 'I was hoping you could put my mind at rest on that score, Josh. Apparently she and Mike lunched together today. I've tried to phone her at the gallery but the line's engaged. I'm just concerned that there's a problem, perhaps with the lease?'

There was silence on the line. 'Josh?' she asked. 'Is everything all right?'

'Fine, but I have to get to a class, Linda. Leave this with me.' She had heard that note in her client's voice this morning when she had been awarded two-thirds of the divvy-up, but had still loved her husband.

The line went dead. Linda replaced the receiver, feeling dirty. She couldn't believe she'd done that. She wiped her hands up and down her skirt. Sally brought in the doughnut: on a plate, like Samson's head. Just get a grip.

CHAPTER THIRTY-THREE

Emily and Josh arrived home together. Fran had a meal ready and a bottle of white wine in the fridge. She had mixed a bowl of salad and served it with a fish pie she had made with tinned pink salmon and a cheese sauce. It was a meal that Jane had always liked. Perhaps Emily would too.

Emily did, but she also wanted wine and held up her glass. Josh shook his head. 'Well, how about a spritzer?' Emily bargained.

Josh glanced at Fran. She nodded slightly. 'Find some sparkling mineral water,' Josh instructed. 'There's no soda, is there, Fran?'

He was tentative and wouldn't look directly at her, just as he had not when he arrived in Emily's wake. He had kissed her cheek then, not her lips, and made to follow his daughter through into the hall but Fran had held him fast and whispered, 'Let's forget about last night, about the whole mess. You apologised and I took no notice. Now I'm apologising and I know it's a pain having the kids, but it won't be for ever. Let's make it up tonight.'

Behind them Emily had made sick noises. 'Must you snog?' But it wasn't venomous, more the ritualistic teenage response to adult affection.

Josh had laughed, but it hadn't been quite right. It would be, though, tonight, Fran thought, as she passed Emily the salt and pepper—Emily, who had made no reference to yesterday, who could only talk of the rehearsal and the new boy, Andrew, who had also come from a boarding school and looked like David Beckham, and was to partner her in some of her duets.

'But you're the star, are you?' Josh sounded tired, the lines were deep around his mouth.

'Of course she is. She'll knock spots off the others.' Fran tore a piece of bread and mopped up the remains of the French dressing from her plate, confident and ravenous.

Josh's meal was only half eaten, and now he laid his knife and fork neatly together and sat back, his hands limp in his lap. To Fran's look of enquiry he said, 'I'm not very hungry.'

Emily snatched a look at him, then pressed Fran's foot with hers. 'He needs a hair of the dog. That'll teach you for ducking out to see Uncle Stan. Mark told me you'd had a session.' She was grinning at Fran, actually grinning.

Fran almost shook her head. So, one David Beckham lookalike came on the scene and the sun rose over Emily's horizon. Fran grasped the moment. 'As he's a little fragile, how about popping upstairs when you've finished and sorting out the remains of your unpacking. I'm still behind with ours, if it's any comfort. I've just been so busy today.'

'Busy?' Josh queried, as Emily huffed and muttered, 'Slave labour, that's what it is.' But she only appeared to be going through the motions.

Fran took the Chardonnay from the wine cooler and offered it to Josh, who refused. My, how bad your head must be, Uncle Josh. She poured another glass for herself. 'We've sold two more O'Reillys and the children romped in the park.' She would save Mike until later when she could also tell Josh how much she adored every part of him, how they could weather this, how things were already

335

turning around, how she was strong enough to cope with anything that anyone threw at them. Look at Emily and Jane. Something's in the air tonight, she'd tell him, and he'd laugh and hold her, and even if he was too pale and interesting to make love, at least they could cling together without disapproval from the stalls.

'I'll have another,' Emily said. 'Just a tiny triple.'

Fran laughed. All Josh could raise was a smile. Emily put down her glass, muttering, 'Well, it was worth a try.'

Josh gestured to the remains of her fish pie. 'Finish up, if Fran's gone to the trouble of cooking, and then what about homework? Love might have reared its head and stardom might be beckoning, but get your priorities right.'

'Oh, Dad, honestly. Love—who said anything about love?'

Josh looked so bleak that for a moment Fran felt as though a fist had clutched her heart. He said quietly, 'Just eat up, Em.'

Em finished, wiped her plate with her crust as Fran had done and looked up triumphantly. 'There, is that good enough, Mr Misery Guts? Mum won't let me wipe my plate, she calls it slumming. I'm going to send off some photos to her and when I do I'll tell her that Fran is teaching me well.'

Fran sighed at the tone. Emily picked up her plate and banged it on to the drainer. 'I won't offer to help with the dishes, as I've my priorities to consider.' With that she swept from the room.

Josh almost stumbled to his feet, taking Fran's plate from her, stacking it on his as though everything weighed a ton. He carried both to the sink, saying, 'She's never actually offered, ever.'

Fran watched him for a moment as he stared out at the garden. He was so still. She loved him so much. He turned, crossed his arms and stared at her for a long moment, and there was nothing in his eyes, nothing—no love, no pleasure, no energy.

Fear came again, the fear of being unloved, of losing him, of not being able to reach him, of not understanding what was happening, of finding her strength too late. 'I love you. Josh, what's wrong?'

He sank his chin to his chest. His shoulders were bowed. He said, and his voice was muffled, 'Are you leaving me?'

She couldn't move, couldn't react. He shouted now, coming right up close, looming over her. 'You've been seeing Mike. You rang him today and you met for lunch. Well, of course you're not leaving, because we're in your house, aren't we? It's we who are leaving, isn't it, so don't bother to unpack our stuff. I'd better call Emily back, hadn't I?'

It was a question, one which she swept aside. 'How . . . ?' she gasped.

'Did I know? Well, not from you, obviously. Yes, you had a busy day selling O'Reilly's cretinous prints, playing with the children, but you left a great wide window out, didn't you?'

He had paced away, to the fridge, then back to the sink. She went to him. He flinched away, just as his daughter had so often done. She took a step back, angry. Yes, angry, not guilty, not afraid. 'If you could stop being the prima donna for a moment I'll tell you. Yes, I rang him. He suggested lunch, to talk about Ken and ask me to chivvy him up, and also to . . .'

337

'Yes? Also to get into your knickers?'

'Oh, don't be absurd.' Her shout was so loud that Mrs Thomas must have heard and she didn't give a damn. The silence that followed was profound as he looked at her. He could read her. She said quietly. 'All right. I needed to talk to an old friend. I rang Linda. She wasn't in. I asked to be transferred to Mike. He asked me for lunch. I don't know what I thought. Perhaps I wondered . . . But he's just a friend, I realise. Just a friend.'

Josh's face was still drawn, his eyes a careful blank. 'He's more than a friend. He's the man you left at the altar for a different kind of life. A life that's pretty much like the old one.' He looked around the room. 'But worse.' He raised his eyes towards Emily's room.

'Josh, I love you.'

'Is love enough, when our lives are falling apart around us?'

He shouldn't be saying this. It was what she had thought this morning. It was what she had talked herself out of. 'Nothing's falling apart. It's beginning to come together. We just need to believe in it, in one another.' She reached for him, gripping his arms. 'I love you so much. You know everything about me before I do, so take a good look.'

He shrugged her off and walked to the kitchen door. 'I can't bear to.'

She shouted at his back, 'So who told you about the lunch, or have you had your spies out? How long have you thought there was something going on?'

He stood still but did not turn. His shirt was almost the colour of Mike's, but faded through

338

years of washing. 'Linda phoned me this afternoon to check that you were all right and, I suspect, to lay claim to any divorce procedure. One more case for Gilbert and Gilbert's books, more money in their till.'

'Linda? Linda phoned you and not me. Why?'

Josh talked to the door. 'Think about it, Fran. Perhaps because she's frightened. Fear makes you panic. It makes you desperate. You should know that.'

He opened the door and walked out into the garden. He stood for a moment staring around, then he made for the side gate and left.

*   *   *

Fran unpacked with a fury. She hung the last of his clothes in the wardrobe, put the last of the linen in the airing cupboard, his bits and bobs in the bathroom cabinet. She unpacked his books and muddled them with hers on the landing bookcase and in the sitting room, and laid down his wine in the dining end. She worked until her arms ached, and her back, and until the light was failing, until it was done. Then she flopped in her armchair, in her house. But it could become his too. It must become his, for as long as they needed it. Because love *was* enough. Without it there was nothing.

She closed her eyes, hearing the sitting-room door open. 'Josh?'

It was Emily, a pale, nervous Emily. A child who stood with her arms crossed, her eyes carefully blank and said, 'I heard you. You've been out with other men. All this fuss about me, all these raised eyes, that amused smile because he got drunk and

339

all the time you've been out with other men. You're a bitch and I hate you.'

Emily stood there, on her beige carpet, the bookshelf to her left, the bay window to her right, with everything in reach worked for by Fran, chosen by Fran and designed to bring her peace, and now Fran was crazily angry again. 'It's time one of you listened to me. Just damn well listened. I've been out with a man who has been my friend for years. I needed to talk.'

Emily turned on her heel. 'Oh, yes. That's what they all say: I needed to talk. So, what about? Where you were going to meet again?' She slammed the door behind her and ran up the stairs. Fran sank her head in her hands. Bum. Just damn and blast and bum. She said it, she did not whisper it, until it became boring, until the words lost all meaning and the raging died.

The house was quiet. There was no banging from Emily. No pulling in and out of drawers, no loud music. Nothing. This was different from all the other times. This must be too much like her mother's home. Josh had always said that no one man would be enough for Catherine. The child must be familiar with the procedure, with the lies, the excuses, the absences and, ultimately, the airline tickets, the packed suitcases, the rejection.

For a moment longer she sat there, too tired to move but when were parents allowed that luxury? They could always move, it was what they did. Fran quietly mounted the stairs and tapped on Emily's door.

'Go away. I'm packing.'

Fran opened the door. Emily had piled everything back into her case and was leaning over, struggling to close it. She snarled, her hair in her face, 'I said go away.' The duvet was rucked up. A trainer lay between the door and the bed. It seemed pathetic, symbolic, tragic, dramatic. Once Jane had done this, when Fran had said she must do her homework instead of going to a party because she had been rude and unpleasant, and must learn that there were consequences to one's actions. After a while, Fran thought bleakly, life became boringly repetitious. She took a deep breath, saying, 'Well, I won't go away and there's no way that will close with all those arms and legs dangling out.'

'Then I'll go without it.' Em continued to struggle with the lid though.

'Where, Em? Where will you go?'

'To Gran's.' She flipped that long hair back over to one side. She'd been crying.

Fran picked up the Nike and pulled a face. 'Well, we'll just have to come after you, because there's no way you're living anywhere but with us. We want you here. Your dad adores you and I'm getting pretty fond of you myself. It's a bit like getting used to a thorn in your side.'

Emily sat on the bed suddenly, her nose red, her face pale. 'So that's what I am, a thorn?'

Fran brought over the Nike. She set it down on the sloping lid of the case. 'Sometimes, just as I am to you. But I mean it, Emily. I really am getting used to you. You're interesting, a bit different, rather fascinating. Very missable. In fact, I'm beginning rather to love you.' It was a lie, but perhaps it could happen.

Emily fiddled with her hands. 'Words are cheap.'

Fran sat down, the case between them. 'So are

341

clichés, so let's avoid them. Now, let's sort this out chronologically. As regards Mike, I phoned to speak to Linda. I was fed up with you all, including Jane. I needed to chat to an old friend. Linda was out. Mike was a friend long before Linda. I was at school with him, believe it or not. I used to copy his maths homework, which is why my appallingly bad exam results were always such a surprise to everyone but me. I should never have said I'd marry him. It would be a bit like the David Beckham lookalike swanning off and Mark stepping into his shoes: convenient, until you stop to wonder what you're doing, or until someone a million times better than even the lookalike comes along and steals your heart.'

Emily sniffed, dragging her hair back from her face. 'Let's avoid clichés, shall we?'

Fran grinned and Emily did, almost. Fran moved now to the door, as though barring the exit, and said, 'Anyway, imagine riding off into the sunset with someone you truly loved, only to have a blistering row, something that knocked you off balance. You'd want to talk, to share the problem, and with Linda in court I thought Mike might still be my friend. He is, but he's moved on too, Emily, and I realised I didn't want to tell him. In fact, between you and me I saw things I'd never seen before. I mean, his hands are sort of white and soft, and I remembered how obsessed he was with work, and he chews his food in the most irritating way and that he'd always bored the pants off me. Well, let me put it another way . . .'

Emily smiled reluctantly. But then she looked down at her hands and began to fiddle again as though remembering other plausible explanations.

Bloody Catherine.

Fran said, 'I really, desperately want to find a way to make the three of us work and I'm sorry if I've put the process back a stage, but I won't give up on us. I don't care how far you go, I'll come after you and drag you back. You belong here with us, though we accept we have to share you two ways, but not three. If Jessie wants to see you, she sends you back pretty quick, is that clear? Now unpack that lot before we have to re-iron it, there's a good girl. Cocoa in half an hour, in the kitchen. All right?'

There was no answer, but she hadn't expected one. She let herself out and heard Emily ease back the lid of a suitcase, heard the thud as the Nike hit the floor. As she shut the door behind her she noticed the rattle of the hangers in the wardrobe and felt as though she'd reached the top of the mountain for the umpteenth time today, and wondered just where all those words had come from, and hoped she would come to mean every single one.

It was then she saw Josh leaning against the banister, his usual smile on his face, the love back in his eyes. He came to her, took her in his arms. 'Is that true?'

'Most of it,' she whispered. 'And the rest of it could be.'

'I adore you. I always will and you haven't put us back a stage, you've leapfrogged us forward. Why don't you and I just land in a great big pile on our lovely bed?' He smelt of linseed oil and turps, and it was so much better than aftershave and so much the sum of their lives.

'Cocoa in half an hour, but after that . . .'

They clung together more fiercely than they had ever done before and she whispered, 'Tomorrow I must paint. Tomorrow we must start again.'

He said, 'I was telling the group today of the way you like to use a single application of colour, rather than layers, of the freshness of your work. I suddenly remembered the early work of Mary Cassatt—same technique though different style. I must show you her work.'

So it continued throughout cocoa and even Emily was interested in the concept of cropping objects at the edges of the composition, making scenes appear candid and realistic.

Suddenly, as Josh collected up the mugs he paused, looked at them both and shrugging, said, 'Mark you, perhaps we don't need much practice in candid and realistic scenes.' Emily was still laughing as she opened up her script.

They both heard her lines, which were far from perfect. 'I've plenty of time,' she said airily.

Fran didn't want to get involved in that one and neither did Josh, because there was not plenty of time. Emily had come into the play late and it was a mere two weeks away but Brian must sort it. Instead they talked of redecorating the sitting room, or rather, Fran did. For this was their house. 'We want it to have some much needed life, Emily, so why don't you choose the scheme?'

'Then can we do my bedroom?' Emily asked, her finger still on a difficult passage of the script.

Firmly Fran said, 'No, not for the moment. It is too early with regard to Jane.'

Emily received the edict thoughtfully and without objection, merely commenting that it sounded as though they were staying put for a

344

while.

'As long as it suits us, don't you think, Josh?' Fran said. 'On the strict understanding that no flying ducks suddenly appear on the wall.'

While Fran and Emily grinned, Josh coloured and swiftly changed the subject by checking his Monet expedition dates on the calendar. It was then that Emily wailed, 'But those are the dates of the play.'

Fran took the mugs to the sink, trying to think quickly but Josh was there before her. 'No matter,' he assured Emily. 'I can leave for home a day early and catch the last night. I'm not missing the chance to embarrass you by wearing my best hat and waving.'

As Fran washed the mugs she looked over her shoulder. Emily was raising her eyebrows at her. 'He thinks he's so funny.'

'Sad, isn't it, especially as I'll have to sort out his matching frock.'

'Oh, p-l-e-a-s-e.'

*   *   *

That night Josh took Fran in his arms, and it seemed like a lifetime ago that she had felt the length of him against her and his hands on her body, and hers on his. Hands that peeled back, layer by layer, the veneer that had been built, stroking away the hurts, the fears, the deep darkness of pain, the flaring anger, the uncertainties until the love was exposed and its power swept them back to St Ives, back to the dreams and the hopes, and skywards, swooping and dipping, higher and higher, until finally it crashed them down, exhausted but together. 'Always together,' Josh murmured, his arm over her body.

CHAPTER THIRTY-FOUR

Linda phoned Fran at the gallery. 'Sorry, Fran. I bet you know by now I phoned him.'

'But you were worried?' Fran silenced Gail with a wave of her hand. Gail mouthed, 'I'll sort it.' She was waving a fax at her.

Linda was saying, 'Yes.'

Fran felt it wasn't a firm yes. It was a 'yes I was worried but not for the reasons you think'. Ah. 'In case I snaffled the man of your dreams from under your nose?' The silence was satisfying. Fran leafed through the mail but the fax regarding the clash of workshop dates had been the only thing of interest.

Finally Linda admitted the truth. 'I've loved Mike for years. Or at least I've fancied him and now I've spent time with him I know its love. If you know what I mean.'

Fran knew exactly what she meant. 'Nice, isn't it.'

'Its a ruddy nightmare, when you don't know if they feel the same.'

Oh, so Mike hadn't committed. Well, just how far had it gone? Fran was curious, that was all. She said, as James made snorting and gushing sounds in front of the desk indicating that a cappuccino was on its way, 'Linda, anyone who could coax Mike into that tie is in with a colossal chance.' She grinned as James now tried to emulate a flapjack. 'Just a minute, Linda. James, go away and come

346

back again with whatever comes to hand.'

She ignored his lecher imitation, returning instead to Linda, who hadn't waited a minute, and had been explaining that Mike had switched into modern man mode in the aftermath of Fran's bolt and that it owed nothing to her.

It seemed strange to be listening to one of her best friends talking of the other in such a way, especially as 'she had knowledge' of him, as her mother would have said. 'But you've spent time with him?' Fran queried.

'I grasped the nettle and said I had tickets for *Les Misérables*, after the Mahler concert fiasco. I could have murdered Ken.'

'We've all felt like that about Ken at some stage of our existence and you're a beast, you could have got tickets for us. You and me.'

Linda laughed. 'Needs must, when the devil drives.'

'Oh, lord. Am I living in a land ruled by cliché?'

'What are you talking about?'

James was placing a flapjack and cappuccino before her with all sorts of flourishes, to the amusement of a party of elderly women who, unknown to him, had just entered the gallery. They applauded. He flushed. Fran enjoyed his discomfort, holding her hand over the mouthpiece, saying to the leader of the group, 'I promise you he's not included in everyone's order.'

'That's a shame,' the group chorused, as they passed on into the coffee shop proper. James disappeared in confusion to the storeroom.

'Fran?' Linda said.

'Yes, I'm here,' Fran reassured her. 'Look, has he returned the invitation?'

'Scampi and chips at a pub, and next week, too.'
'What night?"
'Wednesday.'
'That's bridge night. My word, that's great guns. Look, go for it, darling, then cook him a meal at your place. You're made for one another and I'm sure Cheryl, his daughter, will find you far superior to his last trollop.'

Linda's laugh was reluctant. 'I feel strange when you say that, Fran. I still wonder if . . .'

'Absolutely not,' Fran cut in. 'Mike has no feelings for me beyond friendship and I certainly have none for him. I wonder if there ever was anything else, really. Either way, he's moved on. Maybe one day we could all have dinner?' There was a pause.

Together they said, 'But not yet.' The shared laugh was familiar, as it had always been.

'Go for it, darling,' Fran repeated.

Linda said quietly, 'What about you, Fran? Are you in trouble? Isn't it working? Why did you ask to be put through to Mike?'

Fran told her the story and the aftermath.

'I'm so glad. For you and for me.' Linda said.

'So much so that you will come to Emily's performance, won't you? I need someone with me on the Thursday night to cheer for Em. I'm going to rope in Jane and Ken for Wednesday, Josh will be back from France on Friday. Jessie and Fred have promised to make it that night too.'

James floated past. 'We're on for Thursday too,' he said, holding up four fingers.

Fran nodded, making a note to see which night Edward and Tom wanted tickets, though Mark was in the band so probably the Terrace would be on

348

audience duty throughout. Linda agreed and offered help.

'Costumes,' Fran said firmly. 'She's Esmerelda in a tutu. Jessie offered only this morning but Josh fears the results and you are so, so clever with your sewing machine. Remember Jane's ballet costumes, the robin outfit? That adorable beak.'

'You don't need to market the idea. I'm on board.' Linda was sighing slightly. 'I have a sense of déjà vu.'

'*You* have a sense.'

'And it's OK with you?'

'There will be peaks and troughs, but we'll get there.'

'How about Jane? There's trouble brewing at work. Did you know?'

Fran broke a piece of flapjack and dipped it in her rapidly cooling froth. 'I've mentioned it. She seems more settled. Now I've a huge piece of flapjack to eat and a coffee to drink, a gallery to run and a husband to meet for lunch.'

'Sounds good to me.'

'It is, Linda. Trust me, it is.'

CHAPTER THIRTY-FIVE

The next week saw the end of the O'Reilly exhibition and the installation of the College students' work. On Friday, at the Gallery's evening preview, Ruth licked her lips at the endless stream of students and their relatives, which promised a healthy trade over the next two weeks. The press were supportive. Stan, Josh and Tom played soft jazz, and Jessie and Fred would have attended, they phoned to say, 'And we'll have to buy a video of the prima donna's debut rather than be there, which is tearing us apart. The tourists are baying for pots and we're working ourselves into a lather over a hot wheel. You'll understand, darling Fran, and Em insists she does.' She did.

Mike and Linda attended, holding hands and looking coy. Ken and Jane came. Ken looked pale and tired but he'd found the Mainwaring file that he had mislaid, or so Jane shared with Fran. 'So at last he can sort it out properly, but unfortunately Mike knows. Never mind, he seemed all right about it.'

Fran looked around quickly, fearful of eavesdroppers, for a lost file should never be discussed in public. No one appeared to have heard, most important of all not Mike, who was pretending to admire a brash modern art piece near the window but was in reality absorbed in Linda who stood very close to him. Did he really not mind?

Fran hadn't realised how much her daughter was still on her mind until that moment, and a great weight lifted from her shoulders as Ken drank a glass of wine and wove his way towards Mike, who greeted him with a smile. Presumably not. Nearby, Jane laughed and smiled with the Dean in a way that Fran had almost forgotten. Only Emily, who stood behind Jane pulling 'sucking up' faces, made her shoulders tighten.

The next day, with the first night of the school production a mere week away, Emily put aside her script yet again and volunteered to accompany Fran to the DIY to collect paint. 'It must be exactly right, Fran. Quite right won't do; we must have it mixed, if necessary. You did promise I could choose.' She pointed to the colour chart.

But dark-red? For a sitting room?

'Are you coming, Dad?' Emily called.

'He's packing,' Fran said, looking for her car keys which she found near the bread bin.

'Gosh, Dad. I didn't see your lips move.'

'Don't be clever,' Josh shouted down from the airing cupboard, saving Fran the job. 'How many towels, Fran?'

'For a week in a house with a washing machine? Two.' Fran found the keys. 'Come on, then. Off we go, but this is only going to work if you behave.'

'Oh, for heaven's sake.' Emily slouched out of the front door and stood by the car.

They found just the right shade of red, which at the last minute Emily decided would be more suitable for the dining area beyond the arch, choosing a slightly lighter shade for the sitting room.

'So there definitely is a God,' Fran whispered to Josh on their return.

They ate a last lunch together, and Fran couldn't stop the lurching and missing which had already begun.

Emily spoke enough for the two of them, taking them step by step through the dorkish song she and Andrew had to sing and the choreography the chorus line couldn't hack, and telling of the way Mark had improved since Stan had been coaching him night after night.

Josh muttered, 'We could have done more of that *if* I hadn't been too busy with the scenery.'

'Stop grizzling,' Fran said. 'Emily and I have

managed reasonably well, haven't we, Em?'

'Why did you offer to do the scenery it you make such a fuss about it?' Emily asked, reaching for the butter.

Josh snatched a look at Fran, pulled a face, then laughed. 'OK, OK, because I like it, really. Is that good enough?'

'It'll do.' Fran grinned. To her surprise Emily shared a look with her and a smile. Perhaps they had really sailed in the calm of a miraculously normal teenage bloodiness.

After lunch Josh accepted Fran's Factor 25 with poor grace, stuffing it unceremoniously into the top of his rucksack before kissing his daughter. 'Be good. Learn your lines. Break a leg. I'll phone.' Emily hugged him briefly. Josh said, 'I hope Andrew rings.'

'Oh, Dad.' She blushed and swung away.

Fran shook her head at Josh. Did fathers never learn? He held her to him. 'You're sure about this redecorating on top of everything?'

'It's occupational therapy. I must do something while you're away.'

Emily called from the kitchen, 'If I can't decorate my room because the delectable Jane *might* be thrown into a tizz, then at least let us get the sitting room out of its rut.' Her tone was not actually objectionable, more of a tease.

'Out of the mouths of babes and sucklings,' murmured Fran, trying to defuse the worry in Josh's eyes.

He pulled away, looking closely. 'Fran, are you sure about us altering things and staying on here?' He nodded in the direction of Em.

'We've been through this. Why move when we

can make it ours? We've Mrs Thomas and her gossip mongering to consider too. We haven't given her nearly enough to do and a scarlet sitting room will provide her with a good springboard.'

His laugh was delighted. 'I love you up to the sky and back down again.'

Emily made vomiting sounds from the kitchen. They tried not to be irritated.

* * *

Fran and Emily started heaving the furniture into the centre of the room that afternoon, and covering it all with old sheets. 'We'll paint for a couple of hours and then it's homework. For you and for me,' Fran decreed.

There was some haggling but nothing much, even though she and this child were in the ring together, just the two of them. 'Two hours is the maximum with your work so in disarray. We have all week.'

'You might have, but what about my rehearsals?' Emily pouted, her hands on her hips.

'They're only on Monday and Thursday.'

'Doesn't it get boring?'

'What?' Fran asked as she decanted the paler ceiling red into two roller trays.

'Being right.'

Fran handed her a roller and a headscarf. 'I'm used to it. Now wear this, if you don't want to be a very spotty Esmerelda, whom not even the prince would want to snog.'

'Oh, really.' But the girl laughed. She actually laughed. Fran made a great effort to hide her astonishment.

After the two hours were up, Fran graduated to supper production and then ironing until at last it was bedtime. There was little sleep, though. Just a great deal of tossing and turning, and missing, and aching, and staring at the phone, until she crept into the spare room, set up her easel and tried for Cassatt's balance of rounded forms including an impressionist figure, against a background of vertical lines.

Absorbed, she didn't notice the coming of dawn until its fine light took the edge off the artificial, and then she stood back. This work was more measured, less frenetic. The rounded forms lacked the raw, anguished activity, as though held in check by the verticals. Not held in check. Vanquished.

She showered, letting the water beat hard and fast. She towelled herself dry, clearing the steam from the mirror, looking at herself, searching for a lessening of the bags, of age. She thought she saw it as the phone rang. She dragged on her dressing gown as she flew through to the bedroom, snatching up the receiver, tucking herself into the bed. It was 7.30. Josh's voice was eager: 'Darling, I love you, I miss you. We're here, the kids are settled. I'm not. I ache for you. I adore you and it doesn't seem like Sunday without you and *The Times* all over the bed.'

Emily knocked on her door, calling, 'Is it Dad?'

'Come in, Em.'

Emily came in, her tartan pyjamas rumpled. She sat on the edge of the bed, tutting, slumping, sighing. 'I feel the same,' Fran said into the receiver, 'but the first night is over. Only . . .'

'Six,' Emily interrupted, hovering, reaching out for the receiver.

'Yes, as Emily so rightly says, six to go. I love you, darling.' Fran wished the girl would go away.

Emily pulled a face and took the receiver that Fran offered. 'I'm fine,' she said. 'We've painted half the ceiling, then I had to do homework. She's all right, but missing you. We're both missing you. OK, Dad. I'll pass you back.'

While Fran talked of nothing in particular, Em curled up beside her on the bed, heaping the pillows, Josh's pillows, up behind her. She had brought in her script and when the phone call was finished she handed it to Fran. 'Take your mind off it and help me learn my lines.'

'Please.'

'OK, please.' The tone wasn't surly, it was normal. Emily lifted her hair over her head and avoided eye contact. Fran sat back tentatively, but Emily did not move away and for twenty minutes the two of them sat side by side, and Fran hardly dared move or speak as Emily went over and over the part.

She was hopeless and as far away as ever from word perfect, although Fran had no intention of telling her. Instead she placated, calling herself a wimp and telling Emily that the words would suddenly come.

That evening Fran completed the first coat of the ceiling and rubbed down the door which would have to be some sort of red, but she'd leave the choice up to Emily. Josh phoned again and they talked for longer than they could afford, but promised one another they'd keep it short next time, knowing they wouldn't.

Again she painted at her easel while Emily slept and this time she restricted herself to shades of white, working from the centre out. Only when she was through was she aware that from start to finish she had dictated the concept, controlled it, planned it. She thought it her finest work yet.

On Monday after school they powered on with the decorating in the children's absence, forgetting about lines, as Fran wondered if a day off would give a spurt to the memory bank. They had a break for supper, then went back to decorating and little was said, though they both tutted over the dramas of *Coronation Street* as they worked. As the credits rolled Fran had to say, 'Enough, time for homework.'

She was prepared for Emily's snapped, 'Yea, OK, I'm going, though why I can't prioritise I do not know.'

'Good try. Up you go.'

The stamping was impressive.

Josh rang briefly and Fran simply said that Emily was being more pleasant, and she was. The stamping had been pretty much on a par with Jane's at that age: all perfectly normal. She replaced the receiver, content.

On Tuesday Lucy helped Emily finish off the sanding of the door, while Fran developed an aching neck and shoulder rolling on the second ceiling coat. At 5.45 Jane called to collect the children. As she entered the sitting room her face was more or less what Mrs Thomas's would be, Fran thought.

'Mother, what have you done?'

Quite. 'It's Emily's choice.' Fran hoped her voice held sufficient warning.

Emily dusted off Lucy's hands. 'We're not doing anything to your bedroom, Jane. Because it *is* yours and you should have the final say on that.'

Jane glanced at Emily and then at Fran, a smile growing. 'Well, I'm sure you know how you want to spend your evenings. It must be quite invigorating, I suppose.'

Harry was gurgling in his chair and kicking strongly. 'Soon he'll be walking,' Fran said, coming down the ladder. 'He tried to pull himself up on the coffee table, didn't he, Em?'

'Are you in rush, Jane?' Em asked, reaching over Lucy for the script lying on the dust sheet which covered the settee. 'She's hopeless. Far too busy missing Dad.'

Jane's voice was sharp. 'Who is *she*?'

'Big Job's mother.' Emily ducked the rag thrown by Fran before she had time to think better of it. Emily just grinned. Jane started to speak, but Emily broke in: 'Because if you have time, could you take me through my lines, or you and Ken will cringe on the first night.'

'Go on, darling,' Fran pleaded.

Lucy pulled at her mother's skirts, saying, 'Emily said you could be voices when you came. She said I'd like you to be voices.'

'It really would help me,' Fran said, as she edged the ladder around the dust-sheeted furniture. 'Go on, just ten minutes.' Did her voice reflect the importance of this moment, one that she had not contrived, one that had just happened. Or had it? Was Emily trying to build bridges?

While Jane took on Andrew's part and the Dame's, and the little elf, Emily stopped and started and stumbled through Esmerelda's until they reached the end of the scene. For a moment Jane said nothing, as Lucy shrieked and giggled

357

and said, 'You're so funny, Mummy. Where do the voices come from? In here?' She poked Jane's stomach.

Jane had once been good at drama. She had been excellent in *Lady Windermere's Fan*. It was a performance Fran had forgotten.

Jane was flicking back to the beginning. Slowly she leafed through the script again while Emily sulked and picked at the sandpaper, saying, 'I can't do it. How can I be expected to with all this chaos around?' She gestured at the dust sheets.

Fran rolled more and more vigorously, willing Jane to say something, but please let it be the right something.

Jane said, 'Hang on a minute, Emily.'

Please don't, Fran said silently. Please, please do not wave a red flag at the bull. Jane was holding Lucy's hand, her fingers to her lips. 'Wait, Lucy. Emily, why not try singing it? The rhythm concept always worked for me. Actually, beating out the rhythm of the words on a drum is even more effective. You can make a rhythm for them, you know.'

'No way, a drum,' Fran interjected.

Both girls laughed and Lucy joined in. 'Come on,' Jane said, 'I've a few minutes to spare. Ken's in late. We'll run through once again.'

Jane led the way, singing to a made-up rhythm. Emily followed awkwardly, as though she felt a fool. But Jane was absorbed, uninhibited, and Lucy leaned against her knee and droned along with them both, and by the end Emily was closer to getting it than at any stage over the last few weeks.

'Better,' Jane declared, snapping shut the script.

The ceiling was finished. Fran eased her

shoulders and carried the roller and tray down to ground level, placing it carefully on the newspaper which covered the fireside rug. She wiped her hands free, almost, of emulsion as Jane picked up Harry with one hand and took his bag of tricks with the other. Emily took it from her. 'I'll help. Fair's fair. Come on, Lucy, let's get you to the car.'

Would she thank Jane?

Fran followed them out, saying to Jane, 'You were wonderful in all your plays, but Oscar Wilde brought out the best in you.'

Jane clipped Harry into the car. 'I'd forgotten I'd ever done anything like that.' Her voice was wistful.

Emily was pulling the straps over Lucy's shoulders. 'Sit still, Lucy. I can't do it if you're wriggling.'

'Mummy can.'

'Well, Mummy's very clever, we know that, and she's kind.' Jane glanced at Emily suspiciously. But there had been no rancour, only sincerity. It would do, Fran thought.

CHAPTER THIRTY-SIX

Emily was word perfect by the weekend and Fran could have gone down on her knees to Jane, as she actually did on the following Wednesday evening when the sitting room was finished and Emily was at school with the rest of the cast, confined to the drama room in case they missed 'curtain up' on this, the first night. Jane coloured, almost enough to match the walls. 'Don't be silly, Mum, get up. I should have remembered. It was stupid of me not to think of it sooner.'

She'd called her 'Mum' in that fond old tone. Fran clambered upright, wishing she were ten years younger. 'Darling, it's not as though you haven't a million other things to think of.'

Jane was rushing, piling Harry's things into his bag, unwilling to dilly-dally. Fran said, 'There's walnut cake. Sit down for a moment and tell me all. The good, the bad and the ugly.'

Jane was already hoisting up Harry. 'I can't, Mother. The Head Office position is to be announced at . . .' She looked at her watch. 'Well, right now. I want to be at home. Ken put a bottle of champagne in the fridge last night, to celebrate, and though he'd probably prefer to be out to dinner he's still willing to come to Emily's show. He's so kind.'

Fran led Lucy to the car. 'I hope you've told him that if Emily's any good it's because of you.'

'Don't be daft. I can't do anything, really.'

Fran waited as Lucy clambered into her seat, as those words ricocheted around her head. I can't do anything, really. He's still willing to come to Emily's show. Lucy wriggled. Fran clicked her secure, examining Jane as she strapped in Harry, watching closely as her short-sleeved blouse rode up. Nothing. I can't do anything, really. Again and again Fran had said such things because David had told her it was so.

'Darling?' Fran held the driver's door open as Jane slid in behind the wheel. 'At the risk of repeating myself, is everything all right? You know I'm always here for you.'

Jane's face was radiant as she turned the key in the ignition. 'It really is fine. He's talking of the holiday all the time now. It will be wonderful.'

Fran smiled and slammed shut the door. 'I'll pick you both up, then you can polish off that champagne and anything else you've put on ice.'

Jane drove off and Fran waved until they were out of sight, annoyed with herself. Why hadn't she just asked outright? Because there was no real reason to, she answered herself. No reason at all. It was all down to Mike. To jumping at false shadows. What if she had asked? Jane would have been furious that her beloved Ken was under the microscope; Ken who had been under the strain experienced by most young ambitious fathers; Ken who had found the file and whose wife was radiant with happiness because he probably would get the job now, surely . . .

'Cooee. Fran.' It was Mrs Thomas in her pinny, the one with roses and a huge pocket. What did people keep in them? Mrs Thomas's face was set in that strained 'we must allow others their funny little ways' look. 'Fran, I couldn't help but notice your decorating. My word. Red. It symbolises fire, I think.'

'And sex, Anne.'

Anne Thomas's mouth was a perfect 'O'. Fran didn't wait to see what it became, but swept inside to answer the ringing phone. It was Josh, to wish his daughter good luck. 'Do not say that. She will flounce and lay any failure firmly on your shoulders. I will tell her you said to break a leg.'

'Damn, I'd forgotten she wouldn't be back. Has she had lots of cards? Mum promised.'

'A few. Jessie, Lucy and Harry, Linda and Mike.'

'Ah, a joint one?'

'Absolutely. Their stone seems to be rolling

361

down the hill, gathering stardust nicely.' She should tell him about Catherine's letter. 'Even Catherine wrote. It arrived this morning.'

Josh scarcely missed a beat, but nonetheless it was a beat. 'Ah, after failing to phone for how many weeks? How is Em?'

'Not so good.' She could still hear the savage tantrum, the curt dismissal of the finished sitting room and see the curled lip when Fran said 'Break a leg'. 'She took it to school with her. I wasn't privy to its contents, but why should I be? I must go, Josh, I need to go through the knife edge of togging up to just the right degree, though nothing that could draw attention, or let her down.'

He was laughing as he said, 'I'll be there for the last night.'

'She knows you will and so do I.'

'I love you.'

'Me too, always.'

She had barely put down the phone when it rang again. It was Linda, telling her Mike wanted Fran to know that he had not given the Head Office job to Ken. The loss of the file, in spite of its recovery, had told against him in committee. It was a measure of his limited capabilities and, what's more, according to the Board, a good excuse to turn him down.

Fran was thoughtful as she replaced the receiver. If Ken and Jane had any sense they'd down that damn champagne anyway. Then they could top it with a choc ice and coffee in the interval. Bum and double bum. She lifted the receiver, then had second thoughts. No. Don't make more of it than it already was.

Upstairs, she sorted through her wardrobe,

plagued with thoughts of Ken. But he did not drink, she told herself as she tried on smart trousers, then discarded them. She stepped into a pencil skirt. Yes, that was better. She found a light cotton shirt. He hadn't the time to be a womaniser. She did up the buttons, adjusted the collar. For her daughter to be in the same position she had been in was inconceivable. It couldn't happen and she had already talked herself through all the ins and outs, so shut up. Lastly the shoes.

Downstairs, she snatched a light supper of salad and smoked turkey, and no wine. Best not, as she was driving. Meals with David had been almost the worst: the sense of walking on eggshells. She stared at her empty plate.

Jane had not winced when she had held her, she had never borne bruises, she had never said . . .

The phone rang again. It was Mrs Thomas, wishing Emily all the best. Fran was surprised, but then she remembered how Anne Thomas had always come to Jane's performances. How could she have forgotten? Never mind, she'd get a ticket for tomorrow. She said, 'Thanks so much, Anne. I thought you might like to support Emily tomorrow night. I'll drop a ticket through the letter box in the morning.'

'I did wonder if you'd remember.'

'Got to go. Can't be late.'

'Such a shame her father . . .'

Awful old bat. ' 'Bye.'

She replaced the receiver, yet again fumbling in her bag for her keys. Why didn't she put them away? But perhaps she had.

She tore through to the kitchen. Yes, they were in the fruit bowl, keeping the fruit flies company.

She must chuck the black bananas and that revolting apple. She tore to the front door but as she opened it the phone rang once more. She almost ignored it, but knew she'd wonder all evening who it was.

She doubled back, snatching it up, fearing that at last it would be the call she was dreading: Catherine. 'Fran, speaking.'

'Fran?' It was Ken. 'You sound rushed?'

'Yes, I'm on my way, so don't fret if I'm slightly astray.'

'Look, so sorry. Just relax. We can't make it after all. Poor old Jane's absolutely flat on her back so I've cancelled the babysitter. I don't want to leave her to a teenager's tender mercies. Report back to us, won't you?'

Fran stopped rushing, stopped everything and just stood for a moment. Then she said slowly, 'Flat on her back?'

'Some sort of flu thing, I think.'

'But she was bright. Brighter than I've seen her in ages and it wasn't so long ago she had a cold.' Fran's voice was sharp.

'I think that dragged her down,' Ken said ruefully.

'I see.' Well, there was some sense to that and there was a bug going around. Sally had made Linda's week last Thursday when she had been clobbered with a twenty-four-hour thing that had come on rapidly. Her mind raced. She said, 'Look, as I was coming that way, I'll call in.'

'Of course, why not. Or maybe I can get her to the phone, which would save you passing on germs to the "star".'

Damn, he was right, and there was nothing . . .

There was nothing, only . . . What the hell was there? Nothing. She said, 'Fine, ask her to pick up the extension. She is my little girl, after all. But hang on, Ken. Have you had any news about the Head Office transfer? I must say I think you'd be better advised to stay put. That way you can stay out of the politics and build your own little empire at Crewkerne.'

Ken's voice was smooth. 'Mike's obviously in agreement with you. Yes, I have heard. I haven't been given it. Maybe next time. I'll call up to Jane.'

He didn't seem concerned, so Fran had been doing everyone's worrying for them and more besides, and it was time she stopped trying to solve problems which didn't exist. Wasn't that an apt description of a neurotic? 'Thanks Ken. Lots of love.'

Jane's voice was croaky and feeble. 'Mum?'

Mum again. She felt reassured. 'Darling, what is it, a fever?'

'Something like that.' Jane's voice broke.

Reassurance fled. 'Shall I come?'

'For God's sake, we don't want to give it to little Miss Perfect, do we?' Jane's voice was raw. 'And you'll be late. Ken will look after me.'

Ken's voice broke in. He had been on the extension all this time. 'Of course, Fran. She's my little girl, too, you know. She's streaming, so I'll give her Beecham's. Hadn't you better get a wiggle on to be there for curtain up?'

'Yes, for heaven's sake, Mother.'

Fine. She knew when she was superfluous. 'I'll call tomorrow. Take care.' Fran finally made it out of the door.

Emily quite stole the opening scene and all those leading up to the interval. As others queued for choc ices Fran saw her peering from behind the stage door curtain and waved. Emily tried not to smile in return, but did, and waved a few fingers as a bonus. Fran relaxed, or almost because she could not remove the sound of Jane's voice. Not the harsh dismissiveness, but the break. Nor could she forget that Ken had been on the extension and as she queued for a cup of tea she remembered Jane's answer to her earlier question. 'It's fine. He's talking about the holiday.'

She returned to her seat, not bothering with the tea. Everything was fine, because he was fine. It's how she had felt with David, who could be nice, who could convince her that it was all finished. She rolled and unrolled the programme, wanting to go round, now; this minute. But on what pretence?

The interval seemed interminable. Someone's mobile phone rang. She wanted to snatch it off them, phone Jane. But she already had, stupid woman.

Stupid. That's what David had called her. Stupid, that's what Jane called herself.

The curtains were pulled aside to reveal Emily as Esmerelda, in Doc Martens, and Andrew in a corresponding tutu. Emily hadn't shared this with them. The audience were laughing, kids were whistling. Fran knew the script by heart, and sang it to the tune Emily and Jane had made up. Emily was faultless and now slipped into her duet with Elfie, accompanied by Stan and Mark. The hall fell silent. It was movingly beautiful and Fran stood to

366

applaud as the others did, wishing Jane were here. The success was hers so how dare she think she was stupid?

As the second act continued Fran groped on the floor for her fallen programme, returning it to her lap, not paying attention to the chorus, just wishing the seconds and the minutes away, so glad that Stan always set a cracking pace.

She rolled and unrolled her programme again, tapping it on her leg until the woman next to her tutted. She stopped and as she did so she knew the answer. She'd call round after the show with a programme. It was plausible and when she found Jane crotchety and ill she would accept her scowls and return home, her tail between her legs, which she could take—which she would welcome. And she would not have accused anyone of anything.

But . . . She forced herself to stop the mind game, to follow the chorus as it trilled itself off into the wings and the other acts came and went, but none to compare with Emily and she felt sorry for the absent Catherine.

At last the finale was over. Fran waited in the entrance hall with the other parents and every child, but Emily, seemed to rush out. Fran checked her watch. Ten minutes. It seemed like ten hours. Come on, come on. At last Emily came, to be greeted by a smile which Fran realised was too rigid. She knew Emily noticed.

She forced her shoulders down, made herself relax. 'Emily, what can I say, except that you were wonderful? I was just thinking how awful it was that Jane missed it.' Emily smiled. In the pocket of her blazer Fran saw Catherine's letter. Fran made that tomorrow's problem as she tried not to hurry her to the car.

She need not have bothered, for the world and its wife were trying to escape from the school car park, and it was another fifteen minutes before they were out on the road. Instead of heading towards home, Fran turned right towards Jane's. Emily said, 'What? But its late; she'll do her nut.'

Fran knew her voice was too sharp, too tense. 'Maybe not. Either way, she should know what a success you were, because some of it was down to her.'

Emily slouched back into her seat. 'Please yourself.'

Not now, Emily. Do not do this until I've had an earful from Jane and can go home ecstatic. The traffic seemed ridiculous for this time of night, but that was only because she wanted to scorch along the roads and be there in two ticks, but it was a further ten minutes before Fran pulled the car into the kerb outside Jane's house. There was a dull light on in the bedroom and another behind the closed curtains of the sitting room.

She snatched the programme from Emily. 'Stay here,' she ordered.

She closed her car door quietly and almost crept up the drive. She stood outside the front door, listening. She could hear laughter, music. The television. Once she had heard crying when she phoned. That had been the television. Or . . . She heard soft footsteps coming down the drive and spun round. It was Emily, walking as quietly as she had done. Emily who came close and whispered, 'What's wrong? What the hell is going on?'

'Don't swear.' The response was automatic. 'Nothing's wrong.'

'Why are we whispering?'

Fran looked at the girl in the light from the diamond-shaped frosted front door window. She just shook her head and knocked. Emily was peering through the window. 'Ken's there,' she said, 'he's just come downstairs. God, he's such a pillock. Why doesn't he open the door or does he think we're raping and pillaging when . . .'

'Do be quiet,' Fran snapped.

But Emily was rapping on the glass, yelling, 'Come on, Ken. Let us in. We're totally harmless.'

'Em, that's enough.' Fran felt tired suddenly, wondering what they were doing here in this quiet neighbourhood, with Mike on alert at the rear of the property and children who had mentioned nothing amiss, and a daughter who had no bruises . . .

Ken opened the door. She could smell the champagne on his breath. So he'd been drowning his sorrows after all; how very wise. For a moment Fran could have kicked Mike for not stretching a point for his god-daughter's husband. He was Chairman of the Board, for God's sake, he could have swung it.

Emily snatched the programme and held it out to Ken. 'We've brought a programme for Lucy.'

'No, not for Lucy,' Fran snapped, irritated with the child. 'For Jane.'

Ken looked from one to the other, making no attempt to take it. Instead he checked his watch, squinting dramatically. 'I'd ask you in, but everyone's asleep.'

Fran rubbed her arms. 'Heavens, though. It's a bit chilly out here.'

Emily's expression was one of amazement on

369

this balmy and warm evening. Then, loud and clear, came Lucy's voice from upstairs: 'Grandma, Grandma.'

Ken made as if to close the door. 'I'd better go.'

But Emily was already barging past as only she could and had reached the stairs in one easy movement. She called, 'Hi Lucy. Look what I've brought you.'

In a flash Ken was up the stairs after Emily who had disappeared into the children's bedroom. Fran stepped into the hall, watching, waiting for Jane's irritated shout, for her flu-ridden emergence, but there was nothing. Only Ken, stalled outside their door, taking a step towards the children's room, then returning, like a guard dog, just like Fran had once been, pacing, stalling, defending Jane against attack.

She moved dreadfully quickly now, climbing the stairs two at a time. Oh, yes, she had once been a guard dog and it seemed as though it was only yesterday. She reached the landing and walked towards Ken. 'You go and see to Lucy. I'll just check that Jane has everything she needs.'

How had she kept her voice calm and normal? Because the look on Ken's face was not of a defender, but a predator. Ken put up his arm across the door. 'She's sleeping.' He raised his voice. 'You're sleeping, aren't you, darling?'

In the children's room Emily was telling Lucy all about Esmerelda. From Jane's came no sound. Fran said, 'It's mum, Jane. Are you all right? Remember what I said, I'm here for you.'

Ken seemed very big tonight, his arm well-muscled as he barred her way. His eyes were quick, moving between the two doorways. He was

370

panting; his hair was damp from sweat. Lucy called from her bedroom, 'Hello, Grandma.' Emily and Lucy stood in her doorway, hand in hand. Lucy wore her Paddington Bear pyjamas.

Ken said, 'For goodness sake, she has to be up for Maisie's in the morning. Get to bed.' His voice was so harsh that even Emily froze, blinking. From behind them came Harry's startled cry. Lucy had reddened and now she too was weeping.

Fran said, 'See to your children, Ken.'

She headed as though for the stairs because danger made you cunning. Ken watched her, then hurried to Emily and hauled Lucy into the bedroom. Emily hesitated uncertainly, staring at Fran as she doubled back, trying Jane's door handle. Don't let it be locked. It wasn't.

Jane stood at the bottom of the bed, the duvet dragged around her. She was crying into it, smothering the noise. There was enough light from the table lamp to see the blood. It still oozed from her nose. It trickled from her swollen and cut lip on to the crisp cotton. Her poor arms were already bluing, as Fran's had once done, so very often.

Fran covered the distance between them soundlessly, taking her gently into her arms, so terribly gently. Slowly she pulled the duvet from her, letting it fall to the floor. Jane wore a towelling robe. She was shaking beneath it, shivering and trembling. Behind Fran, Ken said, 'She fell, right down the stairs. From top to bottom.'

Jane stiffened, looked up, pulled away from Fran. Gently but firmly Fran held her by the lapels of her robe, looking into her swollen eyes. Fran held the lapel tighter with her left hand, but reached out with her right, stroking her daughter's hair, her blood-stiffened hair, as she would have a frightened animal.

Jane's head was still the same shape beneath her hand as it had been when she had washed her hair so many years ago. Ken repeated himself. He was so close that Fran could smell his breath, could almost smell the animal fear of her daughter. It was her fear; the one she had lived with. It was one she felt overwhelm her now, but it mustn't. She had managed before to protect her daughter. She would do it again, but this time she would defend herself as well. This time.

Never taking her eyes from Jane for one moment she said, 'I see, Ken. Before or after the flu?'

It was only now that she turned, gripping Jane's belt instead of her lapel, standing between Ken and her daughter. Ken's eyes were just as David's had been: cold, brutal, angry. He was too close. He was within punching reach. He was looking past her to Jane, who was backing, pulling away from Fran. Fran wanted to back with her. But no. Never again. Never, ever again, do you hear. Never.

He said, 'Beecham's made her sleepy and she fell. So stop being stupid, Fran.' His breath reached her. Was it alcohol that sparked it? Or, like David, was it any time, any place, so you never knew when to prepare, expect, hide.

Jane shuddered, stumbled. Fran lost her grip on the belt and just managed to catch the pocket, hanging on, as Ken said, 'Tell her, Jane. Tell her, you fell.'

Jane's voice was thick and hoarse, her tone that of an automaton. 'Yes, I fell.'

Behind Ken, Emily stood framed in the

372

doorway, looking from one to another, horror draining the colour from her face. Fran indicated the children's room with her eyes, with a slight movement of her free hand. Emily was too shocked. She saw nothing other than the tableau. Fran frowned, gestured again. Emily saw but did not comprehend. Fran gestured one more time and at last Emily nodded, as though waking. She slipped away.

Fran put up her hand to Ken, who was even closer. In a moment they could dance. She said, 'She needs to see a doctor, Ken, and don't call me stupid. I will not be called that. Never again. Never. Never.'

Ken wasn't looking at her, but at Jane. His smile was gentle, rueful, but his eyes were the same. 'You said you didn't want a doctor, did you, Janey? You still don't?'

Jane gave one convulsive sob, then fell silent. At last, as her mother dared to snatch a look, she said, 'I don't need a doctor.' She was holding her hands to her face. Poor bruised hands. God Almighty, Fran would kill him. She turned back to Ken. Behind him Emily was tiptoeing past the door, hand in hand with Lucy, Harry on her hip. Don't cry Harry. Not now.

Fran said, 'These things can be sorted, Ken. Ken, look at me. This can be sorted.' She had to hold his attention. She had to talk over any creak of the stairs, any cry from Harry, any sound of the door opening, the children running up the drive.

Jane was sobbing again. Good. Keep it up. Protect your children. The cardinal rule: protect your children. How dare she say that when she had failed? When something she had done had helped this to happen. When she hadn't torn down the barriers, poked and pried until she discovered the truth.

Suddenly, Harry cried. Ken reacted, spinning round, but Fran grabbed him, shouting, 'Hurry, Em.'

Ken tried to hurl her aside. 'You stupid bloody woman.'

She hung on. 'I said don't call me stupid.' He punched her head. Sickened by pain, she hung on. Emily looked up from the stairs. He pushed her, pulled her. He was David. But she was Fran, a different Fran. She was roaring, 'Do not call me stupid.' He slapped her, knocked her with his arm. The pain burst above her eye. Jane screamed. Emily hesitated. Fran yelled, 'Go on, Jane. Help Emily. Help Emily to save your children. Go on.' She clung to Ken's arm, hitting back. 'Jane, I'm telling you to save your children. Get them to the car, Emily. Go. Just go.'

He had her hair, he was dragging her back. She groaned, then swore: 'You bugger. I'll kill you. I'll . . .'

She wrenched round, flailing for his arm, finding it, whimpering with the pain, kicking him. He released his grip on her hair, she dragged him further into the room, clinging on. He tried to dislodge her. He couldn't. Jane was gone, now, out of the door. Still she fought him like a terrier, moving quickly, knowing that if he trapped her she was dead, because these men did kill. And if he killed her he would kill her child. Backwards, forwards and now her children were gone from sight, down the stairs, but not at the car. Not yet. They couldn't be.

Back and forth, her arms aching, her body jolted as he rammed her into the chest of drawers. She hung on his arm, dragging him back as he made for the door. His breath was in her face: the champagne, so like the Scotch. But it made them clumsy, unsteady. Now she remembered it all. Now she kicked as she had kicked David that last time; kicked, hit, bit, barged, butted.

All she could hear were grunts, just as David had grunted. Back, back, back to the wall. She grabbed the table lamp. She crashed it against his head. He fell, shook his head, started to rise. She heard the car horn, again and again. She threw the duvet over him and fled down the stairs, almost falling, gripping the banister, praying her legs would carry her just a little bit further.

Please have the engine running. Please. Out of the door, down the drive.

She staggered to the driver's side. Jane was revving the engine. 'Get over,' she roared. Jane scrambled to the passenger seat. Fran almost fell in behind the wheel, her hands trembling. She couldn't find the gear.

Emily screamed, 'Hurry. He's coming out.'

She found the gear and depressed the clutch, almost stalled. Oh, God. He was coming up the path, staggering, calling, 'Janey. Come back.'

Lights were going on in the houses. The wheels were spinning, screaming on the warm tarmac. Lucy was crying. Harry too. 'Hurry up,' Emily was shouting again and again.

They were off. She jerked into second, then up again, roaring through the streets. 'Hospital,' she said. 'Jane, you need the hospital.'

Lucy was sobbing, Harry was crying. Shut up.

Shut up.

'No, Mum. The children. It'll be hours. They could call in social workers. Your house.' Fran could taste her own blood, but it was only her lips. She drove past Linda's. No lights. They were at a concert. Why tonight?

She drove right up to her garage doors, but why? They should be on their way to hospital. She was insane. She tried to find reverse.

'What are you doing, Mum?'

'Hospital,' she gasped.

Jane's hand covered hers. 'No, I can't. I won't. I'll lie. Home. I want to be at home.' She was pointing to Fran's house.

'Bloody hell, make up your mind,' Emily gasped. 'He could be here any minute and there are the kids.' Her voice wasn't level.

Fran couldn't think, but now Jane was leaving the car, so there was nothing to decide. She switched off the engine. 'Quick, into the house.' Fran's voice was shaking too. 'Use your key, Em. And don't swear.'

She tried to hurry to Jane's side, her own pain catching her. Em overtook, carrying Harry, dragging Lucy, fumbling with her key, opening the door. Fran had Jane now and was taking her weight. 'Hurry, darling. Let's hurry.'

All the time she looked for his car. 'I hope he's too drunk to drive,' Emily said, as she came to help.

David had been too drunk, but he had driven nonetheless, right into a lamp-post. Multiple injuries, the coroner said. Perhaps some of them had been the blows she had finally dealt him when he swore he would 'stop that bloody child from

376

crying' because she could not let him kill another of
her children.

CHAPTER THIRTY-SEVEN

Fran dead-locked the front door, though her
fingers felt too weak, too shaky. For a moment she
stood quite still, panting so hard it seemed she
couldn't get her breath at all. Slow down, she
commanded. Slow down. She did, then pushed
herself upright. Emily, Jane and the children were
huddled behind her in the hall, waiting. For her.

She found a smile, a voice, one which was not
quite hers but it would do. 'Emily, how about
taking the children into the sitting room. Pop them
on the settee, put on a video, your Disney tapes,
anything. Draw all the curtains, double-check the
patio doors. Come on, Jane, into the kitchen. I
want to check your injuries.'

Emily carried Harry and herded Lucy before
her, making a game of it, though she didn't close
the door behind her. Fran could understand her
need to know that others were close by and she, in
her turn, left the kitchen door wide open. She put
the radio on quietly, pulled the blind, checked the
locks. Big Job wound round her legs. Automatically
she put dried food in his bowl as she assessed
Jane's injuries. 'Any blurred vision? Any nausea?'

Jane sat at the table, her head in her hands. 'I'm
fine, Mum.'

'I still think we should take you to the hospital.'

'No.' Jane's voice was strident. 'No, there's no
need. No need at all.'

'Then I'll call the doctor.'

'Mum, just get me some cotton wool. I'll be fine.' Her lips were already swelling and her words were indistinct.

Fran was scrabbling in the pantry for the First Aid box. 'You won't be fine. You are not fine.' Her own lips were swelling too.

First she opened sterilised wipes and handed them to Jane, whose hands were so swollen that she dropped them. Fran took over, gently swabbing away the blood, examining the bruises carefully. Jane's nose wasn't broken; her lips were split, but no worse than Fran's.

She drew open her daughter's robe. Her ribs were red in places, with faded bruises in others. She asked Jane to move this way and that, as the doctor had so often asked her. No broken ribs. All the time she was listening for the car, bracing herself for a hammering on the door. 'Now, I'm phoning the doctor.'

'No.'

Fran ignored her and headed for the hall, but too late, for the phone rang.

'Leave it to me,' she almost screamed, running for it, waving Jane down and Emily back. 'Leave it.' Knowing it would be Ken, for that is how they worked.

She snatched up the receiver. 'Yes.'

'Darling?' It was Josh. For a moment she thought she'd faint, then that she would cry. But she must do neither, not now. There was no time. There was never time, *now*, while they could still reach you.

'Josh. Oh, I'm so glad.' Her voice still didn't sound like hers.

'What's up? Was it as bad as all that, or better than you dared hope?' He was laughing, but wary.

She blurted, 'He's been beating Jane. I've got them here. He might come. I wish you were back.' She could hear the video, Jane's sobs, the silence down the line.

Finally Josh almost whispered, 'Slow down; tell me exactly what's happened.'

She told him very quietly and very slowly, gesturing to Emily to close the door so that the children would hear nothing. For another long moment Josh was silent and she could see his face in her mind, his beloved face. He said, briskly now, 'Listen darling, after you've rung the doctor, phone Linda and Mike. You need Mike most of all.'

She knew she did. 'You don't mind Mike?'

His shout was exasperated. 'Fran, it's your daughter's safety we're talking about and maybe yours. I can't be there. Mike must be. He can reason with the bastard, or he can slap an injunction, anything. I want you all safe. All, do you understand? Do anything Mike says. I'll be there as soon as I can. Phone him now.'

Would they be back from the concert? She gave them another minute by phoning the doctor. He would come immediately. Now she dialled Mike. Only the answer machine. Her fingers were still trembling. Every car that passed seemed to slow down, about to stop. Her lip was throbbing and the side of her head, her ribs, her arms. She dialled Linda's number as Emily came to her, whispering, 'The children are asleep on the sofa. I'll make a cup of tea and sit with Jane.'

The girl looked so tired and she'd been crying. Fran held her close as the phone rang and rang.

'I'm so sorry, Emily. It was your big night and this is the celebration. You shouldn't have to see things like this.'

Emily's arms were round her, her head rested against hers for a moment, then she withdrew. 'Should I put sugar in the tea? It's good for shock, isn't it.'

Linda answered the phone. Emily melted into the kitchen. Linda handed it over to Mike who said they'd both be round.

*   *   *

Mike, Linda and Emily put the children to bed in Emily's room. The doctor checked Jane and all the while she insisted that she had fallen down the stairs. Fran and the doctor glanced at one another as she handed him two more of his miracle 'you won't need stitches' plasters. 'Her husband beat her,' she repeated each time.

Jane winced as he closed the last cut near her eye. 'Mother, please. It was a mistake.'

'You should report him,' the doctor said. 'Take a look at the state of your mother and still tell me it was a mistake, Jane.'

'But it really was. We won't report him. We will not. Is that clear, Mother?' Her voice was rising; she was crying. 'Don't do it, Mum. Don't. Don't. It's not fair. Just not fair on him.'

The doctor gestured to Fran. She nodded, saying gently, 'Hey, come on. I'll do as you want.'

Jane calmed down and Linda entered the kitchen, taking the seat next to Jane. 'Hush, now, the children are asleep. We don't want them to wake, do we?'

The resignation in her voice mirrored Fran's when Jane said, 'He doesn't mean it. It was me. He was so distraught about the job and I made it worse.'

Fran recognised herself and felt the tears running silently down her face, running and running like some endless stream. Had her daughter heard and seen after all? Had she, Fran, created this night, this marriage?

The doctor moved on to her. She wouldn't sit. She stood, because she had failed her daughter and how could she take a chair near her? But Linda was taking Jane past her into the sitting room and the doctor was insisting she sit, and she must do as she was told, and still the tears were running. 'She must have heard David after all,' she stated.

The doctor said, 'It might have set a victim pattern, subconsciously. There are those who think it can. I can't cast a vote. Either way, she can change it. You did.' For this was the younger partner of the doctor who had tended her wounds, far too many times.

But she hadn't. Her husband had died. She had been set free. She had not walked away, she had not found that courage, and it was this that had torn and dragged at her for all the years afterwards—torn and dragged and made great gouges and spirals on so many oil boards.

The doctor finished with her and disposed of his swabs, washing his hands and using kitchen towels to dry them. He poured himself a cup of tea and another for Mike, who had entered and now sat with Fran. The doctor said, 'Will this Ken allow her to go, or will he hunt her into the ground? Are the children safe? Perhaps she fears this? It's often what is behind a spouse's reluctance to leave or attribute blame. Or maybe she's just come to believe she's as useless as he says, that its her fault . . .'

'She loves him,' Fran said flatly. 'She believes this will stop when she starts to "do things properly". She believes that he is a nice man and each crisis is abnormal. She believes . . .'

Now she was shouting and it was Mike holding her, hushing her, warning, 'The children.'

Yes, the children. It must stop. With Jane. It must stop before it reached Lucy. It must never, ever happen to anyone else in her family. Her breath shuddered in and out of her chest. It shook her whole aching, battered body. Emily showed the doctor to the door, then returned and sat at the table opposite Mike, who was mopping Fran's face with his handkerchief. She took hold of Fran's hand, squeezing it. 'So you're used to this. To being beaten. To being brave.' She had heard.

Mike said nothing, just returned his handkerchief to his pocket. Fran said, 'No, I was never brave. I did what Jane has been doing all this time: lying, covering up, finding excuses for him, blaming herself.'

'So it's happened before?' Emily was appalled.

'Her ribs have old bruises, probably old fractures.' Her voice was so flat and cold. 'I just didn't see it, even when you were worried, Mike. I was too wrapped up in myself. I compared her with me and she was different, and I left it at that.'

Fran looked at Mike, who was shaking his head. His voice was sharp as he said, 'I wondered about it once, then I forgot, so don't do this. Everyone has a right to concentrate on their own lives. *You must not do this.'*

Jane's voice was harsh from the doorway and though it was little more than a whisper it sounded savage. 'It would have stopped if you had moved in with Mike because it was what he wanted. It would have reduced the pressure on him. That's what this is, pressure. If only you'd done it, it would have . . .'

Linda was there now, leading her away to the sitting room but Emily was on her feet, the chair rasping as she pushed it back, calling, 'Hang on a minute. Just look what your mum's done for you. Look at her face. My mum wouldn't have. It's time you got some balls and told the bastard to back off or do you like someone kicking the shit out of you? Is that what this is all about?'

She flung her hair over to one side as Fran pulled her back down. 'Hey, that's enough. Mike, can you . . .' Wearily she indicated the sitting room.

'Yes, Linda and I will try and get her to bed. The little room?'

Emily glared after him. 'Well, she *should* tell him to piss off.'

Fran's head was splitting. Her mouth was dry. She sipped her tea. It was sweet and cold and disgusting enough to be a shock in itself. Emily had slumped back in the chair and was kicking the table leg. 'It's not that simple, Em. He's beaten not just the shit out of her, but everything, to use your vernacular. Anyway, even now she'll be rearranging tonight in her head, sorting out *her* mistake, prepared to go on living on eggshells in the belief that all this will pass.'

'Go back?' Emily was shocked out of her slump. 'Go back?'

Fran felt old and tired. 'Perhaps. It's a decision I

never had to make. I mean, will he let her leave in peace, or will he follow her, find her, beat her, even kill her? I just don't know. You can imprison him, but one day he'll come out. He's the children's father, so how do you keep him away? What does it do to them if he's in prison? She loves him, or thinks she does. She'll believe him when he says it will never happen again because what is the alternative? You live in fear, with them or without them. I just don't know.' She mustn't keep saying that, but it was what was going round and round her head, and it was what had gone round it so many times when David was alive.

Again Em said, 'But go back. She can't. At least if she leaves she has a chance.'

'It's not as though he's had an affair or something concrete she can justifiably hate him for, see him as at fault.' Fran thought for a moment. 'Yes, I think she'll go back. It's what I would have done. That way you can see them coming. Though there's therapy now, the police are more responsive . . . Oh, I don't know.'

Fran was so tired. Emily was too. They must go to bed. Emily must sleep. She had school and a show tomorrow. The world would go on. She would look up at the stars and see how small their problems were.

'Go to bed, Emily, darling. Thank you, you've been wonderful in every way.' Emily took the mugs to the sink. 'Leave them, Em, I'll do them.'

Em washed up and left them to dry, saying, 'You've done enough.' She came to Fran and kissed her cheek. 'You've done enough and you should sleep. Don't worry about the children. If they wake in the night I'll sort them. I can always go in to school a bit later.'

Fran smiled. 'It's always worth a try, isn't it?'

Emily grinned. 'Always. It's maths first. I hate it.'

'Go to bed.'

Fran listened to Linda chatting briefly to Emily on the landing before she and Mike came downstairs. Fran met them at the bottom, her hands out. 'What can I say to you both?'

'Nothing.' Linda hugged her. 'Just get to bed. Mike's going to phone Ken, right now, from home. Jane definitely won't take out an injunction against him so Mike will bring personal and professional pressure to bear to keep him away.'

'He'll deny it. He'll contact her. She'll weaken.'

Mike kissed her cheek. 'I'll do it anyway. Get some sleep. Lock up after us. Keep the phone by the bedside.'

She did everything they said, but she would not sleep, could not sleep because she must stay alert. She must listen and wait and guard. The dawn would come, but still she would guard and wait and listen. She would not move from their sides all day and all night, for as long as it took for Josh to return, for he was the proof that hope existed.

CHAPTER THIRTY-EIGHT

Jane struggled to sit. Her ribs hurt too much to lie down, but it had seemed to please Mike and Linda to think they'd tucked her in and left her cosy. She edged the pillows up behind her. There were fewer cars passing, fewer headlights swooping along the curtains. The house had quietened, though she

385

could still hear her mother downstairs, pottering, as she would have called it. It sounded nice.

For a moment the world had stopped spinning. For a moment she was safe, and it was stupid and childish to wish she were in her own room. In fact, it was fitting that her children should be there, asleep and guarded by Emily, of all people. Emily who had been strong, and swept them all down the stairs and out into the street, and then the car. But it was she who had felt for the key in the ignition, praying it was there. She who had turned it and heard the roar of the engine. She who had said, 'Hush, Lucy. It's just a game. It's part of Emily's show. You've been there while we've practised, hasn't she, Emily?'

Emily had been quick. She had said something. Jane had replied, 'See, we're rehearsing our lines, all of us, Daddy too.'

Her mother had come out of the house. There had been blood on her face also. 'The make-up is so good,' Emily had told Lucy. 'It's tomato sauce, really.'

'I don't like this play,' Lucy had said, but she was half asleep already. She would think it a dream.

He had come out into the drive. His expression was so lost. He hadn't hit her before, not really, not so many punches, again and again. Not the kicks. Before he had just grabbed her, shaken her, sort of thrown her, his hand slipping into a punch. This time it had been the shock. She should have warned him that Mike was concerned, as her mother had suggested, but when the file had been found she didn't think there was any need.

She should have warned him. She beat her fists on her knees. She had decided not to and she had no right, no right at all. She shut her eyes, but saw too much: those fists, the shoes, that smell of stale champagne. It had made her freeze. She remembered . . . what?

She stared into the darkness of the room, calculating the shapes. There, to the right the old writing bureau where her mother had kept the bills and letters. Next to it her easel. So that was the smell, the strange smell that was not part of this house when she was growing up. Damn the bloody easel, the painting, Josh.

She covered her face with her hands. But, after all, it was her mother who had come. She had stood in front of Ken. It was Fran who had sent her from the house. 'Protect your children,' she had said. He would know that. He would know it was her mother who had said she had to leave.

She was shaking again. Her fingers were swollen and sore. He had hit them. It had saved her nose. It had saved her cheekbone, the doctor had said. 'Report him,' he had added.

Ken. Ken. She wanted him to hold her as he had once done. By now the shock would have worn off. He'd be in that bed, alone. He'd be crying. Only she ever saw him cry. He'd be so sorry.

She felt sick. It passed. The bureau, look at the bureau. It had stood downstairs in the hall. Why was it up here? The tenants. That's right. Her mother had moved things around. Why was it still up here? Why hadn't her mother married Mike? Of course. Josh. Why had her mother gone to the class? Because a stupid daughter had suggested it. Ken was right.

Why was she here, now? Because she hadn't told Ken how Mike felt. If she'd done that he would have been prepared. Instead, she'd watched him put the champagne in the fridge. But she'd thought he knew something she didn't. 'Stupid, stupid woman,' she murmured, but the words were funny because her lips were so big. When he saw he'd be sorry, again. When he saw he'd never do it again. Never, really never, because now they could plan properly, knowing they weren't to go to Head Office. Perhaps it would be better this way? Less pressure. It was just that there'd been so much uncertainty, so many mistakes. Stupid, stupid mistakes and most of them hers.

He was just trying to keep a roof over their heads. They were everything to him, he said. Everything. It was all for them. It was because he cared so much and everything became so important. 'You do understand?' he'd say. 'You are my world. I can't live without you.'

Her mother was coming up the stairs. Carefully Jane lay down, dragging the pillows with her. She closed her eyes as the door opened. Quietly her mother came in and stroked her head. 'Sleep well, darling girl.' Her kiss was light on her hair. It's what she had done when she was a child.

She crept from the room. Jane watched beneath almost closed lids. The door shut. It was dark again, too dark, and the events of tonight were back: Ken so close; his fist, that awful fist; the pain; the smell of champagne, so like the smell . . . of Scotch. That smell. Where? Some time before? Long before?

Now she remembered. Her mother's voice, the door opening, Daddy standing over her bed. That awful smell. The sound of crying. Her own crying. Her mother pulling him, pulling him out to the landing, keeping him away. The fists. Not for her but for her mother. Her mother struggling to reach the door. Shutting it. Making it dark again. But the sounds . . . 'I'll stop her bloody crying.' She should have stopped crying. She was stupid. It was her crying that made Daddy cross. She knew now what the shadowy thoughts had been, those dark, blurred memories, snatches of sound. Oh, God, she really remembered now.

She struggled to sit again. She pulled the pillows up behind her, flicking on the table lamp. But that was too bright. She reached out and tugged at the curtain. It drew back, admitting moonlight: soft, cool, quiet moonlight.

CHAPTER THIRTY-NINE

Fran was resting, watching the early morning clouds chase across the sky, when a car drew up outside the house. She was off the bed. She was at the window. Ken?

No. Josh. She dragged on her dressing gown and was down the stairs, out into the drive and in his arms. He hugged her gently; she thought she would faint from pain. 'I've been beside myself,' he kept repeating as he helped her back into the house, shutting the door quietly behind them. Her finger to her swollen lips, Fran led him to the kitchen. One of her nails had ripped away from the skin. She hoped Ken had a deep gouge.

He held her now, as though she were porcelain, looking at her face, touching her lips. 'I'll kill him.'

She shook her head. 'Put the kettle on instead.'

389

Could he understand what she said?

'It doesn't suit me.'

They laughed together as she sat down. Josh looked tired. 'I flew back. As it happens, I know someone with a Cessna.'

'As you do.' She was unconvinced.

'As I really do.'

She was amazed. Josh hunted in the pantry and finally emerged with the instant coffee. 'Art dealer friend. Useful contact.'

She put up her hands. 'I do hope you said *art* dealer.'

'I swear.' He raised his eyes to the ceiling. 'How goes it?' She told him. It was Josh who said, 'Have we any bottles for Harry?'

They hadn't. Jane usually brought them with her in the booty bag. Immediately he dug for the car keys in the fruit bowl, emerging triumphant. He pecked her cheek. 'Back in a minute. Safeways have them. Are stewed pears his favourite, and a bit of Farex? Let's spoil him.'

She took over on the coffee front and now it seemed a sun-filled day, though the clouds hung low. Her beloved hadn't failed her. He had simply surpassed everything she had hoped for.

*   *   *

By 9.30 the children had been fed and watered, and appropriately dishonest excuses made to Maisie and Emily's headmaster, accompanied by assurances that she would appear in all her glory tonight. 'The show must go on,' Emily said to Lucy, as they snuggled down with Harry on the settee.

Josh watched from the doorway with Fran. '*This*

is my daughter?' he whispered.

'Oh, no, this is a star.' Fran didn't whisper and shared a snatched grin with Emily. 'The one who chose the colour scheme.'

Josh puffed his chest. 'I meant to comment. You have my artistic sense, my girl. It's pretty great.' Then he turned to Fran, concerned. 'You *do* like it?'

It was a real question. Of course it was.

'I love it. It's us.'

Upstairs Jane had moved into Emily's room, a room that Emily had just this minute tidied, treated to clean linen and which was now the proud possessor of all Jane's knick-knacks. 'In the hope that she will stay away from that raving bastard,' she whispered now, as she came to where they were standing, slopping her tea on the carpet. It was tea into which she had ladled far too much sugar. Fran sipped the chocolate milk drink Josh had brought back, complete with straw.

'Is it more comfortable than a mug?' Josh asked as they stared at the television, though taking nothing in.

'Yes,' Fran said, though the drink had stung her cut tongue.

Harry started to make hungry noises. 'Let's try him with another bottle.'

Fran collected Harry, leaving Lucy with the television and yet another Disney tape they had found, and trooped into the kitchen. Emily added another spoonful of sugar.

'Hey,' Josh said, as he took a bottle from the fridge.

Emily responded, 'Well, I still feel bloody shocked.'

So did they all. 'Don't swear,' Fran said, plonking Harry on the girl's lap and pushing the tea out of his reach, while Josh tested the bottle against his cheek. Leaving them to it, Fran took a chocolate milk drink up to Jane, who managed to drink a little, before pulling the duvet up to her chin and resting back on the pillows, half sitting, which seemed more comfortable, she had explained to Fran.

'You don't have to explain,' Fran had insisted. 'You have every right to what is best for you.'

'Don't, Mum.'

Was she that transparent? 'Yes, probably,' Josh had said as she returned downstairs. 'But you're her mother, so why not?'

Mike phoned. Linda too. 'Just starting the day,' Fran said. 'I'll keep in touch. Thank you. Both.'

In the afternoon the doctor called again to check mother and daughter, forbearing to comment on the fact that Jane was still adamantly opposed to 'causing waves', as he so succinctly put it.

As he drew away and Anne Thomas made it her business to come into her front garden to clean already perfect windows, the florist arrived with two huge bouquets. Fran took them, knowing who they were from, wanting to say, 'Take them away and shove them up his arse.'

Anne Thomas said, 'My word. Was the show that successful? I can't wait until tonight. Can you take me in your car? Goodness, have you been in the wars?'

The bouquets crackled in their cellophane. The red bows were obscene. They were all Jane's favourites: lilies, sweet peas, cornflowers. Josh stepped past her, out into the dull day. 'I'll have the honour of escorting you, Mrs Thomas. It's my support stint tonight, especially after the shunt these two had in the car. Jane's car,' he amended quickly, as Mrs Thomas peered across at Fran's. 'Darling, you're needed; Harry you know. It never stops, does it, Mrs Thomas? Wonderfully clean windows, they must brighten the day.'

He was steering Fran inside the house, waving to Mrs Thomas.

Emily waited in the hall, spinning her finger against her temple. 'Wonderfully clean windows?'

'Attend to your duties, wench. Leave the play-acting to me.' Josh pointed to the sitting room, then took the flowers from Fran. 'What do we do with these?'

She read her card. 'So sorry. Far too much to drink. Isolated incident. Can't begin to apologise enough.' It was in his own handwriting. He must have woken up, thought how do I handle this? Two bloody women to hoodwink. But he hadn't phoned the order. Too wise. How do you tell a florist to write such words. It was proof, wasn't it?

She reached for Jane's card, then stopped. No.

She took that bouquet up to her daughter. She watched her read the card, but couldn't stand the tears and looked out at her garden: the garden she had carved for herself once she had been given the peace in which to do it. *Given* the peace, so how could she tell her daughter what to do, what to take for herself? For in that way she might be able to rebuild her self-worth.

She heard the phone ring.

Jane was still staring at the card she held with swollen and bruised fingers. 'It'll be Ken,' she said.

'It might not be.'

Josh had picked up the phone in the hall. Fran held Jane's stare. *Don't go back. Do not go back*, were her silent commands. Jane said, 'Mum, I don't know what to do? I just don't know.' All the fear and uncertainty were in those words.

'I know,' Fran told her. Because she did.

Josh called up the stairs: 'Fran, it's Ken's father for you.'

Jane dropped the card. It slid off the cellophane on to the pale-yellow and blue duvet. Fran didn't want to speak to him, or to anyone from that family, but she didn't say that, for Jane might see it as weakness—Jane, who must be strong.

She took the flowers. Jane sank back against the pillows. Fran said, 'I'll put them in water. They're beautiful. None of this is *their* fault. Neither is it yours.'

'Don't, Mum.'

She must. 'It's his. Get out. Sell the house. Divide the spoils. Start again.' But would she? Would he let her? How could this ever end?

She took the call on her bedroom extension. Ken's father was all injured innocence, all bluster and incomprehension, all wild explanations about the awful effect of drink. She said, when he had finished, 'Last night Ken was drunk. The other times he has been sober.'

'But he's never actually hit her before. She's just fallen, when he's tried to make her see sense.'

'Ah,' Fran said. 'I see. That's not quite true, I feel, and even if it were I don't consider it a particularly thrilling distinction. Well, I have to tend to my daughter, now. Goodbye.'

She was shaking, with rage when she put the phone down. It rang again immediately. It was

Ken's mother this time. 'Fran, may I speak to Jane?'

'I would rather you didn't,' Fran said.

Jane called from her room, 'Who is it, Mum?'

'Joyce, wanting to speak to you.'

'I'll come.'

Fran didn't want her to, she wanted to keep her from them all, but Jane wasn't a child any more. Her daughter wasn't going to be given her peace. She must take it, if she would. She must stand against them all and take it.

Jane's walk was unsteady. Her left eye was blacking nicely and swollen shut. She sat on the bed. Fran handed her the receiver, standing over her as though she could protect her, knowing she could not.

Jane straightened as she said, 'Hello!'

She used both hands to hold the receiver, those bruised and swollen hands into which her wedding ring cut. 'Yes, I know, I know. Perhaps he's right, but I thought I had. I did try, I really didn't intend for him to feel left out.'

Fran tried to contain herself in the face of the 'have you shown him enough attention' line, but she could not and moved forward, her hand outstretched for the receiver. Jane ducked away, waving her mother back. 'It's difficult with the children and work. Yes, I love him too. I know there are no other women. Yes, I know what some women have to put up with. Yes, I know I don't. I couldn't bear that. Yes, you're right. You're right.' Her voice was a whisper, the formation of her words an effort, the final result indistinct. 'Tell him . . .'

Fran snatched the receiver now, saying into the mouthpiece, 'Tell him nothing. Do you hear?

Nothing until she has her mind together. And reorganise your perception of your son, for the love of God.'

She slammed down the phone.

Jane was hunched, her hands in her lap, Emily's tartan dressing gown too much a part of the livid colour scheme that made up her daughter this morning. Fran sat next to her, tentatively holding her, choosing her words very carefully, keeping her voice quiet and calm. 'There is no need to make a decision until you are well. You must understand that.'

She helped Jane back to bed, tucked her in and drew the curtains, hearing Josh playing ball in the garden with Lucy, her granddaughter's laugh. It seemed unreal.

*   *   *

At four they made tea. Emily and Lucy had baked a walnut cake, and Linda had phoned with the shelter number. 'They're experts and will call on her. She needs to talk and to listen, Fran.'

Did Linda think she didn't damn well know this?

Jane wouldn't. She said, 'I'm not one of those people. I'm not. He doesn't drink like Dad. He's not the same.'

So she did remember.

'Darling Jane, they don't have to be drinkers. You *are* one of those people.'

'No, I'm not, Mother.' Her enunciation was as distorted as Fran's. 'His parents are right. Ken is a good father and husband. We've a nice house. He comes home at night. He works hard for us, all for us. We're a family.'

Fran was sitting on the bed. Her hand was throbbing, her head too. Everything seemed to hurt more as the day wore on. She wanted to sleep. Just for a moment, but she must not relax. She said, 'You are a ravaged human being, pretending everything is all right, just as I did.'

Jane flung her arm over her eyes. 'Shut up, Mum. Just shut up. He's right, don't you understand? I just don't cope. I get hysterical. I drive him to it. He hasn't gone in to work, he's at home crying.' She leaned forward, her hands out to her mother. 'We can get it back to where it once was. We really can.'

Fran thought her head would burst and her lip explode. Jane's was bleeding again. The blood trickled down her chin. Fran reached for the tissues on the bedside table, handing them to Jane, saying wearily, 'I'll leave you to sleep. Try and drink a little tea, clogged with sugar though it is. It's Nurse Nightingale's brew, I'm afraid.'

Jane half laughed into a tissue. Fran left the room. How could laughter exist any more? She shut the door, leaning against it, her legs turned to water. To her surprise Emily was beside her in a moment, taking her weight. 'Come into your bedroom, Fran.'

Fran straightened immediately. No one must see her weakness. For the moment no one must see that. 'What on earth are you doing here, Em?' She walked ahead of the girl into the bedroom, making it to the bed. Just. She sat upright, very, very upright.

Emily said, 'Eavesdropping on your opinion about my tea-making.'

Fran braced herself. Not now, Em, absolutely

397

not now.

But Emily was bending over, touching Fran's forehead. 'You look so hurt, Fran.'

Fran laughed shakily. 'Well, I am a bit battered and bruised, let's face it.'

'Can I get you some hot tea rather than that chocolate muck. Without sugar, as it's you. I'll rinse out the straw.'

'Not at the moment, darling.' She felt unnerved at such kindness from this girl and it made her resolve weaken, and she longed to lie back on the bed. But no, it was too soon, it was not yet safe. 'Where's Josh?'

'Reading to the children in the sitting room. He's just rung Mike. They're talking of going round to see Rambo. Then he flipped through my lines with me.' Emily drew out a piece of paper from her pocket. She rolled and unrolled it.

Fran said, 'OK, you want to try your lines?' This was more like Emily; a deal was imminent. She was disappointed, but why? She could not have asked for more from anyone since this had happened. 'Where shall we start?'

Emily held the sheet of paper out to her. It wasn't a page of script, it was a letter, Catherine's letter. Fran didn't understand.

Emily said, 'I heard what Jane said to you about that bastard Ken.'

'Don't swear.'

'Fran, I sent Mum some photos as I said I would, some were of the wedding party, your wedding party. Read what she says about Paul Davies.'

Fran thought she'd missed out on a part of the conversation. Paul Davies? Who on earth was Paul Davies? Fran touched her eye, which felt as though

398

it was swelling even more. Emily pulled her hand away. 'Don't touch, it'll become infected. I'll sort out a salty water wipe and get my own back on you.' She was smiling a little, but still she held out the letter. 'Read this, Fran.' She stuffed the letter into her hand, her voice urgent. 'Read it. It might make Jane think again.'

The words Fran read took a moment to come into focus, then they danced in time with the throbbing of her head. San Diego seemed wonderful, the mountains behind striking, the desert awe-inspiring. Exasperated Fran handed back the letter. 'Come on, Em. I haven't time for this.'

Emily returned it, her long-sleeved T-shirt pulled down below her fingers. 'Just read the bit about the photos.'

Fran scanned down. There, three-quarters down the page.

What a scream. Fran looks suitably ridiculous. Honestly, your father's taste has gone downhill.

Fran looked at Emily. 'Why are you doing this, Em?' She was close to tears at last. She handed it back, although she would have preferred to tear it up.

'No, Fran, not that bit. She's an idiot. Read on.' Emily pushed the letter into her hand, pointing to the line below.

Who is that man with the child in his arms? He's a friend of mine called Paul Davies. Next time you see him ask if he knows the Fairmile Hotel. Watch his face, little one! Report back. I shall be agog . . .

The letter went on about something and nothing. Emily craned over, so she could read it again, aloud this time. 'Don't you see, Fran? Mum's friends were the leg-over sort. She was always at it.'

Fran released the letter. Emily tucked it away in her jeans pocket. 'I want to phone her, Fran. I want her to tell me Paul is Ken, and Ken has been screwing her, then we can tell Jane. It might make her see sense.'

Josh called up the stairs, 'Emily, come and eat because we need to get you to school for the performance. Stan's picking you up and you'll have the pleasure of Thomas the Teasmaid's company. It should be me, but I don't want to leave the others tonight. Mike and Linda will be there. Is that OK?'

Emily pushed her hands into her pockets, standing in front of Fran. 'Can I phone? I need to know what time it is over there . . .'

Fran shook her head. 'Don't do this to yourself, Emily. You don't want to know this. It could ruin your relationship with your mother. Dad and Mike said they'd go round, that might be enough.'

Emily coloured. She rubbed one Doc Martens against the other, looking at them, not at Fran. 'I sort of know a lot anyway.'

'Sort of knowing is different from hearing it from the horse's mouth. Trust me. Trust your Dad and Mike.'

At this Emily flung her hands wide. 'That might work for a while but what are they going to do, mount a twenty-four-hour watch on a marriage? You can't, even I know that, because I've tried with

Mum. Look, Fran, just think. If Mum says Ken has been bonking her it means he isn't doing everything for them. It means he really is a slut. Or is she going to say she's driven him to that as well? We've got to change who she thinks he is, haven't we? I mean, you need to look at things head on, don't you?'

Fran picked a white thread from Emily's blue T-shirt. 'Not at your age, darling.'

'If you won't let me phone, let me e-mail?'

'No. Lets just leave you out of this. It simply isn't fair.'

Emily looked half relieved, but nonetheless her shoulders slumped and that look came on her face. 'I thought we were a family,' she muttered as she stalked from the room.

CHAPTER FORTY

Catherine drew on her menthol cigarette, glad that Roger trotted off to work early and arrived home late. He didn't like her to smoke: 'Bad for the baby.' She'd gone on to menthol, for heaven's sake. Wasn't that enough?

The sun was out, but then it almost always was. The Mexican maid was mopping the tiles in the kitchen. Soon she'd be in here getting in the way, talking that incomprehensible language. Honestly, it was a pain.

She wandered on to the veranda, looking out across the gravel garden. Well, at least there was no grass to cut, nothing to make Roger break into a sweat. He was at his least attractive with beads

401

rolling down his face, though she thought he probably felt it manly.

She sat in the recliner. It was going to be another interminable day unless Manuel called. Perhaps she should lunch after all. Polly had called yesterday afternoon, whittering on about a bunch of company wives who had a luncheon reading group which met once a month. But that meant they would jaw-jaw about whatever crap they'd been reading. She'd passed on it but perhaps she should have gone.

She drew on her cigarette, watching a eucalyptus leaf dangle on its branch as though exhausted, or terminally bored. She knew the feeling and it was one that would not have been solved by yacking on about books. Neither would the conversation have stayed with matters concerning books. No, the talk would have veered towards babies, escalating to children, and everyone would poke and pry about Emily.

Inside the phone was ringing. Juanita brought it to her, shoving it into her face, unable to answer it herself. Why did Roger employ these people who couldn't speak the language? What was needed was someone who could monitor calls. Madam is not in residence, they could say. She snorted with amusement.

'Yes?' She inhaled again.

There was a transatlantic pause, then a tinny 'Mum?'

Instinctively Catherine stubbed out her cigarette. Damn it, had the phone eyes? 'Emily, poppet. How is the show?' She sat upright, but then relaxed. For God's sake, it was only her daughter, not a headmistress.

'You remembered, then. You didn't mention it in the letter.'

Oh, well, how bloody marvellous, Em might just as well be a headmistress, since she seemed to be catching her father's prune voice. 'Did I not? I had a card I thought I'd put in.' Of course she hadn't, but when you were pregnant your mind went woolly. But she'd lied now, so she could use that excuse another time.

'Look, Mum, it's late over here and I've just finished a show, and Linda wants to get to bed.'

'Linda? Who the hell is Linda?'

'A friend of Dad's and Fran's. She said I could use her phone.'

Catherine's heart sank. Oh, God, if she was making secret calls it meant she wanted to come over again but she couldn't. Not now, not when it looked as though the pot was beginning to boil. She stroked her stomach. Manuel said he liked fecund women. She said, 'Darling, whatever's wrong? Do tell and I'll have a word with your father. He's got to take your needs into consideration and when I've finished with him he will. Never fear.' She adjusted the shade attached to the lounger because the sun was too hot, now, and she didn't want to risk lines or age spots. Some of the women here were just like walnuts.

After the time lag Emily said, 'Mum, listen. I need a faxed note to Linda's number, which I will give you in a moment.'

'What note? What are you talking about?'

'Paul Davies.'

An aeroplane was creating a trail across the sky. Juanita had some ghastly Spanish rubbish on the radio and she wouldn't have it blaring out in this way. She'd only been told about it last week. Paul Davies? Oh, Paul Davies. 'Darling, I'm agog. What have you found out? Isn't it a scream? I thought he might have kids, not that there was Farex down his tie or . . .'

'Mum, he's Jane's husband and . . .'

'Jane?'

Again the lag. 'You know, Fran's daughter. He's . . .'

'Do not take that tone with me, Emily. I will not have it.'

The time lag was longer. Had her daughter hung up? Well, obviously she was still a little prima donna and there was no way she was coming over here to tax her mother's patience, especially in her *fecund* condition. She sniggered. Let Fran and bloody Josh . . .

'Mum, listen. He's a batterer. I know you were sleeping with him. I want you to write a fax saying that. I want you to say what presents he's bought you. I want you to write down where you had him.'

Catherine was struggling to sit up again and, once up, she swung the shade away. 'What on earth . . . How dare you be so insolent?'

'Shut up, Mum. This is serious. I want it. I want it now, in your handwriting. You must describe him. Anything about him. His clothes. A briefcase. You've already as good as told me the hotel.'

Catherine was pacing up and down the veranda, the cordless phone wowing and whistling. 'I'm going to put this phone down until you have collected yourself, Emily. I can hardly bear to think what sort of a life you've been living with that woman if this . . .'

'Mum, if you hang up I'll e-mail Roger. I'll tell

him about your little friends. About the cigarette case. About the baby. I mean, whose baby is it, Mum? Would Sue know, not that it can be hers unless you were doing odd things with a yoghurt pot and turkey baster.'

Catherine was standing quite still and sweat was breaking out, rolling down her face and back and belly. She felt as though she had been punched in the throat. She stared at the lounger. It seemed an awfully long way away.

'Mum.' Emily's voice was breaking. She sounded as though she was crying.

'How could you, you little bitch?' Catherine said as she finally managed to sit down.

'Mum, I love you, but you've got to do this and now, this minute. Jane's in real trouble with this bastard and it could have been you. It still could be, if you're still at it. Mum, you've got to stop. You've got to be careful. You should see Jane and Fran. Mum, please.'

Juanita was coming on to the veranda with a steaming cup of coffee. 'Get out of my sight,' Catherine screamed.

'Mum,' Emily protested.

So what if she thought she meant her. She was just a shabby little blackmailer, just a . . .

Juanita scurried inside. Emily said, and her voice was strong now, 'I'm telling you to do it, Mum. Do it now. Or I will tell Roger.' She gave Catherine the number. 'Do it, or I'll e-mail. And please stop. Please be careful. I do love you so much.'

CHAPTER FORTY-ONE

Fran and Josh phoned Linda's house again. The line was still engaged. 'So they are still there,' Josh tried to reassure Fran.

'You've second sight, have you? It could be someone phoning and leaving a message. It could . . .' She stopped. 'For heaven's sake, Josh, it's late. Why Linda had to take her back for cocoa after the performance I can't imagine. Why did Mike have to go off to a meeting and miss it, leave them alone together for the drive home? What if they've broken down and Ken's found them, what if . . .?'

He was holding her, stroking her hair, kissing her swollen eye very gently. 'Why on earth would he want to do that? Now come and sit down. You're absolutely done in. Besides, they have the mobile and would have phoned if there were a problem.'

They returned to the sitting room. She straightened the picture Josh had painted of her so long ago. It had been returned to its position over the mantelpiece this afternoon, at Emily's suggestion. Lucy had been thrilled and asked when she could make a picture for Grandma on the nice red wall.

Everyone had laughed.

Fran could not sit down, but walked from bookcase to bookcase as though marking her territory, warning strangers to keep away. She swung round. 'I mean, why didn't Stan stay with them?'

Josh was sitting on the sofa, watching every

move she made. 'He had to drop Teasmaid home, darling. Not to mention his son. She'll be fine.'

Fran kept her voice low. She knew she sounded fierce but he didn't understand that only when Emily was here, only when they were all here could she keep them safe. 'We don't know that.'

'I know that. I trust Linda. Good heavens, Ken isn't a monster who's going to stalk everyone who has anything to do with him. He's a bastard who thumps his wife, and anyone who comes between him and that wife.' His face had hardened. 'Em is quite safe, but we need to decide what to do about this Paul Davies thing. Em's right, it could make all the difference to Jane's perception of her knight in shining armour.'

'We can't use Emily.'

'There's no one else. Catherine will laugh in our faces if we say we'll bring pressure by dobbing her in to Roger and he'd think it was just another round of a mind game.'

'Not tonight, Josh. I can't think of it tonight.'

It was half an hour before they heard a car pull up. Fran was at the window in a flash. Linda. Josh was already on his way to the front door, but she beat him to it, opening it just as Emily reached up to press the bell. 'Where the hell have you been?' Fran heard the wail in her own voice.

Emily said, 'Don't swear.'

Linda grimaced. 'I knew I should have thrown my hat in first but this girl is as stubborn as anyone I've ever come across.'

Emily was waving a fax. 'Are you going to let us in, Fran, or do I have to spend the night on the doorstep. Dad?' she pleaded over Fran's shoulder.

Fran stepped aside, half laughing. 'You are such

a baggage, Em. Why on earth couldn't you both have cocoa here?'

Emily and Linda exchanged a look. Linda followed Emily into the house.

Fran said, 'Hey, it's time you were in bed, my friend. You're not having another round of cocoa here.' She held the door open. 'Home. James.'

Linda stood her ground. 'Not quite yet, Fran. We've something to show you.' She held up both her hands in surrender. 'I admit I had to be persuaded and I'm still not sure I've done the right thing.'

Emily had disappeared into the sitting room. Josh followed, his voice urgent: 'Em, what's happened? What have you there?'

Linda joined Fran, her face apologetic. 'She *was* determined.'

Fran shut the front door, glancing up the stairs. No sound. 'Determined?'

She already knew.

Josh was reading the fax when they entered the sitting room, his arm around Emily. He handed it to Fran and it was Linda who had her arm around her as she read Catherine's detailed account of her liaison with Paul Davies, aka Ken Swanton. Fran shook her head when she had finished, letting Linda take the paper, listening as she said, 'It was the manager of the Fairmile Hotel who returned Mainwaring's file. That's the link Mike can use.'

Fran wasn't interested in Mike, the hotel, or Ken. She was only interested in Emily who now knew details which, though thankfully not explicit, certainly left nothing to the imagination. Emily smiled wearily. 'It's all right, Fran. It might make Mum stop and think, because it could have been her all bruised and cut. It honestly is all right, a sort of relief.' They shared a long moment.

At last Fran said, 'Let's hope that Jane is able to feel that too.'

* * *

The next morning they kept the two children at home again, rather than risk a snatch from Maisie's by Ken, while Emily returned to school and normality with excessively bad grace. Jane had spent a better night, and the swelling and pain were marginally reduced. Mike phoned at eleven. 'Fran, Linda's briefed me. What I can do is keep Ken in employment on the proviso that he behaves just as we wish. I'll talk to him now, reveal all we know and insist he seeks therapy. Ideally, I'll get him to suggest to Jane that they live apart, to save her from that decision. His access to the children will be confined to supervised child visitation. Failure to agree will end in an injunction, his career in ruins and a messy divorce in all probability.'

It was all so easy, so cut and dried, all taken out of Jane's hands. Nothing for her to do except get on with her life, just like Fran. She said, 'Mike, let me talk to her. I was going to show her the fax this morning and let her make the decision I didn't make. I want *her* to be in control.'

'If she won't?' Mike's doubt was evident.

'I don't know.' That idiotic phrase again.

'Talk to her, then to me, my dear. Josh phoned first thing, did you know?'

She did not.

'He's even more adamant that he wants to be in the frame, if there's anything to be done. I'd like

409

that. He loves you all.'

'That is something I do know.' It was what she'd clung to every second of the last few days.

*   *   *

Jane pretended she couldn't read the fax with her eyes as they were. Fran sat next to her on the sofa, pointing out each word, reading it aloud until Jane hit her hand away. 'Mum, no. No.' She tore the paper in half. Fran held her wrists, her poor bruised wrists. 'Linda's made photocopies. You will read it.'

She took another from the coffee table and forced it into Jane's hands. 'Read it.'

Jane tore it again and again.

Fran took another and another. Still Jane tore them, sobbing. Undeterred Fran read the fifth copy over the sound of her daughter's tears.

'You see the dates. The phone call. It was our wedding. He walked to the bottom of the garden, beyond the molehills to take the call. Remember the painting; Catherine nude. He missed that, or he would have recognised the body as one he knew intimately. Remember the date when she stood him up at the Fairmile Hotel. Did he hurt you that night? Were you more stupid than usual? Is that what he said, Jane, darling? Think of the dates, please. Think of the Mainwaring file. It was sent to Gilbert and Gilbert by the hotel after they discovered it in a drawer. They had a Paul Davies booked in for that day. Now, read it for yourself, Jane.'

*   *   *

410

Jane was glad her mother had left her alone in this sitting room where she had done her homework, watched the television, learned her lines, grumbled about Anne Thomas, had Christmas with Linda and Mike—Mike who liked the parson's nose; Linda who always pulled a face because it was the turkey's bum. They had worn hats from crackers and laughed at the silly jokes. It was so long since she had really laughed.

Her mother was wrong, though. He hadn't beaten her on the day his mistress had left him. He had just pushed and pulled her and shaken her, finally throwing her against the chest of drawers and punching her just a few times. He had only punched her, again and again, and kicked her on the night he had not been given his promotion. He'd only done it so dreadfully badly that once.

She watched Josh playing in the garden with Lucy. They had a striped ball. If that big stripy ball went over the fence the old dragon would make them beg for its return. Too many people made you beg.

She went to the patio doors. Her hands were too swollen to open the latch. They'd been too swollen to hold the papers her mother had read from and tear them. But she had.

He had only beaten her properly, really properly, once. Once. The promotion.

He had not beaten her when Catherine left him. Not really.

Lucy was chasing the ball. She was laughing, really laughing. Josh was running after her. He caught her, held her high in the air. She squealed with delight. Fran had held Jane in the air. She

411

remembered it. She had been chased, held, kissed. Josh was kissing Lucy.

Ken didn't kiss Lucy. Ken shouted. Ken didn't kiss Harry.

He had not beaten *and* kicked her when Catherine left him. Only when he lost the promotion.

She circled the room. The pain was less. In the bookcases Josh's books were muddled up with her mother's. There were a few of Jane's old ones. A Catherine Cookson paperback, all worn and dog-eared. She and her mother loved Cookson's books. At home, Ken's books were all together, in alphabetical order. They were not to be touched. His stereo was not to be touched. His socks must be neatly paired. The mugs must be spotless and facing the right way. The towels straight.

Here they weren't and the sky had not fallen. Here they never had been straight. She had forgotten. In this world her mother had said no to Mike but they were still friends. No, the sky had not fallen, things had become better. Josh played with the children. Emily played with them. Linda and Mike were happy.

She stood in front of the painting of her mother, reaching out, touching the thick palette strokes, the red paint of the walls. Again she circled the room. It was the same room which had sheltered her as she grew, but it was different. Things could be different, but sort of the same. There could be change. There *could* be.

The doctor was coming this afternoon. He would look, talk and listen. She had the phone number of the shelter. They would talk and listen. Soon her mother would come in, and she too would talk and listen.

She was at the patio doors again. Harry was in his pushchair. Fran was crouched at his side, pointing to Lucy and Josh, to the stripy ball. Harry had a ball too. A red one. He was holding it out to Fran but before she could take it he dropped it. It was too soft and sluggish to bounce. Long ago it had fallen into the rose bed and been punctured, making it easier to grip. Fran was reaching for the ball, the red ball. She gripped, pinched, lifted and threw.

He had only shaken and thrown her when Catherine had dumped him, and punched just twice. He had pushed and pulled and shaken, and his fingers had dug in like her mother's. He had not cared enough about the woman with the beautiful naked body to change from shaking to beating, really beating. He had cared enough only about his job, so there really was no heart in that fine body and how could something change that did not exist?

She had a heart, though, and it was breaking. It had been breaking and crumbling for so long. Too long.

Her hands were on the latch, scrabbling, releasing. Now the bottom bolt, the top. It hurt her fingers. The doors were open. She was running and it did not matter that her ribs hurt, because this was the worst they'd ever be. She'd make sure of that.

She snatched the ball from Fran and hurled it into Anne Thomas's garden. She ran to Josh, grabbed the stripy ball from him and threw that too, turning to shout to her mother and Josh: 'No one is to beg for their return. No one is ever to beg again. Is that clear?'

CHAPTER FORTY-TWO

Catherine waited for Manuel in the hotel bedroom. Air-conditioning kept the room cool but it would be nice to be on the balcony and smell the sea. Not that it smelt of brine, like Hive Beach where she had taken Emily as a child, with Josh. The child had built sand castles, but not very well because it wasn't quite the right sort of sand.

Emily, who had been so cruel to be kind. Yes, that's what it was, cruel to be kind, but there was no way she could be hurt by someone like Manuel. For God's sake, she hadn't been born yesterday. I mean, looking back on it she could see that Paul, or Ken, or whoever he was might turn nasty. There had been that bit about wanting a whip. For a moment she felt a chill, so pulled the hotel robe tighter.

On the television there was some ridiculous game show. She missed UK television, where even the advertisements were better. Sometimes Paul would like the television on 'to cover your noise'. Yes, perhaps he had been rather rough, but somehow it had hit the spot. She laughed.

Well, he was on his own now, tucked away safely in Crewkerne, seeing a shrink, according to Em. Would he and that little wife of his get back together? Wonder what they'd get for the house? Enough for Jane to buy up that little hovel of Josh's, or that was the plan, apparently. Enough, plus maintenance, to stop working to give herself time to think.

Outside the sky was impossibly blue, and the sea,

414

too. Tomorrow Roger would take her up into the mountains for a Sunday brunch as usual, but he shouldn't leave her alone so much. He had only himself to blame if he worked weekends; it stood to reason.

She ran her hands over her stomach, sighing. Next week she would write a magnanimous letter to Emily, healing the breach properly. She could come, if not at Christmas, then in the spring and help with the baby. I mean, what sort of daughter did not want to fly to the sun to see her mother at Christmas? It was outrageous. Then Catherine shrugged. It would be easier, actually. No lies to make up.

There was a light tap on the door. 'It's unlocked, Manuel,' she called.